The Herlequin
Pitch & Sickle
Book Six

D K GIRL

.

The Herlequin© 2023 by Danielle K Girl

Cover Art by Deranged Doctor Design

Edited by Inspired Ink Editing

ISBN: 978-0-6453274-8-9

CHAPTER 1

A metallic click roused Pitch from the depths of heavy slumber. He fought back a dart of panic, one that always came with waking in a room shrouded in rich shadows.

He blinked into the quiet dark, his thoughts racing against a rush of fear. This was *not* the asylum. They had escaped the Fulbourn.

Nor was this Arcadia. He had *not* returned to the blackness of the abaddon.

He was safe, for now.

Pitch lay in a stranger's bed in a modest country house somewhere in the eastern sprawl of the British Isles. The home belonged to an acquaintance of Nancy and Ada, a gentleman who was very conveniently abroad, with no plans for a return in the foreseeable future. Old Bess had approved of the location, suitably isolated in the countryside, and set about forming it into a Sanctuary. One that would not, preferably, collapse in on them and present them with an array of horrors.

Pitch released his lip from between the clasp of teeth, relaxing a little beneath the weight of the bedcovers. It was near on a week since the debacle of the Fulbourn. Since Edward had spoken of the Holy One. Since the lieutenant, a purebred, had cast divine magick.

Pitch's throat squeezed.

Fuck.

It was so very unlike him to be...afraid...*this* afraid. But then, he'd had no reason to be so unsure of himself before. He was the spawn of a daemon king. He was Dominion. He was created to destroy the enemies of Arcadia.

But that was before he'd been handled by a Seraphim.

Breathe, gods damn it.

Breathe.

With a few measured inhales, the tightness of his muscles eased, as focusing on his breath, like Silas so often espoused, worked its gentle magick.

Pitch steered his thoughts away from the Fulbourn.

Edward was still unconscious. The man was seriously unwell, despite Sybilla's care. The toll of the Fulbourn, and the pendant watch, had fallen hard upon him. And Pitch, rather ungraciously, relished the fact. For now, he could remain in a happy no-man's-land between what had occurred and what was to come. A land where the turbulence of the wildness, for once, did not find him. There had been scant sign of that unbridled power since Edward's touch in the collapsing asylum had subdued the beast, as Pitch's flames sought to burst into uncontrollable wildfire.

The Fulbourn had been a nightmare of a place. Pitch did not understand so much of what had happened in that labyrinth. And was not sure he wished to.

Perhaps he'd experienced a madness there. Everyone else in the infernal place certainly had. Perhaps he'd not heard Seraphiel's voice at all, nor seen the angel's familiar intolerance in elements of Edward's behaviour. Perhaps the lieutenant, the *prophet*, might never wake up and Pitch would never need to learn what the fuck all this meant.

He could just stay here and ignore Lalassu and Sanu when the Lady finally deemed it safe enough to send them. It was not as though anyone knew where to ride off to. The location of Seraphiel's Sanctuary was known to Edward alone, and Edward was dribbling and thrashing in his sleep right now.

Pitch would stay here, quite happily.

Once he'd thinned out the number of residents, of course. This Sanctuary was far too overcrowded. Silas and his privates could stay, but Pitch would evict Nancy and Ada at once.

In the rush to secure a hiding place, and Silas stubborn in regard to the security of Tilly and her mothers after their involvement in the Fulbourn, Old Bess and Mr Ahari had agreed they were safest here in the immediate aftermath. But a week later, they were still damned here.

Pitch was driven to distraction by Tilly and her obsession with bringing him trinkets. He'd stepped on more piles of rubbish than he cared to count. And with the Fulbourn having left him bone-weary and unable to sleep a full night through, having his feet stabbed by Tilly's latest assortment of found items– everything from saplings to hairbrushes– whenever he stepped from his bed or armchair was testing the limits of his barely-existent patience. Gods forbid if he left the amber earring on a dresser or tried to hide it in a drawer. Tilly had cried – *cried*, for crying out loud– when she'd found it down the crease of a couch cushion two days ago. A right bloody fuss that had Silas's face bunch with concern, and seen Pitch do something ridiculous in order to stop the flow of tears. He'd pierced the earring's pointed clasp through his right earlobe, there and then, ignoring the sting of such a penetration.

'There. I shan't lose it again.' He'd glared at the snivelling child. 'Happy?'

The smile that shone from her had made his chest feel odd.

Pitch slipped his fingers between the pillow and his ear, touching at the earring that had seen him and Silas found at the Fulbourn, when even the ankou's hound had been fooled into believing they were not hidden in its depths.

It was six days since he'd woken upon the window seat downstairs, feeling rather the worse for wear, only to find himself perking up, in all ways, when the ankou suggested they bathe together.

Six days since Silas's attempt at bravery in the shallow waters of a copper tub had gone horribly awry. What should have been a luxurious, well-deserved descent into debauchery began rather less outstandingly. Silas's bone-deep fear of being submerged, even with one of his heads

3

still above the surface and a naked daemon between his legs, had proved too much.

Pitch might have been gravely insulted that his cock didn't provide a suitable distraction had he not known how set-fast this fear of Silas's truly was. He knew how valiantly the ankou fought to get himself into that tub, and how utterly mortified he was when at last he had to admit defeat and clamber out in haste, his body shaking, his legs too weak to hold him as the fear, the old and burdensome fear of the water, overruled all else. It left him an apologetic, near-to-tears mess upon the pale yellow Savonnerie carpet.

Pitch sighed into his feather-stuffed pillow. He had not trusted himself to find the right words to soothe. So instead he did what he knew himself best at, and the blow job he bestowed upon Silas had replaced one type of trembling for another.

That memory had much of Pitch's bleariness vanishing now. His appetite for sweet things had taken a severe dive since the Fulbourn, but that was not to say all his desires were subdued.

Surely it was not too early to roll over and nudge the ankou awake? Silas lay behind him, somewhere in the ridiculous amount of coverings and throws the bed was piled with. The bed was enormous, enough so that even the ankou with his heft and spread could stretch out or curl up to one side and disappear beneath the blankets. Pitch listened for sign of breathing, but Silas was remarkably quiet when he slept and did not toss and turn anywhere near so much as Pitch. He knew himself to be a terror to sleep with– actually *sleep* with– which was why, normally, he'd have his lovers vacate the bed as soon as they were done.

He exhaled, grinning. His preference for sleeping alone had taken on a mighty transformation of late.

Pitch rolled onto his back, his head slipping between two of many pillows, blocking his view of Silas's side of the bed. The sheet clung to his naked body like the wrappings on a damp gift, teasing at a half-roused cock that saluted the morning. Pitch touched himself, a quick slip of fingers along hardening flesh.

'Sickle,' he whispered. 'I have quite the stiffness that needs tending.' Pitch's mood was light despite his tiredness. His dreams had been so dull as to be forgotten already, with no nightmares of burning angels to speak of. 'I wish those hands of yours upon me...mouth too, if you'd like your breakfast in bed.'

He expected a snort at that, a chuckle even, but no sound came from the ankou. Pitch spread his leg, stretching pointed toes, searching for sign of the oaf beneath the copious, heavy coverings.

'Did you hear me?' He rolled to his side when his reconnaissance turned up nothing of note: no solidity, no give of flesh or grunt of irritation at being disturbed. 'I have need of you, Mr Mercer.'

For carnal pleasure of course. That was all. Silas could cuddle him and whisper silly things as he was wont to do, if he must. Pitch did not care either way.

He wriggled from beneath his pillowy confines, blinking into the dullness. The curtains were a burgundy so deep as to appear black in such light, and well suited to holding back the day.

A day likely wet and miserable, thanks in no small part to Matilda. The elemental had added her damp touch to their fortifications, for visitors were far less likely to come knocking in such inclement weather.

Pitch propped himself onto an elbow and saw at once that he was alone.

His gut swirled with unpleasantness, but he could not pretend the silent wildness was to blame for this ill-feeling. The emptiness of the room swooped in at him, and he pulled the covers closer to his chest.

So it was the click of the door that had woken him, the ankou doing his best to be quiet while he slipped away. The same thing had happened yesterday, too. Silas gone, the cool sheets telling Pitch he'd been abandoned for a while before he woke.

He admonished himself for being so bothered, but need Silas be so damned furtive? Not so much as a pat to the backside and a *good morning*? For Pitch knew Silas liked touching his arse. It was an established fact. The ankou liked to do other things to it as well, though he'd showed his full appreciation for Pitch's fine entrance only once since they'd arrived here in this overcrowded place.

Tilly's love of a game of hide-and-seek had the all-too-sensible Silas fearing she would be scarred for life should she decide the cavernous space beneath their bed was a prime location for concealment.

Yet another reason the dryad brat and her family should leave as soon as possible. Pitch was craving a repeat of the languid, slow fucking that had come the night after the debacle of the tub. A lavish affair, unhurried and thorough, exploring every inch of each other. The exact opposite of the whirlwind of the Crimson Bow, but each encounter as superb as one another.

Feasts for an incubus.

But he'd not fed on Silas at the Bow, nor had he here. Sating his incubus blood might see Pitch rid himself of his exhaustion, but the Alp daemon's marks ran deep. He could not bring himself to take... as he'd been taken from. Knowing first-hand that to feed upon another was to dominate, to possess, to steal control. He'd not do that to Silas. Not again, at least. No matter how willing he knew the ankou to be.

Pitch punched at Silas's pillow as his mood tugged him downward.

'He could have at least brought me a coffee before he found better things to do,' he muttered. 'He's probably brewing a fresh pot for the vagabond as we speak.' Pitch pushed the pillow away and sat up, scowling at the unlit hearth. Silas fretted too much over Charlie, who had not left the lieutenant's sickbed in days, insisting on sleeping in an overstuffed armchair at his side. 'Didn't even stir the bloody fire. Selfish bastard.'

If Silas wasn't with the lad, fussing and bothering, he was probably out walking his ugly, drooling hound. Throwing the skriker a ball when he should have been handling Pitch's.

Now he was slipping into a downright foul mood, and even though he knew his thoughts and grumbles not entirely reasonable, he let them overtake him. He threw back the covers. Surly or not, his morning glory had not eased: a fine tent pole of pink and rose hues, dashed with the faint trace of blue-green where veins ran close beneath the skin.

'Fine. I shall deal with this myself.'

Pitch lay back down and took hold of himself with an irritated hiss, cursing the ankou for a serious neglect of duty. He gave himself tight, angry jerks that bordered on unpleasant but, admittedly, only roused him further. He cleared his mind, focusing upon one need alone. Pitch arched the small of his back, grunting up at the canopy which shuddered a little as he worked himself, his breath coming in shorter and shorter gasps. The seeing-to would be brief.

Pitch bent his knees so as to allow for more violent jerks of his hips, finding an urgent motion that had his balls ready to burst.

'Ah, oh gods...fuck...' The rest of his words melted into incoherent groans as Pitch soared high, where a base fire burned his belly, spreading desirous flames towards his cock.

He cried out, bracing for the unstoppable release.

Two sharp raps on wood and the door swung open.

Suddenly, abhorrently, he was no longer alone.

'Tobias, you must...oh sweet Jesus!' Charlie shouted. 'Oh god, I'm sorry...oh god.'

Pitch rolled to face away from the door and balled up as tight as one of the akaname who had fed on the Gu. But it was too little, far too late. The torrent spilled from him, making his body pulse with fracturing jerks.

The door slammed, the lad still uttering frantic apologies from beyond the barrier. 'Tobias...I...I'm so sorry...'

Not sorry enough to leave, evidently.

'What the fuck is wrong with you?' Pitch grabbed at the blankets, breathless, heart pounding, his belly slippery with a mess he'd have preferred to avoid.

'I need to talk to you,' Charlie fairly squeaked.

'I was fucking busy.' His body tingled, but the bliss was already fading.

'I know...' The lad's voice was small and, oddly, came from the bottom of the door, as though he'd buckled with the horror of what he'd just seen. Good. Pitch hoped it gave him nightmares. 'Tobias...it's Edward.'

He considered telling the vagabond to piss off. Pitch inhaled. 'What about him?'

'He's calling your name.'

There was no brush of concern at hearing Charlie's words. Just a numbness.

'Tobias? Did you hear me? Would you please come and see him?' Charlie's request wobbled from him. 'I know you've been avoiding him, but please. Perhaps it will help for him to see you. I don't know...I don't know how else to help him.'

Any pleasure that had come from spending all over himself whittled away. Charlie sounded as exhausted as Pitch felt, and as despairing.

He slid from the bed and padded across the pleasingly thick carpet over to the elaborate Indian rosewood wardrobe. It had been empty when they arrived, but Old Bess had set up a clandestine Melusine delivery service between here and Harvington Hall. A way of moving inanimate objects, food and clothing, from one Sanctuary to another, delivering them into a trunk in Bess's chambers. Which meant Pitch had, at least, a suitably lovely selection of clothing to choose from.

'Once I've wiped myself down,' Pitch said. 'I'll consider it.' He heard the hitch of the lad's breath, but Charlie made no further protest. Pitch reached for a pair of pale lemon trousers that had arrived yesterday. 'Is Silas with him?' Now it was Pitch who held his breath, awaiting the reply.

'He's not with you?' The lad's voice rose with surprise, but he was quick to smother the moot question. 'No, no. I've not seen him since last night. Perhaps he's gone for a walk. You know how he is with the garden.' Pitch certainly did. It had not stopped raining for days, the ground was sodden, the December air was punishing, but Silas walked every day. 'He won't be far, I'm sure. Tobias, please, will you come and see Edward?'

Pitch slammed the wardrobe door closed and was faced with his own reflection in the mottled mirror. A calamitous sight, for sure. His hair, with its ever-encroaching waves of gold in the natural mousier brown, stood haphazardly, as though Matilda had struck him with her damned lightning. There was no denying the smears of grey beneath his eyes, nor how his emerald irises did not shine so brightly as before the Fulbourn.

Pitch dragged on his trousers with a fierce wrench. 'I'll be along momentarily. Now piss off.'

'Thank you. Thank you.'

The quick, dull padding of bare feet upon the hall runner declared Charlie's departure.

Pitch dressed slowly, taking his time to decide between shirts, deciding on a white affair with voluminous sleeves and a collar trimmed with light blue lace. So far there had been no sign of the corsets he'd requested, despite Bess's insistence he'd ordered them from the Hall. Pitch bent to put on his shoes, their polished black leather gleaming. His belly rumbled. But it was just simple hunger. Not appetite, just the basic need of a body for nourishment.

He was too distracted for appetite.

The wildness was quiet, slinking so deep in the shadows of Pitch's innards that he wasn't sure if he imagined its faint stirrings or if it was real.

The fear that simmered inside him fed on the silence.

He touched the dangling earring, smoothing his thumb over the amber before untangling a strand of his hair from around its fastening and heading downstairs.

CHAPTER 2

The drizzle was his only companion as Silas made his way to the back of the garden. The expanse of untended rose gardens and waning orchards was not inconsiderable. To reach the pond at the outer perimeter meant losing sight of the squat Georgian house they were currently calling home, with its chocolate-coloured slates and white-paned windows, a low parapet around the eaves to create the distinctive square shape of the era.

By the time the neglected groundsman's cottage he'd discovered on a stroll the day before came into view, his greatcoat was double its weight thanks to the saturation of the woollen weave. And his hair, which had grown at a fast clip since Tyvain had cut it for the soirée at the Charters' household, was plastered against his skull. A firm shake of his head sent water flying in all directions. He swiped his hand across his chin, grateful for the ever-increasing length there too. Not least of all because Pitch had told him a few evenings ago, as they lay beside one another, in a room that had become theirs, that he enjoyed the roughness against his skin.

If not for the circumstances which made them both unable to sleep readily, Silas considered those hours of idle chitchat and comfortable silence to be among the most perfect he could recall. Certainly far more pleasant than his appalling loss of control the first evening here, when he'd been puffed up with relief, bravado, and lust, only to step foot into the warm waters of the tub and make an absolute tit of himself.

Silas wiped at his nose, freeing ice-cold droplets from the tip. He shrugged, against the rain, his embarrassment, and the swaddling of worry that had not left him since the Fulbourn.

The constant niggle of dread plagued him, an itch he could not reach, a worm of reticence that was intent on burrowing deeper. But there was something more to the sensation than circumstances might dictate. Of course their situation was dire, their task mammoth, their enemies formidable. But this dread he could not shake...this despair...sat upon him strangely.

Silas did not feel quite connected to his mood. As though his mind had forgotten something he was terribly morose about but his heart had not. He flicked his fingers in annoyance, sending droplets scattering.

Every single resident of this house was not quite themselves. They were all frightened. Unsettled. Why should he be any different?

Silas pushed on towards the cottage, a basic wooden structure that could not seem to decide if it was meant for storing gardening accoutrements or housing a living soul. Inside, he'd found piles of discarded gardening equipment, empty wooden crates, and some crudely carved furniture: an impressive dining table, though with only one chair; and a bed frame with the sad remains of a straw-stuffed mattress. The rustic nature reminded him of Ottelie's forest home, sadly without the fantastical floral carpeting or her wonderful cider.

Silas pushed against the swollen door and stepped inside.

He took off his greatcoat and frock coat beneath. The greatcoat was courtesy of the absent owner of the residence, but the forest-green frock coat, which fit him perfectly, had come via Old Bess's marvellous magick. The Child of Melusine, as different to his dastardly sister Palatyne as light was to dark, had transformed a steamer trunk he'd found in one of the rooms into a mailbox of sorts. Clothes and necessities for the empty larder had been appearing in the trunk for the past few days. A secure system of delivery, Silas was assured. No living creature could travel between the Sanctuaries this way, and even if Harvington Hall was found and then breached, the passageway between the Sanctuaries had been described by Old Bess as a combination lock, and he the only one who knew the sequence.

Ronin, Old Bess's dour but handsome tsukumogami, was keeping constant watch for any signs of trouble beyond the boundaries of the hall and its village when he was not seeing to the lists of requirements Old Bess was sending. The poor chap must be run quite ragged by now. Silas managed to find some sympathy for him, even though he recalled very well how the tsukumogami had thrown himself into the task of convincing Pitch to bed him at the hall. Ronin had been waved beneath the daemon's nose like a treat when Sybilla and Bess were trying to persuade the ailing incubus to feed and restore his strength.

Silas was foolishly grateful they'd not returned to Harvington Hall.

He set his greatcoat on the solitary hook by the door and draped the frock coat over the lone chair. He removed his socks and boots and stepped back out into the drizzle. With a suck of the air against his teeth Silas traipsed bare feet along the haphazard lay of a stone pathway that was mostly swallowed by fallen leaves and creeping weeds. Mud oozed between his toes, raindrops scurried between the collar of his shirt and his skin, and a blackberry bush tried to lay claim to his trousers and the skin beneath.

Silas moved through the leaning ghost-white timber of a rose arch. Several paces later he found himself staring down on the pond. Its size was unpleasantly similar to that of the pond he'd been forced into at the greensward. It blotted the garden like smudged paint on a watercolour.

Just the mere sight of the body of water set a wave of trepidation rolling through him, and he swallowed against an appalling whimper.

'Get ahold of yourself, man,' Silas hissed. 'You are no use to him if mere pond slime renders you catatonic.'

They were headed to a place called Blood Lake, for goodness' sake. What choice did Silas have but to quash his marrow-deep fear?

The water had stolen the sky's dull grey hue and mingled it with a tinge of green. The colour matched the skin of a sailor roiling on a monstrous sea.

Silas curled his fingers but could barely feel the tips against his palms. Bloody hell, it was cold.

'This water is a home for eels and frogs,' he muttered, to keep his lips from freezing shut mostly. 'Nothing more. Now get in there, Mercer.'

It was very unlikely an insidious panlong hid in the murky depths. Old Bess would have noticed that surely when he wove the Sanctuary's walls about this place.

Silas nodded to himself. 'Certainly he would have noticed.'

He continued closer to one of the few gaps in the wreath of bulrushes surrounding the pond, where the ground sloped and the water lapped at the drenched soil. He was unprepared for how slippery it was there. He lost his footing, only just managing to halt his slide where the shallows lapped the edge with a thin film of liquid that could not have drowned a mouse. He set his jaw, teeth grinding hard to stop their infernal chattering, and took a step forward. Then another. Until his feet were covered entirely, barely seen through the heavy silt, the icy-cold water encircling his ankles.

He bent to roll up his trousers. A senseless act really, considering the entire point of this was to get himself soaked.

The pond's surface was a patchwork of waterlilies and duckweed and floating pennywort, each fighting the other for space. The pennywort was winning the battle for the most part. Fortunate, he supposed, for it was a much finer plant, with delicate tiny leaves that should cause little bother to push through. He shuddered. Damn, this idea of his was terrible.

The rain dimpled what clear surface there was, giving the water a life he'd rather it didn't have. The downpour came from a sky streaked with stormy colours reminiscent of Lalassu's coat. He faltered, with the water lapping at the bottom of his knees. He hardly needed another concern right now, but there it was. The absence of his horse, of Sanu too, tugged at him daily. If Sybilla knew why they were absent, she wasn't saying. But then the Valkyrie wasn't saying altogether much these past few days. She was as distracted as the rest of the household by her concerns. They were anchorless, drifting as they waited for Edward to wake and give them direction.

Silas's resolve faltered. Between forcing himself into dreaded water and the heavy settling of gloom that would not leave him, he felt bloody wretched.

He pulled at his shirt, wincing as the material drew off his nipples, which were so hard from the cold that they could have cut glass. The rub of the material was painful in a not-so-pleasing way. Though Pitch would disagree, he was sure.

He closed his eyes.

And took himself to a much more pleasant place.

Silas took another step. Another followed. The ground sloped beneath him, and he fought back the stirring of a very familiar terror. He drew back his shoulders and pushed on.

One step after another. The weeds beneath the surface rather unsettling against his legs. But onward he went. The same act repeated over and again, until the water encased Silas's thighs, caressing them with cruel hands of melted ice.

No matter how lovely his thoughts, the cold could be ignored no longer. He halted, shivering hard, his teeth dancing against one another behind lips that must surely be blue by now.

The pond was roughly the length of four rowboats. A swimmer would take a handful of strokes to move from one side to the other, but it seemed much deeper than he'd imagined. There was no letting up of the slope of the ground, and he was still a decent way from the centre. He crossed his arms and shoved his hands into his armpits, where there was no more warmth than anywhere else on his body, but at least embracing himself felt more fortifying. Something soft brushed at his inner thigh, and his shivering burst into a jerky movement that unsettled the water lilies about him.

Pond weed. Nothing more.

'Go in, Silas. Don't be such a dolt.'

Hidden frogs croaked their agreement. Apparently a crowd of them had gathered to watch this show.

Silas shook himself, prepared to move. 'He'll not see you lose your senses again over a tub. I'll not have it. Now bloody well get in and get it over with.'

Certainly, he'd rather eat one of those raucous frogs than allow the daemon to see him brought to tears again by a harmless body of water.

Harmless body of water? Good god, who was he kidding?

Silas swallowed hard.

He did not truly see a weed-laden pond or, the other night, a copper tub filled with steaming water. What Silas saw was a massive, frightening, churning body of water. A loch. A grave.

His fear was a tattoo set beneath his skin by hundreds of years of pressure. Christ almighty, of all the memories he could have lost, why not the one that contained his death?

But resenting his lot would not protect Pitch. The Morrigan were many things, but Silas doubted they were foolish enough not to understand Pitch was the Horseman they should fear most.

That the prince was their nemesis.

'Finish this, man,' he hissed at himself as something splashed further out in the pond.

Pitch was coveted. By the Morrigan. By the Seraphim who still plagued him. And by the Order.

None of them wished him any peace. None loved him. So far as Silas could see, he was alone in that.

He put one foot in front of the other. The water rose, crept up his belly, played at the bottom of his ribs.

His fears darted about, swift as minnows, but he was not yet paralysed by them.

'You are braver than a fish, you fool,' he muttered. 'And they don't mind the water. Move your grand arse deeper.'

The silt was disconcerting, thick in an unpleasant way, like he'd stood in a heap of fresh dung.

Another splash. This time closer to where he stood. The strangled croak of frogs lifted higher. Silas paused.

He should not have done so.

The hesitation gave his fear a place to settle its claws, rousing the murderous weight of a thousand deaths.

'Fuck.' Cold as he was, he grew colder still. The type of chill that only the mind could muster. 'No. No.'

Silas dug his feet into the silt, desperate to ground himself somehow. The chorus of the frogs grew in unison with the rise of his terror. The rain drummed a shallow beat upon his skull. Hammering him down.

Memories, as brutal as the Dullahan's whip, tangled about him. Over and over they wove.

His brother pushing him from the boat.

His cries that tore his throat to shreds.

The *knowing* that he would not be saved.

Oh god, he couldn't do this. He was failing.

Silas bit his tongue so hard his mouth filled with copper and heat. A scream built in the middle of his chest, and the water shook as he began to rattle himself to pieces. Silas closed his eyes tight. Staring straight into the monstrous eyes of his fear which roared up to meet him.

He was sinking, but not in the way he'd intended.

The choir of frogs hit their high notes. A piece of the real world seeping into the darkness he was drowning in.

The real world, where he stood waist deep in a harmless body of water.

Where his true enemies were not the shades of a past that couldn't be changed.

He grabbed at the stem of a nearby water lily, anchoring himself.

With a sharp intake of breath Silas let his knees buckle, and sank into the water.

CHAPTER 3

E dward's room held the unpleasant tang of the ill. The room was a small one on the ground floor, tucked behind the kitchen and larder. It was clearly for house staff, considering its undressed walls, plain linens, and thin curtains, but Charlie had decided upon it, pleased with the firmness of the mattress and the view out onto a neglected kitchen garden.

The lad shared Silas's barbarous love of the outdoors. Which was not irritating at all, of course.

Mutual interests and an ancient history. Wonderful.

Pitch's sour mood curdled a little further.

Now he not only must endure Charlie's company but a sickroom ripe with the scent of sweat and unhappiness. The window was cracked open, the chill reaching Pitch where he hesitated in the corridor. He was not fond of the human body's propensity for illness. He himself was not prone to the more severe ailments of the purebreds, of course: the colds and influenza and debilitating diseases that felled them by the cartload. But he knew what it was to be unwell while in human form. The Gu had made him party to that delightful experience, a fucking dreadful few days made worse by Silas's insistence on coddling him, despite the disgusting mess Pitch had been.

His gaze shifted to the window, beyond where Charlie whispered to the lieutenant while mopping his brow with a damp cloth. There was a considerable downpour outside, the sky low and heavy. Where the blazes *was* Silas? Surely even the garden-obsessed ankou would not consider this a good day for a damned stroll?

There'd been no sign of him as Pitch made his way through the sleeping household. No clomp of boots to suggest he moved anywhere about. The only other living soul awake at the ungodly hour seemed to be Forneus, the hound lying upon the window seat in the parlour where Pitch had first woken after the Fulbourn, opening one red eye to watch him pass by.

'Please come in, Tobias.'

Charlie's quiet summons drew Pitch back to the room.

He laid his hand against the doorframe but could not quite find the wherewithal to step across the threshold.

Charlie selected a bottle from the plethora set upon the tilted pine bedside table and squinted as he allowed a few droplets onto the cloth. The liquid spewed a bitter scent, a mix of the gods-knew-what Old Bess and Sybilla had deemed necessary. The bottles on the tabletop were joined by a clutter of floral posies, dried and curled but their scent still evident and mingling with that of the lieutenant's overheated body: lavender, a tight bundle of sage, and another clump of something Pitch couldn't name, bergamot perhaps. Silas would have known.

He watched as the lad tended the lieutenant. Charlie was painfully gentle with the ailing man, who muttered at his touch but did not open his eyes. There was a second cloth across his forehead. The pendant watch that Lucifer had delivered, the fine gunmetal trinket that had changed everything in the Fulbourn, was pinned to his nightshirt, its gold accents and swirling metalwork ludicrously out of place there. Edwards's eyelids were a discomforting hue of blue, one that matched the shade of his lips, as though he were freezing despite the layer of sweat that coated his equally grey-tinged skin.

'He does not look well.' Pitch stated the bloody obvious, for lack of anything better to say.

'His fever will not break.' Charlie swapped over the cloths and dunked the one that had just been against the lieutenant's skin in a basin of water balanced on the bedside. As he wrung it out, the trickle of water seemed to bother Edward, who groaned and rolled his head side to side. His pillow was patched with damp blots where his sweat-dampened hair stained the cream-coloured material. 'No matter what has been tried, we cannot seem to ease his temperature. He's suffering nosebleeds too, but Sybilla's tincture helps with that at least. He's not eaten properly in days.'

There were fine cracks in Charlie's words. The lad looked almost as wretched as the lieutenant, worn out and in great need of a hairbrush through his curled auburn strands. How he was not shivering himself to pieces in this room, Pitch had no idea. The bite of the December morning slithered in through the opened window, managing to find even a fire daemon, who so rarely felt the cold.

Pitch shivered, regretting his decision not to dress more fully. 'Perhaps his eyelids are frozen in place. It's awfully cold in here.'

'He becomes more restless when I close the window. I think he feels too closed in without it open. Tobias, you will need to come closer,' Charlie urged. 'He does not say much, and when he does, it's not much more than a whisper.'

'Yes, yes. I'm coming.' He tried for an air of comportment but doubted the act was convincing. If Edward suddenly opened his eyes, Pitch was not sure he wouldn't screech like a maid sighting a mouse.

Charlie sighed. 'Today? Or are you waiting for me to escort you in?'

'I don't wish to catch what he has.'

'Tobias, please.' Charlie blinked bright blue eyes, steely with impatience. 'I may not understand all that is going on, but that does not make me a fool. Edward's illness is connected to you...don't you dare turn away from him now. You've not once come to see him. How can you treat a friend so?'

The lad was quite forceful by the end, and Pitch did not like what he had to say at all. Mostly because the accusations were not without merit.

'Careful, boy.' He glared. 'You have seen what I can do. I could turn you to ash before you could turn a heel to run.'

'Perhaps, but you won't.' Charlie's hand tightened around the cloth, but he held Pitch's gaze. 'When it comes to those close to you, your bark is far worse than your bite.'

'You overestimate yourself in my considerations,' Pitch said. 'I care not a whit for you.'

'But you care deeply for Silas,' Charlie cast right back. 'And he and I share a friendship. I know I am quite safe with you because of that...if nothing else.'

Care deeply? Just because he enjoyed Silas's hands on him, the rumble of his laughter when the ankou somehow found Pitch amusing, did not mean they should find the nearest vicar and get wed.

'No one is *quite safe* with me, little boy.' He thought the threat sufficient, but the lad rolled his eyes and returned to his lieutenant.

Pitch reaffixed his collar for the seventh time. Damning his feet for not moving. Glancing one last time up the hallway. Searching.

Clearly the ankou did not *care deeply* for *him*, or else he'd be here right now, instead of poking at moss in the rain. With his irritation rising, Pitch crossed the threshold and strode to the bed.

His eyes fixed on the pendant watch.

Pitch had not given any specific instructions that it be kept with the lieutenant. Charlie had simply done so. On one of many failed attempts to visit Edward's bedside, Pitch had overheard an exchange between Bess and Charlie.

'No. It needs to stay with him.' Charlie had been firm.

'Are you quite sure?' Old Bess had returned.

'It is the only thing I am entirely certain of. The watch must stay with him.'

Pitch reached Edward's bedside now far too quickly. He'd hoped he might escape the uncomfortable prickling beneath his skin that came with being near the watch, but a touch of it arrived as he came to stand behind Charlie's chair.

The sensation tapped at the back of his neck but in truth it was not nearly so horrid as it had been in earlier days. With some effort, he might forget it bothered him at all. That should have pleased him, but it bothered him instead. First the wildness being subdued, now this? Pitch was so used to being uncomfortable that the absence of any pains was as close to troublesome as pain itself.

'Well then,' he said curtly. 'I'm here. Speak up, Lieutenant.' Pitch frowned. 'I thought you said he was awake?'

'I said he called your name,' Charlie said.

'Well I don't hear it now. I should go.'

The lad sighed, again, rising from the chair. 'Here, have my seat. Take his hand.'

Pitch recoiled. 'No. I don't want to touch him.'

'Tobias, is everything all right?'

He stared at the lad, blinking into the astounding question. 'Is everything all right? Are you a bigger imbecile than you look? A week ago you were pulled out of a magickal prison by a giant fox with nine tails. Before that you were attacked by walking corpses and rescued by a faerie hound. I understand that your feeble purebred brain is not seeing things entirely as they are, but I think even you can grasp the situation by now. No, Charlie, you daft idiot, everything is far from all right.'

The lad twisted the cloth in his hands. 'Do you know that of all the things Old Bess has tried to explain, the fact I had the least trouble believing was that you are a daemon. I had always assumed such creatures to be spiteful, arrogant bastards, and you do not disappoint.' He dragged in a breath, seemingly surprised at his own vehement words, a little unsteady on his feet. Charlie appeared so infinitely frail in that moment. Too delicate to deserve a tongue lashing for his harsh assessment.

Damn him.

'I am very pleased to have met your expectations.' Pitch was dry as sand. 'Your opinion is so *very* valuable to me.'

Charlie lifted his hand to scratch at his forehead. The movement slid the cuff of his sleeve back, exposing Ottelie's bracelet. It was threaded with more green than Pitch recalled, like there were hints of new growth through the twigs Ottelie had handed over. The lad tossed the cloth aside.

'Take his hand,' he said.

'I will not.'

'Why do you fear touching him?'

'I don't bloody–'

'You do. Take his hand.'

'Why are you so obsessed with hand-holding?'

'Because I know it is what must be done.' Charlie's cheeks reddened, eyes bright. 'I don't understand why...or what it means. Fucking hell, Tobias, take his bloody hand. Has he not endured enough?' He grabbed Edward's hand, lifting it. 'Stop being a pompous, stupid arse and just bloody fucking do it.'

Pitch folded his arms across his chest in one tight, controlled movement. 'I beg your pardon?'

The lad crumpled, sitting heavily on Edward's bed, laying the man's hand down gently in his lap. 'I'm sorry. That was unfair. I am just so tired...'

Pitch's fingers twitched, and he considered for a fleeting moment putting a reassuring hand upon the lad's shoulder. Luckily the nonsense idea fled before it could embarrass him, but he was gentler when he spoke. 'Yes, well, none of us have had an easy time of it.' He'd not say so aloud, but the fact that Charlie, after all he'd endured, was not as wrecked as those patients at the Fulbourn was impressive. Perhaps it was Ottelie's forest magick, or the ghost of the angel in the man he clearly cared for, giving him strength. Perhaps Charlie was just very used to fighting to protect himself. 'You're a stubbornly resilient thing, aren't you? Silas thinks you remarkably brave for staying true to your preference for'– he sent a vague wave the lad's way– 'a man's life over a woman's.'

Charlie shook his head. 'It is not a preference. It is simply what should have been. What is. I don't expect you to understand.'

'Don't expect me to understand a desire to have been made a different way? No. I don't suppose I could ever understand that.'

Charlie glanced away. He stroked an errant hair away from Edward's sweaty neck. The lieutenant's normally clean-cut hair was straggly and longer than Pitch knew the man preferred. 'I'm sorry –'

He sighed. 'Gods, I already have one man in my life who apologises too much. I don't need another. Are you recovered from the Fulbourn...the tree and all?'

It was a stalling tactic, but Charlie did not challenge him on it. 'Well as can be expected, I suppose.' He tugged at his cuff, hiding the bracelet.

'There are a few aches and pains still, but who does not have them after that place?'

Pitch grunted, a vague acknowledgement of the understatement.

'What of yourself, Tobias?'

'Fine. I'm really not so delicate as a certain ankou would treat me. The man is a fiendish coddler.'

Charlie's smile reached one side of his mouth only, tired as he was. 'I will not disagree with you there. If Silas asks Bess one more time when I can be moved somewhere safer, I think I shall clobber him. I know it must be far worse for you. Can you even take a piss without him worrying?'

'Only if I piss *on* him. Which he really doesn't seem to mind.'

'Oh Jesus Christ,' Charlie cried, a grimace and a smile contorting his lips. Pitch's intentional vulgarity working its dubious charms. 'You really are appalling.'

'Says the one who invaded my privacy terribly, not a half hour ago.'

'Oh, don't worry, I shall pay for that mistake the rest of my life. I am scarred deeply, I assure you.'

'Come now, we both know what you'll do with that memory when next you are in your bed alone.'

Laughing softly, Charlie glanced down at Edward. The lieutenant's eyes darted beneath his lids, his fingers twitching as though he were typing out a manic Morse code. Charlie caressed his hand, and at once Edward sighed, the tension in his body easing.

'You are fond of him,' Pitch said quietly.

It didn't need to be a question. Charlie looked on Edward with far more than a doctor's concern for a patient.

'I am.'

'You barely know the man.'

'I'm not sure that matters.' Charlie spoke softly, touching a fingertip to a bead of sweat running along Edward's cheek. 'But we had some time....before all this...to share some pints and conversation...and I couldn't remember when I'd last felt so at ease, so very sure I did not wish to be anywhere else.' His gaze flicked to Pitch. 'You know how that is, I'm certain. You soften when you are with Silas.'

Pitch had leaned in to listen, but now he took a firm step backwards. 'Gods, I'm not a soufflé. We have been forced into each other's company. Fortunately he's not a terrible man to be stuck with. Nor to fuck. As you would know.' He wasn't sure if he'd kept the brittleness off those last few words.

Cornflower-blue eyes fixed on him. 'Tobias, there is no competition between us when it comes to Silas.'

'Is there not?' Pitch bit the inside of his cheek, abhorring how readily Charlie had seen through his charade.

The lad regarded him, freckles bright on pale skin. 'Did that flame of yours fry a part of your mind? I know you are astonishingly powerful, but bloody hell, I didn't think you were so stupid.'

Pitch stared, aghast. 'Do you have any idea whom you are speaking to?'

'A daemon with outstanding insecurities who needs his eyes checked. Because if you are missing the way Silas looks at you, then you are in dire need of a monocle at least.' Charlie stood up while Pitch rather embarrassingly mimicked a carp, mouth opening and closing with no words coming. 'What is between Silas and I is very different. We shared an instant closeness, I don't deny that, but we misread it. We were both vulnerable and took the ease between us to mean one thing when it meant another, but by then we'd ventured where we shouldn't have. I mean that's not to say sleeping with him was terrible. He is a wonderful–'

'What is your point, Charlie?'

'My point is the love between us is like that of brothers.'

'So you enjoy incest, then?'

'Tobias!' Charlie laughed and seemed poised to say more when he wavered on his feet, pressing a hand to his belly.

Pitch reached for him before he could think better of it. 'What's wrong?'

'A little faint, that's all.'

'When did you last eat something?'

Charlie frowned. 'Do you know, I'm not really sure...'

'Then do it now. I'll not have them blaming me for you passing out. You're right next to the kitchen, for fuck's sake. Go and find something to eat. Nancy has baked all manner of atrocities this past week.'

The lad's smile was fragile but it was there. 'All right, so long as you'll stay with Edward.'

'Yes, yes.' Pitch waved the lad away.

'Shall I bring you something too? You haven't had breakfast.'

'No. No, it's fine. I'll have something later perhaps.' He'd likely do no such thing. 'Go on. Go. You could do with a wash, too.'

That had Charlie's weariness vanishing beneath a look of horror. 'Oh bloody hell.' He sniffed his armpits. 'Perhaps you are right.'

'We spiteful, arrogant bastards usually are.'

Charlie gave Pitch's arm a quick squeeze as he passed. 'Arrogant but very brave. I'm glad Silas has you at his side. I'm glad we all do.'

Before Pitch could bluster a reply, Charlie was gone, taking the basin with him and leaving the door ajar. Leaving Pitch alone with the lieutenant and his secrets.

He gripped the back of the wooden chair, keeping it between him and the bed. Charlie's misplaced but charming words rang in his head. Brave? Fuck, if the fool only knew.

'Edward?' Pitch cleared his throat. 'Can you hear me? It's Tobias. You were asking for me. Well, here I am.'

'William Black.' The lieutenant's dry lips cracked just wide enough for the words, and Pitch almost squealed. Edward's eyelids fluttered but remained closed.

'What did you say?' His pulse raced a little quicker to hear the old name. The one he'd borne when he'd been free to indulge in this world at will. The name he'd worn when he first met Edward, several years past.

'William Black.'

The rain tapped at the windows like a bunch of piskies wanting in from the miserable weather. Pitch had been William Black too, when the Seraphim first toyed with him in his Sanctuary.

'What do you want, Seraphiel?' He might have sounded firm if not for a slight tremor on the name.

Edward shook his head, a slow back and forth. 'The angel isn't speaking, it's me. Edward.' Gods, the man sounded rough. Like a worker from one of the smoke-spewing factories which grew like mould over England.

'That was you, wasn't it? That man I knew as William. You are one and the same.'

'We are.' Pitch wet his lips before he spoke again. 'The angel told you?' Edward breathed. In and out. Each breath a laborious scrape of air. 'Not by way of words...no...it doesn't work like that. I just...understand things that once puzzled me. When we first met in January, at the Cyprians' Ball, you seemed so familiar. I couldn't take my eyes off you.'

'Well, you were hardly alone in that. I looked a dream that night.' Pitch's laughter was embarrassingly frail. Little wonder Edward did not join in.

'Why didn't you tell me, Tobias?' The lieutenant's eyes were yet to open. 'Why did you allow me to believe myself going mad, when you knew all that had been done to me...you knew I was not imagining him?'

Pitch shifted back, away from the lieutenant and his questions. 'I'm...' What? Sorry? Was he to be as full of apologies as the ankou now?

Edward's plight was not a pleasant one. He'd been taken over and used without hint of consent. But, gods damn it, the same had been done to Pitch. He had very little pity to spare here.

'How could I speak of such things? Tell you that your freedom had been stolen by such a creature. Your body used in an act of supreme selfishness.' Pitch swallowed. 'I know how that feels. You are a decent man and did not deserve such cruelty, even if you had believed me, which is unlikely. You had never recalled the possessions in the past...I thought it best left that way.'

Edward's lips parted, but there was a long delay before he spoke, and still he did not open his eyes. 'Were we ever true friends...lovers? I liked William Black very much. But did he ever truly like me?'

That was the man's question at a time like this?

'Yes. I liked you...I *like* you, Charters.' Pitch's fingernails dug into the wood. 'We were good friends, first, before that bastard complicated it all. We drank and gambled and fucked, and your company was a pleasure.' The mindless debauchery, a world away from the Hellfield and the drama of Arcadia, was what Pitch had craved. Humankind adored frivolity and trivial, pretty things, as much as Pitch craved them. 'I did not know...I did not know the angel would choose you. He does not ask for permission from anyone, least of all me, and he certainly didn't care if I disapproved. But still, I fucked up, Edward. When I saw that it was not going to be once or twice...I should have done more than just believe him when he said you would not be harmed by his possession.'

He stopped, just shy of saying sorry, the word snagging at the base of his throat. A tear rolled from the corner of Edward's closed eye, slinking like a crystal slug down his temple.

Shit. Sending Charlie away had been a mistake. Pitch was readying to make a dash for the door and retrieve the vagabond when Edward spoke.

'I've not been harmed. I've been blessed, to know you both.' They were not the words Pitch had expected. 'I know you tried at Mordiford to distance yourself for my own good. But you need not feel any guilt. The Holy One is so brilliant, so sublime...you both are. I'm walking where no mere human has a right to walk...amongst the gods, the creatures of the heavens. I am a vessel for the divine. How can I grieve what I might have lost when I am gifted with such treasures as you and he?'

Pitch sighed. The man was in a rapture, surely. But was that such a terrible thing, considering his plight? If Seraphiel had him blinded by reverence, then it was the first mark of kindness the angel had shown.

'Are you in any pain? Do you need more tincture or something?' Pitch touched at some of the bottles, like he actually had a clue which one to use.

'Charlie has told you what I need, Vassago.'

'Don't call me that.'

'I understand it is your true name.' Edward swallowed and it seemed to pain him. 'A daemon prince of Arcadia. The one who shall save this world from a great evil.'

Pitch slumped against the chair. 'He told you all of that, did he? A pity half of it is utter bullshit.'

Edward opened his eyes and Pitch tensed. But it was not Seraphiel's citrine, drilling gaze there, only Edward's calm grey. Remarkably clear.

'I need to take your hand, Tobias.'

'What bloody for?'

'I'm not sure.'

'Well, the *Holy One* has never been big on explanations. Ask him again.'

Edward grunted, eyelids heavy. 'I told you, it is not like that...not exactly...we don't converse...there are visions. I see what it is he wishes me to do. When I touched you in that horrid asylum, it was because I had seen that it must be done. That it was right, even if I didn't truly understand the wheres and whys. It is a wonder the angel has chosen me as his vessel –'

'I pity you for it.' For he knew what it meant to be at Seraphiel's mercy.

Edward broke into a feeble smile. 'I told you, I am humbled that he has chosen me.'

Sweet mercy, the angel had worked the poor man over. 'Fuck, Edward, you are being deluded.'

'I am as clearheaded as I've been since I started dreaming of a beauty beyond imagining. I have been made a part of something...' Edward searched for the words. 'Noble...righteous. He is glorious. And neither you nor he frighten me.'

'Well we bloody well should, Edward. And whatever this is he's doing to you...it will kill you.' He should not have been so harsh, so blunt and brutal, but his anger was directed at the angel beneath Edward's skin. Whatever form he might be in.

'Then my death shall stand for something significant. This cause is far greater than me. *You* are far greater, Your Highness.'

Pitch's empty stomach churned. Edward was by nature a noble man. Decent and mindful of the greater good. Seraphiel...Seraphiel's ghost...whatever this was...was taking advantage of the man's shining attributes.

'I am neither great nor high. Though I wish I was the fucking latter, let me tell you. Don't ever address me that way again if you wish to keep your divinely anointed tongue.'

'You are resplendent, even if you refuse to see it.' The lieutenant pushed himself onto one elbow but did not look fit to stay there long. 'He wishes to see how you fare.'

'How I fare?' Pitch spat. 'I'm tired and sore, as we all are.'

Edward's stare was discomforting. If Pitch was not mistaken, there was a tinge of citrine now spreading through the grey. 'You know of what I speak. Time is of the essence. We have already delayed here too long–'

'Because you are lying half-dead in this bed, Edward. You cannot be moved, and you are the only one who knows where we must go next.'

'The escape from the Fulbourn taxed me greatly.'

'Taxed us all fucking greatly.'

Edward carried on as if he had not spoken. 'The divine magick of the Holy One is not meant for one such as I, just as the burden you carry is not meant for a creature even so powerful as yourself. You are at your limits, Vassago...Tobias. You must know it. But there is much to be done. Give me your hand. Let him see how you fare.' Edward gasped and his body jerked, a hard contorting shift that bucked his hips off the bed. His head slammed down against the pillow.

'Shit.' Pitch shoved the chair aside. 'Charlie! Bess!'

'Not yet. Your hand.' Edward panted, eyes rolling in his head, unable to find focus.

'No. You need help, Edward.'

'Please, Tobias...he must see the flame.' A savage spasm rent through him and he cried out. The veins in his neck bulged. 'Your hand.'

Every fibre of Pitch's being was repelled at the idea of letting Edward touch him. He wanted the angel–or whatever the fuck was consuming Edward–nowhere near him or his flame. The creation flame was for a daemon as a heart was for a purebred. The source of life, the core of being.

At least, that was how it usually was. That was how it *should* be, if an angel did not meddle so thoroughly that a daemon couldn't be sure which, if any, parts of himself were truly his own.

'He intends no harm, Tobias,' Edward gasped, his legs twitching beneath the covers.

'Harm is exactly what he intends. Is that not the whole point of this?'

Edward grimaced, rolling onto one side, causing the pendant watch to dangle and swing. Footsteps came from further down the corridor, perhaps Charlie or Bess heeding Pitch's summons.

Perhaps Silas returning.

But the bedroom door swung shut, closing with a definitive click. The lieutenant's discomfort gurgled from him, along with a thin trail of blood from his nostrils.

'Shit.' Pitch abandoned thoughts of telling Seraphiel, or whatever had Edward writhing, to fuck off and leave them all be. The idea was as ludicrous as his notion of running away.

If the Fulbourn had taught him nothing else, it was that pretending something didn't exist did not make it so.

'Enough. Stop, you bastard. Seraphiel let him be.'

Pitch snatched up Edward's hand.

CHAPTER 4

Silas sank beneath the surface and his scream bubbled and boiled. The cold struck his heart, squeezed his lungs and cries from him until he was empty and desperate for air. He clawed at the surface, a rabid wild animal seeking escape from tall grass in a jungle. Silas erupted from the water with a holler that barely tainted the air, for there was no breath to strengthen it.

Panting, dribbling the gritty pond water, Silas inhaled until his chest puffed and his nostrils could flare no wider.

Christ.

He was upright. He was jellied by fear, but goddamn it, he'd done it.

Silas's laughter was sharp. He raised his arms and punched at the laden sky. 'Did you see that?' He hiccoughed his ecstasy. Asking the question of mindless clouds and the hidden frogs, the only audience to his great feat. 'Did you all see that? I was under...I was under...and I did not lose my mind.'

Not entirely.

He was, though, in danger of losing the tip of his tongue with how violently his teeth chattered. Silas shoved his hands through his hair, slicking the finger-length strands tight against his skull. The grit was a pumice against his skin.

Shit, he was cold, but one brief moment submerged would hardly suffice. He must go again. Further out.

The loch that had taken him was unfathomably deep. There had been no hope of finding solid ground. He should go deeper this time, somewhere he could at least pretend there was an abyss beneath him.

Silas pushed on before his fear could melt through the ice in his veins. He waded deeper, and something weaved about his legs, making his pulse race until he spied the spiky water milfoil which had made a dense home where he stood. The lacy fronds moved like sluggish flags.

'Weeds, nothing more.'

Silas was determined now to hold the reins on his terror. It was *he* who would must taunt the waters. *He* who must bolster the prince when they at last came to this dreaded Blood Lake.

There could be no repeat of the debacle of Goodrich Castle, with Silas clinging to Pitch like a petrified, oversized monkey as they traversed the moat.

He blew out a breath, a blaze of white coming from between his lips, heat defying the chill...as he defied the weight of centuries past.

His life had been taken from him violently–over and over–and his memories stripped by time until he was bare. But nothing could change what was done. And he'd been given life in return, survived where all others had long since succumbed. And Silas did not need to ask why, anymore.

He knew it was for this.

This dreadful, vital moment where he must not just survive but slay those who sought to take from him again.

He was the Lady's Horseman, death's chosen messenger, and the lover of a most undeniable prince. Silas must be ferocious when their enemies came to take what...*who*...was most precious to him.

Silas inhaled, clearing the last of his doubt from his lungs.

And dove beneath the surface. Wide, sweeping strokes took him down. Down further.

The pond was deep at its heart. Far more so than its outward appearance belied. The water clamoured at his ears, forcing its way in and deafening him until all he could make out were the sounds of the bubbles he released and the restless hum of his own mind.

They were there. The memories. Most punishing of all was that very first, when the terror of the masses had seen him banished to a watery grave as the Lord of Arcadia rained down his fury.

Silas knew now it was the fear of the gods he'd seen in his brother's eyes that day. A fear of the monster that lurked in Silas's veins.

The monster perhaps he was.

He had torn teratisms apart with his bare hands and thought nothing of it. Christ, a part of him had relished that violence...until he came to realise he was fighting the wrong enemy.

Down Silas swam. The strokes coming easily.

When had he learned to swim? Was there a lifetime where he'd staved off a summer day with a dip in the sea or a lazy paddle in a lake? And with whom? Perhaps that woman in lavender and her companion had joined him?

Considering how often he had drowned, he was likely a terrible swimmer when it came down to it. But might he have tried to learn? When he had lived, did he sense his great weakness and seek to override it, or did he scramble from bathtubs like a great babbling fool each time?

The flurry of questions was a welcome distraction as he moved downwards. A shame no answers were to be had.

Silas's lungs ached, warning of a need to head back to the surface very soon, if he did not turn into an ice-block before that could happen. He shook so hard that it was as though his organs shuffled about inside him, his heart rattling down to his stomach, and his stomach shimmying its way up to his throat. All the rest tangling together like the milfoil and mare's tail plants that played at his limbs.

Bloody hell, it was like being lost in a forest of weaving eels. The paltry light from the pale winter sky barely penetrated the mass of shifting lengths.

Silas grasped hold of a bunch of frothy mare's tails, wrapping one leg about the gathering of stems to anchor himself.

He floated there in the icebox that was the pond. The quiet was so thick he could hear the faint pulse of his heart in his ears. The weeds touched at him, tendrils that found their way to the back of his neck, snagged in his hair, and touched at his bare feet.

But he had been under water for some time now. And was doing a fine damn job of things, if he did say so himself.

Silas glanced down. And did not expect to find such utter darkness there. Such a clear reminder of the blackness he so often sank into.

He gasped, releasing the very last of the bubbles his lungs could fuel. The panic sneaked in through the swaying mass of weed, darting to find him.

His scream was short-lived, his parched lungs very much done for. Oh god, he was afraid.

Silas kicked out, but he could not seem to separate himself from the milfoil. It was everywhere. He'd free one limb only to have another taken prisoner. Christ almighty, where was the fucking surface? The light had dimmed. The darkness swept up from below, coming to claim him.

Thrashing about was only worsening things, he knew it, but the terror was making a fool of him, and wrapping him more fully in the dense branches of this underwater forest. His vision was spotting, his head light, his lungs empty.

Silas's struggle weakened.

He did not recall which way was up now, even if he could fight his way free. A fool. He was a fool to have done this alone. But surely this could not be his new grave? His hourglass could not have run out so ingloriously. Not right now. With so much left undone. Unsaid.

A spark of indignation tried to catch in the dampness. No. He'd not bloody well die here. He'd made Pitch a promise. Told the prince he'd not navigate his fate alone.

Silas bucked about, his whole world oozing back and forth as breathing became a distant memory. Surely Forneus at least would sense his distress? What good having a fae dog if the bloody thing ignored you when you were clearly in desperate need?

A press at his neck came as tendrils of milfoil wrapped there like ugly, slippery scarves. Silas's eyes flew open as he reached for the slimy noose.

He came face to face with living horror.

A creature swam towards him, illuminated by its own dull light. Large as a badger, it had eyes like saucers, black as the darkness that clawed at Silas's feet. The head was too inflated for its own body, with a skull that was cratered at the top, as though a huge weight had been dropped upon the bone but not killed the unsightly thing. A mosslike substance clung to the rim of that crater, delicate as the lace on a widow's veil.

As Silas struggled against his binds, a huge tongue shot from the creature's mouth, a glint of quicksilver brightening the sombre surrounds.

Silas threw back his head. The creature's tongue sliced against his neck, and Silas feared it was his own blood that would muddy the waters next. Instead, the strangling hold of the milfoil eased.

He'd been freed.

A second creature, smaller than the first but with the same misshapen head and gleaming snakelike tongue, darted in at his side and made quick work of the mare's tail that embraced Silas's waist. Severed chunks of weed floated around him. Spindly arms reached for him, grabbing Silas's shoulder and hauling him upwards. They moved at a startling pace and burst through the surface.

Silas's inhale was like the screech of an ungodly spirit. His ribs flared as though they wished to split his skin wide open and search for yet more air.

The creature still held him, though it stayed hidden just below the surface, only some of its thin arm visible. Where a man would have skin, this strange beast had algae, all shades of green and dirty browns. Silas was propelled towards the shore, coughing and spluttering like the near-drowned man he was.

His throat stung as though all the grit in the pond had streaked it as it drove into his lungs.

The creature's grip was at Silas's collar. He could feel pressure beneath his chin as his head was kept raised from the water. They were moving along at a great clip, fast enough to create a bow wave as Silas's body was pushed through the water and lilies. At his side the water rippled with the presence of the other bowl-headed creature, cruising along like a seal.

Distracted by his swimming companions, Silas startled when the bottom of the pond suddenly pressed against him. He was in the shallows, returned to the gap in the bullrushes where he'd entered the water. Silt forced its way in at the waist of his trousers as he was hauled along the bottom. The hand clenching his shirtfront released him, the ripples spreading away as the creatures turned back towards deeper waters. Silas rolled over. His buttocks sank into the mud, which squelched between his toes and fingers as he sat up, seeking to see who had rescued him.

And that is when the tune began. A slinking, weaving melody that ebbed and then flowed. Subtle, and quite pleasing to the ear.

Water elemental. Undine.

Had he just met Matilda? The last of Holly Village's elementals he was to be acquainted with was not quite what he'd been expecting.

'Noble, but there are warmer baths to take, Mr Mercer.'

Silas jerked about.

A dark-haired woman stood not far from where he sat, and she was every bit as drenched as he was. The long lengths of her hair hung like a small cape over her shoulders and down her back, all the way to the backs of her knees. Her plain cotton gown, a startling white that would challenge a summer cloud, was clearly without corset or crinoline beneath. The material clung to her willowy figure, to the point of indecency. The low cut of the bodice, loosely laced, highlighted the path of water that dripped in a near constant stream from the tip of her aquiline nose to the shallow, exposed valley between modest breasts. Her saturated nature did not seem to faze her in the least. She stood with hands at her sides, quite relaxed despite the downpour.

Here was the undine the notes sang of.

'Matilda?' Silas drew himself onto his knees, trembling like a rain-struck leaf. Thankfully it was mostly cold and not fear that bade him do so. 'It is wonderful to meet you at last. I have much to thank you for.'

'Yes. You do.' The undine's eyes, a fetching shade of blue a few hues lighter than Charlie's bold cornflower shade, flicked down to Silas's chest. When she did not look away as quickly as was mannered, he glanced down at himself.

'Oh my, I'm terribly sorry.' The top buttons of his shirt must be buried in the mud, for they were certainly not at their posts. A good portion of his chest was bare, the curls of dark hair stained with all manner of pond unpleasantness.

'What for?' Raindrops dripped from her lashes, splashing against her cheek in great pronounced displays. 'The view is hardly terrible.' Matilda's way of speaking was deadpan, to say the least. And her words rather embarrassing.

Silas pushed to his feet, gathering his shirt folds, covering himself. 'You must be wondering what on Earth I am doing–'

'No. I am not wondering that at all.'

'Oh...very well, then.' Silas cleared his throat, wincing at the reminder that a short moment ago he'd been drowning. He glanced over his shoulder. The pond's cluttered surface held small patches of lacework where ripples disturbed the surface as the rain continued to fall. 'There are creatures living in that pond who–'

'There are creatures living in all ponds.'

The rain slanted towards Matilda as though seeking her out.

'Yes.' Silas nodded. 'Of course...but I meant these were naturals.'

Matilda arched a thick eyebrow. 'Are naturals not allowed to live in ponds?' The water followed the reshaped contour of her brow, a tiny waterfall streaming near her temple.

'No, no, that's not what I'm saying at all.'

'Are you ungrateful for the kappas extricating you from the pond? Would you prefer they had left you there to dither about in a frenzy?'

The undine's comments were sharp as hail. Silas had the sense of being a child reprimanded by a governess. A few months ago such a retort might have had him cowering. Not now.

'Kappa?' he said. 'Was it you who bade them assist me?'

Matilda's eyes narrowed, though her expression did not change from utterly blank. 'That is not what I first asked you.'

Was it Silas's imagination, or was the downpour more ridiculously heavy now? Soon he'd be in danger of drowning without need of the pond. 'I am most grateful for their assistance,' he said. 'There were more weeds than I'd anticipated, and I did have myself in rather a muddle.'

'But you wish to be in that muddle again.'

Silas stared at the elemental. She was precisely right, and appeared to know it. 'I do. I must.'

The droplets were not only drawn to Matilda, they shrouded her, a watery aura that managed to catch light in the dull surrounds. The beauty contrasted her rather plain features and dour expression.

'You need not fear the water, Mr Mercer. You are a child of its womb.'

That was not a way he'd ever thought to look at it. 'Unfortunately I'm also a corpse in its tomb.' He swallowed. 'I do fear it...terribly so. And I am not proud of it.' He shivered so hard that it was making his muscles ache, those he could still feel at least.

Matilda stood, stoic as any tree in the nearby copse which marked the boundary of the estate. 'So you wish to drown yourself until the fear is parched.' The elemental tilted her head, exposing a wet and glistening throat.

'I must.'

'You keep saying that.'

'Because it is true,' Silas replied. 'I cannot have such a weakness.'

'Strength would snap us in two if not softened by a touch of weakness.'

Silas exhaled. He was cold and very wet, and in no mood for such deep conversation. 'This is more than a touch, I'm afraid. I must be capable of more.' He spoke firmly, Pitch on his mind, and fixed in his heart.

A loud croak came from behind, the guttural bellow of what must be the largest frog in existence. It made Silas's ears ring. So much so he could barely hear the melody that played in the chamber at the back of his mind. A tune that did little more than mimic the bellyaching croak of the kappa itself.

Kappa. Yokai. River child.

Mud wiggled between his toes as Silas turned. His panic must have deafened him to the creatures' naming tune earlier, but it was very clear now.

The kappa, the larger of the two, was in the shallows. Christ, it was an unappealing thing. Squatted down on amphibious haunches the colour of gutter water, the creature peered up at him with its saucer eyes. The concave skull was filled with pond water, which was yet to settle after the kappa's emergence from the depths. It seemed a specimen of confused design. From the waist down it was without doubt an oversized frog, but there was a turtle's carapace upon its back, rough with barnacles, and humanness to the front limbs, arms of a sort, with dubious hands, webbed in the way of a frog.

Staring at it, Silas knew what it was he must do. Mad as it was. 'Would...would you help me?' He turned back to Matilda. She stood in an ever-growing puddle that was glass smooth, despite the steady downpour. 'Would you all help me? I wonder...if the kappa might agree to holding me beneath the water, and ensuring I don't wind up in a tangle again. Would they do that for me?'

Silas balled his fists. Sweet mercy, the mere idea of being held beneath the surface terrified him. But that was entirely the point. He must be fearless.

'Chinami,' Matilda said, flat as a lake on a still day. 'Mr Mercer would like you to help him drown. What say you?'

The reply to the request did not sound favourable: a series of rumbling regurgitations. Silas glanced Matilda's way, inordinately anxious that the elemental and her water children would see fit to help him. 'Was that a yes or a no?'

Matilda did not blink. Had not done so since he'd first set eyes on her. 'That was an angry muttering about how much silt you churned up on your first foray and all the frog spawn you ruined.'

'I'm not sure I can't promise that won't happen again, not to begin with,' Silas said. 'I'm terribly sorry for ruining their pond, truly, but I am in a grim predicament. You know what we face, Matilda. And I want what the kappa want, after all: to be able to enter that pond without losing my mind.'

He tried to imagine holding perfectly still beneath the surface, the crush of the water upon him. Oh shit. The thought was nothing but acrid horror. Best they get on with this before he turned tail and fled back to the house.

'He is right. You do apologise far too much,' Matilda's voice was monotonous to the point of distraction, but he had no doubt of whom she referred to. And reminder of the prince only girded Silas's determination to carry out this god-awful idea.

'Chinami, please,' he beseeched the kappa. 'If you wish to rid your pond of my presence, then assist me now. For I shall plague your waters with or without your agreement. I'm sor...' Silas left the word on his tongue. No more apologising. 'It must be done. That is simply that.'

The kappa tilted its head, a move that should have spilled the water from its bowl cavity, but the liquid caressed the edge and went no further. Chinami opened its mouth and darted a rather putrid green tongue over its own eyeball, the quicksilver gone. A bark came from further out in the pond, the cough of a gentleman who enjoyed cigars too much. The smaller kappa peeked its head out of the water, the soft frond of pond slime around its crown floating atop the surface.

'Ezume says it is best you stop loafing about on the mud then,' Matilda said. 'If you wish to love the water.'

'"Love" is rather a strong word,' Silas replied. 'But they are not wrong otherwise.' He waded in until the water cupped his knees. Perhaps he was entirely numb because the touch was not so icy as before. But he hesitated, rubbing at his bearded chin before turning back. 'Matilda, I wonder...if you have the time...might you stay with me?'

Silas was drawn to the undine's unflappable manner, to her curious talk of him being a child of the water. It calmed him in a way that surprised him. Not to mention, he expected she could deliver quite the harsh scolding should he resurface in a mindless panic. A good incentive to hold it together.

'I am not leaving you, Mr Mercer.'

'Thank you, very much.' He turned back to the pond, which did not seem quite so fathomless now.

Chinami croaked and sprang from the muddy shallows, leaping into the depths with a great splash. Ezume barked and performed a splendid flip before disappearing too.

Without hesitation, barely a hint at all, Silas dove in to follow.

CHAPTER 5

Pitch took Edward's hand, and the wildness charged from its hiding place.

Plunged its claws into his heart.

And the room gave way to fire.

Pitch winced beneath the roar, the crackle and hideous snap of an inferno that consumed all in its path, including the daemon who bore it. He bowed beneath the onslaught, curling his shoulders against the blaze, melting away into nothingness as his world, his existence, became a raging fire. He was the core of a sun that had erupted, and its molten innards spewed from him, spreading over him in enormous wings of flame.

If this was the wildness, it had not only stepped from its cage, it had incinerated it.

Pitch bent beneath the great weight until he thought he would break in two. He was no stranger to this formation of his flame. The winged expanses had been useful at Goodrich Castle, certainly at the Fulbourn. But even on the day his control had abandoned him, the day Seraphiel fell, the flames had not been so riotous as this.

These wings could shadow the world. Reach all the way into Arcadia and brush their tips against White Mountain. They were all-consuming. Overwhelming. A wingspan far too magnificent for any paltry daemon to control.

The wings began to beat. Stirring hurricanes around him. Horrendous blasts of heat that sought to eviscerate all.

Pitch thought he was screaming. His mouth was wide open, his throat ached, but he could not say if he made a sound, for the tremendous hunger of the flames ate at everything.

There was no containing this monster. This wildness.

Pitch sank to his knees.

Your avoidance of the prophet is costly. The Seraphim's voice slipped through the fire, and his words burned. *Your endurance falters, and the prophet is of weak flesh. You are failing me.*

Gods, the angel was a cunt even now.

'How I've missed you.' Pitch's words, but he could not say if they were spoken or merely thought as he cowered inside a firestorm. *'Were you ever fucking dead? What is this?'*

I am neither life nor death.

Though still ever the arcane bastard. Gods, Pitch abhorred the opaque nature of the higher angels.

But whatever Seraphiel might be, he was not happy. Beneath the roar of the winged bonfire Pitch was alerted to a sensation he knew well. The simmer of the angel's anger. The Seraphim may claim to be neither here nor there, but he was still capable of being pissed off.

The rage was palpable. The wings beat harder, strained further, grew ever more gigantic. And Seraphiel's fury built with it.

Pitch realised, with no small amount of sheer delight, that he was struggling. Gods, was the wildness too much, even for the angel who manipulated it? If only Pitch did not feel like he was swimming in the primordial flames under the Ophanim Throne, he would have cheered the beast on.

'What have you done to me?' His jaw was turning to stone beneath the heat.

Cultivated a last hope. The voice came like air escaping a bellows, strong to begin but dying quickly. *The prophet must reach the Sanctuary, he is the key. No more delay, daemon.*

The arsehole could turn him inside out but couldn't give Pitch a name. *'I don't know where your fucking Sanctuary is, you prick. I was more prisoner than guest, do you recall?'*

Seraphiel, the undead cockhead, didn't answer that. *The prophet knows the way.*

'And *the prophet is dying,'* Pitch thought-said. *'You're killing him.'*

You forced my words from his lips in the home of your enemy. The blame is yours. The angel's voice dropped low beneath the savagery of the fire. How Pitch despised this holy arsehole.

'Tell me *where your fucking Sanctuary is. Let Edward go.'*

The Sanctuary calls to him alone.

'Well that's a stupid fucking idea–'

Enough. The bellows exhaled a mighty blast, causing even the wings to miss a beat where they sought to melt all the known worlds. *He hunts for you, the Watcher King in his lake. The behemoth you carry must be silenced, lest its cry be heard. With this last seal, you will know true weakness. See you are guarded well. Prepare the prophet to ride this day.*

Pitch's ire was as red hot as the flames encompassing him. He yearned to say so much more, but the conversation was over.

The language of the higher angels whispered through the flames and reached out to shape themselves around the wings. Drawing them in. Dragging at their titanic reach, pressing them back into Pitch in a tidal wave of firelight. The heat was astounding, eviscerating his insides, taking him over, the wildness...the behemoth...snapping back at the angel who sought to cage it.

Seal it away.

Divine magick hissed around him, rain on hot rocks.

The angel's monster fought its master. And Seraphiel...dead or alive...was much displeased.

I am your master. His voice roared in Pitch's head. *You will heed me.*

Much the same words as he'd uttered that day on the cliff. And there, in the midst of the inferno, Pitch understood.

The angel's own Cultivation was testing the limits of his control.

And the struggle was not new.

Seraphiel had *always* been barely in control of his own beast. This behemoth. Maybe that explained so many secreted trips to the blasted Sanctuary. The angel had overreached, and couldn't quite bring his invention to heel. Still, he'd forced the burden on Pitch regardless. Left a daemon prince to drown in his own nightmare.

The heat vanished; the cage slammed shut. And the real world returned, with all the force of a slap to the face.

Actually, no. Someone *had* just hit him.

Pitch's eyes blazed. The view he saw through narrowed lids was sunset red.

'Pitch...go!' someone shouted. 'Just bloody well...go.'

Pitch shook his head. No...that wasn't what was said.

'Let go.'

'Let him go, Tobias. Bloody hell.' Frantic, panicked. Charlie. 'Let go of Edward, now.' The lad hissed a curse. 'Bess! Someone help me.'

Pitch blinked his eyes wide. The light was dull, no longer incandescent. He knelt on the floor, straddled over the lieutenant, the man's nightshirt bunched in his fists. Pitch had Edward's shoulders lifted off the floor, and the man just hung there, not resisting. Not moving at all. Dry lips slack and parted, the blood from his nosebleed streaking his cheeks with the lolling of his head.

Charlie grabbed his arm. Nothing too forceful, but Pitch was in no mood for punishment of any kind.

'Don't touch me.' A feral snarl if ever there was one. He knew his eyes were alive with flame, his *own* flame. And clearly he had just attacked Edward, but Charlie did not run away screaming like so many did from Vassago when he was in such a mood. Pitch was struck again by the lad's courage.

'You need to let him go, Tobias,' Charlie said quietly. He sat back on his heels, hands raised as though to show he held no weapon, the weave of the rowan wood and holly bracelet peeking from beneath his sleeve. 'I know you do not truly wish him any harm.'

'You know absolutely nothing, you fool.' He could not shift the image of those monstrous flames from his mind.

Charlie edged a hand towards the lieutenant's head, but seemed undecided if now was the right time to move. 'I know you are decent,' he said. 'Despite your best efforts to prove otherwise. I know I've seen you give everything to protect those around you, me included. And I know you see something in Edward...in what is happening to him...that frightens you terribly. It frightens me too, Tobias.' The lad touched his wrist. 'Please let him go.'

Pitch licked his lips, lowering his gaze. His pulse was still racing, hammering nails into his temples. But the space in his head the angel had filled was gloriously empty.

He released the lieutenant's shirt. Charlie caught Edward's shoulders before his head was in danger of striking the floor.

'Charlie?' The soft voice came from behind Pitch.

'It's all right now, Bess,' Charlie said, carefully. 'Edward had another of his fits, and he fell from the bed.'

The pregnant pause told Pitch that Old Bess recognised the lie. He turned.

The mistress of Harvington Hall hesitated in the doorway. Pitch drank in the familiarity, using it to anchor himself back in the world. The Child of Melusine's usual glamour was absent, his silver-grey hair unhidden by any elaborate wig, his earlobes not troubled by impossibly heavy earrings. He wore not a whit of makeup, having just been rudely awoken, and wore a splendid nightgown, the laciest, frilliest piece of apricot-hued linen Pitch had ever laid eyes on.

'Right then,' Old Bess said, assuming a cheeriness that was no more than skin deep. 'Shall we get Edward back into bed?'

Truly it was no better being condescended to than being feared. 'He didn't fall from the fucking bed.' Pitch dragged himself off the lieutenant, bracing against the edge of the bed to pull his sorry arse upright. He was utterly wrung out and filled with an unsettling quiet after the chaotic angelic interlude.

'Care to share what did occur then, Tobias?' Old Bess spoke gently, which made Pitch suddenly, inexplicably enraged.

'And then what? You sell our secrets to the Morrigan, or pass them to your dear sister who is clearly their whore for hire?'

Charlie took a sharp breath. Bess's unusually bare face reddened. He clutched at the delicate lacework of his gown with too much fervour. 'I know you suffered at Palatyne's Sanctuary, but you go too far, Astaroth. I would never betray you or the Order. I am not your enemy.'

'How can I be sure of that?' Pitch was high on the wave of his confusion and trepidation now, channelling all his terror at the Child of Melusine. It was undeserved. He was a bastard. He could not stop. 'Your kind are easily swayed by deep pockets and flashing gems, all know it. Perhaps your sister Jacquetta is not disappeared at all but at this very moment tending the Sanctuary she built to hide the sorcerers in. The Morrigan were not born fully grown, they had to shit their pants and learn to walk somewhere.'

Bess's angry blush deepened. 'Look to the UnSeelie Court if you wish to find the nursery of maleficium. Look to the Watcher angel Iblis. And don't you dare sully my sister's name again in such a way. Jacquetta loves this world. Loves the part of her that is human, with a passion even *I* do not share. She would never, ever side with those who seek to allow maleficium to endanger the purebreds.'

Pitch was spoiling for a fight to vanquish his own distress. 'You don't even know where the fuck she is, let alone what she is doing with her spare time–'

'Stop, both of you,' Charlie cried. 'Bloody hell, Edward is still on the blasted floor and you are throwing stupid tantrums.'

As he spoke he was gathering the lieutenant up, an arm beneath his shoulders, the other beneath his knees.

'Fool, he's too heavy for you,' Pitch sniped.

'I can do it, Tobias.' Charlie moved to lift the man, who must be near double his weight, however undernourished Edward had become. 'Just leave me be.'

He shouldered Pitch away, who watched in some small astonishment as the lad did indeed lift the lieutenant, senseless as he was, and place him on the bed. It wasn't graceful; it was more a heave and drop than anything, but it was done. Pitch glanced at Old Bess, who was watching the display with equal surprise. He made a face when he caught Pitch's gaze, as though to say he had no idea when Charlie had become a weightlifter either.

Pitch deflated, all trace of his irrational fury slipping away. It was a terrible accusation he'd just levelled at a man who'd tended him so carefully at the hall. Who'd been there to help haul his disastrous arse out of the Fulbourn, and who was keeping them safe now. Not to mention clothed and fed.

Pitch should have offered an apology. Silas certainly would have nudged one out of him. But Pitch was tinder dry and more exhausted now than he'd felt all week. What he wanted most of all was to crawl back into his bed, hide beneath the covers, and pretend the angel had never spoken. Never given the beast a name: behemoth.

Pitch suppressed a shiver. He needed the ankou in that bed with him. It would not be so cold then.

'What?' Bess lifted a heavy brow. 'Why are you staring at me? Do you wish you had a nightgown like this one? I could have Ronin send one for you if you like?'

It was a return to their normal inane banter. Old Bess graciously letting go of Pitch's brutal accusations. But mention of the tsukumogami evaporated his considerations of an apology.

'I don't want anything from Ronin.' Memory of their fuck on the stairwell at Harvington Hall left him oddly uncomfortable. He wondered if Tyvain had told Silas what she'd seen. He wondered why he cared either way. 'Nor do I desire to wear such a ridiculously frilly nightgown.' An utter lie and everyone in the room who was not unconscious knew it. 'Where is Sybilla?'

'She needed some herbs Harvington Hall couldn't provide. She rode out on Hastings in the early hours, but Matilda says she's on her return now.'

The Valkyrie must have been desperate to risk riding out, though between her own magick and the horse she rode, Sybilla could hide herself well.

'She needs to see to Edward the moment she returns.' Pitch hesitated. He had considered saying absolutely nothing about the angel's directions. But the only one who would truly suffer with that was the lieutenant. 'We must ride out today.'

'Today?' Charlie was alarmed. 'Edward can't be moved–'

'We go today.' Pitch tucked in his shirt, where his encounter with the angel had made him into a slovenly mess. But even such a small effort left him drained.

Old Bess frowned. 'Surely you cannot ride out before the Lady's horses arrive?'

'They will find us when they deign to grace us with their presence. We cannot wait.' With Edward unfit to travel, Sybilla had told Pitch and Silas that Sanu and Lalassu were aiding in the Order's search for the Morrigan. And for the kitsune, Ernest Weatherby, who had been sighted just outside of Cambridge, attempting to weasel his way onto a coach he had no payment for. Whether he was seeking to rejoin Dr Severs or fleeing for his life was yet to be determined. 'Bess, do you know where Silas is?'

It was Old Bess's Sanctuary, after all. He probably knew where all the mice in the house were.

'Well, not exactly. Somewhere in the garden, I think.' The half-blood fae was not so good a card player as he thought. He had a tell when he was lying: the tiniest twitch in his left eye.

'Why are you lying to me?'

All manner of wild thoughts gripped him. One shouted loudest of all. The ankou had left him, he'd had a gutful of all this, packed his bags and gone.

'Now, now.' Old Bess tutted. 'Don't be worrying yourself so. I know he is in the gardens, but I think perhaps he needs some time on his own.'

Silas hadn't left. Pitch's pulse beat out the declaration, chasing some of his weariness away.

'Well, that is too bad, for we need to begin preparations for our departure, and he can't be out talking to pine cones while we do all the work.' He moved to the doorway. Bess stood aside to let him pass. 'See to it that those corsets you promised are delivered at once. I shall not ride off to my certain doom unbound, it just wouldn't do.' He glanced at Charlie, who was occupied with resetting Edward. The lieutenant seemed peaceful enough after his latest trials, lying very still, his lips slightly parted. Pitch turned back to Old Bess, keeping his voice low. 'The coat...I know there's hardly been time, but is there any chance–'

'I put Lim and Xian onto it as soon as you asked a few days ago. They're in Mustow Green and an absolute wonder, Lim especially, with a piece of cloth. They've made good progress I'm told. The coat will be ready for him before you set off, I'm certain.' Bess was tired too. Pitch saw it now that he was close. His beard needed trimming, his brows a decent pluck. 'It's a very thoughtful gesture, Tobias.'

Concern and something softer, more like affection, mingled with the lines at the corners of his eyes. Old Bess reached for Pitch, likely going to say something appallingly sentimental.

'Get Sybilla back here quickly, Bess.'

Pitch was out the door and down the corridor before the mistress of Harvington Hall could say another word.

CHAPTER 6

O utside, the rain was absolutely pelting down. As Pitch stepped out onto the verandah, his skin was shot through with goosebumps from the freezing air. It was bloody wonderful after the heat of those flames. He was shivering. A fire daemon was shaking like the leaves on the trees as the rain pummelled them.

Pitch moved to the edge of the modest verandah and stuck his hands out into the icy rain, teeth chattering. He did not recall ever being so cold in his life, and was caught between a deep, snaking concern and utter exhilaration.

'Fire man funny.'

The giggle came from up in the branches of a mature birch tree that leaned in close to the house.

'Tilly?' Pitch peered through the haze of rain. 'What the fuc...blazes are you doing up there?'

The dryad changeling could not have gotten more drenched if she'd been sitting in a washing tub. Tilly's snow-white hair was flat against her skull, stuck to her cheeks. Her nightdress was a sky-blue wrapping about her small body, her feet bare, her lips bright red despite the cold.

'Look me, look me,' she demanded and got to her feet, bouncing on the branch, sending new showers downwards.

'I don't want to look at you.'

'My tree. I'm dancing.'

'Is that what you call it?' Pitch ignored the child's dubious ballerina skills upon the thin branch. Nancy would have a heart attack to see it. Tilly was at least ten feet off the ground. She wobbled and giggled and threw her arms about like she would be happy to tumble off at any moment. The dryad was in her element of course, one with the trees.

Which gave Pitch an idea. 'Do you know where Silas is, in the garden?'

'Yes.' A pirouette, a light leap onto a higher branch.

'Where?'

'In the water.'

That had Pitch's head drawing up. 'What?'

'Silas in water.'

Another day he would ask why the blazes she could say the ankou's name, yet he was to be known forever more as 'fire man.' 'Don't be ridiculous,' Pitch retorted, blinking through the fine mist of sodden air. 'He hates the water.'

'Yes. He hates sinking.' Tilly leapt, grabbing easily at a neighbouring branch and swinging like the trapeze artist she would likely become.

'Sinking?' Pitch was not going to panic just yet. His information was coming from a child that still likely wet its bed, fae or not. 'Stop talking utter nonsense. If you don't know where he is, just say so.'

The changeling plonked onto her backside on a particularly straight branch and toppled backwards. Pitch gasped and took a step forward. Tilly locked herself around the branch, hanging by her knees, regarding him from her upside-down position as she swung there. 'Silas in the pond. Sinking. Wet lady make him.'

'Wet lady?' Pitch was all manner of uneasy. 'Tilly, stop fucking about.'

The changeling giggled. 'Bad fire man.'

'Tilly,' Pitch snapped. 'Where is Silas?' His temper unfurled right alongside his fear.

The child pouted, and damn it, if she started to cry, he would consider slapping the sense into her.

'That way.' A chubby finger pointed down towards the far end of the garden. 'I take you.'

'I don't need you to escort–'

Tilly waved her hands at the ground, and the drenched, packed leaves there rustled in their muddy confines. A clump rose up, gathering like a sickly-looking bird in the air.

'Silas don't like sinking,' Tilly said, with a touch of sadness that had Pitch's gut lurching.

'No, he bloody well doesn't. Show me where he is, Tilly.'

This didn't make any sense. Who the hell was the wet lady? Bess would know if Silas was in danger, surely?

The cluster of leaves shot off, headed where Tilly pointed. Pitch ran into the rain, chasing the enchanted debris. His heart was already slamming as though he'd run a mile. Sinking? Fuck, this had better be a child's gibberish. The wet woman could be a silly imagining of an infantile mind. Or more nefarious, like a Jenny Greentooth or, gods forbid, a siren, seducing the ankou into the depths.

Pitch barely noticed that his boots were double their weight with mud. His worries came at him, charging in like a bull, piercing him through.

Wet lady make him.

'Fuck. Fuck.'

There was a traitor within the ranks of the Order. Macha had known of Pitch's recovery from illness in the Village, and the ill-fated phone call to the Atlas from the Crimson Bow. So did the Morrigan already know of their hiding place? Had he been lying languid in bed while Silas was tormented? Why hadn't the imbecile woken him? Pitch would have been persuaded to take a bloody stroll eventually. Silas need not have gone alone.

Pitch struggled to catch his breath, his thoughts in a spin as he ran behind the leaves that whirled about one another like a flock of sparrows. A pressure sat on his ribs, growing heavier with each step, as though the mud clung there too.

The garden was terribly overgrown. Silas had moaned about it several times the past few days, attempting to regale Pitch with his ideas for its improvement. As though he actually believed Pitch gave a shit about plants. Now the poor upkeep had him fuming. Pitch stomped over the brown skeleton of what might have been a rose bush and slapped at a birch that dangled its winter-silent branches in his way. He slipped in exposed patches of soil and stumbled over abandoned garden beds that sucked at his boots as though they intended to eat them.

The fucking rain was intolerable. He was as soaked as if he'd been standing out here all day naked. Ahead, a rundown cottage poked its roof through the clutches of a hedge of blackberries. Tilly's guiding flurry of leaves jabbed itself towards the left-hand side of the cottage and then collapsed upon the ground, its work done.

He was close.

Pitch raced ahead, considering burning his way through the blackberries rather than taking a widened path around them. He called the flame to hand. And by the gods it must have been as exhausted as he was, for he'd never known it so slow to heed him.

'Come on, come on,' he snarled at his own hands, his own ineptitude. Seraphiel's words curled at the back of his mind.

With this last seal, you will know true weakness.

Pitch banished the thought with a flick of his wrists and was rewarded with the hint of flames at his fingertips. He skirted around the blackberries, close enough to curse them as they grabbed at him, scratched their thorns across his lightly glowing hands. Too damp to be under any threat from his fire.

'Hold him down longer this time.' The dreary voice came from up ahead.

Matilda. The wet lady.

'And hold him at the bottom. No matter how he might protest.'

Incandescent anger bloomed, sucking what air there was from Pitch's lungs. He raced through a lopsided rose arch, brushing the rotten timber as he went, making the whole structure tremble.

Matilda stood at the edge of a pond, an unimpressive body of water that was stifled with bullrushes and a carpet of green upon its surface. At its heart the liquid bubbled.

As though someone screamed from beneath.

'Silas!' Pitch roared.

But his hands did not. A single, contemptible flame at his forefinger. Nothing more. Fuck, what was wrong with him? His lungs were tight, his body constricted as though he already wore the severest of corsets.

'What are you bellyaching about?' Matilda cast a sideways glance, as though he wasn't worth the effort to turn for.

'Let him go, now.' His shout was not so formidable as he'd planned. It was hard to bellow when you could not draw breath. 'You traitorous bitch.'

Matilda's disdain wrinkled her face, her hair hanging like wet lengths of liquorice to the backs of her knees. 'Are you drunk again?'

Fuck the flame, he'd use brute force instead. Panic reared. A stallion kicking at his innards. But not the fucking stallion he needed. 'Let him go.'

'You need to calm down.' Matilda was droll, and painfully unthreatened.

Calm down? While she held Silas in his greatest nightmare? While the great and terrible Prince Vassago could do nothing but point a flame-ridden finger to terrorise her? 'What have you done, Matilda?' That time he nearly ended up on his arse, his foot catching in dense ground matter.

'Stop shouting like a maniac and I shall say.'

She was so fucking patronising. It was infuriating. Pitch's throat tightened with mindless rage. He *should* have been burning the pond dry too. 'I swear, if you have harmed him...' Gods, was this possible? Matilda stealing the ankou from him right beneath his nose? A quieter part of his mind cast doubt but could barely make itself known over the fear.

Silas is gone. You are alone. Pitch's heartbeat tolled.

'I do not have the ankou.' Matilda folded her thin arms, her dour expression saying clearly she thought him out of his fucking mind. 'Astaroth, you should take a breath before you make more of a tit of yourself.'

But he had no time for the trivialities of breathing. Matilda stood between him and the water. Between him and Silas. Pitch lunged at her, a woman who could run like a river. Matilda was gone before he'd taken three steps. He charged at empty air, rain-soaked but empty air. His feet hit the mud at the edge of the pond; his boots flew out from under him. His arse hit hard enough to make his teeth clatter, and he slid until he was waist deep in the water.

'Fuck.'

The water was beyond cold. And Silas was likely beneath it.

Pitch rocked onto his knees, the silt claiming them, and launched himself at the water. He crashed into it with all the aplomb of a brick.

The shock of the cold stole what vapours were left in his lungs. He was light-headed nearly at once. His arms slashed at the veritable forest of water plants. The pond was choked and murky as a London fog.

The merest glow came from his eyes, but the flame was as useless there as elsewhere. The sickly yellow pallor illuminated no more than a few inches ahead of him.

Useless, useless godsdamned flame.

Tiny bubbles escaped from the corners of his mouth. Pitch's lungs were two chunks of lead in his chest. The thrash of his pulse was at heady gallop. His heart wanted out of its ribbed caged.

A strange hysteria crept over him.

Useless, useless daemon.

Slimy wrappings tangled around his legs, teased at his elbows. The gritty water stung his eyes. He had no idea where he was going. What he would do when he got there.

No idea if he was too late.

He couldn't defeat a pond on a country estate, let alone Blood Lake.

Gods, Silas.

The pond wrapped about Pitch, constricting him. The hysteria tapped its fingertips over his spine. Over the marks of the amuletum that had been etched there to keep a wild daemon subdued.

Now the Seraphim had added his own measure. Put fresh chains upon a captive prince.

And Silas would pay the price for it.

The water vibrated with Pitch's scream.

CHAPTER 7

Silas settled upon a rock at the bottom of the pond, the very deepest point, he was assured. Which, considering the body of water's modest size, was quite deep indeed. A kappa held him at each arm, anchoring him. But they were quick to release him the moment he signalled it was time. He'd tested the signal several times to be sure.

This was his third attempt at being held in the murky, icy, and quite unpleasantly slimy depths, and so far this time he managed to keep his pulse to a reasonable clatter and not yet pushed Chinami aside to claw his way to the surface.

To say Silas was calm would be a blatant untruth. His past rumbled in his head like a horrific shadowbox playing out the scenes of his final moments. It would take more than this single morning in a neglected garden pond to overcome the terror of all his deaths...but it was a start.

He closed his eyes, mostly because the silt was so bloody thick, but also because the darkness behind his lids was not filled with so many shadows as the abysmal pond.

At once he was in the boat on the loch. The first boat.

Back at the beginning, where he so often was dragged.

The water was frothing, rebelling against the land as the rains came down. All was shrouded in silence. But the fear was there alive and well.

As was his brother, a slighter man than Silas. Time had smoothed down his features, and the colour of his eyes was lost, the contours of his face unclear. Like watching someone through tears. The boy with the cornflower-blue eyes huddled in the crudely shaped bow of the wildly rocking boat.

And he was frightened. Terribly so.

Silas's brother and another, a man worn to a silhouette by the passage of the years, took a hold of the young man. Sought to drag him to his feet.

The boy fought like a lion, trying to fend off the much stronger men.

Silas did not recognise this version of events.

The time was the same, certainly, the feverish gallop of fear exact, but Silas did not recall sitting in the boat, watching the boy kick and fight to keep his place.

Charlie's ancestor screamed. Silas's eyes flickered open, half expecting to see the child beside him. He could swear he'd heard the scream, while all else in the vision was silent.

He blinked at the harsh caress of the water and closed his eyes once more.

Watched as grown men sought to hurl a child to his death to appease a deity that could not have cared less if they had all drowned.

But Silas had not just watched on that awful day. The memory dislodged from where it had snagged in the recesses of his mind. Silas had pleaded. Begged for the boy to be spared.

The breath he was holding slipped between his lips as he exhaled. Christ. Yes.

He'd begged them to sacrifice him first. Offered the boy the only thing he could. More time.

Silas's shocked cry drew the last bubble from him. He realised now what this meant.

Charlie's ancestor, the sweet young man who had tried to save Silas in return with the futile casting of the bandalore, had survived. And Silas's sacrifice bound them.

A strong current pushed at Silas, and Ezume's hold on his arm released. He opened his eyes anew. Chinami babbled incoherently, bubble bouquets erupting from its wide mouth. The kappa jabbed its webbed fingers into the murkiness.

There was something tangled in the weeds, fighting to free itself. Silas pushed off his rock, using the stem of a water lily to pull himself forward and see what had invaded his pond.

But it was not *what*.

Who.

Pale skin and slender arms, a glint of gold in his hair. Silas spat a curse, his lungs reminding him there was no air left for such things.

Pitch was in the goddamned water.

Chinami reached him first and was deft with freeing the jerking, thrashing daemon. Broken water-lily stems joined a mesh of slashed milfoil as the kappa released Pitch.

Silas grabbed at one of his arms, pulling his slender body close. He rushed them to the surface. Ezume grabbed hold of Silas's shirt and pulled him along. Pitch's body spasmed once, then stilled, adding a further chill to Silas's already-frigid bones.

They broke the surface, and Silas felt the kappas' amphibious hands at his arms and his back, sending him at speed towards the shallows. He concentrated on keeping Pitch's head clear of the water. All too concerned with how quiet the prince was, how slack his body in Silas's hold.

'Pitch? Can you hear me?'

There was no reply.

Silas felt the ground beneath him at the same moment the kappas backed off, releasing him and letting him glide in to where the water lapped at the mud. Matilda stood there, arms folded. No bloody help at all.

He settled Pitch on his side, conscious of how full of water he must be. He nearly buckled with relief when the daemon coughed out a great brown mouthful of putrid water.

'What happened?' he demanded of the water elemental.

'He thought I was killing you.' Matilda was unperturbed.

But Silas less so.

That may explain why the prince was in the water. But why the bloody hell was Pitch shaking so hard, his eyes clenched shut, odd whispers coming from between chattering teeth?

'Pitch, I'm here. Take a breath now. You're out of the water.' Silas knelt over him, water raining down onto the oddly unresponsive daemon. He should have been cursing at the very least, bellyaching about being in the mud for certain. But instead there was only strained clicks coming from his throat, as though a blockage stopped the slightest hint of air moving down. 'Pitch, take a breath now. Come on.'

That seemed to shift the daemon from his frozen stupor. He rolled onto his back and opened his eyes, revealing the merest hints of his flame through the emerald. The prince clutched at Silas's chest with one hand, while the other did the same to his own, pulling at the sodden fabric of his shirt. The prince's lips were blue as winter lake ice. He was gasping something incoherently. The traces of his flame evaporated from his gaze, and in their wake was left behind a most peculiar look. One so at odds with the daemon himself that it took Silas too long to see it.

This was sheer panic.

'Easy now.' Silas tried to stop him from scratching at his chest, but his frantic effort was strong. 'Pitch, please. What is wrong?'

'He worked himself into a state looking for you. Acted like a bloody madman. If I thought him capable of such things, I'd say he's hysterical.'

Pitch let go of Silas's shirt to grasp at his own collar, his fingers tearing at the lacework there. 'Can't breathe.' He sounded like a steam train hissing, but Silas caught the prince's words sure enough. And he realised Matilda was absolutely right.

Silas knew Pitch capable of working himself into an agitated state, he'd seen it when the daemon and Lucifer shared harsh words. But then the panic had manifested in flame and bitter words, not this frailty.

'Pitch, listen to me.' Silas took hold of his chin, careful to be soft about it. He made sure they were eye to eye. 'You *can* breathe. I assure you. This is an attack of panic.'

'No. No air.'

'There is plenty of it for you. Easy now.' Silas moved his hand to lay it over Pitch's, where the daemon seemed still intent on tearing off his clothing. 'Steady, my dear. Breathe with me.'

Silas inhaled deeply, dragging it through his nostrils loudly to make his point. He made sure his exhale could be felt, sending warm air against

Pitch's eyelashes, making them flutter. He abhorred the fear he saw in the prince's eyes. 'Pitch, my darling, you are safe. I promise you.'

Silas tensed, realising what he'd said out loud. He'd gotten away with the endearment once, leaving the Fulbourn, for Pitch had been unconscious. He was certainly not now.

A strained inhale came from the daemon, as though he were as shocked as Silas to hear such pretty talk. His breathing evened.

'There, you see?' Silas said softly. 'You are safe.'

Matilda made a sound that could pass for amusement or ridicule. Whichever it was, Silas startled to hear it. He'd forgotten his audience. But he did not look away. Pitch stared up at him as though he were the only star for his ship to navigate by.

'I don't think it was his safety he was worried about, Mr Mercer.' For a water elemental, Matilda was very dry. 'You didn't tell him about the pond.'

It was not a question, so he gave no answer, but surely the prince was not so concerned that he'd become paralysed with fear?

Silas raised Pitch's hand to his lips and pressed a kiss to his knuckles, which were small hills of ice. 'Is that what caused this? I'm so sorry, Pitch. I should have told you what I intended to do...I thought you'd think me foolish.'

He'd been a fool all right. He'd sought to make himself more useful to this glorious creature, not render him incapacitated with worry. Silas's gaze slipped over soft, full lips that now held a hint of their more desirable pinkness. 'I'm sorry,' he whispered again.

The prince nodded, and when he blinked, the last of the shadows were wiped from his gaze. They breathed in unison for a few breaths, the prince finding a stronger rhythm with each rise and fall, his eyes never leaving Silas's face. But blast it was cold, and they were both saturated. Pitch's shivering would not end if they stayed here. Silas set aside the niggling voice that wondered why a fire daemon shook so.

'I should get you back to the house,' he said.

He was not prepared at all when Pitch freed his hands and shoved them against Silas's chest.

He let out a startled cry, rocking back on his heels, barely stopping himself from being thrown back into the water. The prince scrambled away as though he'd been held a prisoner in Silas's arms.

'What the bloody hell was that for?' Silas demanded.

Pitch's rise to his feet was made inelegant by the slip of his boots in the slime and mud. 'Being an idiot.' He was hoarse, coughing his words. Pitch gestured at the pond. 'What the fuck do you think you were doing, Mercer?'

Oh the daemon was himself again all right. Silas sighed. 'I will explain it to you when we are drying by the fire.'

The prince flinched and his scowl deepened. 'You'll explain it right bloody now, ankou. I'll not be ordered about.'

'I'm not ordering you about, Pitch,' Silas replied.

But gentle as he sought to be, irritation stirred. Silas had the grit of the pond in all the wrong places. He'd barely managed not to have become a mindless mess of nerves himself at the bottom of that pond. He wasn't steady enough yet to handle the return of the daemon's sharp tongue.

'I've enough to be bothered with, Mercer,' Pitch said. 'I don't need to be racing around after you when you decide to take swimming lessons from toads.'

The kappas, watching the show from where they squatted on either side of Matilda, clicked their jiggling throats in annoyance.

'Mind your pretty mouth, daemon,' Matilda said. 'I tire of your theatrics.'

'Oh, fuck off.'

Matilda's eyes narrowed. She flicked her fingers at the air. Sharp pellets of frozen rain drove down at Pitch– but missed Silas entirely.

The prince launched into a dance of many curses, flailing his arms about and coming up with a multitude of ways he was going to put an end to the water elemental, which only caused her to hurl larger hailstones at him.

'That is quite enough,' Silas declared. 'Matilda, I appreciate your assistance, but I'd say we are done here.' He strode to the prince's side, grateful when the hailstones ceased. In one precise move, Silas took hold of the flailing daemon's waist and lifted him, casting him over his shoulder.

'What the fuck do you think you are doing?'

'Putting an end to this, Pitch. You are freezing.'

'Set me down, you bastard.'

The prince slapped at his back, a halfhearted effort at best, considering his strength. Pitch could extricate himself from Silas's hold in a heartbeat, if he so desired.

'Stop wiggling about.' Silas, acting on sheer impulse and mild exasperation, slapped Pitch's arse, a sharp flick of the wrist that rang out against pert flesh. The most adorable sound of astonishment escaped the daemon.

'How dare you, Mr Mercer.' But the barbs had smoothed from Pitch's tongue.

Silas, his own angry mood considerably dulled, turned to Matilda and the kappas, who watched the whole spectacle intently.

'Thank you, to you all, for the help you gave me today.'

Ezume did something odd with its lips, a smile, though it was a gruesome thing to behold. Chinami croaked, nodding its head, the water sloshing about in the cavity.

'Matilda, if you will please excuse us? I think perhaps I should like to have a few words with Mr Astaroth, alone.'

Matilda's bland expression did not alter. There was no telling what she thought of this...of anything at all really.

'Fine. But if you'd be so kind as to stay out of the pond, the kappas would appreciate it. It will take a good hour or so for all that silt the daemon churned up to settle.'

Chinami croaked its agreement, a sound like a broken town-square clock. Pitch wriggled about, taking a breath to reply.

But Silas was in no doubt it was high time for a departure, and he hurried away with his bristling, shivering passenger.

CHAPTER 8

Silas had them inside, out of the elements, as quickly as he could. The run-down cottage consisted of a single room with one very smudged window, making the cluttered interior dimmer than the grey morning outside. He was trying to decide where to set Pitch down when the daemon delivered a vicious slap to his backside.

'Jesus,' Silas cried.

'No, only me. I thought you might like to see how it felt.' Pitch's voice slunk low. 'I do think there is some pleasure amongst the pain.'

A lovely heat rose to Silas's cheeks. 'Do you now?'

With his skin smarting, and likely some water in his head making him a bit foolish, Silas landed another slap against delightfully firm princely buttocks.

'You prick!' Pitch cried.

'What? You said you liked it.' He readied his hand, enjoying this far too much.

Pitch swore and laughed and turned into a daemonic octopus, his arms and legs everywhere at once. The prince found his way off Silas's shoulder and ended up somehow clinging about his waist like a fetching wet towel. Silas held him easily with one arm, the other darting in to try to deliver another slap.

'Stop it, you bastard.' Pitch was hollering the words but really not fighting as hard as he could to escape.

'Where do you think you're going?' Silas tried for stern, but could not suppress his laughter. 'Christ, you're like a bloody squirrel on a tree.'

'Is that so?' Pitch was breathless now in a much more pleasant way. 'Then where shall I hide my nuts?' Somehow he managed to keep ahold and send his hands into uncouth places at the same time. 'Oh, this seems a promising spot.' His fingers danced pressure between Silas's legs.

'Don't you dare!'

Of course the daemon dared. Fingers squeezed tight, and Silas's balls fired with a pain that was only partly unpleasant. He hollered, dropping to his knees upon a rug made of pieces of interwoven rags, a wonderfully soft place on which to dump his royal load.

Pitch landed with a dull thump, laughing with far too much gusto.

'That was truly unkind,' Silas groaned, hands hovering over his pained balls. A pity his cock seemed to enjoy their discomfort, stiff and wholly roused.

'I could kiss them better if you like?' Pitch still lay on his back, his head slightly lifted where it rested against a pile of empty hessian sacks stacked beside the table.

Silas swallowed. 'Oh...bloody hell.'

Pitch sat up, using the edge of the table to steady himself. He rocked onto his knees, shuffling in so he was right up close. The warmth of his breath and the dank scent of pond came at Silas in a rush.

'Would you like that, Mr Mercer?' There was enough tightness beneath his trousers to make it clear that *he* would.

It was as though the entire incident in the pond had not happened at all.

'I think I would like it very much.' The reply came with a shiver, but not one born entirely by the suggestion of Pitch's mouth between his legs. Silas was very damp and cold.

He traced his fingers over Pitch's cheek. His skin was only faintly warm, tugging Silas's thoughts away from what those bowed lips could do to his balls and back to what had brought them to this cottage to begin with. The prince had been in a terrible panic, which was very unlike him. 'But I am coated in silt and god knows what else...and you...you need warming up.' Not four words he ever thought he'd say to a daemon with fire in his veins.

'Don't be ridiculous. I'm fine.' Pitch ran his finger over the waist of Silas's trousers, homing in on the button. 'And I hardly care about a little mud.'

Silas bit at the inside of his mouth, chasing away the image of Pitch's mouth upon him. He knew the daemon, and Pitch very much *did* care about a little mud in normal circumstances. It took a large measure of self-control to gently stop Pitch's hand where slender fingers worked at undoing Silas's trousers.

'Could we talk first perhaps?'

The gleam of amusement vanished from Pitch's gaze. He snatched his hand away. 'I wish to suck you off and you wish to *talk*?' He pushed to his feet. 'Are you worn out? Was that what that was out there?' He stabbed a finger at the dirt-streaked windowpanes. 'You, Matilda, and the kappas fucking in the duckweed? Nothing like a decent orgy to while away the time, I suppose. Good for you, Mercer.'

Silas took his time to answer, lest his rising temper get the better of him. He despised it when Pitch called him Mercer. It was meant to serve as a wall to shut him out, but he was done with having any distance between them.

'You know very well we were doing no such thing, Pitch.' He watched the prince stomp over to the hearth, where yesterday Silas had tried and failed to start a fire, the kindling too damp. 'I'd like to tell you why I was there, if you will listen?'

Pitch leaned against the small cast-stone mantelpiece. He scowled down at the wood but made no move to try to light it. Silas felt a tingling of concern, but it was possible, with the daemon's sour mood, he left it unlit to ensure Silas kept shivering.

'I don't care what you were doing out there,' the prince retorted.

'I think you do.' Silas got to his feet, grimacing at the unpleasantness of wet clothing and a half-aroused member rubbing against them. 'I believe I made you terribly worried, and I'm sorry for that.'

'Fucking gods, I'm not going to stand here and listen to you apologise ad infinitum.' Pitch shoved away from the mantel, turning towards the door.

Silas stopped him before he'd taken two steps, planting himself between the daemon and his escape.

'Move out of the bloody–'

'I wanted to be unafraid.' Silas raised his voice over Pitch's demand. 'That's why I asked to be held down in that pond, because I cannot stand being this afraid. I wake up with my heart in my throat because I've dreamt that I am drowning, that the sorcerer holds me under, as they did at the greensward, and they take you from me, Pitch. They hurt you and take you away from me and I can do nothing to stop it because I am afraid of something so utterly piss-weak as water.' At some point during his rant, Silas had planted his hands on Pitch's shoulders, where his too-cold flesh was pricked with gooseflesh. The prince kept quiet, staring up at him through twin pools of deep viridian. 'When I could not bathe with you that night in our room...when the terror overcame me, even as you lay against me...I have never felt so desolate.'

Pitch did not blink, barely seemed to breathe. The quiet stretched out.

'You don't know that for sure,' the prince whispered finally.

'What?'

'You're very old, my dear. You've likely felt just as desolate a hundred times over. I'm hardly a special case.'

If Pitch sought to break some of the unbearable tension, he succeeded. Silas relinquished a reluctant smile. 'Perhaps. I have my doubts though. I think you are quite the special case.' He flushed with saying it, with being so blatant.

And it seemed to catch even Pitch off guard. He picked at his nails, dirty with the pond. 'Well, there you are, proving yourself the oaf I have always claimed. You do carry on with such nonsense.'

Silas frowned, irritated by the dismissal. 'We have been through much. Why do you find it so hard to imagine I might care for you?'

'You have spent this much time in my company, and you can ask such a question?' Pitch kept at his nails, hands visibly shaking. 'Your special case is most certainly very hazardous to your health. I nearly got you killed in that asylum.'

Silas cupped a hand to the back of the prince's head, but Pitch still kept his eyes downcast. 'We set foot in the Fulbourn together, you did not coerce me. And horrid as that place was, I do not regret all of what it meant to be trapped there, because I emerged from it stronger than I entered. The Morrigan sought to weaken me. Instead, they made me better able to protect you.' He touched a light finger to the daemon's lips, stopping what he presumed would be a protest. 'I know, I know, you are more than capable of handling yourself. You are magnificent, I've said it once, now again.' He traced the curve of those lips, down to the corners where there was hint of Pitch's wet warmth. 'But humour me with this. Let me believe that you need my help just a little.' The daemon's gaze was still lowered, and Silas could not see beneath dark lashes. 'Matilda told me I am as much a part of the water as it is of my past. That the water itself is not my enemy. I find great comfort in that.'

Pitch relaxed and leaned into Silas. They melded together in that way they seemed to have mastered. 'Did you recall any more of your lives,...your deaths?' He set his forehead against Silas's chest as he spoke.

It was a good thing the daemon was not looking at him, for Silas feared betraying any hint of the Nephilim secret he guarded. He still could not bring himself to speak of it. 'I believe I may understand more of the connection with Charlie's family.'

'Oh wonderful.' Pitch sighed. 'What marvel did you learn about the vagabond?'

Silas kissed the top of his head. Not so pleasant as usual, on account of the grit. 'I believe I may have saved him...his ancestor I mean. They were to be sacrificed first, a mere child, for goodness' sake.' He shuddered. 'I think I may have offered myself up in their place. Somehow that has bound our fates to this day.'

'They owe you their life.' Pitch thumped his fist gently against Silas's chest. 'My knight. You have been valiant and noble and too bloody good from the very first breath you took.'

'I doubt that very much.'

'I do not.' Pitch pressed in harder against Silas. A fresh wave of shivering moved through him.

'We really need to get you warm.' Silas frowned. 'I set everything for a fire yesterday, but the wood was still damp... Do you think you could light us a fire?'

The daemon tensed in his arms and stepped back with a suddenness that stopped Silas from preventing his escape this time. 'I'm not cold.'

Silas tilted his head. 'Pitch...you and I both know that is a lie. Will you tell me–'

'Silas, for the gods' sake...it is nothing...'

'It is not *nothing* if it's bothering you so. We must be open with each other. We have come too far for anything less.' He was very aware of his own hypocrisy. 'Speak your mind.'

Pitch waved his hand, seeming to battle with himself a moment. 'Fine. You wish to know what is bothering me?'

'Yes.'

'Here.' Pitch threw out his hands, palms raised. A weak sheen of golden light lay beneath his skin. 'Here is what is fucking wrong, Silas. *Me.* I am wrong.'

The glow was barely strong enough to reach into the narrow space between them.

'I'm not sure I understand,' Silas said carefully.

Pitch growled and turned to thrust one hand towards the kindling. A thin weaving flame sprouted from a single fingertip, not much bigger than that of a simple night candle. 'I am stifled, Silas. Look at this piece of piss my flame has become. I can draw it out no more than this, not even when I knew you to be at the bottom of that fucking pond.' He snapped his wrist, like he were trying to cast off his hand entirely. 'Fuck, he has cursed me. The arsehole has fucking cursed me.'

Silas struggled to follow. 'Who has done such a thing?' He longed to be closer, to wrap his arms around the daemon who was so clearly in distress, but such a move was not wise when the prince was in a temper.

'Who do you think, Silas? I went to see Edward!'

Silas waited, giving the daemon time to gather himself. Hating that he'd not been there. Pitch had been avoiding Edward's sickroom like it truly held the plague.

'The lieutenant has stifled your flame?' Silas asked quietly.

'Edward is a tool. Seraphiel did the stifling. I've heard him, again. And he had a lot to fucking say...' Pitch paused, staring at the small flame he'd made.

'Pitch? Go on.' The daemon had told Silas of hearing the angel speak to him through Edward, at the Fulbourn. And with the divine magick used to ultimately save them from the asylum, it was clear that something monumental had occurred when the lieutenant received the watch. But what exactly? Even Pitch seemed at a loss to say.

'The angel wishes me muzzled and the monster inside me buried deep.'

Pitch curled his fingers into a fist, extinguishing the flame. He stepped around Silas, who did not try to stop him, and made his way over to the most impressive piece of furniture in the room: a rectangular oak table with carved sleigh feet, far too elaborate for such a space, likely gracing a room in the main house before a new purchase had seen it abandoned here.

He stopped by a bucket which sat atop the table. A few days ago Silas had decided to begin conquering his fear by dunking his head in a bucket of rainwater. It turned out to be an embarrassingly inadequate solution. The daemon stared at his reflection in the water, the surface as still and blackened as night.

'The angel gave my monster a name. Isn't that nice? Behemoth, he called it.' Pitch's ridicule was rife. 'Gods, the idiot was always one for grandeur and hyperbole.'

'Behemoth? Are they not a creature of the Bible?' Where that tug of knowledge came from, Silas did not know or care.

'And as mythical as most others you shall encounter in the pages of those books.' He took hold of one of the dun washcloths Silas had seen fit to bring down here when his dunking idea had seemed reasonable. Pitch balled up the cloth like he wished to squeeze the colour from the thread.

'There is no such creature?' Silas asked.

'Not until now, apparently,' Pitch replied. 'And whatever it is, the Seraphim does not think me capable of carrying his burden so well anymore. He has sealed the wildness in. He told me it would weaken me but failed to tell me it would make me next to impotent.' Far more than the chill caused Silas to shiver. 'I thought you were drowning, Silas. I thought you in harm's way...and I could not do a fucking thing to help you. I could not do anything but lose my bloody marbles.' He shook his head, gripping the table. 'You were seeking to make yourself stronger for me, while I was being made a greater burden for you.'

'You are no burden, Pitch.' Silas stood close, but not too close, behind the prince. Trying to fathom why the angel would disable the daemon so.

'Says the man who carried me like I was a sack of fucking grain because I could not manage to walk myself.'

'Well, I don't mind carrying you, if I'm honest.'

Pitch teased the flame from his fingertip, singeing a black mark on the tabletop. 'If you intend to find a silver lining with this, I think I shall throttle you.'

Detecting a lighter note in the prince's tone, Silas moved up behind him and wrapped his arms about his waist. Pitch went stiff, and Silas enveloped him tighter.

'With what you have just told me, it is certainly understandable that you feel so disconcerted. But we have been sorely tested before, we shall see our way–'

'If you say "our way through this," I swear, Silas, I'll fry your eyeballs with this ridiculous flame.' He lifted his hand, bringing his flaming fingertip close to Silas's face. The heat was immensely satisfying.

'That is hardly ridiculous.' Pitch's midriff was hard beneath Silas's hold, and though he certainly was not afire with heat, the prince's body was warming him very nicely.

'You can look at this mere sliver of fire and say that after what you've seen me do?' Pitch said. 'Shall we discuss your need for spectacles yet again?'

Silas touched his nose at the dampness behind Pitch's ear, setting the amber earring swinging.

'No. I see perfectly well. That blasted angel has never gotten the best of you, he shall not do so now. I am certain.' Silas made sure he sounded utterly certain of it. There could be no room for any hesitancy, even if his throat ran dry at the thought of the prince's flame being stolen from him. What in the name of all that was holy was truly going on?

The daemon believed himself a vessel. *A part of a monstrous whole,* he'd said, waking at the Crimson Bow in a pool of sweat after a dream of Seraphiel's final moments. Now the angel, supposedly long dead, was to stifle not only the wildness but the daemon's own flame too? What madness would possess the angel to make Pitch so vulnerable now? Was the wildness...the behemoth...so near to consuming him that there was no other choice?

'Whatever the angel's plan is here,' Silas continued, 'then we shall navigate it. If anyone thinks us a pair of lily-livered dolts, they shall be sadly disappointed.'

Pitch's ribs flared with what might have been suppressed laughter. 'By you, certainly. I know what it took for you to be in that water, Silas. It was idiotic, but brave.'

'It was idiotic not to have attempted it long before now. And the bravery only came because I knew my purpose. I knew exactly who I was in that water for.'

He sealed the declaration with a kiss to the side of the prince's neck. But Pitch tilted his head, jerking away from Silas's touch.

'Well, my dear oaf, you wasted your time in the end, for you are not going any further on this quest with me.' He tried to slip free. 'Damn it, let me go.'

'Certainly not while you are talking utter nonsense. Of course I am going with you.'

'So I might stand by with my pissy little finger flame and watch you get torn to shreds, before the Dullahan whisks me away to become a plaything for the UnSeelie Court?' Silas's mood darkened. Christ, he'd not stopped to think on that cursed debt the Erlking claimed. 'It's bad enough that you made me bloody senseless by that pond.'

The daemon fought to free himself, and Silas slackened his grip, aware of the perils of holding on too tight but not keen to allow the prince to run from him either. He did not wish the daemon to be paralysed by such fear again but couldn't stifle some delight in knowing Pitch had been so concerned for him.

'I dare the Dullahan to touch a hair upon your head,' Silas said, with a boldness he usually found uncommon. 'He'll have an army of teratisms upon him before he can raise that infernal whip an inch.' That slowed Pitch's struggle to escape, and Silas took the opportunity to pull him closer. 'You shall never be the UnSeelie Court's plaything. And you will not speak again of continuing alone, do you hear me?'

Pitch's inhale was slight and sharp. He returned to leaning against Silas, sinking back into the place he fit so well. 'I hear you.'

'Good.' Silas laid another kiss to the back of his head. 'Now shall we return to the house and get cleaned up? Have some breakfast?'

At once the prince pulled away, turning to face him. 'I'm not hungry, and I don't want to go back to the house. I don't want to be near him.'

Pitch's faded appetite was a concern, but Silas had hardly been ravenous himself. He put it down to the trials of the Fulbourn like much else.

'You'd rather stay here? Among the cobwebs?'

'Yes. I would.'

'All right. Here we stay, then,' Silas declared. 'But we must get dry.' He paused and decided to return to boldness. 'We should likely get out of these wet clothes. I doubt they'd take long to dry by a fire. Perhaps you could just give it a try?' He touched his fingers to the few remaining dirty buttons on his shirt, as though intending to undo them.

The prince lifted his head, emerald eyes sharp. 'Are you trying to seduce me into starting a fire?'

Silas's skin prickled as he feigned seriousness. 'Mostly I'm trying to seduce you into taking your clothes off. You are beautiful in them but breathtaking without.' Silas winced and turned away. 'Oh god, that was terrible, I'm sorry.' Suave master of seduction he was not. 'And it's hardly the time for such things.'

He felt the daemon move up behind him, and touch fingers to the small of his back.

Silas sucked in his breath, his hands twitching to reach for him. He waited.

'It was not terrible,' Pitch said softly, tracing the muscled lines on Silas's back. 'And I think now is exactly the time for such things. There is just one change I would request. If I can manage to light that fire, would you take my clothes off for me, Mr Mercer?'

Silas swallowed down every single worry he held– for the prince, for the sense of dread that would not leave him, for what lay beyond the comforts of the Sanctuary, and for what lay in store for those who sheltered within. Each concern grew pale and fine.

'I would, Mr Astaroth. Most certainly.'

CHAPTER 9

Pitch knelt at the hearth and raised his hand to the pile of kindling. Crouching was made difficult by the rigid length in his trousers, but he'd endure worse to see this fire lit.

He stared hard at the bright and sure flame that came from his finger. It *was* more than enough to have this hearth crackling, Silas was right. They would be warm, and warm themselves further in more pleasant ways. And eventually he'd tell Silas what else the angel had said...about preparing to leave this day. But not yet. It was early, Sybilla had not yet returned. And Pitch needed this time with the ankou in this dusty, cluttered place at the bottom of the garden.

His cock twitched at the thought of what was to come. He glanced over his shoulder. Silas cradled the bucket of water in his arms, sloshing it over the sides as he sought to move it.

'What are you doing?'

'If we warm this water,' Silas said, 'then we can use it to bathe...I don't know about you, but I have silt in some very odd places.'

'A good idea, but Silas, I have fire in my fingers, why are you lugging it about? I'll warm it where you set it. You're going to slosh half the bloody water out at that rate.'

'Oh, yes. Of course.' Silas blushed, and Pitch's balls inched a bit higher, squeezed a bit tighter. 'I'm rather distracted.'

He laughed in that uncertain way he had. Gods damn it, this was going to be the quickest fuck known to humankind, for just the sound of Silas's voice had Pitch leaking, hungry for the distraction and the intimacy. If the ankou tried to wipe him down with a warm wet cloth, the game would be over.

The flame snapped from him, doubling its size, swelling as impressively as Silas's cock was doing in his trousers. Pitch dragged his eyes from that sight to regard the fire coming from him.

Fucking gods, despite its growth it was still pathetic. He jabbed his finger into the kindling. The time for worrying over Seraphiel's monumental meddling would be later. Pitch had other needs right now.

The wood caught and flared. He set his finger to the other end of the pile and soon had a pleasant hissing fire glowing in the hearth.

He rose to his feet, feeling happier than he'd done since he'd left the house.

'Well, I shall be useful in a forge at least.' His grin snagged as he set eyes on Silas.

The ankou had peeled off his sodden shirt. The dark hair on his chest glistened as the fire's light caught at the dampness. His light brown eyes were bright with his desire.

'Come here, please.' Silas was throaty and altogether too wonderful to deny.

Pitch did as he was asked, moving to the table where Silas waited. The ankou did not take his eyes from Pitch's face, but he tilted his head towards the bucket he'd placed on the chair. A forest-green coat, the brightest colour in the room, hung over the back. 'Would you mind warming the water?'

Loath as he was to do so, Pitch tore his gaze from Silas. He placed his hand in the bucket and sent the flame beneath his skin, grimacing with how slow the glow was to arrive.

Silas moved in closer, the dank scent of the pond moving with him. 'May I?' He set his fingers upon the surviving buttons on Pitch's shirt.

'You may.'

Silas began to undress him. He shifted back the collar, lifting some of the torn lace from where it was plastered to Pitch's skin. The ankou's fingers brushed collarbone, and Pitch sucked in a strangled breath. Silas had discovered his weak spot at Harvington Hall, the place to touch to turn a daemon to jelly. And never forgotten.

Without a word Silas leaned down to kiss him. A tantalisingly subtle brush of lips that had Pitch straining on tiptoes for more. The ankou eased back, a teasing, yet shy, grin rising. His hands slipped lower, taking in turn each button that had survived the mania of the pond, pausing to rub his fingertip over Pitch's cool flesh, before moving in for another feather-light kiss.

Over and over he teased, drawing whimpered protests from the daemon he tortured.

By the last button, Pitch breathed like a post boy on his last run of the day, groaning against the torment of kisses denied. His prick was crying tears of frustration, making a warm damp patch in his already-soaked trousers.

'I think that is warm enough,' Silas whispered, running his hands up Pitch's chest, slipping fingers beneath damp fabric clinging to his shoulders.

'What?'

Silas pushed the shirt clear and grazed his lips over Pitch's skin. 'The water.'

The bucket of water was bubbling.

'Oh shit.' Pitch withdrew his hand, droplets speckling the tabletop. 'Damn it.'

'Never mind.' Silas smiled and with fiendish ease removed Pitch's shirt entirely, tugging it free where it snagged on one of his wrists. 'It shall have time to cool before I need it.'

'Is that so?' Pitch could taste Silas's iron-tinged kisses. The ankou was bold today. Sitting at the bottom of that pond had done him well.

'It is.' Silas nodded.

He unbuttoned Pitch's trousers, brushing his knuckles at the stiff pillar awaiting him, easing the clothes down low until the sodden material hit the rug with a wet thump. The fire had not yet managed to warm the cottage interior entirely, and the brisk cut of air against Pitch's bare skin made his shuddering intensify.

Silas moved swiftly, gathering Pitch up, one arm cradling his arse, the other bracing his back. Pitch looped his legs around the ankou's waist, his cock bobbing between them, showing off its glistening top. The ankou carried him to the end of the table closest to the fire.

'Warmer?' Silas asked.

'I am.' Pitch nodded, grateful the ankou did not voice a concern that the fire daemon felt the cold at all. Those worries had no place here.

Silas turned so that Pitch was hovered over the edge of the table and seemed ready to set him down before he frowned. 'No, that won't do. Wait a moment.'

Pitch hissed his annoyance. 'Can you not see I am ripe for spilling?'

Silas's laughter was weighted with lust. 'Oh, I see. And I am going to celebrate every lovely inch of that ripeness, once we have you properly settled.'

Settling was the very last thing Pitch wanted right now. But Silas backtracked to the chair, removing his hand from Pitch's back to lift the green coat. Pitch clung to him, amused with all the wobbling about, relishing the tangle of Silas's chest hair around his fingers.

'What on Earth are you doing?'

'This.' Silas returned them both to where the fire's warmth was evident, spreading the coat over the end of the table. At long last he set Pitch down. The fabric was dry and remarkably soft. 'If you are uncomfortable, you will tell me?'

'It depends what you want me to do.'

'Nothing, nothing at all.' Silas kissed the tip of his nose. 'Save for allowing me to indulge you. Would that be all right?'

Pitch could barely manage to nod. His body was a nocked arrow. He wasn't sure he wouldn't just explode if he tried to utter a word.

He very nearly did when Silas went to his knees.

The ankou kissed the top of each of Pitch's thighs, then moved to his knees, bestowing more kisses there before urging Pitch's legs to part. He obliged willingly. So willingly it was a wonder his bloody hip didn't seize up. He spread wide as a king's mistress and watched as Silas kissed his way up the inside of his thighs. Moving from side to side, making sure neither were neglected.

'Sweet gods...' Pitch shoved his fingers into Silas's hair. He felt the ankou's grin against his skin. 'Silas, damn it.'

The bastard had the audacity to laugh quietly before he finally ended his journey at the jutting pillar between Pitch's legs. Silas flicked his tongue over the reddened tip and almost received a black eye, Pitch's hips thrusting so hard with the pleasure. Grinning like a fool, Silas waited till he caught Pitch's eye before he sank his mouth down over a cock that fairly burst out of its skin to greet him.

The shocking combination of heat and softness had Pitch spineless. 'Shit. Christ' were the eloquent words that left him.

The ankou sank his mouth all the way down, lips tight around rock-hard flesh, throat squeezing. Pitch groaned while the ankou's tongue rubbed at the especially sensitive underside and his fingers danced against tight balls.

The ankou dragged his teeth over Pitch's length, asserting just enough pressure to be dangerously arousing. A familiar, delicious tingling erupted at the base of Pitch's spine. He rocked against Silas's mouth, felt his prick touch at the back of the ankou's throat and the rhythm quicken. The slick work partnered with the pops and sizzle of the fire warming his curled toes.

Up and up Pitch went, losing sight of the known world and racing towards that pinnacle where climax lived. He sank onto his back and thrust into Silas's sucking hold, listening to the ankou's own groans of pleasure as he tasted the spoils.

Pitch bunched up the coat in clawed fingers, wriggling his arse as Silas devoured him. He was one meagre step from losing his fucking mind when the ankou's fingers left the firmness of his balls, scissoring around the thin skin that held them. He clamped his fingers tight and pulled down. Pitch cursed, knowing the move for what it was. Exquisite torture. The press of Silas's fingers stamped out the charge that had begun. Held back the imminent eruption.

Silas withdrew the sinful pleasure of his mouth.

'You bastard.' Pitch gasped, propping himself on his elbows.

Without a word, and with his devious finger trap still in place, Silas stretched to reach for one of the dun cloths. He leaned, twisting at an angle to dunk it in the steaming water.

'Sickle,' Pitch moaned. 'I thought you meant to indulge, not torment.'

'And I'm a man of my word. Hush now. You'll like this, I'm sure.'

'I *liked* your mouth on my cock.'

'I know. But I suspect you'll be favourable to this. And if not, then we shall explore other options.' The ankou's grin was devilish as he loomed, his fingers still keeping their tight hold on soft skin. He pulled the cloth from the water with his freed hand, tight-fisting it, the heated water releasing a fine white vapour as the excess trickled into the bucket. 'Now, would you mind turning around, please?' Silas kissed the trembling tip of Pitch's cock and finally released his hold on the daemon's balls.

'Fine.'

With a huff and much show of inconvenience, but with his curiosity piqued, Pitch did as he was asked. He slid himself off the table, making sure to brandish his considerable wares in Silas's face, just in case the ankou decided to return his tongue to work.

'Are you going to fuck me now?'

'Not yet, but soon.' Silas licked his lips, casting a wretchedly beautiful smile at the daemon who taunted him. 'Unless you prefer that I bend for you this time?'

Sweet taints of the gods, what a thought that was: his cock buried in Silas's arse, the ankou's face twisted with the pleasure and the pain of it. He'd thought about it more than once. But Pitch had been spoiled. He knew what it was now to be filled by Silas, and he was greedy for it.

'I...no, me. I bend.' Clearly his tongue was broken. Pitch tried again. 'I'll take your offer, but not today.'

'Very well.' Silas kissed the crease of Pitch's thigh. 'Around you go, then.'

Who was this man? Pitch could not decide which Silas he preferred: the reserved, reticent man who would do exactly as he was told, or this specimen. The man who held his hips to guide him, asked him to bend over slowly, and told him to place his forearms on the table.

The man who knelt once more behind him and bade him spread his legs wider.

That devious man who took the warm cloth and brushed it over Pitch's arse cheeks in smooth circular motions, wiping away the remnants of the pond, skimming his lips over the damp places.

Pitch balled his fists, his cock touching at the edge of the table as his hips refused to remain still. The cloth teased at his crack. Water trickled into the gully between tight mounds, making him hiss.

Silas pressed the cloth in deeper, near to where tight muscle twitched. He must have squeezed the cloth, for all at once Pitch was dripping, the water running down the inside of his thighs. Silas captured the running water at Pitch's knee and dragged the cloth all the way back up again, making his legs tremble and delirious shaft jerk.

But Silas was not done. He sent the cloth deeper this time, a gentle pull at Pitch's cheek easing the way open. The ankou touched the warm material against Pitch's entrance, causing the daemon's back to arch, a long drawn-out moan to escape him.

'This is what I had planned for our bath.' Silas was throaty, his hand busy.

He cleaned his daemon with fastidious care. Pitch was splayed out like a royal feast upon the table, being taken care of one gentle stroke at a time. He wriggled at the attention like the damned weeds in the pond, but there was no fear here. No panic. If Pitch were any calmer, any looser, he'd collapse.

He moaned and stretched his arm, intending to reach for his prick and ease some of the formidable pressure. But Silas was not having it.

He took hold of Pitch's wrist. 'I'll take care of that,' he whispered. 'But you can help me...here.'

Silas drew Pitch's hand back until it brushed the daemon's arse cheek. 'I want you to hold yourself open for me.'

Pitch nearly choked on his own astonishment. The ankou was superbly wicked. He followed orders, spreading himself open. He let his head drop, his hair surrounding his face like a veil. Waiting for what would come next. Right now there was nothing beyond these walls, gods, nothing beyond the fire's swaying light. The ankou's presence vanished all else.

Silas's breath came first, warm against hidden places.

His tongue was next, running over the swirl of tight muscle between Pitch's cheeks.

'Oh fuck.'

The ankou, damn him, laughed where he was buried, puffing warm air against Pitch's entrance before returning his tongue to work. He traced its tip against curled muscle, teased at the tiny weakness at the centre, pressing in deeper, seeking to enter.

Oh, fucking yes.

Pitch pressed his chest to the table, and his free hand joined the other in pulling himself as wide open as his flesh would allow.

'Silas...damn it...Silas.'

He sputtered the name over and over, in that foolish way that came when all sense fled. Pitch pressed his hips back, pushing himself against the ankou's tongue.

Silas reached around to take Pitch in hand and worked him, back and front. Relentless in both areas. Stroke after stroke, both exquisitely placed. The ankou's thumb rubbed over the weeping slit on Pitch's prick, while his tongue lapped at his entrance like a cat on cream. Pitch grew frantic as the ankou maintained an even pace. The small of his back was afire, but not with any bullying flame. Just good old fantastically delicious lust.

'Oh gods...Silas...I can't...' Pitch bit at the coat, a mouthful of woollen material all that anchored him to the room. He was ready to fly off to a far distant star. One more tease of Silas's tongue, one more brush of his fingers against the underside of a straining, dribbling cock and Pitch would be soaring.

But the ankou knew exactly what havoc he was creating. And precisely when to stop so as to create the most torment. His tongue and hand fell still.

'No,' Pitch whimpered. 'More.'

Silas hushed him. 'We are not done.'

He touched a cautious, easing fingertip at Pitch's entrance, while his lips returned to his first love. Kisses. A bounty was bestowed on Pitch's cheeks, joined by tiny nips of teeth as Silas worked his fingers into the heat and press of resistant flesh.

The ankou made soothing sounds as Pitch begged and hissed and pleaded. One finger became two, sinking deep. But it was not enough.

Pitch squirmed. 'You...I want you.'

Silas's groan came from deep within his chest, and his fingers drew free. He swept an arm beneath Pitch and flipped him over, as though he were no heavier than the coat he lay upon.

'And I need to see you.' Silas's growl went straight to Pitch's balls. The ankou's eyes were brightened, almost amber in their lustful vibrancy. He had discarded his trousers at some point, and stood bare, his desire thick and nodding against his belly.

'Hurry.' Pitch lifted his knees, opening himself wide, not giving a fuck at being seen so desperate and needful.

The table was too low for Silas, who had to bend to find his place. Pitch wriggled his arse closer to the edge of the table, frantic until he felt the tip of Silas's shaft nudge deep between his cheeks.

'There you are,' Silas whispered.

'Here I am.' The blood pounded in Pitch's ears, between his legs, and beneath his ribs. 'At your mercy.'

'Oh Christ,' Silas groaned. He lifted one of Pitch's legs, draping it over his shoulder. There was little doubt he'd chosen that leg on purpose, the one whose hip did not bother Pitch so. Silas wiped at himself quickly, discarded the cloth, and took himself in hand.

Pitch's own prick throbbed, yearning for the ankou's hold.

'Damn it, there's no oil,' Silas said. 'We–'

'Forget that!' Could the man not see him going out of his mind? Pitch lifted his free leg and clamped it against the ankou's backside. 'Just fuck me.'

He thrust against the pillar taunting him, his heel driving Silas forward. The impale went deeper than Pitch had intended, the sting of such a widening eye-watering. Silas was significant in all ways.

'Oh. Shit.'

'Pitch, are–'

'I'm all right.' He clasped Silas's face and smothered his question with hungry lips. 'All of you. Now. Don't be gentle about it.'

The ankou's gaze flared, dark and rife with hunger, but with an added mischief. 'You need to ask nicely to get what you want, daemon. What do you say?'

Pitch stared at the brute leaning over him. The great mass of a man who was playing games with him. Wonderful, rousing games.

'Sickle, will you fuck me?' The play had him panting, desire making him shake.

The ankou raised a dark brow. Still not satisfied, curse him.

'Please?'

'Good boy.'

Silas drove into him, powerful, relentless motions that might have slid him off the table entirely if not for the ankou's hold on his leg.

'Fuck...fuck...' Pitch grasped at the wood, at Silas's arms, hanging on for dear life as the pummelling found its rhythm.

The ankou drove deep, glancing at the hidden place in Pitch's passage that rendered him truly insensible; shouting and crying and whining like a maddened farm animal. His sounds stuttered by the brief, brutal thrusts. Silas worked his hips, grunting like a beast, the slap of flesh loud and primal.

It was ugly and base and utter paradise.

Pitch could not catch his breath, could do little else but hold on as the ankou owned him. He arched his back, losing himself in the reckless rhythm played.

Silas's usual gentleness was wondrous, but this...sweet mercy...this rough consideration drove the daemon mad with pleasure.

The ankou leaned closer, planting a hand against the table. The nearness drawing Pitch's knee down until it almost touched his own shoulder. His cock rubbed against Silas's belly and he let loose an unholy sound of longing. The ankou found his mouth, kissing him, not missing a beat with his thrusts, the table creaking beneath them.

'My god, you are heaven.' Silas slid the words between their lips. 'Every inch of you.'

Pitch's cry caught in his throat. He used his heel to urge the ankou on, like a rider nudging the flanks of his stallion. The pace quickened, the fuck deepened.

The far legs of the table were shoved off the rug, finding floorboard as the ankou's pounding treatment moved mountains.

Silas slipped his arm beneath Pitch's shoulder, as though he feared he'd thrust his lover clear off the tabletop. And well he might.

'Yes...yes...' Pitch whimpered into the crux of Silas's neck where he was pinned. Where he was buried in the scent of this man who girded him like a living fortress.

Silas panted with his efforts, with the beautiful confusion of approaching climax. All the while he whispered endearments: how stunning Pitch looked when he was being fucked, how perfect it felt to be inside him, and other words, far too pretty for the creature they were gifted to.

Pitch was alight with carnal hunger, inflamed enough by desire to offer a gift of his own to the man who filled him. He pressed his lips to Silas's ear. 'I need you, Sickle. Please don't leave me.'

Silas cried out and broke, spilling everything of himself into the daemon. Pitch was close behind, his spine on fire, his thankful balls releasing. White-hot lashings shot from him, slicking the skin between him and the ankou as climax engulfed them.

The room blazed.

The table shifted against the floorboards, the raucous grind of wood on wood mingling with their cries, their moans and whimpers as they spent themselves. Bodies pressed as close together as the flesh could be.

They panted like raced horses and returned to their senses slowly. Pitch prayed his words had been lost in the maelstrom, for he already regretted their foolish release.

Silas eased his weight away and gently lowered Pitch's leg from where it still draped his shoulder. The ankou's thick fingers were light as they rubbed his thigh, as though knowing how the daemon's muscles ached. Silas gazed down at him, his pupils blown wide, sweat at his brow.

'I shall never leave you, Pitch,' he said. 'I love you.'

CHAPTER 10

O ne moment Silas was buried in his lover, the next he was abandoned, raw and still shuddering with pleasure. Pitch snatched up the coat and wrapped it tight around himself, moving away. Startled as a deer, running for cover.

Bloody hell, Silas should have kept his mouth shut. The daemon had made one mention of needing him and Silas had lost his damned head.

He reached for the second cloth, still neatly folded and untouched. He was desperate to clean up both the messes he'd just made.

'Would you like this one? It's unused.'

'No, no. It's fine.' Pitch waved off the man who had just been inside him as though he were a buzzing fly. 'You see to yourself. I've left quite the stain.'

The prince busied himself with gathering up their sodden clothes and arranging them where the fire's heat could dry them. He dragged the chair over to the hearth, doing so one-handed as he kept the coat clutched tight. He kicked over one of the crates and used his foot to push it near to the hearth.

Silas set down the dry cloth and took up the one he'd used earlier. He wrung it out in the bucket where the water was still pleasantly warm and set about cleaning himself up, scowling at the limp and sated length between his legs. Silas cast all blame on that rod of flesh for making him no master of his senses. Why had Silas muddied things by carrying on about love? He shifted attentions to his belly and chest, where Pitch's release glistened in the sweep of curled dark hair. Christ almighty, it was intoxicating to lie with the prince. But, *I love you*? Bloody fucking hell, he was a fool. The daemon was manipulated so badly that he could barely keep ahold on himself, and now it seemed he'd been robbed of the flame he treasured. The flame that was as much a part of him as the scythe was for Silas.

The weight upon Pitch's shoulders was enormous. He needed an ally, a protector. Not a smitten ankou mouthing off sweet nothings and getting jelly-legged when they touched.

Silas squeezed the cloth like it was his own neck. He deserved a throttling for sure. He set the cloth to his balls. Scrubbing hard.

'You said you loved me.' Pitch's words made him jump. 'But you seem to be trying to geld yourself to remove all evidence of me.'

While Silas was lost in his remonstrance, the daemon had moved to his side.

'What? No, no, that's not...no...' Silas's tongue tripped over his teeth. 'You must pay my words no mind, truly. I was simply caught up in the moment.'

The denial would have continued– had he not looked at the prince just then and caught the brush of uncertainty sweeping his features as Silas took back what he'd said.

His self-directed anger faded. If this was his last ride as a Horseman, he'd not fill it with lies.

'No...that's not right.' Silas shook his head. 'I *do* want you to take heed of my words, because they are true. I love you. I adore you, quite frankly. And I'm sorry if that bothers you, but I can't change it, nor do I wish to. You don't need to do or say or offer anything in return. You need never think on it again, for I shan't burden you with any more outbursts. I just wanted you to know, Pitch, that I care for you deeply and will not leave you.'

The prince was, in that moment, the rarest of things: so very unsure of himself. His teeth toyed at his lower lip, his gaze a fluttering butterfly of indecision on where to land.

He was delicate when he spoke. 'I don't know what to do or to say to that, Silas. I'm not...I'm not familiar with...this.'

This what? Being cherished? Having a besotted oaf stuck to his side? It made Silas's chest ache to imagine the prince knew not what it was to be cared for.

'Not familiar with a man making a dolt of himself over you?' Silas forced his laughter, heat striking his cheeks. 'Come now, I'd say you are most expert with it.'

He moved to where his trousers lay over the seat of the chair. He longed to cover up, to cease feeling so exposed.

'Expert with an enchantment perhaps, but it's not that.' Pitch turned away, dropping the coat to return himself to stunning nakedness once more. He stepped closer to the fire, holding his shirt where it might dry. The tattoo he bore on his back was so faint as to be confused with a shadow. Seeing the faded state of the amuletum tinged Silas's unease darker. Sybilla had not attempted to reapply the strange ink after the Fulbourn. Not after Edward's touch. The *angel's* touch. But Silas found no comfort in that, for it did not mean that all was fine and dandy for the prince. Far from it.

'I'm not familiar with all...this...' Pitch paused, picking at a piece of milfoil that clung to his shirt. 'The time spent thinking about you. Worrying about you. Getting annoyed when you aren't in my bed. Playing the fool to make you smile. Feeling as though I'd burn this world to cinder if any harm comes to you.' He paused again. His hands glowed bright. 'I said I need you. But I don't know if I *like* needing you. I certainly don't know if I love...being this way.'

Silas blinked, his heart thumping like a battalion's drum. The daemon had said far more than he dared imagine possible.

They both stood, stark naked and dishevelled. Silas watched the light dance over Pitch's lean body and envied it for its closeness.

'I seek no answer. You have far greater things to concern you.' Silas turned over his trousers, well aware they were still too damp on one side to justify the switch. 'I didn't intend for any of this to add to your burdens. But with how our days are going...well...I didn't want important words left unsaid.' He tensed, realising a painful truth. 'And that was selfish of me, wasn't it? Damn it, I truly did not intend to make you uncomfortable on top of everything else. Bloody hell, I am so–'

'Stop.' Pitch flicked the sleeve of his shirt, and the material slapped Silas's bare thigh.

'Ouch, shit.' Silas flinched, rubbing at the reddened patch of skin. 'That seems unnecessary.'

'It had to be done to stop another of your endless apologies. Tell me I am wrong, and that was not a *sorry* about to leave your lips?'

Silas fell into his smile, grateful for the sign Pitch was not so terribly unhappy with him. 'I suppose we shall never know.'

'I suppose not.' Pitch hung his shirt on the handle of a rake that leaned against the mantel, then held out his hand to Silas. 'Here, give me your trousers. You weren't wearing any drawers?'

Silas duly handed over the trousers. 'No. They were in the wardrobe, and as the door creaks, I did not wish to wake you.'

'Well, we shall have to install a creaky wardrobe at Holly Village, then. I favour the notion of you wandering about with your jewels dangling.'

Silas could do little but stare at the daemon. Not because he was being salacious, that was a given, but because he seemed to suggest a coexistence would continue after all was said and done. The longing for such a future was painful as a knife strike.

Pitch gave Silas a sideways glance and a crooked smile. One Silas tried to return, lest his melancholy be seen. But Pitch's smile split into a grimace as the daemon seated himself.

'What's wrong?'

'Do you not recall how it was after the Bow? You're a large man, Silas.'

Silas blushed, down to his gums it felt. 'Oh –'

'Don't say it. And it is not a complaint, by any stretch of the imagination.' Pitch laid the trousers across his lap, stealing Silas's view of all the resting beauty between his legs. 'But seeing as there was no oil...'

'Oh bloody hell, I knew it was not right to continue without it.'

Pitch's laughter held a whisper of meanness, a devilish delight in the taunt he'd just delivered.

'Bastard,' Silas muttered, crouching by the fire, scowling at the flames as he stirred them. 'That was not nice.'

'No, but it was amusing. Your face.' He chuckled to himself as he spread his hands over the shirt, using the heat of the flame like a washer-woman might use her iron.

'It is pointless to dry everything,' Silas said, still grumpy. 'We shall get soaked again on the walk back to the house.'

There was no laughter now from the prince. 'I don't intend to go back for a while. But I'd like to be dressed in dry clothes in the meantime.'

They could not avoid the house and its occupants forever, but what was a few more moments?

'Might I stay here with you?'

He could not read the look on Pitch's face as he nodded.

For a while they remained in comfortable, and mostly naked, silence. The rain continued to fall outside; there seemed no stopping it. The sun might as well have packed up its bags and headed to the continent. It was only when Silas's stomach made an impolite growling sound that either of them stirred.

'I'm rather hungry.' He patted his belly. 'What about you?'

'Not really.' Pitch handed over his trousers, the material warm against Silas's fingers.

'Thank you.' Silas shook them out, balancing on one leg as he dressed. 'I suppose you are quite filled to the brim in all manner of ways, after what we've just done.' He grinned, expecting something lewd in return.

'I am not a parasite.' Pitch was sullen, working upon his own trousers with his flame-warmed hands. 'I did not feed on you while we fucked.'

'I've never considered you a parasite. And I have no qualms with you seeing to your incubus needs with me, you know that.'

The daemon scowled down at his clothing. 'I had no interest in gorg-ing on you in that way.'

'Do I taste unpleasant?' Silas tried for lightness.

'Being death and all? Surprisingly, no.' Pitch ran his hands along the length of one trouser leg, a light steam coming from the dampness meeting the heat. 'Your kisses taste like iron at times, loam on the odd occasion. And your spend is much the same but with an added saltiness that wakes the senses. You taste sublime.'

The daemon's bluntness still caught him off guard. 'Right...flattering certainly but not quite what I asked. As an incubus, I understand you need to take–'

'I didn't *take* anything from you, Silas.' Pitch's irritation strangled his words. 'A feed and a fuck do not need to be one and the same thing. I'm not a whimpering babe that needs a tit every five minutes to survive –'

'You know that is not what–'

The prince waved an imperious hand. 'Sweets and liquor do just fine in the right quantities.'

'But you're not eating very much of late.' And he'd not been drunk all week.

'Because I'm not fucking hungry. What is this interrogation in aid of?' A rather large flame erupted from Pitch's forefinger, catching on the hem of his trouser leg, setting the fabric alight. 'Fuck, gods fuck it.' He jumped up from the chair, dropping the burning material to the floor, stomping on it. 'By Enoch's balls, I've never seen a man so eager to be treated like a milking cow. If you wish to find a daemon to hold you down and drain you dry, then go and find the Morrigan. They have just the bitch for you.' His voice broke and he coughed, patting at his chest as though there lay the problem. 'Fucking smoke, getting to me.'

Silas could have wept. He was light-headed with realising why Pitch refused to feed from him. To *take* from him.

Her name was Onoskolis.

'I have been an ignorant fool.' He could not say how sorry he was. Pitch would despise it, and rightfully so. 'I should never have pushed you on the matter.'

'Forget it.' Pitch kept his eyes down turned, fixed on the trousers. 'You weren't to know I'd still be carrying on over such a matter.'

Carrying on? He'd been violated and abused, left black and blue, inside and out.

'It was a grave matter,' Silas said quietly. 'And cannot be set aside easily. I am here for you, just know that, Pitch. And when you are ready, I am willing. You can't steal anything from me, for it is already yours.'

The prince turned away, his shoulders tight. Silas feared he'd said too much, yet again.

'You talk such nonsense.' Pitch pulled on his trousers, and though he did so quickly, it was clear his hands were shaking. 'But thank you, Sickle.'

The moment was so very delicate, until Silas's stomach growled once more. 'Oh, bloody hell.'

But the ruckus spliced the tension nicely. Pitch scoffed as he made his way over to where his shirt hung. 'Go and get some damned food, man.'

'Perhaps I should.' As Silas bent to reach for his own shirt, the room seemed to tilt. A shiver ran its way down Silas's spine, as though the last drop of pond water slid from his hair. He clutched at the mantel. Christ, he was practically on top of the fire, how was such a coldness possible?

'Silas, are you all right?'

'I'm not...sure...I don't feel quite myself.' Trepidation waltzed across his skin like a ballroom full of inept dancers.

'Nor do you seem so.' Pitch moved to his side, the buttons still undone on his shirt, firelight caressing his smooth chest. 'What is it?'

'Nothing...a chill from the pond, perhaps.' Silas shrugged off the half-truth. Pitch had been brutally honest with him, he deserved the same in return. 'No, that's not so. I've felt off for the past few days, a strange sense of...well, despair, if I'm honest.'

'I doubt you are the only one feeling such a way.' Pitch was subdued. 'Does this mean you think this quest utterly hopeless?'

'No, no, I do not. We have endured so much and still stand strong.' He shovelled on the reassurances, sensing the prince's fragility. 'That's the thing, you see. The feeling does not seem mine. I'm certain this dread...this hopelessness...does not come from me.'

'Then who?'

'I don't know.' Silas sighed. 'Those teratisms I freed from the Fulbourn, perhaps? Maybe I have a connection with them now?'

An exquisite dimple formed in Pitch's cheek as he wrinkled his face in consideration. 'That seems possible, considering you said you were drawn to where they were in the Fulbourn. But how could they find the Sanctuary? We are in trouble if a handful of corpses have traced us.'

'And that seems highly unlikely. Forneus would have let me know if they were about.'

'Or he brought them here, so they'd be close to their master.'

'Their master?' Silas raised his brows in surprise as he realised who that master was. 'Oh, me. Very strange all of that business, but even if I could be called their master, I'm not convinced it's them. The feeling is different. It's...' He searched for the word. 'Bigger.'

'How eloquent you are.'

'It's hard to explain. But I suppose its as though the Fulbourn was a quartet and this a full choir.' The rumbling erupted at his belly once more.

'Oh for fuck's sake.' Pitch returned to his chair, pulling his mud-caked boots from beneath it and taking his socks from their place on the hearthstone. 'You are completely ruining the ambience of this place with all the ruckus. Shall we find you something to gnaw on?'

'It is probably best.' Silas *was* famished, loath as he was to return to their troubles.

'I believe Ronin should be sending those corsets for me today, at long bloody last.' Pitch bent to tie his laces.

'How wonderful.' Silas scowled down at his own boots. He pictured the tsukumogami sorting through satin and lace and boning. How he might hold each design, imagining how it would suit the daemon's body. A body Ronin may know intimately.

'Ronin does have fine taste,' Pitch said. 'I'll say that much for him.'

'I wouldn't know.' Silas nearly snapped his lace. 'So long as you are happy with what he sends.'

A good thing the tsukumogami wasn't hand-delivering the goods.

He looked up to find Pitch regarding him. 'You'd do a much finer job of dressing me, I'm sure. Perhaps, when this is all done with, a trip to Fortnum and Mason is in order.' Pitch's smooth, seductive manner was well-returned. 'You can decide what I must wear. Seeing as you have found a fondness for ordering me about, Mr Mercer.'

With a gratuitous wink the daemon cast the coat over his shoulders, turned on his heels, and strode out the door.

CHAPTER 11

Pitch reached the house with no sign of Silas behind him, even though he slowed to a near snail's pace on the walk through the garden, waiting for the ankou to catch up. Pitch decided he must be ensuring every ember in the fire was out. It was the sort of thing Silas would worry about. And as the rain was incapable of letting up, Pitch kept on, holding the ineffectual coat over his head in a vain attempt to keep dry.

He was tired of being drenched this day, in all ways but one. He was decidedly damp between the cheeks and pleased about it, still floating on the high of being fucked by the ankou. Even if the encounter had Silas saying all kinds of foolish things. None of which Pitch could expel from his thoughts.

He bypassed the verandah where he'd met Tilly in the tree and continued around the side of the house to where a door would lead him directly into the kitchen. Going the other way would have meant walking along the corridor past the lieutenant's room, and Pitch was not ready to have his day ruined again by that place. He was almost at the door when the thump of footsteps came from behind. Someone at a run.

Pitch tensed, whirling about, his pulse racing.

'Just me,' Silas called, the topcoat streaming like a banner over him as he moved. 'Sorry, I should have called out.'

Had Pitch looked as concerned as he'd felt? Blast it, he could not be jumping at shadows like this. 'I thought a bloody Nephilim had been set loose in the garden.' He glowered through a poor display of nonchalance. 'All that pounding about.'

It didn't seem that great an insult really, but a pained looked swept Silas's features and he was rather quiet as they stepped into the kitchen.

The room was gloriously warm and smelled like a pie shop. Bess was rolling out dough at the long table in the room's centre, the front of his impractical blush-pink silk gown covered over with a garishly floral apron. Wearing a far more sensible set of trousers and a brown shirt, Charlie was over by the kitchener, stirring one of the blackened pots.

'Get that door closed,' Bess cried. 'Blast it's chilly out there.' Either his entire face was smudged in baking flour, or he'd been too generous with his powder this morning. Two bright dots of rouge highlighted his cheeks. 'Not exactly a fine morning for a walk. What were you two doing out there so long?'

'As if you don't know it all.' Pitch headed straight for the black kitchener in its alcove of heat. Charlie was at one end with his pot, stirring a caramel-brown broth that smelled of mutton and cinnamon and cloves. Sharing the same heat plate was an enormous black kettle, steam beginning to hint from its spout.

Pitch busied himself with untying his laces, steadfastly refusing to look the lad in the eye. He did not feel good, being back in this house, the lieutenant and his angel nearby. Pitch's earlier foul mood and violence were likely not forgotten either.

'How are you feeling?' Charlie asked quietly. And something about the gentle way he did so made Pitch rile with sudden, blazing anger. There was only so much care and concern a daemon could handle.

'Fine. Very fine. Silas just fucked me to within an inch of my life, and told me he loved me, can you imagine? Have I not said from the start he is an idiot?' He tossed his boots to nowhere in particular and thrust his hands towards the kitchener's warmth.

It took a moment to realise the room was silent, save for the bubble of the pot and low hiss of the kettle. He looked up to find Charlie staring at him. By the table Bess was patting Silas's arm with flour-smudged fingertips. The ankou's head was lowered and his wet hair long enough now to conceal his face. For which Pitch was grateful.

He had just been an unforgivable bastard.

Charlie left his stirring to join the consolation party. To add insult to injury, he enveloped Silas in a hug and said very pointedly, 'You are no fool, my friend. And he does not deserve you.'

Well, Pitch had never contested that. He counted the seconds, waiting for the ankou to say something, but it was Bess who spoke first.

'That kettle is getting ready to scream, Charlie. Best get to it before it wakes Edward. He's barely settled. He must be rested if he's to leave today.'

'Leave today?' That was Silas.

Pitch's mood scuttled deeper. He'd failed to mention the angel's instructions to leave at once.

A terse situation was about to become even more so.

'That is what Tobias said, you are to leave today. We have Sybilla at a gallop to return.' Bess blew out a breath to shift a strand of grey hair hanging over his nose. 'She'll be here within the hour. I intend to send you off with some of this pie, and the broth shall be ready by then. You must have Edward eat some, however you can manage. He's barely had a mouthful in the past week.'

Pitch felt Silas's hard glare upon him. He shifted so he had his back to the ankou, pretending he was greatly interested in the jars of preserves and jams assembled on the sideboard.

He had no appetite for any.

'Pitch, are we to leave today?'

He'd never heard Silas speak in such a sullen way. Pitch clenched his fingers around a cloth-covered jar of raspberry jam. He picked it up, simply because he had no idea what else to do.

'We are. Did I not say?'

'You did not.'

Pitch slipped the cloth free and jabbed his finger into the scarlet stickiness. Sugar may make him less of a foul creature, he supposed. 'I thought I had.'

'It must have slipped your mind.'

'I was preoccupied, that is certain.' Pitch sucked down a blob of seed-peppered jam. He was every bit the swimmer out of his depth now, as he'd been in the fucking pond. He owed Silas an apology, he absolutely did, but could not assemble any of the words in his mouth. He blamed the jam. And the damned audience.

'Well, you know now,' Old Bess said. 'So best you both get yourselves cleaned up properly and start thinking about what to pack.' Pitch had never wanted to kiss Old Bess so fiercely in his life. 'Charlie has already started gathering a few things for the journey, blankets and the like. Edward will need to be kept warm when his fever finally breaks and you...' He paused, so long that Pitch turned around to see to whom he referred. And damn it, it was him. 'Make sure you pack long johns, plenty of wool shirts too. I had more than we need sent over. Nancy and Ada are feeling the draughts of this place, just as you.' Wonderful, Pitch was placed in the same company as the purebreds. 'I'll come and help you when I'm done here.'

'I don't need a valet.'

'You do when you have no idea what it is to be cold, Tobias.'

Bess did not bother to conceal his concern. No doubt he knew of Pitch's performance in the pond and could see with his own eyes how desperate Pitch was to warm himself – the fire daemon with flames in his veins trembling with cold. But Pitch was only half listening now. Silas had moved to Charlie's side, insisting on lifting the heavy black kettle despite the lad's protests that he was quite able. The ankou took the hot metal over to the bench where a more delicate floral teapot was ready for the boiled water. How long until Charlie prattled on about Pitch trying to strangle Edward in a rage? Another detail he'd kept from Silas.

'Tobias...'

He started at the name, realising it had been said several times already. Bess gave him a tight smile.

'Give him a moment, it will be all right.' He darted a look towards the others, over the far side of the kitchen, before waving Pitch closer.

'What?' Pitch grumbled.

96

'Come here, damn it.' When Pitch acquiesced, Bess leaned in to whisper. 'The coat you requested. Lim finished it, and I believe it arrived while you were...' He wrinkled his nose. 'Occupied.'

'The Inverness?'

'Shhhh. It's a surprise, is it not?' Bess glanced at Silas, but the ankou was absorbed in his discussion with Charlie. 'And I'd say it couldn't come at a better time. A nice peace offering, after being such a cunt.'

A fair assessment. Pitch put up no protest at the insult. He nodded, quietly elated at the prospect of the coat's arrival. The Inverness he'd arranged to have made may as well be the crown jewels right now. He'd requested an exact replica of the ankou's beloved coat. The original was far away in Holly Village, likely a home to moths and silverfish, nibbling away at its fetching cape and black trimmings. Silas adored that coat. And in the strange ways of the ankou, he missed a piece of clothing the way Nancy and Ada might miss Tilly. Hopefully he adored it enough to cease being furious with a thoughtless daemon.

Bess returned to assaulting his dough with the rolling pin. 'Up you go then. And be sure to see if Ronin has found the mushrooms I need. No point making this mushroom pie otherwise. Nothing can top a Mustow Green mushroom, something in the soil.' He gave Pitch a wink. 'Nancy said Ada's partial to mushrooms. If this doesn't get her eating, then nothing will.'

But Pitch had little interest in Ada's lack of appetite. He had enough issue with his own. Pitch set down his jar of raspberry jam, glanced once more at Silas and Charlie, who paid him no mind, and made his way towards the door.

'Tobias, dear,' Bess called. 'Do be sure to wash, you are rather pungent, and I'm not talking pond water.'

Pitch made his way along the corridor and into the main section of the house. He passed by several empty rooms, a sitting room where much of the furniture was sheeted, a dining room where candlesticks and condiment jars and a couple of fine glasses still remained from last night's attempt at a meal. His sock-covered feet made him silent, only the occasional creak of a floorboard to betray him.

Tilly's giggle announced the changeling's presence up ahead. He was very grateful to find her far too distracted to notice him pass by the parlour, where she busied herself with arranging an appalling selection of gleaming trinkets in Forneus's coat.

'Pretty, pretty puppy,' Tilly declared, adding a pearl-embellished hair-pin to the arrangement dangling from the hound's shaggy coat.

The child, thank all the gods, had her back to the door and did not notice him pass by, but the skriker did. His red eye followed Pitch's movement, tongue like a drooped black flag hanging from his mouth. They regarded each other balefully, and Pitch had the horrid idea that Silas's hound might know exactly how mean-spirited he'd been to the ankou.

'Fucking dog,' he muttered, and broke into a jog.

That didn't last long though. Pitch grimaced, grabbing at his hip, the resistance in the muscles causing him to stumble. Seraphiel had stifled the wildness, whittled Pitch's flame to nothing, but had left Pitch with this godsdamned dodgy hip. Not so bad as before, he'd barely noticed it on the walk from the garden, but it was still going to be an issue if he could only stroll away from mortal fucking danger and not run away screaming in panic, as he seemed prone to do these days.

He negotiated the stairs with trepidation. But here again the hip was not so bothersome. His legs were just stiff from being contorted as Silas fucked him. And he'd not complain about that.

Pitch turned right at the top of the stairs, heading away from Nancy and Ada's room, which lay the other way.

Old Bess had claimed the largest of all the rooms, despite the fact that Ada and Nancy and the changeling were rather cramped in their quarters.

He pushed open the deceptively heavy mahogany door and stepped into Bess's bedchambers. The room was thick with the odour of perfume, Bess's preferred sandalwood. The curtains were all pulled wide open, allowing in what light the struggling day held, the windowpanes smeared with the incessant rain. The room was considerable, the hearth alone double that of the one in the room he shared with Silas, and the bed...good gods, what exploits could be had in such a space. It had posters thick as small tree trunks and a mastery of carving upon them, vines of ivy brought to life in the rosewood. The bed was covered in blue satin and strewn with enough pillows to bury oneself in entirely.

Pitch's attention moved to the trunk which took up a good portion of one corner of the room. The steamer trunk had been set up on one of its ends and fanned open to reveal a tier of wide drawers on one side and an open section on the other, where hangers would normally be fixed in readiness for the clothes to be hung. No wonder Old Bess had chosen this particular trunk, for the inside was covered in a floral wallpaper that nearly matched the bright and busy design on the apron he wore.

But Pitch was much disappointed to see the hanging section empty. He'd been expecting a splash of royal blue there, double folded to accommodate the great swath of material it took to cover the ankou. He knelt between the two widened sections of the trunk, and opened one of the drawers. A paper-wrapped parcel sat there, tied with a purple ribbon. He was hit by the pungent odour of fresh-turned dirt and a more resinous waft. Pine needles, he suspected. Ronin had found the mushrooms.

Pitch lifted the bundle from the drawer, the mushrooms soft lumps beneath the paper. There was a bag of sugar too, and a mother-of-pearl inlaid brooch. A gift for Tilly, he suspected. Pitch set them all aside and moved to the next drawer. His eyes widened.

He let out a cry of delight. A corset. Indubitably fine. He pulled it from the drawer, pressing it against himself, rising to his feet so he could admire himself in the mottled mirror over the rosewood dresser. The corset was glorious. A sublime maroon, embroidered with silver lengths of ivy and wheat stalks, and edged with a cream-coloured lace at the top. It flared a little at the hips and tapered down to a long point at the torso. Likely the tip would press at the bone just above his cock. He'd be tightly bound from tits to balls. It was perfect.

Pitch dragged his shirt over his head, forgoing unbuttoning, grumbling as the fabric caught at his earring. He'd take the blasted thing off the minute they left the Sanctuary and Tilly wasn't there to see it. Shirtless now, he set to putting on the corset at once. Its hooks were sewn at the front, so he needed no assistance to put it on. Another great delight.

He exhaled deeply, ridding his lungs of air, pulling in his stomach, growing a little light-headed as he fought to make himself small enough. The effort it took to bind himself in the corset was far more than it should have been, because he was far less than he should be.

Which would have made him far more irritated had he not caught sight of himself again in the mirror. He was a picture. Pitch breathed in short intakes as he accustomed himself to the tight press at his ribs once more. It had been a good few days since he'd been restrained, but now that he was back in the embrace of a corset, he could not imagine why he'd not demanded one sooner.

He smoothed the satin, ran his fingers over the embroidery, brushed his knuckles at the lace which sat just beneath his exposed nipples. Pitch was pale, he'd not noticed quite how much so before. It must be the particular hue of the fabric. And there were some fine scratches upon his shoulder that marred the perfection of his skin, a bruise too upon his arm. That was likely from Silas, dragging him from the weeds or pounding him into the table. Subtle things, really, that shouldn't have caused any marks at all.

Pitch turned away from that thought. Back to the corset.

Ronin had done remarkably well in choosing it, not that he would say as much to the tsukumogami, or to Silas.

Satisfied, Pitch returned to the trunk, searching for signs of the coat. He opened the third draw, releasing the hint of strawberries. A handful of strawberry tarts sat beneath a glass dome. They were arranged on an ornate plate, ivory ground with finely crackled glaze, hints of a turquoise and yellow scene painted beneath the tarts.

He lifted the plate from the drawer and removed its dome. A dollop of clotted cream sat in the middle of each tart. They were all but perfect, the pastry golden, the filling a deep shade of pink, one that teetered on the edge of red. Old Bess must have arranged this surprise. He suspected they were fresh from the Mustow Green bakery where he had eaten the poor baker clean out of tarts on a daily basis during his stay.

Pitch took one, dabbing its pastry at his lips. He *was* hungry. But his appetite had no depth to it. He did not crave as he was wont to do. Pitch inhaled. Perhaps one bite. He felt compelled to at least try. More so than he'd done in days.

He widened his mouth, the cream in danger of catching at his lip.

'No!'

A figure exploded out of the trunk, coming at him from the section where garments should hang. They collided and Pitch was thrown onto his side, the plate of tarts sent flying. For some bizarre reason, he refused to let go of the one he still held, squishing it in his hand, despite the stranger's shouts.

'Let it go, let it go.' The stranger went for his face, grabbing at his chin. 'Did you eat any? Spit it out. Now.'

What in all the imagined realms of hell was going on? 'Let me go, you fucking arsehole.'

'Did you eat it, Tobias?'

Although startled to hear his name, Pitch lashed out with hand and foot, punching and kicking his way free of the imbecile who clambered all over him. A well-placed kick to the gut had the attacker grunting and withdrawing. Pitch leapt to his feet, tart squeezing between his fingers, staring down at the man huddled on the rug.

'Ronin? What the fuck are you doing here?'

'Did you eat any of the tart?'

'What was wrong with the tart?'

'Did you eat any?' he shouted.

'I fucking did not!' Pitch shouted right back. 'What are you doing here? What is going on, Ronin?'

Old Bess's favoured footman and Pitch's momentary lover, was somehow, unfathomably, here. Pieces of pastry stuck in his jet-black hair as he gasped for breath, rolling onto his hands and knees. His clothes were worse for wear, great tears in the sleeves and a rip over his right butt cheek. There were some cuts upon his face that Pitch was certain he'd not put there.

Had not Old Bess said only inanimate objects could pass through the faerie tunnel between Harvington Hall and this place? Nothing living and breathing could do so. Ronin may be a sake pot at heart, but he was very much living and breathing. Gasping for every breath, actually.

'Where is she?' Ronin demanded. 'Where is her plate?' He still found the wherewithal to slide his gaze over Pitch's body.

'Could you focus enough to be clearer?' Pitch said darkly. 'Whose plate?'

But Ronin was already panting his way across the rug. As he moved, the floor seemed to crack beneath him. Not a creak of wood though, something sharper. More disconcerting. He cursed under his breath.

'Thought I'd have longer.'

'Ronin, are you all right?'

'I'm fine. There...there she is...take her to Bess. Before any more damage is done.' Ronin lifted his hand and pointed.

His forefinger snapped at the knuckle as though an invisible hand had wrenched it backwards. The tsukumogami fell forward and screamed his agony into the rug.

'Fuck.' Pitch raced to his side, catching sight of the plate. It had ended up half-hidden beneath the bed, scattered tarts staining the rug around it.

The clatter of hurried footsteps echoed in the corridor. A moment later, the door opened and Old Bess flew into the room in a rush of skirts.

'Ronin? Oh gods, dear boy. What have you done?'

Ronin had no chance to answer before another of his bones broke. He had his arm stretched to reach for the plate, and so Pitch had a very clear view of his thumb as it snapped, the nail touching at the inside of his wrist. But worse was the muffled crack that came from beneath the tsukumogami's shirt. A rib, or two, Pitch suspected.

The man was breaking apart.

Ronin's squashed cry vanished into Old Bess's bosom as the half-fae wrapped up his footman, gathering the slight figure and heaving him onto the bed before Pitch could try to assist.

'Hotaru,' Ronin breathed. 'She is with them.'

'Hotaru?' Old Bess appeared as confused as Pitch, which was no comfort at all.

Ronin's ankle turned, in a way no ankle should when it was simply resting upon a bed. The tsukumogami gritted his teeth, hissing through the rest of his reply. 'The tarts for the daemon...I forbade them. Astaroth didn't deserve them, I said. Then I heard a housemaid gossiping that I must have changed my mind...and was trying to woo this bastard with a fresh batch.' He laughed, short and snappish. 'I know well enough when I'm not wanted. Wouldn't waste a single strawberry on him.'

He fixed Pitch with a glare that was truly quite admirable, considering the pain the man must be in. Or perhaps it was because of it.

'Who sent them then, Ronin?' Bess held the tsukumogami's wrist, tracing all manner of shapes upon his skin. But Bess was no healer; whatever he sought to do might dull the pain at best.

'Who *brought* them.' Ronin coughed. Most unpleasant. For both him and those having to listen to the snap of more ribs. He groaned but kept on. 'The plate, Bess.'

Ronin's body stiffened. His hips shifted one way, his shoulders twisting the other. He was a dishcloth being wrung out.

'What is happening to him?'

'He's dying,' Bess said tightly. 'Nothing living may pass through the tunnels. He might have stood a chance if he'd kept to being a sake pot, but he's thrown himself in full bodied. Where is the damned plate?'

Pitch stood at the foot of the bed. The damned plate was right at his feet. Its intricate artwork was a garden scene, with birds of yellow and turquoise settled among oversized scarlet roses, the painting edged with gold gilding. Hardly a formidable monster, unless birds frightened you.

Pitch snatched it up. 'This?' He waggled the plate. 'Ugly enough, I don't understand–'

Old Bess belied his namesake, moving from where he sat on the bed to launch himself at Pitch in the blink of an eye and snatching the plate from his grasp. Bess held it towards Ronin.

'This is Hotaru? Another tsukumogami?'

His nod was laboured. 'A sister turned deceiver. You'll find those tarts poisoned, I'm certain.'

Pitch stood still, a sickening certainty gripping him.

With the way Bess held the plate, Pitch could only see its back. A plain surface, save for two holes at opposite sides of its circumference. Perfect placement for screws, so as to tie wire or string between them and mount the plate upon a wall. In a ballroom perhaps.

Fuck.

'Is that a Satsuma plate?' Pitch asked tightly.

Bess cast him a curious look, one not half as unpleasant as Ronin's.

His eyes were shot through with blood; he was weeping crimson at the ears and nose. But he answered. 'It is. Hotura is young. Barely a hundred years since her spirit formed, and I had not seen her in at least half of that.' The man was rough as loose gravel. 'But it is the way of a tsukumogami to be moved about. We are but objects, after all.' He coughed again, and blood sprayed the air. They waited while he endured the breaking of his little finger, the last on his right hand to succumb. 'When she sought me out in Mustow Green, I thought it the visit of an old friend. We drank, we spoke of Japan...'

'Your *old friend* is an ally of the Morrigan.' Pitch was grim. 'And just tried to infiltrate the Sanctuary to kill me.'

'It seems so.' A bloodied tear slipped down the side of Ronin's face. 'But if it was just you the Morrigan would harm, I might have turned a blind eye. Let them be done with you, for you are the root of all this madness.'

'That's a hell of a grudge to carry because I wouldn't fuck you again.'

'Enough.' Bess tugged at the ties of his apron, pulling it off and wrapping it around the plate. 'Quiet, the pair of you. Tobias, are you certain she is with the Morrigan.'

'I'm certain.'

Bess brushed his hand over the concealed plate. 'Foolish little one,' he whispered. 'You cannot hide deep enough to escape this.'

There was no fae magick whispered, no building of any prison to hold the tsukumogami in. Bess let the plate drop to the floor. He lifted his skirts, revealing a low-heeled boot. With grim determination, the Child of Melusine brought down his heel upon the centre of the plate.

The crack of earthenware joined that of Ronin's slowly shattering body. And above it all, a high-pitched scream, so high and distant it barely sounded as though it was in the room at all. Ronin let out an anguished cry to join it as the gooseflesh rose along Pitch's arms.

Bess waved his hand over the apron with its pile of ruined tsukumogami. Glittering flecks of silver fell from his fingers, dusting the material in a thick coating of prettiness it did not deserve. That done, Bess turned his attention to the trunk. He went to it, fluttering his fingers to order all the drawers open at once. They shot from their slots. Pitch had emptied all but one. Royal-blue fabric unfurled, sinking to the ground like a grand petticoat.

Silas's coat had been neatly folded up in the very top drawer, the only one Pitch had not yet searched. Bess kicked at the empty drawers, as though not convinced the Morrigan weren't in the gnarls in the wood.

'Can we be certain she was not spellbound?' Pitch gathered up the coat, clutching at it like a life vest. 'Could the sorcerers be tracking her location?'

Bess flicked his fingers, and the steamer trunk slammed shut with all the finality of a sarcophagus. 'She could not be spellbound and pass through the tunnel. Magick is alive. I would have known of its arrival, just as I did Ronin's. But even if by some miracle they could manage such a feat, we are in my Sanctuary. There is no hiding nefarious magick in a place where I am privy to every crack and crevice. The Morrigan can send their rats, but there is a trap for each of them.'

'Then why send the bloody plate at all?' Pitch said. 'Why not just a load of poison-encrusted tarts?'

Bess's gaze darted to Ronin. 'Because it would not likely kill you, as you've proved.' Pitch was frighteningly unsure of that himself. 'And they'd still not know where we were. Hotura's death would not be immediate, as you can well see. Once she learned our location, there would be time to send word of it before she...' Bess tugged at the frilled collar of his dress, his words fading.

Pitch had heard enough anyway. The tsukumogami had been on a one-way journey. He wiped his strawberry-tart-encrusted hand against his trousers.

Ronin groaned, and Bess hurried to his side, settling himself on the bed. He brushed back the damp black strands off the tsukumogami's forehead. 'I'll do what I can for you, my friend. The angel will be here soon. She will take away your pain.'

'And Hotura...' Ronin rasped.

'Of course.'

'She's not dead?' Pitch glanced at the apron with all its shattered pieces.

'No. I've done a terrible thing, to break her while she is in true form,' Bess said, solemn and low. 'I'll not be so cruel as to leave her that way. Sybilla will aid me in finishing things properly.'

'No choice, Bess.' Ronin's lips trembled, and blood peaked from their corners. 'I'm so sorry.' He was so pale as to be translucent. His veins stark. 'I should never have allowed her in.'

'No, you bloody well should not have.' Pitch was desperately on edge, and unnecessarily cruel, he'd not deny.

Ronin jerked, lips tight. His fingers bent at excruciating angles. Bess fussed over him, whispering encouragement to hold on. Be strong. And when Ronin settled again, Bess turned on Pitch.

'Since we are throwing blame about, how long have you known of a tsukumogami being amongst the Morrigan?'

The accusation stung. 'Silas informed the Lady of it, he told me as much.' Pitch hid behind Silas's sensibility, cut by the cold way Old Bess regarded him. As though he were at fault for all that had happened. Despising the fact he could not decide if Bess was right or wrong. 'The necromancer taunted us with it in the Fulbourn–'

'Why the fuck was nothing said to me?'

'I don't know. Perhaps it was. You are old–'

'Fuck off, Astaroth. Why would *you* not say anything?' The heat grew behind Bess's words.

'Me? I've had other fucking things to preoccupy me, aside from filling you in on all the minute details.'

'A minute detail that put every single soul in this house in danger, and is killing my friend.' Bess's voice was clenched between a wild whisper and a shout. He was being unreasonable, the accusations terribly misplaced, but Pitch understood the agonies that drove him on. He'd done his fair share of lashing out to soothe his own pain. 'Why are you not gone from here, Tobias? You said you must go, then fucking go.'

He'd not expected the vitriol though. Pitch held so tight to the coat that the ribs of the corset bit deep.

'Bess...' Ronin lifted his hand, though it barely resembled one now with all its fingers contorted, and sought to reach for the half-fae. 'Enough.'

Bess slumped, covering his face with his free hand. The tears loosened in a rush, as though he'd piled them all behind his eyes till now. 'I should have been able to protect you. They have killed you, Ronin.'

The tsukumogami had come to the aid of someone he despised, to protect the one he loved. And the price was hefty.

What the fuck had Pitch been thinking, hiding away in the cottage at the bottom of the garden? Bess's blame may be misplaced, but he wasn't entirely wrong in it. Pitch *had* put every single soul in the house in danger with his determination to deny his fate.

'We shall be gone within the hour.' He turned away from Bess's tears and swallowed against a throat run dry with the weight of things. 'It should have been sooner...forgive me.'

He struggled to keep from running to the door, but it felt an eternity before he was closing it behind him. Shutting away Bess's words and Ronin's sacrifice.

Pitch leaned against the wall, so preoccupied that he did not notice he had an audience.

'Fire man, all right?' Tilly and Forneus watched him, the hound on his haunches, the little fae beside him, her neck adorned with multiple necklaces.

'Not really. But you'll all be safe soon. I promise you, little one.'

Tilly took his clean hand. She was warm. 'Not your fault.'

'I think it is though.' The changeling's tiny hand rested in his palm. 'Where are your mothers?'

'Sleeping.' She patted her chest. 'I help them. Better they sleep.'

The fae was sedating her parents to help them through this. How blissful a thought. To go to sleep and only wake when all was well.

'Clever girl.' He squeezed her hand. Tilly's eyes were on the earring Pitch wore. She tugged at one of the necklaces, dragging its pendant from beneath her nightshirt. The matching amber earring dangled there.

'Friends.'

'You have dire taste in friends, changeling.'

Tilly smiled, and Pitch could not stand there another moment.

'Get away with you now.' He nudged her aside under the watchful eye of the hound. 'And you...fetch your master from where he's playing housemaid.' Pitch was not going to enjoy telling Silas all that had happened. 'There is much to be done if this house is to be rid of me.'

CHAPTER 12

S ilas and Charlie readied the horses and carriage, the sizeable brougham belonging to Adamaris and Nancy, each lost in their own troubled thoughts. The lad had quickly given up instructing Silas on how to settle the horses into their straps and cinches, for it was evident almost at once that he held innate memory of it. Silas had gathered up the breeching and settled it on one of the bay's hinds, buckling it in place before Charlie had finished tying up his horse.

'You've done this before, then?' the lad said.

'It would appear so.' Not so surprising, considering his lives lived, Silas supposed. Though it would have been nice to be equally so adept with riding from the outset and have saved himself a few falls.

The stables were quiet, with only Hastings in residence, sucking down her chaff greedily after being ridden hard, and the building was luckily grand enough to allow them to prepare the horses inside, avoiding the drizzle beyond the wide-open doors. The silence was broken only by the click of buckles and the snorting of the pair of bays as they were strapped up. Silas would have preferred more noise, anything to distract him from what Pitch had told him about the events in Bess's room. Anything to wipe from memory what he'd heard as he passed along the upstairs corridor, drawing near to Bess's chamber. The tsukumogamis' ghastly rattling tunes were like none he'd yet heard nor wished to again. Whatever melody they'd held before was made grotesque by their strange, lingering deaths.

The bay stamped his foreleg, and Silas barely moved his boot in time to avoid a crushing.

'Easy there, nearly done.' He rubbed the gelding's neck, as much to soothe himself as the horse.

How sickening it was to think on how close the Morrigan had come to Pitch. Indeed, to everyone in the household.

Silas glanced at the stall where Hastings ate her chaff. A lucky thing there had been a stall without a gate. The massive mare's hindquarters stuck out into the walkway as it was. She was still damp with sweat, despite a rub down.

Sybilla had come in at a gallop and had barely slowed to a trot before she leapt from the horse's back and rushed into the house. That was half an hour ago. He'd seen no sign of her since, but the grim sounds of distress coming from Bess's chamber had ceased.

'Are they certain there is nothing to be done for Ronin?' Charlie asked. 'Surely amongst all of you, with all your preternatural powers, someone can help him?'

Silas lost hold of the tug buckle he'd been securing. 'I am told there is not.' He knew it to be true. He'd heard the hopelessness in the inevitable fading of Ronin's song. 'It is a terrible state of affairs.'

One Pitch was not dealing with well.

He'd looked a beautiful, wretched sight, startlingly pale against the maroon corset he wore as he relayed to Silas what had happened while pulling their clothes from the wardrobe and tossing them in a pile. The prince barely seemed able to stand unaided but warded Silas off the moment he drew close.

'Tend the horses, I'll see to our clothes, and have Sybilla ready Edward as soon as...' He'd drawn in a breath. 'As soon as she is done.'

Charlie secured the bridle of the second bay. Both were done now. The horses need only be settled between the shafts and the reins run through the terrets and the brougham was ready to be taken over to the house where it could be loaded.

'But Tilly and her mothers, Bess, too, they will all be safe here once we are gone, won't they?'

Charlie's question had Silas stepping around the horses to find the lad. 'You will *all* be safe here, Charlie. The Morrigan have not found us, Bess is certain of it, and the tunnel between the Sanctuaries is now severed. Once Pitch and I are gone, the Morrigan's interest will follow.'

The lad stared Silas right in the eye as he declared, 'I shall be with you, Silas.'

'You absolutely shall not, Charlie.'

The lad set his jaw, straightened so he was as tall as he could make himself. 'I can be of help. You don't understand how things have–'

'Silas, are they ready?' Sybilla moved into the stables like a low-lying storm cloud, her black leather coat fanning around her, stirring the hay-strewn floor. She held a rigidness about her that stopped Silas from asking after Ronin. He knew enough anyway. With death that close by, he'd know when its last notes were played.

'I need a minute, no more,' he said. 'Then they can bring out the carriage.'

'Good. Bring them around to the front of the house. We will load from there, and I'll mark the carriage with some runes that will serve to make us less observable. I've tended the lieutenant. He's as comfortable as I can make him.' She wiped the back of her wrist over her brow, and Silas thought he heard her sigh. 'Would you see him into the carriage, Silas? I just need a moment to catch my breath.'

'I can do that.' Charlie tossed Silas the rein he'd just clipped to the bridle. 'Let me handle getting Edward sorted.'

The lad raced off, turning heel so fast that Silas barely had his lips parted to tell him the man was too heavy to move alone.

'He'll be fine, Silas.' Sybilla sat down with a grunt on a hay bale, rubbing at her face.

Silas decided against voicing his disagreement. Frail as Edward might be, he was far more than the slight lad could handle alone. Charlie would realise that soon enough. Just as he'd realise he was not coming on this fraught journey.

While he threaded the reins, Silas watched the angel, who sat with her face pressed into her hands. 'I would ask if you are all right,' he said gently, 'but I know what the truth is. I'm sorry, Sybilla. You must be exhausted.'

'No more so than anyone else.' She raised her head. 'But thank you, Silas.'

'Is there any chance Sanu and Lalassu will join us soon?' He half expected the angel would not answer him. She was very intent on the straw for a while before she did so.

'Not yet, no. It is just Hastings for now.'

'What is keeping them?'

Sybilla bowed her head, scratching at the back of her neck where the tight curls of her pearl-white hair were thinnest. 'I don't know where to start with my answer to that. The world is a wound spring out there, Silas. Never have I seen it so unsettled.'

'How so?'

'You won't like it.'

'I don't doubt it.'

'The Blight. It is so rife, it seems it is not just your dead who feel its touch. The tales I'm told speak of hauntings among the purebreds, of people becoming possessed by daemons.'

Silas stopped his work, the very last buckle undone. 'Daemons? Is such a thing possible?'

'Not daemonic possession, no.' The emphatic shake of Sybilla's head was somewhat reassuring. 'They could perhaps manipulate a person into *believing* themselves possessed, and I suppose the Morrigan may count a daemon among their number, they have all else. But that is not what this was. I was longer last night than intended as I heard tell of a village where there was a man claimed to be possessed. I rode there, and watched from afar. What I saw was not a simple illness of the man's mind, nor was there any trace of a daemon within the village. I fear he *was* possessed by something bleak, something of your world, Silas. And he is far from the only one.'

'Possessed by a lost soul?'

'Is there a chance of that? I do not recall you ever speaking of the dead stealing the bodies of the living.'

Nor did Silas. The notion did not trigger any sense of memory. Only that of trepidation. 'Even if it had occurred on occasion, surely such grave numbers is far from natural?'

'Exactly. There is chaos out there, Silas. More to occupy us than we can handle.'

'An intentional play by the Morrigan?' Silas asked.

Sybilla nodded. 'Start so many small fires that we cannot see the blaze, for they without doubt have greater plans afoot. And the UnSeelie Court's aid is undeniable now, if it were ever in doubt. Marcus brought word of the Wild Hunt plaguing the west. The Herlequin is terrorising the areas around Bristol.'

Silas was not familiar with either the Wild Hunt or the Herlequin. One he could imagine well enough, but the other gave him pause.

'The Herlequin?'

'You do not recall? It is the name given to the leader of the fae's Wild Hunt. We have dealt with them here and there in our times together. Chased them back to court when they overstayed their welcome. A bit of sport really, nothing of serious consequence.'

'I don't recall,' Silas said, not bothering to hide his annoyance. 'What does this fellow look like?'

Sybilla pushed to her feet, stretching her arms overhead. 'There is no way to know, not for this particular one at least. The Herlequin is chosen at the Erlking's pleasure. It has never been the same creature twice. And it was not Lokke who sent the ones we dealt with, but his father, Farbauti. The Order eventually managed to convince that old bastard to stop kidnapping purebreds simply because he wished to decorate his court with those that intrigued him.'

'That is the purpose of the Wild Hunt? Kidnapping purebreds?'

'It's purpose varies according to the Erlking's whim. Sometimes they are bounty hunters, chasing down runaways or traitors of the court. Right now, the Wild Hunt is yet another hindrance for the Lady to deal with. Another banging drum to draw their attention.'

'Then best we move very quietly amongst all that noise.' Silas took hold of the reins. In his mind hovered the disturbing image of Pitch in the grip of wild panic, his flame reduced to candlelight.

'My thoughts exactly. Are you ready?'

'Almost. Would you mind passing my coat, please.' He nodded to where the Inverness lay on one of the stacked bales behind her.

'Certainly.'

She handed it over. The touch of the thick wool was heavenly. Just to see that splendid work of tailoring brought Silas some measure of calm. The unexpected thoughtfulness that had brought the coat into existence made his pulse quicken.

While Sybilla settled herself beside one of the horses, Silas shrugged on the coat with practiced ease. The fit was possibly more perfect than the original. He transferred the bandalore from his trousers into one of the deep pockets. 'Right, now I'm ready.'

They led the horses on, the brougham settling in behind them. The carriage house was a decent distance from the house, with a wide sweeping drive that would bring them around eventually to the front door.

'Silas, I must tell you'– Sybilla was sombre, which raised Silas's concerns at once– 'that the tarts were indeed poisoned. A considerable amount of Gu.'

A muscle in Silas's jaw ticked as pressed his teeth. Might the Gu have done its worst this time?

'I see.'

'And something else–'

'Good god,' he muttered.

'Blood.'

Silas peered over the bay's ears. 'I beg your pardon?'

'The tarts were baked with blood. It was in the icing too.'

'Whose blood?'

'I have no way of knowing.'

A flash of the greensward came to Silas. The poor young man with his throat slit. 'The tarts were filled with blood magick?'

'No, magick does not do well in the Melusine tunnels, as any living thing, and would not have been able to breach Harvington Hall's barrier. I can't say for certain, but I think perhaps the blood was set there in readiness. If their plans had gone another way...they would have had it there at their disposal. Ready to be used for casting perhaps? But I truly can't say for certain. Blood magick is unique to maleficium. I know very little of its intricacies.'

'And they knew Pitch to be partial to those sweets. If he had eaten the blasted things...Christ, if anyone else in the household had eaten them...' Silas held so tightly to the reins that his nails bit into the palm of his hand. 'Sybilla, there is something you should know about Pitch's situation. I doubt he will have told you.'

'Told me what, Silas?'

'Pitch is not quite himself.'

They were almost at the turn that would take them to the front of the house.

'Silas! Are you building the fucking carriage?' Pitch's voice carried high and loud across the damp air. 'Stop patting the fleabags and bring them at once. We are ready to leave.'

Sybilla sighed. 'Sounds himself to me. Are you right with this pair? I best tend to Hastings.'

'Yes, yes. I'll be fine.'

Silas led the horses on, quickening their pace now. He rounded the side of the house, to where the front door with its fanned stone steps and white railings came into view. Pitch was at the open doorway, arms full of bundles of who-knew-what. Tilly sat upon Forneus on the gravelled drive, smiling broadly as she caught sight of Silas. But it was Charlie, making his way down the steps, that had Silas's attention.

'What the bloody hell is he doing?'

But it was very obvious what Charlie was doing. He was holding the lieutenant. Standing there with Edward cradled in his arms, and showing no sign that the man was any burden at all.

CHAPTER 13

The travel trunk at the back of the carriage was filled to the brim with blankets, clothing, and food. Plenty of sugar-rich cakes and honeycomb, Pitch had been told. Though eating was the last thing on his mind. All in all, enough supplies for a good week if they were careful. But no one seemed to know how careful they needed to be, because no one had a fucking clue how long the ride would take.

And it was beginning with Silas in a sulk.

The ankou was still attentive to Pitch's needs, of course, aiding him up into the driver's seat when he refused point blank to ride in the carriage where he'd be knee-to-knee with Edward. But that was not to say the ankou was in a fine temper.

Silas handed Pitch a blanket, one foot upon the pedestal step, the other still firmly on the ground. His gaze fixed on the cabin's open door where Charlie knelt upon the floor, his feet sticking out and revealing well-worn soles on his boots. He and Sybilla were busy making Edward comfortable inside, but Silas had taken great issue with the way the lieutenant had been moved from bed to carriage. Charlie had carried the man alone and manoeuvred him in through the narrow doorway single-handedly.

'You can stop glaring at me, Silas,' Charlie said from inside the cabin. 'I am coming with you and that is that. We are almost ready to drive on, do get in the seat.'

'Do you have any idea how dangerous this shall be?' Silas said.

'Have you forgotten I was at the Fulbourn? And set upon by ash men with you? But you saw me just now. I seem to have the strength of an oak. I told you I can be helpful, now you see it.'

'He has you there, my dear.' Pitch added his contribution to the pointless argument. Charlie had emerged from the Fulbourn as changed as the rest of them, and the lad was utterly set on travelling with them.

'I cannot allow this.' Silas, bless him, thought he still had a chance.

'Do you think yourself my master, Mr Mercer?' Charlie returned with steel of his own. 'Let me disappoint you right now with the truth.'

Pitch had to grin at that. And the horror on Silas's face at such an accusation. But Pitch's amusement was short-lived when he caught sight of Old Bess in the upstairs window, arms folded tightly across his chest, his hair askew. His despair reached all the way down to where Pitch sat.

'Silas, enough.' Pitch tugged at his cloak, a hooded black affair he wore over the top of a dull beige herringbone tweed coat. It had killed him to don such a plain ensemble, but they needed to be the height of uninteresting for the journey. The corset hidden beneath would keep him sane. 'Get in the seat and drive, man.'

'But it's not right, it is far too dangerous.'

'Driving a carriage? You said you know you've done it before. Another of your hidden talents. Much like your tongue upon my arsehole.'

He was vulgar with the intent of drawing the ankou's attention away from the blasted vagabond and onto the road ahead. Northwest were the scant directions provided. Told to Charlie, of all people. Whispered through dried lips by Edward when the lad lifted him from his bed.

'Arsehole,' Tilly declared, swinging her legs where she sat upon the skriker nearby.

Fuck.

But Pitch had Silas's attention at least. Even if it was a glare. Pitch shrugged. 'What? Everyone has one...'

'Tilly, please go inside.' Silas took his foot from the pedestal and moved to the child's side. 'Stay with your mothers, and listen to Bess. He will look after all of you. You will be safe here.'

'I help.' Tilly splayed her chubby little fingers, brandishing them towards the house.

There had been no ivy upon the walls when they first arrived. None a day ago. But there certainly was now. Swaths of it covered the red brickwork in vines of the brightest green, as though summer and not the dullest, dreariest winter's day surrounded them.

'That is very helpful.' Silas knelt on one knee, like he were in the midst of an inappropriate proposal. A giant alongside the petite dryad. 'Take care, little one.' He planted a kiss on the top of her head, and she pressed her hands to his cheeks.

'Bye-bye, Sy.'

The ankou enveloped the little girl, his solid arms wrapping her gently. All Pitch could see of Tilly was her tiny hand patting at Silas's back.

It hurt his eyes to watch. He looked away.

The cabin doors clicked closed, almost in unison.

'We are ready,' Sybilla called.

'Bye-bye, fire man.'

Pitch glanced down. The hug was done with, Silas rising to his feet. The changeling smacked her hand over her mouth, then released it, blowing Pitch a sloppy, irksome kiss. If she were wanting one in return, she'd be waiting for some time. If Pitch so much as moved an inch right now, he might break, like the man he'd killed upstairs.

'Silas.' Pitch pulled up his hood, gripped all at once by bleakness. 'Let's go.'

'Yes, of course.' For someone who could not read a letter, Silas read his daemon superbly. 'Forneus, stay with them for now, until Bess and Matilda are certain there is no threat. Join us as soon as you are able.'

Forneus didn't bark or growl, but Silas must have been satisfied he'd been understood, for the carriage rocked as the ankou hefted his weight up the step.

The driver's seat was barely suitable for two average-sized passengers, let alone one of Silas's large scale, which meant they were pressed up against one another from the outset. The ankou gathered up the reins, clucking to the horses, speaking to them in that deep, rumbling way that was his. And the bays responded as well as anyone who'd been encouraged by Silas's dulcet tone. The harness jingled, the wheels turned, and they were at last on their way. Hastings was tied to the back of the carriage, saddled and riderless, but her tethering was for show only. The mare would go wherever Sybilla was.

Pitch edged back his hood as they passed the end of the house, daring one last glance up at the window. Old Bess still stood there, and he thought they would pass right by without the man doing anything but stare. But at the very last moment, Bess shifted, raised his hand, and blew a kiss.

To Silas, certainly. Sybilla and Charlie, no doubt.

Silas flicked the reins, drawing a greater speed from the horses, and Pitch was turning to look away when Bess pressed a hand to the window and mouthed a few words.

Words that moved through the air of the Sanctuary to find Pitch and whisper, *I'm sorry. I was cruel. Go well. Give them the hell they deserve.*

Pitch twisted in his seat, keeping his eyes on the half-fae. He watched until the curve of the road took them from where he could see Old Bess, who did not move from where he stood at the window. No more whispers came as they drove on, down a straightening road flanked on either side by a hedgerow and row of leafless elms.

'Pitch?' Silas's hand pressed over his blanket-covered knee, giving it a gentle squeeze. 'Is everything all right?'

Pitch resettled in his seat, Tilly's earring catching at his hair as he moved. 'I'm fine.' He freed a strand from the gold leaf clasp that dangled the amber-encased flower. He must take it off soon. There was no need for the charade now that the changeling was gone.

Silas rubbed at his leg. 'We shall see them again, I'm certain of it.'

Pitch wrinkled his nose. 'As well as a carriage driver and man of the dead, you are a soothsayer now too? Tyvain will be pissed off beyond measure.'

Silas laughed, a soft exhale of air. He pulled away, and Pitch fought the urge to draw him back. The ankou needed to focus on handling the horses, not warming the hand of a daemon who should be able to do so himself.

Silas clucked his tongue, giving the reins another flick to move them on faster. The horses broke into a trot, and the ankou kept them running straight down the middle of the drive. His movements were subtle, coming easily, and he did not seem bothered by the fact that they could barely see the path ahead as Matilda's work layered the grounds in a thick mist.

'At least she has stopped the bloody rain,' Pitch muttered.

'I think Matilda intends to stay with us awhile.'

'What a formidable army we are. The Morrigan will think twice before they attack this carriage of warriors.' If his sarcasm were porridge, the spoon wouldn't be able to dig through the thickness.

'An army would stand out like a hammered thumb.' Silas's porridge, on the other hand, was decidedly watery. 'I think there is something to be said for keeping low to the ground and quiet.'

'Oh, you were a major general in a past life, then?'

Silas fought down a smile. 'I can't discount the possibility...' He turned suddenly, brow raised as though startled by his thoughts. 'But you were, most certainly...how remiss of me. You led a legion–'

'And did so appallingly badly. I tended to destroy first, find out if anyone followed after. Don't ask my advice.' He rubbed his hands together and could see he'd brought those lines of concern again to the edges of Silas's eyes. 'But yes, there is something to be said for being unobtrusive, I suppose. Not so wonderful if you are discovered, though.'

'Lalassu and Sanu will find us before long.' Silas sent his gaze forward, jaw tight, a tilt to his bearded chin. He was so bloody handsome when he was determined. 'Forneus too. The Lady knows that we are on our way –'

'Towards certain doom, yes, yes. She's been such a wonderful help so far. Oh wait...no she hasn't. We've seen neither hide nor hair of her in a while. Perhaps she's gone off to Spain, sunning herself and enjoying a sangria while learning to play the castanets.'

That had Silas throwing his head back with laughter. Pitch scowled at the start it gave him, but there were few lovelier sounds.

'You are ridiculous.' Silas moved the reins into his left hand and lay his right on Pitch's thigh. His smile faded. 'But she has much to occupy her, I'm told.'

Pitch bobbed against Silas as the rollicking movement gained momentum. The ankou filled him in on what Sybilla had said about the Blight and the Wild Hunt. Talk of the fae brought to mind the Dullahan, which did not make for pleasant memories. Pitch resettled his blanket on his lap and lay a small portion over the ankou's as well. Grateful when Silas did not make a song and dance about the gesture.

They reached the end of the long drive, and Silas turned the horses left onto a narrower cart track. 'That is due north,' he said. 'But there's no other option for now. We'll turn westerly as soon as the road allows.'

'You're a compass too. My, my, what talents you have.'

Silas gave him an indulgent smile. 'No, sadly not. But Matilda knows her way about. She's spent much time watering the countryside and will guide us. There is a crossroads about eight miles ahead where we can adjust our course.'

They travelled on awhile before they passed beyond the borders of the Sanctuary. Bess had spread their haven wide.

The departure from that haven was extraordinarily subtle. Or it would have been if Pitch were not scrutinising every tiny sensation, searching for a sign he was not so deadened inside as he felt. He knew precisely when they stepped beyond Old Bess's borders by the gentle tug at his senses, the slight pressure against his eardrums.

Though they could not see it for the fog, the breadth of England lay ahead. Seraphiel's Sanctuary lay hidden in its curves and folds somewhere. Blood Lake too. Pitch sank into his seat, hunched further under his cape. He felt himself an emptied container, dulled at the edges. Gods, what fool's journey was this? He was exposed now in a way he'd not dealt with before. In turn, so were all those around him. Pitch's heart betrayed him with a foolish, hurried thud.

He did not know he was clutching at Silas's greatcoat until the ankou touched him.

'Hey now, one mile at a time.' Silas rubbed his hand. 'Remember to take a breath.'

Pitch glowered. 'I am taking a bloody...' He exhaled, his lungs rushing to expel the air he'd held too long.

'There you go. Well done.' How did Silas manage to say such things without sounding like a condescending prick?

Pitch released his hold on the dull greatcoat. Stiff and the colour of pea soup, it covered over the royal-blue of the Inverness and would keep the ankou dry should Matilda see a need to piss upon them. His presentation of the new coat to Silas had not been pretty. He'd practically thrown the Inverness at the man and yelled at him to gather their belongings. But he'd not been so blindsided by Ronin's horrid demise that he did not notice how Silas's eyes glistened as he stared at the blue tangle in his arms, caressing a cuff as though Pitch had just presented him with their newborn son and not a piece of clothing.

Silas pushed the horses into a trot. Pitch leaned into the ankou as the horses drew them on, from one Sanctuary to another, and tried very hard to ignore how cold he was.

CHAPTER 14

For some time now the grumble of far distant thunder off to the west had bothered Silas. It announced itself again now, but thanks to a copse of trees and Matilda's gloomy, drizzling fog, there was small chance of observing the storm. He shrugged his shoulders, seeking to shift the weight of his unease. The weather was as unsettled as he. The dread that had accompanied him since the Fulbourn anchored deeper with every mile.

He turned his attention back to the road ahead, fighting the urge to set the horses into a gallop, run them all the way to this blasted Sanctuary. Move Pitch to the safety it might offer.

He blinked, his eyelashes damp.

These steeds were not Lalassu and Sanu. He'd be sending them to an early grave, and likely before they even reached the Sanctuary. Bloody hell, he missed his pale horse. It had been far too long without her. Every moment passed in Lalassu's absence gave him greater cause for concern as he imagined what she encountered in a landscape run riot by the Blight.

The carriage moved on at a sure but reasonable pace, through a day tart with winter's touch. There was no breeze save for the one made by the carriage's movement, but more importantly, there was an absence of heavy rain. Matilda, wherever she lurked, deigned to keep them relatively dry.

Silas flexed his hand where it rested on Pitch's thigh, his fingertips near numb from the cold. He wasn't certain if Pitch slept but he'd been silent a long while.

Another half hour passed before the prince shifted against him, raising a slender hand to tug at his hood and tilt it down further over his face.

'Do you need another blanket?' Silas asked.

'No' came the sullen reply.

Silas pressed no further, though he heard the lie. And he felt it. Pitch shivered every now and then, sniffing with a nose that ran with the chill.

Seraphiel, blast him to all hells, had been heavy-handed with this seal of his. And at a time like this. The angel had essentially gagged and bound the very power he'd created. Why?

Silas inhaled and blew a breath between his lips. The familiar white of winter's speech billowed in the frigid air. He touched at the hint of a black cuff that peeked from beneath his more rigid greatcoat. Pitch's secretive arrangement of a new coat, a replica of Silas's Inverness, had caught him utterly by surprise. Turned him speechless, really. He wasn't even sure he had thanked him. He'd been unable to do anything but stare like a fool and fight back tears. The gift was superlative, thoughtful, and if he made too much of a fuss of it, the prince was likely to rip it up in front of him.

So far the road had been devoid of other travellers. Silas had spied some far-away farmers tending flocks, and at one point noted a party of riders off in the distance, travelling a parallel road. No sooner was Silas thinking how pleasant the ride was and the clatter and whine of an approaching wagon pockmarked the air.

The wagon thundered over a low rise, drawn by four large workhorses at a trot that looked set to spill into a canter at any moment. Their driver appeared to be a great pile of brown cloth, with very little sign of the man who sat beneath the layers, reminding Silas of Isaac, the Village's miserable coachman. The driver whistled sharply at his horses and shouted at them to move along. His barked orders echoed across the sparse landscape.

'Bloody hell,' Silas muttered, taking his hand from Pitch's thigh.

He guided his pair towards the edge of the road. There was likely space enough to pass one another if they moved cautiously. Something the other driver seemed intent on *not* doing.

The wagon was laden with wooden barrels, empty judging by the manic tempo with which they knocked against one another.

'Is this chap going to slow down?' Silas asked.

Pitch's weight shifted. 'Hold our horses steady where they are. It will be fine.'

'Fine? He's in the middle of the bloody road. There's not enough room for us.'

There was no way possible the driver could not see the approaching carriage by now. Silas was going to be run off the road entirely at this rate. As it was, he was keeping a nervous eye on their wheels which ran closest to the soft edge. Silas reined the bays in further, slowing them nearly to a halt. But still the wagon thundered on.

Silas's heart was in his mouth, a cry set to burst from him to warn the driver of their presence. Pitch laid his hand on Silas's thigh.

'Hold steady,' he said.

At the very last, with Silas's shout filling his throat, the wagon shifted over. Not much, granted, but enough that the likelihood of a head-on collision vanished.

'Get on, get on with you!' the driver shouted, slapping the reins against the straining horses.

Shires, all four, great splendours of horseflesh with lavish feathered feet and plaited tails. The wagon was calamitous as it passed by. The blinkered horses frothed at the mouths, their chests lathered. Their driver cast Silas and his carriage a disinterested glance, as though they were some dull part of the scenery unworthy of acknowledging. The dour-faced man cleared his throat so noisily it could be heard over his wheels. He spat into the narrow section of road between him and the carriage before whipping his unfortunate horses into a canter. Well laid as the road may be, the pace was reckless over such uneven terrain.

'What a damned idiot.' Silas guided the bays back towards the centre. 'I swore he was going to run straight through us.'

'I told you he wouldn't,' Pitch said from beneath the shelter of his hood. 'The Valkyrie has marked the carriage with hexes to make us unremarkable. We are nothing but a flutter in the corner of the eye. That idiot saw enough to avoid us, but he will have forgotten seeing us within a few turns of the carriage wheels.'

Silas chewed back his annoyance. 'I see. I wish Sybilla had seen fit to tell me that before I had major palpitations. I thought I'd die of fright.'

'Fright will hardly kill a dead man, Silas.' It was not said in jest; there was no hint of amusement in the tone.

Silas glanced at the prince, who simmered in his melancholy. 'No, it will not, that's true,' he said carefully. 'But I was worried nonetheless.'

'As you so often are.'

Silas sighed inwardly, feeling the precipice of Pitch's mood keenly, the daemon's use of acerbic words to barricade himself. Perhaps Silas was unrealistic to assume the habits of four hundred years so easily altered, simply because he declared his affections and proved himself a reasonable lover.

He reached to touch the prince. Pitch slid his hands beneath his cloak and lowered his head. All at once he seemed unacceptably fragile and lost.

'You are cold.' Silas threw caution to the wind, his concern overriding sense. 'I can see it. You are very uncomfortable.'

'Hardly an unfamiliar state for me.'

Silas licked his lips. It was like having a storm cloud sitting beside him. 'No, and that is terribly unfair,' he said. 'But will you allow me to help you? Even if it is just with a silly blanket. You know I am here for you. I have prattled on about it often enough. Made a right tit of myself, I'm sure.' He tried for brevity and hoped for at least a mild response. Pitch stayed still beneath his folds. 'But it's true...anything at all I can do—'

'Oh, by all that is unholy, will you stop?' There was a sound that might...just might...have been quickly deadened laughter. 'My gods, man. You must learn to write, for you would be a wonder with a romantic novel.'

Silas delighted in what he hoped was a shift in daemonic mood. 'Really? Do you think so?'

'You shall be famed for all your sickly-sweet notions. I know your nom de plume already.'

The storm cloud beside him was lifting. Silas smiled. 'And? What do you suggest I use?'

'Written by a Silly Fop with a Splendid Cock.'

Blushing but quietly thrilled, Silas replied, 'You think it splendid?'

A grunted laugh came from beneath the hood. 'Your pillar does not displease me. Even if I am finding the cushion on this seat far too thin.'

Silas was quite sure his face was ember red, but the foolish nature of the conversation was wonderful. 'Well, I am very glad to hear it,' he said. 'Not about the seat of course. We shall organise another cushion at once. But the literary world is quite safe. The silly fop with the splendid cock intends his whimsies for you alone, I'm afraid.'

He did not blame Pitch for groaning. His words were sickeningly sentimental, but what did he have to lose? The truth was out, and Silas had not expected how freeing it would be to admit to such an intimate thing as love.

'Stop.' Pitch's hood shifted as he shook his head. 'You are embarrassing yourself. Something is truly wrong with you.'

'Oh, definitely.' Silas nodded, most solemn. 'I'm mad as a March hare when it comes to you. And a hare, not a rabbit, you will note.'

Really, he was acting quite insane. And did not care a whit. Why had he ever thought to hide his feelings, when they faced such peril? He of all people should know that endings were inevitable. Time was not unlimited.

Pitch's laughter was sharp. He jabbed his elbow hard against Silas's side. 'Stop, I am quite serious. I honestly will push you off the carriage and leave you here if you don't shut your trap.'

Silas's grin tilted as he rubbed at his stomach. The blow had been very halfhearted. 'You sound very serious indeed,' he said. 'I shall cease. At least until we stop to rest the horses. Then it won't matter if you throw me off. If we aren't moving, I shan't be left behind.'

'Utter fool.'

The prince pushed the hood off his head, freeing himself, the lingering remnants of a smile on his full lips, his eyes pleasingly bright and clear of shadows.

Good god, what Silas would not do to protect this man. Playing the fool was the very least of it.

A sigh almost escaped him when Pitch settled in and slid his hand to rest against the inside of Silas's thigh.

The thunderous storm off to the southwest made itself known again, and they both turned at the noise. With the road snaking its way up a hill, and the view suitably clear, the flicker of lightning was evident.

One of the bays shifted sideways, pulling at his riggings. Silas put some reassurance into the reins, urging them on as the slope of the hill grew more pronounced. They were soon afforded a decent view over the terrain. Farmland made a patch-quilt of the landscape, with far-reaching expanses of tilled, barren land, the occasional crop of winter wheat evident, and more rarely the deeper hues of woodlands. No farmhouses were evident so far as Silas could see to the east and north, where there were hints of blue sky about, but the west was very different.

A broiling bank of cloud sat on the western horizon. A dark ash-coloured canvas that draped like a curtain hung from the heavens. To look west was to watch night creep in like a giant in a huge cloak. If he'd known the unsettled weather to be Matilda's doing, Silas would have been suitably impressed. Instead, it only gave him reason to worry.

Hastings whinnied, bringing Silas from beneath the weight of his thoughts. The mare had drawn up alongside the cabin and seemed to be intent on the interior.

A resounding thump came from within, followed by a muffled cry.

'What's happening?' Silas gathered the reins. 'Did I run us over a pothole?'

'Halt the carriage,' Sybilla shouted. 'Halt it now.'

'Whoa, whoa there.' Silas dragged at the reins.

Pitch sat up, twisting about to peer back at the cabin. 'What is it, Sybilla?'

The horses were no keener on slowing than they had been an hour ago, and this was hardly the right place for halting, being on the slope as they were.

'It shall be hard to stop here,' Silas muttered.

Which didn't really matter in the end, for the carriage door flew open and Sybilla stepped, or rather took a small leap, out of the cabin, skipping the pedestal step altogether, unfurling like a black flag, her coat rather dramatic in its flourish.

'Stop the bloody carriage, Silas.' But Pitch wasn't waiting either. He jumped down from the seat, not such a difficult thing considering how slowly they rolled along, but still.

'Christ, give me a moment.' It took another tug or two to halt the horses. 'Is Charlie all right?'

'I'm fine,' the lad called from inside the cabin. 'I'm not really sure what's happening...I was dozing. Sybilla are you okay? Did I hear Edward speaking to you?'

'I hope he told you this fool's errand is forfeit.' Pitch made his way around the horses, waving off one of the bays, who tried to nuzzle him, and coming to stand on Silas's side of the carriage. Sybilla stood a few feet away, pressing at her temples.

'Why would you not tell me?' she hissed, her gaze darting between Pitch and the cabin.

'Tell you what?' Pitch said.

'Edward...the...that's...he's not just...I was ordered away...by...he was in my head. The Seraphim...how can this be, Tobias?'

Sybilla was, for the very first time since Silas had met her, quite thoroughly rattled.

'Could you perhaps form a proper sentence?' Pitch was holding the rein where it ran along the horse's shoulder. 'If you are having a fit, we shall have to leave you here.'

Sybilla strode up to him, looming over the slighter, shorter daemon. She leaned in very close, but Silas was near enough to hear.

'Seraphiel spoke to me.' Sybilla's eyes showed more white than Silas recalled. 'I was trying to bring Edward around, at my wits' end with it...so I used a stronger casting...' She swallowed, her fingers still bothering her temples. 'Then all at once...there was a Seraphim in my head. A Seraphim, Tobias. It may be some time since I've been in Arcadia, but one does not easily forget what it is to be addressed by such an angel. And I can assure you, he was not pleased with my nursing skills.'

Silas listened in some astonishment, realising the Valkyrie knew nothing of Seraphiel's possession of Edward.

'Well, don't glare at *me* because he'd not bothered to shout at you before now.' Pitch puffed up like an indignant cockerel. 'And I've barely been able to speak with you. You were either out on your pony prancing about, or you were by Edward's side. Which is the very last place I wish to be. Besides, I thought you must have surmised already. You knew divine magick was used at the Fulbourn –'

'I did not leap to the assumption it came directly from Arcadia's highest angel, who died, more than a year ago.' Sybilla's attempt to whisper was failing miserably. 'I thought the magick came from the watch, a dormant Cultivation that would unlock in times of mortal danger, perhaps. Or from you...'

'Me?' Pitch nearly choked on incredulity.

Sybilla glowered. 'Well, you are quite set apart from all others. And there is the halo's mark upon you...'

'Half of Arcadia's legions have halo scars, so do those of Elyssiam, for that matter. Do you see those imbeciles Cultivating magick?'

'This is not the same and you know it.' Sybilla raised her voice. 'You are an anomaly among all angels and daemons. You are...'

'A freak? Go on, you can say it.' Pitch was dark with poorly suppressed fury. Silas considered stepping in to halt the conversation here and now, but the daemon was not yet done. 'I may not know half of what I am, angel, but I assure you I'm no Cultivator. You are to tell me that you've been using your blasted angelic voodoo on Edward for days and you've noticed nothing of his passenger?'

'That is exactly what I'm saying. Of course I knew there were traces of divine magick making Edward so ill, but never did I imagine...' She ran her hands over the top of her head, clasping them there. 'I'm still not certain what I imagine. For the human to be the Seraphim's prophet was strange enough, but I thought Edward's contact with him in the past might make it possible.' Silas glanced at Pitch. He was intent on the ground. 'But that...that was not Edward who spoke to me.' She was staring at the cabin as though she expected it to suddenly turn into the angel himself. 'What is this, Tobias?'

'I was rather hoping you would tell me.' Pitch was sullen, still fixed on the soil as they spoke of the angel who had changed him to the very core.

Sybilla took a few steps away from the carriage, her hands working at her hair as though she sought to rub the curls off. 'This all began after the watch reached Edward. I suppose their union may have triggered a Cultivation of some kind...' she said, almost to herself. 'Like a phonograph playing the tune etched into its cylinder. Except that was no recording ordering me to cease and desist.'

'And I heard our dear departed angel before I'd reached Edward with the watch,' Pitch returned.

Sybilla nodded. 'It was in your possession though.' She bit at her nail. 'A shade perhaps? Though it boggles the mind to imagine the strength it would take for the angel's shade to find its way here and haunt the man.'

'Shade?' Silas asked.

'What Arcadia call one of your ghosts,' Pitch replied.

Silas frowned at that. 'I have no sense of any soul within the lieutenant. The scythe gives no hint of it. And surely one from such a powerful being would be evident?' He touched at his pocket, reassuring himself the bandalore was still there.

Sybilla considered for a moment. 'You are an ankou for the purebreds. Seraphim are one step from godliness, made in the image of the Celestials. Seraphiel was as far from human as one can be. Perhaps that is the reason?'

'Or it is something else entirely.' Pitch was grinding a hole in the dirt with his heel. 'Seraphiel used Edward's form in the past to exist in this world, but this is different, clearly. For starters he had a lot fucking more to say in those days, and he used Edward's mouth and lungs to do so. He's not *here*, as he was then, but we both agree...something of him *is*. Perhaps it's his shade. But how did it get here? A world away? That pissy watch carried him from Arcadia to here? Sitting on Lucifer's bedside table until my sire thought, oh what a lovely day to take a stroll with my dead lover to the cesspit of Earth and piss off my Dominion spawn.'

Despite how very serious it all was, Silas had to bite back a smile. There was nothing amusing though about the sudden ache behind his eyes. He pinched the bridge of his nose as the conversation continued.

'Granted, it is unlikely to see a shade so removed from where its death was met,' Sybilla said. 'But we are talking about Seraphim, Tobias. It might be possible.'

'What if this is scrying?' Pitch said, low and hurried, as though he wished to release the words before they disappeared. 'What if he has his hand up Edward's arse, using him as one big puppet to make sure I've washed my hands before dinner and said my prayers before bed?'

'Scrying?' Sybilla stared at him. 'Then he would need to be alive.'

Pitch shrugged, biting at the corner of his lip. Silas gripped the reins. Only the faint twittering of birds and throaty rumble of thunder disturbed the air for a few long moments.

'Tobias,' Sybilla said, very quietly. 'You were there...that day. Are you suggesting he survived? I'm told Enoch still mourns deeply. All of Arcadia has done so.'

Silas shifted uneasily, a fresh chill sweeping over him. He knew how well her questions must pain Pitch.

But the prince put on the airs and graces he wore so well as armour. 'And a waste of tears that is. Alive or dead,' he replied, 'that pompous arsehole made his own fine mess, both at the Day of Ruination and when he fucked around with my flame. But could he have survived when I blasted him out of the sky?' Pitch paced a few steps, rubbing at his arms. The air held the weight of approaching rain. 'It did not seem so to me, but I've learned that very little is as it seems where he is concerned.'

The Valkyrie looked as though she were chewing upon a stick of cinnamon, trying to sort through all the pieces. Silas glanced between them, only to cringe at how the movement worsened the ache behind his eyes. He did not feel right at all.

The carriage rocked beneath him, and Charlie stepped out of the cabin. His auburn curls were pressed flat on one side of his head where he'd slept. He was awfully pale, every freckle remarkable. 'Do you think you could discuss all this while we are riding on? While you are all playing detective, Edward is trying very hard to do what the Holy One, whoever or whatever that may be, demands of him.'

Pitch made a very indelicate noise. 'Of all the names–'

'What is the demand?' Sybilla asked.

'To stay alive. Which is infinitely more difficult with every moment wasted. The sooner we reach the Sanctuary, the sooner Edward's task is done in this strange endeavour. And I would very much like to have the man I know returned to me.' Charlie might have looked a little ruffled, and definitely in need of more sleep, but Silas had never thought him more immovable. Rooted in place. 'I accept that I am involved in a circumstance far beyond my comprehension. I feel as though I'm sucking on an opium pipe, and all this, all of you...the strangest of dreams. But in that dream I know what must be done, and it is not standing about bemoaning your issues with your dearest pappa. Even if he is Lucifer...which I am trying very hard not to think about right now.'

Charlie, to Silas's utter astonishment, looked Pitch right in the eye when he spoke about fatherly issues. Silas sucked in a worried breath. Which only seemed to aggravate his headache further.

But any fear he had for the lad's safety abated when Pitch released a sigh. 'Oh fuck, what I wouldn't do for a pipe, right now.'

Silas braced his hands on the seat, a sudden wave of melancholy driving at him. Every fine hair on his body seemed to tug at his skin, and the prickling at the back of his neck grew into a scratching. He touched his fingers to his throat, where the tightness made it hard to breathe.

Christ, he felt low. Caught by a sudden, vicious despair. The bandalore shifted restlessly in his pocket. He felt its heat against the crux of his thigh. But he could not reach for it; he was too heavy with sorrow.

'Silas?' That was Pitch, somewhere far away.

The pain forced Silas to close his eyes. And waiting behind his lids was all the gloom, the terrible dread that hindered him. It flew at him, an enormous flock of crows, pecking at his nerves as though they sought to snap them one by one. He opened his eyes, to where the world was turned watercolour by a flood of tears.

'Silas.' Pitch was rather more alarmed this time.

'Pitch...I just need a moment.' Silas reached for the daemon, or at least tried to. His arm didn't appear to have registered the request at all. 'I don't feel quite myself.'

The world tilted dangerously. He was fairly certain he was toppling out of the driver's seat, but his arms refused to do anything but hang like limp branches by his sides.

'Shit,' Pitch cried. 'Silas.'

He wished he could reassure the prince all was well. But it would be a lie.

'Catch him,' Charlie shouted.

Yes. Silas was definitely falling. And he could find no will of his own to do anything at all but wait for the ground to meet him.

CHAPTER 15

He was close to the ground. Silas could just glimpse the unevenness of it through a yellowed haze, less than a foot away. He'd not fallen completely somehow. Perhaps Pitch had managed to stop him from planting his face in the dirt. There was a rhythmic inhale and exhale surrounding him, filling his ears. But was it him? Silas did not sense any pressure at his lungs, no breathlessness. He was numb of body. But not of mind.

His thoughts were wrapped in dismay, and he knew at once what it was.

The same disconnected sense of anguish that had teased at him for days. Silas closed his eyes, trying to dislodge the haze ahead of him, trying to find some solace. At least...he tried to close his eyes. He knew it was what he wished to do, but the damned things were wide open, refusing to shift. As though they were quite disjointed from his body and any orders sent from his mind.

'What the...' The worlds bubbled and died. Not on his tongue, for he could not feel his mouth any better than he could his feet.

What the bloody hell was happening here? And why was Pitch not shouting at him to get up? There was no sound save for the odd huffing of breath that surrounded him. Like an exhausted messenger trying to catch their breath.

Wherever this was, Pitch was not here. Nor Charlie, nor Sybilla.

Panic scampered spiderlike through Silas's mind.

Had the carriage been attacked? Had the Morrigan snuck up upon them while they discussed Edward?

No. He shoved at the panic, stashing it away as he'd learned how in the pond with the kappas.

Anger took its place, and found a foothold in Silas's numbed world.

The murkiness cleared in one sharp rush, rising like a curtain. The straw-yellow haze remained, as did the sense of wishing to cry for all eternity, but Silas's view ahead cleared as the dragged breath grew louder, louder until it clanged in his head like a drummer's beat.

Silas's view of the world lifted. He had the sense of standing, though he had no feet to do so with.

The panting shifted to rough, quick puffs of breath. And Silas's view tilted suddenly towards the ground.

Christ, those feet. Bare, scratched till they bled, and covered with unsightly warts. His view tilted a little more. A long chin, skin like melted wax, touched at a chest where black lengths of hair, coarse as rope, were stuck fast to wet skin the colour of lichen, blotched and greyish green.

Good god, this was no more Silas's body than the emotional despair was his own feeling.

The panting gave way to a grunt, like an old man rolling over in his bed, and the creature that Silas shared eyes with lifted their head. They were bracing themselves against the ivy-covered low ruins of a small cottage. And as Silas peered at the overly long fingers, gnarled and swollen at the joints, the pieces of this puzzle slipped into place.

He knew those hands. Black fingernails upon half the fingers, the others torn free. The muck and dirt of endless years discolouring the skin, which was rough and dry as tree bark.

This teratism had reminded him of Black Annis when first it lunged at him in the monopteros at the Fulbourn.

Silas peered through the eyes of a creature that had once sought to tear him limb from limb, only to end up becoming his guide through the collapsing ruins of the Fulbourn's horrid Sanctuary.

Last he'd seen of this teratism, it was, along with three other of its kin, being rounded up by Forneus in the asylum's corridor like a farmer's dog on the sheep. *Wait for me. Be at rest,* Silas had said then to the Blight-borne monstrosities.

But if they had waited, then this one was certainly not at rest.

Do you hear me?

Silas could still think well enough, even if it took some doing with the misery trying to sink him. Perhaps he could make himself heard?

Did you summon me? Where are we?

The countryside, that much was clear. Beyond the cottage's bare remnants there were stretches of pasture and fields, until there, in the distance which made them small specks, lay a smattering of other houses. A village perhaps, set at the foot of a hill, wide and tall, with a decidedly flattened top.

The teratism showed no sign of hearing him. A broken growl left the creature, its fingernails hissing against the stone. Silas needed no words to understand the teratism was tormented. Uncertain too. Rocking on its feet as though both forwards and back were equally unappealing directions to travel.

Its gaze was wholly fixed on the hill, which meant Silas had no choice but to stare there too. What were they looking at? Several of the chimneys had curls of smoke rising from them. He might have caught a movement or two as the villagers went about their day. To the eye there was nothing untoward to be seen.

But to the mind... The intense sense of unhappiness was difficult to bear. The teratisms? Or something else?

Silas watched on with growing alarm. How the bloody hell did he separate himself? Return to the body which must be crumpled up beside the carriage like a corpse.

Pitch and Charlie and Sybilla would be frantic. The daemon would forget how to breathe, as he so often did.

Will you let me go? Do you hear me, I cannot be here. Silas tried to shout his thoughts, tried to move some small part of the wretched body he was held in. *Damn it, enough.*

The view of the hill came apart, splintering into shards, which twisted, turned, and blurred again with the same sickly yellow hue of earlier.

Silas was in a downfall. A plummeting that yawned beneath him like the blackness of the waters. The descent was, thankfully, brief. The broken pieces reassembled. And he was on his knees in the centre of a great cavern.

Grief bowed him over. The monster gnawing at his innards.

No.

Not his knees. Not his innards. He was still numb. Silas was still trapped.

But at least this was not his grief. He doubted any one creature could carry such a burden alone. Christ, it was monumental. Despair knitted with agony, and buttoned up with regret. A cardigan made for smothering all hope.

Little wonder the creature he inhabited now fell onto its hands. The fall was silent. As indeed was the entire cavern. The creature's breath did not come as the other's had done.

Knuckles bulging, fingers twisted, skin like pond scum. He was with another teratism.

Another of the four? Perhaps. But there was far less chance for consideration here than there had been with the other creature.

They were one among many that were gathering, Silas realised, glimpsing what he could through the teratism's barely raised gaze. They were surrounded by other teratisms in all their grotesque glory, along with lost souls. Untold numbers of them. Far more than could possibly be natural.

But gathering for what? His teratism was steadfast in keeping his head down, but Silas needed to see.

Had to see.

He pleaded, he shouted, he cursed the creature that would not obey him. And, as a very last resort, he whistled, pursed together lips he was not sure he even had, and tried to find a way through the silence. Sought to reach that note that had saved him at the Fulbourn.

The teratism's head jerked up.

An altar sat at the far side of the crowded chamber, raised up on a high platform. The entire structure was a simple design of sandstone that was carved with all manner of shapes and designs. Letters perhaps? He did not know enough to recognise them if they were.

A flutter of darkness behind the altar drew his attention. And wherever Silas's body might be, he was certain it shuddered now.

Ravens.

A great flock perched on the rocky crags of the dolomite wall that stood behind the altar. Dark stains against the paler stone.

Silas's soundless world rippled with movement. The ravens rising as one.

A teratism, a spindly creature with one arm missing and deep, terrible lacerations upon its face, climbed onto the altar. It laid itself out on its back.

The birds descended as one, wings clashing as they fought to reach the altar first.

The teratism was covered in a writhing mass of beaks and claws. Torn to pieces before the creature Silas shared eyes with could look away. His teratism cowered, bracing, as though sensing what was to come.

The wave of anguish hit hard. And Silas's silent world was ripped open by a terrible chorus of death notes. So many, many death notes, caught up in the screams of the ravens as they devoured the unfortunate teratism.

The hatred, the rage, the utter desperation embedded in the cries of the birds could crack holes in the earth with their wretchedness. But those terrors of emotion did not belong to the flock.

Silas cowered along with the teratism. Understanding dawned, a fragile flower beneath the cloud of grief.

Macha had been gathering souls, but not purely to create an army of teratisms. That was part of it, but hardly the whole.

The Fulbourn was only ever meant to hold your ghost and corpses, it was never meant to be a battleground. That was what the Alp had said when the sorceress refused the order to evacuate the collapsing Sanctuary. The Fulbourn had been a holding facility for whatever bloody, loathsome hell this was.

The dead were being offered up to the ravens. But for what purpose?

Silas.

Pitch's voice came from a distance, unpicking the threads that wove Silas into the teratism.

Silas. Damn you.

Pitch's voice was like a blade glancing against him. Demanding to be heard. Fighting to keep itself from wavering.

But as desperate as Silas was to relieve the daemon of his concern, he wanted the secret of this cavern almost as much so. What Macha was doing here was a tragedy of unspeakable proportions.

Silas, please, wake up.

Not Pitch this time, but an equally familiar voice. Charlie was frightened, his fear sitting in the cracks between his words.

Open your eyes. One of those cracks split wide open with a sob. *You need to wake up now.*

Silas, damn it. Come on now. That's enough. Sybilla's deeper notes struck at the ties that bound Silas. *Don't you dare bloody leave us... The daemon will not survive it.*

Her words– the very last especially– severed Silas's ties with the teratism unequivocally. He slid free of the bone-crushing horror of the cavern.

And came around to a world blazing bright. He blinked. Bloody hell, his chest ached. Silas squinted up at the pair of concern-wrinkled faces hovering over him.

'Oh my god, Silas.' Charlie collapsed onto him, burying his face into his shoulder in a hug that was far more painful than it ought to be. Silas dragged a breath between his teeth, his chest on fire with the pressure. 'You scared the bloody hell out of us.'

Silas could barely answer for the pain. 'Charlie,' he rasped. 'Can you...'

'Come now, give him room to breathe.' Sybilla was on her knees on Silas's other side. The leather of her coat creaked as she moved to extricate Charlie from his vise-grip on Silas. 'Charlie, let him go.'

'I'm sorry.' Charlie settled back on his heels, wiping his sleeve across a damp nose. 'I'm sorry, Silas. You were just so...you were so still. I truly thought you were dead.'

The poor creature didn't know the half of it. 'Not yet.'

Sybilla eased her hand in between Silas's shoulder and the ground, applying gentle pressure as she helped him up.

'Oh shit.' Silas grabbed his ribs, eyes watering. 'My chest...did I fall on something?'

Sybilla sighed. 'Tobias did not deal well with you lying there like a corpse.'

'He did this?' Silas rubbed at his bruised ribcage.

'He lost his head when you first collapsed. And seemed to think he could make your lungs breathe and your heart beat for you.' Charlie's cheeks were still damp with his shed tears but he scowled.

'I had to apply some means to get him off you, which did nothing to alter his foul mood.' Sybilla looked over at something behind Silas. 'He's not happy with you, I'm afraid, even though I assured him it was highly unlikely you were properly dead. I thought I might have to protect you from being brought round by a scalding.' She paused, giving Silas a meaningful look. 'But I barely saw trace of his flame.'

Silas swallowed. 'Well, I'd say that's fortunate.'

'Indeed.'

He glanced away to escape the Valkyrie's scrutiny. So, Pitch had not seen fit to tell Sybilla of this secret either. Not so surprising, this one at least. The prince was mortified by his sudden weaknesses. 'Where is he?'

Sybilla pointed at a place over his shoulder. 'Sulking behind that juniper. For the gods' sake, Tobias. He's fine, can you not see?'

'I don't want to catch what he has,' the daemon called out, and Silas heard the gouging anger. 'We can't all carry on, dropping like sacks of fucking grain.'

Charlie glared over Silas's shoulder. 'Ignore him. That is Tobias's way of saying he was desperately worried for you, Silas. As we all were.'

Silas touched the lad's hand, a tired smile rising. 'I'm so sorry to have upset you all.' Louder, he said, 'But you won't catch anything from me, I promise you.'

He twisted around, ignoring the ache at his chest. To his surprise he saw that they were no longer upon the rise of the hill but in the midst of a copse of trees, a small clearing giving them enough room to start a small fire, which danced away merrily beside him, bringing welcome warmth. 'How long have I been out?'

'An hour,' Sybilla replied. 'You were quite unreachable. What happened, Silas?'

But he needed to deal with other matters before he explained. 'Pitch?' Silas searched for a sign of him. 'Will you please come over?'

'I won't. What the blazes was that tomfoolery all about, Mercer?' The prince stood half-hidden behind the juniper, its evergreen leaves concealing all but his head as he peered over its top.

'I'm not certain how it happened...' Silas moved onto his knees with Charlie's assistance. 'But I found myself merged with one of the teratisms that we led from the Fulbourn.'

Sybilla raised a brow. 'Has anything like that happened before?'

'No. I mean, I've had visions when I've been submerged, but they were memories. Nothing like this.'

He arched his back, trying to work out the stiffness there. He spied the lieutenant, bundled up in blankets and laid out with his head resting upon cushions on the far side of the fire.

How had an hour passed so quickly? No wonder the prince was barely speaking to him.

'I'm going for a walk,' Pitch declared from behind his juniper.

'Don't be ridiculous,' Sybilla returned. 'I haven't shielded the whole copse.'

'Go ahead and try and stop me, Valkyrie. I dare you. For fuck's sake. Do I have no right to a moment of peace?'

Silas opened his mouth to caution the angel, hearing the acidic note in Pitch's voice. This was a mood he'd not be swayed from easily. But Sybilla had known the daemon longer than he.

'Fine. Go and pout elsewhere. Don't go too far though. We won't stop long now that all is well.'

Silas lifted his hand as Pitch's gaze found him. On noting the furious gleam in the prince's eyes, he abandoned the silly notion of waving.

But anger was better than blind panic, Silas supposed. Though hardly fair. He'd had no control over his turn.

The faint echo of the ravens toyed with him, their anguished sound fouling his mind. He watched as Pitch stomped away from the clearing, uneasy with letting him go but knowing to try to follow would likely see the daemon bolt off like a hunted deer.

Silas returned his attention to Charlie and the lieutenant. The lad pushed up his sleeve as he sat beside Edward.

Ottelie's rowan-and-holly bracelet was snug around Charlie's wrist. Silas frowned. He was certain he spied several tendrils of new growth meandering along the pale white of the lad's arm, the holly leaves more vibrant than he recalled. He'd have preferred Charlie take the bracelet off. For all the gift had done at the Fulbourn, for which he was eternally grateful, and for all it seemed to do still, with Charlie's sudden astonishing strength, Silas worried at the price of such assistance.

'So, would you like to tell me what happened, Silas?' Sybilla's voice, right at his shoulder, startled him. 'You truly did look dead, I have to say.'

Silas scratched at his chin, now almost as fully bearded as it had been before the soirée.

'I think the Morrigan are up to something most nefarious.'

'You needed to be in a teratism's head to surmise that?'

'No. But there is a dark magick at play, I'm certain. One that is devouring souls.' He told the angel all he had seen. Every pang of misery felt.

'An unkindness,' Sybilla whispered.

'I'm sorry?'

'An unkindness...it is the name given to a flock of ravens.'

'A name never more apt. But it was far more than unkindness being shown to those souls there.' Talking of what the teratisms had shown him made him sick to his stomach. Those were *his* souls in desperate need, and the urge to go to them pained him. 'I've felt their torment for days...' He slid his hand into his pocket, handling the bandalore as he'd come to do when he sought calm. 'We need to discover what the Morrigan are doing there. Do you recognise the place by how I have described it?' A long shot, but worth the question.

'I truly hope I am wrong.' A muscle in the angel's jaw flexed. 'But that hill...it is quite distinctive. I believe it may be Pendle Hill.'

A twinge of recall came at hearing the name, but too faint for anything but a sense of vague recognition. 'Is the place significant?'

Sybilla bothered at her coat's flared collar. 'Perhaps.'

'Sybilla?'

The angel narrowed her eyes, her tension palpable. 'There may have been some incidents of witchcraft there in the past that I had to deal with.'

'Maleficium? There were sorcerers at Pendle Hill?'

'There *were*, yes. The very last of the witches...or so I hoped.'

The memory shifted into place with her words, Silas recalling the conversation at Harvington Hall where he'd first been told of maleficium. The Pendle Hill witches were the last known manifestation of Azazel's divine magick, and the Valkyrie, a witch hunter, as it turned out, had dealt with them accordingly.

'It was one of my simpler assignments. The purebreds themselves noticed a strangeness among their villagers,' Sybilla continued. 'And their thirst for casting out the devil made my job easier. I did not need my blade, only my tongue. I whispered in a few ears, raised the heights of their fears. Perhaps too high.' She glanced at the ground. 'They hung ten of their kin in the end, but only four of them were true carriers of Azazel's maleficium.'

'And you could not save the innocent?' Silas pressed his lips. The question sounded every bit the accusation it was.

'I was tasked with eliminating the sorcery in Pendle Hill. It was done.' The Valkyrie regarded him, a dark and unshakeable presence. 'The purebreds should have been the ones to save their innocent. I cannot be blamed if none of them gave voice to protest or reason. The net of fear is cast by the masses, and the innocent are always tangled in the rope, are they not, Silas?'

'Indeed,' he said simply, for he knew it well. Silas held his hands over the fire, wondering if Pitch was cold wherever he paced down his own fears. 'Four sorcerers in Pendle Hill. Was that a large number for one place?'

Sybilla nodded slowly. 'It was, and from different families too. I kept an eye on the place for a long while after, but there was no sign of maleficium again. No more children of Azazel.' She paused and there was so much weight in that silence. 'Or so I believed.'

Silas glanced up from the flames. 'Do you think that is where the sorcerers come from? Or their forebears at least. Macha is fond of her mask but even with it I could tell she is not old. Certainly not two hundred years old. Maybe a child of one of the witches survived? And you simply did not...I mean to say...'

'Go ahead, Silas, say what we are both thinking.' Sybilla's mouth was tight, her eyes darkened. 'I overlooked one. I failed in my duty. Someone survived my last purge.'

'I'm simply trying to understand what I saw, what the importance of the place might be...I am casting no blame, Sybilla.' He was certainly not wishing a massacre had been more thorough.

The Valkyrie scratched at her curls, heaving a sigh. 'I know...I know...I am simply vexed that there has been a nursery for maleficium right beneath my nose. Iblis raising damned witches with the Erlking in the UnSeelie Court. And perhaps Pendle Hill is where he found what he was looking for, I don't know...the witches were certainly among the most powerful I'd known. Perhaps now the Morrigan have returned to their birthplace out of some mangled sense of nostalgia. Who bloody well knows. And we don't know it is the place in your vision for certain anyway.'

Thunder stirred beyond the trees. The storm still bothered the air. Silas peered up at the sky, just visible through the trees. Hints of blue amongst the white and grey.

'Matilda has gone to study that storm a little closer. I'm expecting her back soon,' Sybilla said.

Silas nodded, but he still mulled over what he'd seen. 'There were so many souls, Sybilla.' He swallowed, his throat tight. 'And all of them so burdened by their mortal coils. As though the Morrigan required the most destitute for what they intend. Macha has been gathering souls for a long time. And those ravens...they were something dark and terrible. Macha can manipulate corpses into mindless soldiers, and the Fulbourn taught us the Morrigan are masters of the Blight. Wherever that place is, I fear what they do there. The Lady must be told.'

Sybilla nodded. 'I've left Hastings with the carriage and the other horses nearer to the road. There was no chance of bringing them in through the trees, but they'll not be noticed with the hexes in place. I'll go now and have her pass on what we know.' She paused. 'I have to tell you, it is becoming harder to know if the Lady has received my messages. I think she is much preoccupied. We are more on our own than I would like. We should ready to depart at once, now you are on your feet. Can I leave Tobias to you?'

Silas glanced over to where he'd last seen Pitch. 'Of course.'

CHAPTER 16

P itch had not intended to run. In fact it was a bloody awful idea to do so in the damp and uneven woods. He also knew at once that the decision to wear a coat of paler hues while travelling was appalling. Old Bess certainly would have admonished him for his choice of the beige herringbone had he and the fae been on speaking terms while the preparations to depart had gone on.

Instead, Bess had been holding a man together as he inevitably fell apart. By now Ronin would be shattered and returned to the sake pot from whence he'd come, nothing but broken pieces of stoneware.

Pitch pushed faster, gritting his teeth at the protest that came from his hip, and his lungs. He was out of breath faster than he'd imagined, though he'd remove the corset only on pain of certain death.

He lashed out at an innocent birch, snapping a thin branch as he passed by. Silas had fallen. Lain there like a fucking...well, a godsdamned corpse. Even the blasted vapid Valkyrie hadn't bothered to hide her shock at the ankou's sudden, dramatic fall.

Once her composure returned, Sybilla had tried to reassure the frantic prince, who had been, quite frankly, embarrassingly inept in the emergency. Silas was breathing, she said, shallow but steady, his heartbeat faint but evident. And it would be best if Pitch did not shake him any more. He'd wake when he was ready.

This was hardly the time for sleeping.

And Pitch did not want *faint* or *shallow*. Fuck.

The ankou's heart usually thumped like a hammer on an anvil, and the man was capable of taking breaths so deep it was a wonder any air was left for others.

And through it all...every awful moment as Charlie and Sybilla loaded Silas into the carriage, then dragged him out again when a more concealed resting place had been found...Pitch had been utterly useless. He'd not even been able to focus long enough to start the godsdamned fire. Charlie had done that, though his hands shook with his own fears.

Pitch had been replaced by a packet of fucking matches.

He leapt now over a pile of mulch and spat a few prime curses as the landing jarred muscles in his back. Beneath his armpits it was a squalid damp mess, his shirt clung to his back like a passenger desperate to hold on, and he was fast wishing he'd taken off his coat before he decided his walk should become a mad dash.

Stay close, Sybilla had warned.

Well, the Valkyrie could piss off.

Pitch's boot sank into a patch of mud concealed by autumn-rotted leaves. His precarious balance collapsed. He cried out, going down hard on his knees and sending a thousand vile curses at the dirt, the sticks that poked him, the trees that just stood there around him, watching on. Doing absolutely fucking nothing.

Just as *he* had done when Silas fell.

Pitch punched at the dirt, where hidden stones were harsh upon his knuckles.

Useless. He was fucking useless.

His stomach had turned in a hundred knots as he'd stood over Silas's body. The Gu had been horrendous but it was nothing, *nothing* compared to the sickness that engulfed him when he thought the ankou gone.

Pitch got to his feet, feeling the same tightness in his chest that had come before his panic overrode him at the pond. He broke into a run once more. He had no bloody idea where he was going. It didn't matter. So long as it was away.

Away from Silas. From the Valkyrie and the vagabond. From that creature in the carriage that was forcing them all onwards. Forcing those imbeciles to play nursemaid to a daemon who was about as useful at protecting them as Nancy or Ada.

He might as well be a fucking purebred. Pitch winced at the thought of the women, and their fae brat. Fucking gods. There was nowhere to turn where his troublemaking spectre did not loom.

He grabbed at the earring where it dangled from his ear. Pitch wrenched at it. Too hard, evidently, because the hook ripped through his lobe.

'Shit,' he hissed, the sudden burn most unpleasant. 'Piece of utter crap.'

He raised his arm, intending to hurl the earring away. But by the Archangels' festering boils, he could not do it. 'Fuck!' he shouted, shoving the trite piece of amber into his pocket.

This must be another of Seraphiel's curses. Such worries had never troubled Pitch before. He'd killed with a smile on his ugly daemonic face. Now his eyes stung and his throat refused to allow him to swallow without effort.

Pitch lashed out at a defenceless hawthorn as the deepness of the copse stole away the light. The woods were more expansive than he'd imagined and thick enough to steal a good portion of the light. Maybe he could just disappear here.

Another sodden patch of soil nearly made a new mockery of him, but Pitch was far too enraged to go down to his knees again. He lunged at the nearest support, a spindly tree that shuddered at his weight. A lime. He knew that because the bloody ankou thought it important to point out every damned thing that grew and name it.

He carried on. But the pace was definitely slowing. His cock and balls were very unhappy about his decision to forgo drawers, and his ankle had turned several times now.

The woods grew ever darker. Sweat tickled his temples. At least he wasn't bloody cold for the first time in days.

Pitch barely heard the sound over the rasp of his own turbulent breathing. A shivered cry holding poignant notes of distress. An animal certainly, the bleating made it clear.

Pitch veered away from the noise.

The cry rose high, as though his redirection was unwelcome. The animal appeared in some amount of pain, but he was in no mood for sorting out another's discomfort. He was having enough fucking trouble as it was with his own.

He'd gone not more than three steps, and the mournful sound came again. Playing through the trees, slipping around the trunks and filtering through the undergrowth.

Pitch's hurried walk slowed. Only because the terrain was particularly awful here. Nothing else. Certainly not because the cry was so bloody pitiful that it made the hair on the back of his neck stand up. 'Oh, for fuck's sake.'

He slipped off his coat, tossing it over his shoulder. The brisk air took no time at all to tease at him, his sweat-ridden body coming alive with gooseflesh. Gods, he reeked. Just as well he'd not have Silas anywhere near him. Ever again.

Pitch trudged towards the sound, grimacing at a stone that had managed to find its way into his boot.

The reason for the pained cry grew evident quickly enough. A young doe lay beside a decaying fallen tree. Her front right fetlock was grasped cruelly between the steel jaws of a trap. A rusted trap at that, showing signs of having been laid in nefarious wait for a long while.

The animal had some sense about her. She'd not churned the earth up into a frenzy trying to escape. She lay quite still, calling out for help, her blood darkening the fallen leaves around her. It seemed an odd placement for the lump of steel, nearly hidden beneath the rounded bulk of the trunk. Likely the tree had fallen after the hunter had set the trap, and they'd not returned to retrieve it.

Pitch sighed– to steady his run-weary breath, of course. Not to ready himself for wrestling with the spring-set steel. 'Stop that noise.'

The deer shuffled herself about, enormous brown eyes fixed on him, a small pink tongue teasing at the edge of her mouth. Her ribs flared wildly. The injured animal snorted, concerned at his closeness. Her short tail twitched unhappily.

'Stay quiet…I'll not do a thing if you keep screeching like that.'

How did one talk to a deer? He shrugged off the thought. It hardly mattered. She would need to stay still while he freed her, or he would just leave her to bleed out. He laid his coat on the log, hoping he'd found a suitably dry place to do so.

Pitch moved in quickly and quietly. He could be featherlight when he so desired. At least that particular talent had not abandoned him.

The doe dug her hind feet in, lifting her haunches to push herself from his reach, dragging her belly through blood-soaked mulch.

'Stop moving, stupid animal. You'll cause more harm.' He crouched down and settled onto his hands and knees, moving slowly towards the stricken animal. 'Easy now. Easy.'

He sought to mimic the reassuring tone of the ankou. The low timbre Silas adopted when he spoke to horses, or to spooked daemon princes.

But the deer showed no appreciation for Pitch's interpretation of a dead man's steady influence. The pretty animal, her colours the shades of a new autumn forest, wheezed and snorted and shuffled more vigorously, rattling the chain which anchored the trap to something now crushed beneath the fallen tree. Her cry rose as the steel fangs dug in more fiercely.

'No, no. Stay still.' Pitch's well-worn patience lost another layer, dangerously thin. He sat back on his heels, wiping off his dirtied hands and reconsidering his rescue.

As he pondered why the blazes he'd stopped at all, a fluttering of light drifted over the trunk: will-o'-the-wisps all the shades of a rainbow. An odd time of day for them, the critters usually preferring evening when their auras were on finer display. They breezed around him, parting in two waves like he were a giant stone in a stream.

'Will you piss off?' He waved at the gossamer orbs of light, but they darted easily away from his reach, flowing down around the frightened deer. They swarmed her, but the creature seemed unperturbed. In fact, she relaxed notably, giving up her frantic struggle to escape him. She still watched him closely though, unblinking, damp nose twitching.

One of the will-o'-the-wisps broke free of the group, a curious little thing that held a multitude of colours, a rare sight. It zipped towards him, dancing in the air right before his eyes before slipping back to hover over the trap.

The message would be plain to a blind man. Hurry on and release the deer.

Pitch shifted onto all fours once more. The ground was incredibly unpleasant, and his sweat was cooling too fast. 'Fine, but you had best not be luring me in for a concerted attack.' He crept forward slowly. 'I know you little bastards have teeth when you need them.'

He was less than a foot from the deer now, the will-o'-the-wisps settling on her neck and the crown of her head like a delicate, colourful veil of light. She panted hard, her tongue lolling further from her mouth, but she did not struggle.

Close enough now, Pitch settled back slowly, carefully onto his knees. 'Easy now. Easy.'

This time round the doe seemed more appreciative of his reassuring tone and did not try to dismember herself to escape him. Her tongue slipped back into her mouth, her black lips closing. But not once did her gaze leave him.

'Ready for freedom?'

A pang struck at him. A deep anguish that slithered from the hole he'd thought he'd buried it in. Freedom. What an unreachable treasure. And all the running in the world would not deliver it to him.

Pitch bent forward, flexing his fingers as he took hold of the jaws of the trap, having a brief panicked moment where he wondered if the angel had stolen his strength as well as his flame. He ground his teeth, settled his fingers in between the cruel prongs, and took hold. 'Steady now,' he whispered.

And heaved. His muscles tensed, the metal bit into his skin. The will-o'-the-wisps trembled and their colours danced across his pale skin. The colourful critter who'd urged him on came to settle near his shoulder. He strained. But it was not enough.

Pitch bore down harder, anger stirring.

His anger. *His* indignation. Not that of the wildness, sleeping so deeply he could pretend himself free of it.

There was that fucking word again.

Pitch stifled his shout behind clenched teeth, conscious that startling the deer now would only bring greater harm to the creature. And he was so fucking sick of bringing harm.

The metal made no sound as it bent to his will. Slowly, infuriatingly so, the folds of the trap peeled open. It was like trying to part the fucking heavens.

But he'd not be made a fool of by a godsdamned man-made pile of shit. Pitch gathered himself and threw his full weight against the trap. The jaws gave way, slamming back into their horizontal positions, a tiny clack heralding the catch of the locking mechanism.

The deer slid her injured leg free, pushing up a clump of dirt as she fought to distance herself from her temporary prison. The will-o'-the-wisps whispered like a hundred pixies tittering in delight. They swirled about the doe, who made a calamity of getting to her feet, legs akimbo, body shaking, her tiny tail bobbing like a maddened hare stuck to her arse.

He expected she would dart off at once, and she was certainly readying for it, but at the last moment she twisted in close to where Pitch rested on his heels. A pink tongue licked his cheek, and before he could expel a cry of distaste, she was gone. A hobbling, unsteady, but *free* creature disappearing in the trees.

The will-o'-the-wisps danced around him, the rainbow-hued creature being so bold as to brush at his nose.

'Bugger off, you little prick.' His swipe was not nearly so firm as it could be.

The deer made the undergrowth crackle as she fled, the sound growing fainter and fainter as Pitch contemplated getting to his feet once more. He was tired. To the marrow. He'd not stopped being tired since the Fulbourn. Christ, since that day on the cliff over the Lethe River.

Pitch reached for the trunk to brace himself. The deliberate snap of a branch pierced the settling quiet. He stared hard into the surrounding woods, certain he was being watched. 'Who is there?' he called.

The pause was pregnant with indecision, he could practically hear the cogs of his watcher's mind clacking over as they tried to decide whether to reveal themselves or not. The will-o'-the-wisps scattered, hiding away.

'Someone who is not much pleased about what you've just done.'

A man stepped out from behind the swell of a juniper bush, a bow slung over his shoulder, a pair of hares strung up and dangling from his hand: a huntsman, who appeared not to have ever caught sight of himself in a mirror, for he could surely not intend to look so unsightly. His eyebrows were black as soot and so overgrown they teased at his eyelids. His hair was a calamity too, resembling more of a bird's nest even than Marcus's, the snow-owl djinn.

The hunter's beard had clearly not seen a blade since Enoch was a lad, its tip resting against the middle of his chest, flecks of the forest caught in its wiry, dark curls.

'Is that so?' Pitch got to his feet, fighting not to stagger as he did so, his hip stiff from all the running about. 'And what is it I just did that has you displeased?'

'That was my dinner you just let run off.'

The man was solidly built, or at least it seemed so. He was clad so thickly in various layers that it was difficult to be sure. He wore at least two shirts Pitch could make out, and perhaps three vests, as though he kept on all the clothes he owned. His coat was patched to within an inch of its life, with no care taken to try to match the fabrics. A shadow stretched from his heels. A purebred.

'Perhaps you shouldn't have left your dinner sitting about, then,' Pitch replied, dusting off his hands.

'I don't like a smart mouth.' The stranger scratched his neck, finger-nails coarse against his skin. 'And I don't like a fucking dandy playing about in my forest.'

'Oh, dear chap, you'd quite like my mouth, I assure you. It's the ones who protest the loudest who often do. But as for your forest, well it is rather dull, far too much dirt about.' Pitch brushed off his knees, eyeing his coat, which lay closer to the hunter than it did him. 'I'll just take my coat and be on my way. Leave you to finding your dinner.'

He was not keen on stepping closer to the fellow. And the moment he did so, the smack of beer struck him. The hunter enjoyed his ale.

'Oh, you think so, do you?' For a solid chap, the hunter could move quickly. He snatched up the coat, raising it like a trophy. The hunter grinned, which was unfortunate, for it showed how many teeth he was missing. 'This be the coat you wanting? A nice fancy coat, for a fancy pretty man.'

'Oh my dear.' Pitch sighed. 'I do suppose a man such as yourself might consider that coat with its silk and velvet trims fancy. Goodness, you probably think this waistcoat with its mop buttons the very height of fashionability, but I assure you, you're an idiot.'

But the idiot proved again how very deft he could be. The hunter tossed the coat in the air, a clever distraction admittedly, for when it fell back over his arm, he now stood with a small revolver in his free hand, taken from one of the endless hiding places in his layers.

'Well, that all seems a tad dramatic.' Pitch sniffed.

'You do like to use that mouth a lot, don't you?' The hunter cocked the gun with practised ease and aimed it at Pitch's chest. 'But I don't much like the sound of your voice. Now how's about you take the rest of those fancy clothes off.'

Pitch folded his hands behind his back, feigning coolness. This encounter was fast becoming irksome. 'I'm afraid I've had enough of being on my knees today, if you're hoping for a fuck.' If this bastard so much as took a step to try to touch him, Pitch would not need his flame to tear him apart. He had teeth and nails, and scars. 'Now do be a good chap and hand over the coat.'

The hunter's expression did not change, despite the taunt. 'Spend a lot of time on those knees of yours, I bet. But your hole ain't what interests me here. Your clothes on the other hand, now there's something I'd like my hands on. These threads will fetch a fine penny, I'd say, and who knows what a gentleman like yourself has in his pockets. Coins, no doubt. A silver comb for those pretty curls, perhaps. Come on then, strip them off. I ain't mucking about.' He tossed the coat back over the trunk, and with the gun still trained on Pitch, he searched the folds of material.

Pitch was busy watching for the moment when the man would be distracted enough for him to lunge. The hunter's gaze darted to the coat, his hand sinking into a pocket, but just as quickly his attention shifted back to Pitch.

'What have we here, then?' The hunter pulled his hand free and held up his prize. Tilly's stupid bloody earring. 'Now ain't that a lovely thing. You one of them freaks then, who likes the ladies' things?' His toothless grin sent a lick of cool fury through Pitch's veins. And when he moved to tuck the earring into the folds of his own attire, it was too much.

Pitch ran at him. 'Give that back.'

The sudden move shocked both of them.

The hunter's eyes widened, and the gun wavered for a brief second. Enough for Pitch to reach him, strike at his arm, and knee him hard in the balls.

The gun went off.

Right at Pitch's ear.

The noise stunned him, had him staggering. But the hunter was faster to gather himself. He struck out, pistol-whipping Pitch across the side of the head.

Deafened and seeing stars, Pitch's balance was nearly nonexistent. He staggered backwards, clutching at his head, oblivious to where he was stepping.

The trap slammed shut around his ankle.

An agonised cry tore from him, a sound deadened beneath the ringing of the gunshot.

Down he went, his arse striking the ground first, his shoulders hitting hard enough to wind him. His trapped foot could not move with him, and Pitch's leg wrenched at an eye-watering angle. The sound that clawed up his throat was unearthly. He saw more stars, more flashes of white. And felt nothing but pain.

No stirring of chaos, of wildness rising from where it was hidden deep.

The hunter shouted and stood over him, fury lighting his face. His fucking gun still poked toward's Pitch's face, his other hand covering his offended balls.

'Fucking cunt.'

Pitch heard that much.

The hunter drew back his arm, the revolver's dull grey metal contrasting the lighter shades of the woods behind. Another strike to the head and Pitch may be knocked unconscious– not so terrible, considering the pain he was in – but he had no intention of waking up naked and trapped like an animal.

He brought the flame to hand, having to concentrate far harder than he would have liked. Too much effort for so little result. A humiliating experience all round.

But one that caught the hunter's attention.

'What the fuck?' His raised hand wavered.

The glow of the flames played at his face, which made it plainer to see when his gaze suddenly shifted away from Pitch. The hunter peered out into the woods, eyes narrowing.

Pitch turned his head, following the man's line of sight. Something solid moved through the undergrowth. He caught a glimpse of twisting branches atop a massive moving shadow before they were set upon.

CHAPTER 17

Pitch covered his head with his hands, and sent the flame spilling beneath his skin. The trap's fangs dug in as instinct saw him curl away from the rushing shape.

The hunter shouted at whatever charged forward. 'Back, you bastard. Go on with you!'

His warning went unheard, and his cry was cut short by a heavy, unforgiving thump. The trunk rocked in its mulch cradle. Another weighted sound came, like a tossed hay bale meeting the ground.

Then, just silence, almost complete save for a soft exhale that shifted Pitch's hair. He peered through the gap between his forearms, and the pair of legs he saw was not what he'd been expecting at all.

Not human. Animal. For a moment he thought it was the doe he'd rescued, but these forelegs were thicker, the brown hue of the fur darker. A damp nose touched his arm, and more heated breath flowed, warming his skin.

Pitch lowered his arms. A stag stood over him. And quite a bloody magnificent one at that, with a chest broad enough to use as a dartboard and antlers that reached higher than Pitch could crane his neck.

As it seemed the animal was not about to shove a hoof in his face, Pitch sat up. Impossible to do without shifting his trapped leg. The metal sank deeper.

'Shit.' He bit at the inside of his cheek so hard that he tasted blood at once.

The world tilted so madly he went back down onto his elbow. He could barely see for the white dots filling his vision. And red dots, and green, and yellow. Tinkling bells could be heard, tiny sounds that might just be in his imagination alone.

Good gods, maybe he was dead already?

The stag's waft, rich with the dampness of earth and decaying wood, brought Silas to mind. If Pitch had managed to get himself killed, the ankou would be furious.

Pitch swallowed against the strange sob that worked its way up his throat, turning it into a strangled grunt of irritation instead.

'Take care, take care.' A gentle whisper came from close by. Right at his shoulder to be exact. Pitch shirked away, peering through the rainbow of light that surrounded him.

He was certainly not dead; there was far too much pain for that. The colourful air was courtesy of the will-o'-the-wisps' return.

'Since when do you speak?' Pitch tried again to sit up.

'Take care, I said.' This time there was a soft pressure at his shoulder, urging him back. 'Stay still. We will deal with the trap.'

A snorted breath right overhead made him jump, which in turn made him curse all manner of nasty things. The stag tossed its head, as though personally affronted, but took a step back.

'Now that's enough of that language around the young ones, thank you.' The same gentle voice, a honeyed timbre that could have put a thousand babes to sleep. But who was the irksome little shit? Will-o'-the-wisps, so far as he knew, did not speak, not in a language he understood, at least. They tended to prefer squeaking and squawking like irritating chicks.

'Show yourself,' he demanded. 'And the rest of you bloody well back off. I can't see a fucking thing.' He was lying in a damned rainbow.

'Stop wriggling about, young man. You're spilling enough blood as it is. I am trying to help you. I want you out of here as much you want outing.'

His tired, pained brain considered the idea that it was the stag talking to him. Perhaps the hunter's blow *had* knocked him out. Either way, he'd had enough of this place.

'Leave me be.' Pitch pressed himself into a sitting position and lurched forward, reaching towards his imprisoned ankle.

The scenery tilted so violently that he grabbed fistfuls of dirt to try to anchor himself.

'Sit still, silly boy.' The honey-talker clucked their tongue. 'Let you be? You sure about that? Didn't seem you were doing so well without us.'

Pitch's vision drew back into focus. And he had a disturbing view of great antlers lowering down towards his feet. The stag's bone set was mightily impressive, like a rangy, leaf-bare forest upon his head. The animal lowered his head until the hairs on his nostrils were scraping the undergrowth, and the tips of several antlers were far too close to Pitch's bloodied ankle.

'What the fuck are you doing?' There was nowhere to go. The chain anchoring the trap was already stretched long, any further and he'd dig the teeth in deeper.

'Let him work,' his whisperer decreed.

'Work on what?' Pitch grabbed at his knee, cupping it with both hands. 'Eating my foot?'

'He's not going to do any such thing.' The talker was amused, but they were the only damned one. 'Now just keep still, and he'll have you free.'

Before Pitch could splutter any sort of reply, the stag slid several of the longer curves of his antlers in between the steel jaws. They glanced against the metal, causing a tiny shudder to run through his bone.

'Oh fuck, no. Stop.'

A weighty sigh scored the air. 'Do you want out of these woods or not? Cripes, maybe you aren't a daemon. I imagined them tougher than this.'

Now that he could see a little straighter, it truly seemed as though the stag was speaking, for the whispering came from him certainly. But there was no natural aura surrounding the beast, no suggestion he was a shape-shifter. This was a stag, plain and simple.

Pitch squinted through the candy-coloured light. 'Who the fuck are you?'

The tinkling of tiny bells played around him. Very distinct now, clearly not a figment of his imagination.

'Settle down, all of you.' The creature's honey voice was smooth even when stern. 'Stop that foolish giggling and don't even think about using his language. If I hear one filthy word repeated, you'll be sent to the bog for a week. Now, come on. Let's deal with that trap, Cornelius. This blood's no good for anyone.'

The will-o'-the-wisps gathered at Pitch's feet, and the tinkling bells rang out anew.

The stag, Cornelius presumably, tilted his broad head. Bone scraped against metal, and the pressure at Pitch's ankle eased. He dug his fingertips into his knee, bracing for more hurt.

'That's it, that's it. A little more,' the hidden instructor coaxed. The stag's head tilted further, forcing the folds of the trap to open.

Pitch whimpered at the dreadful sensation of metal dragging from flesh, the steel slow to pull from where it was embedded deep. He was woozy, set to topple back if not for holding so fast to his own knee. A tug came at his trousers, the material tightening around his calf muscle.

'Pull clear now, quickly as you will.'

He thought the instruction meant for him and braced to do as ordered, but his leg moved of its own accord. It lifted from the vicious embrace of the trap, shifting until his knee was sent towards him. Pitch groaned into the back of his teeth. Fuck, he'd never felt so bloody human, so more aware of their delicate constitution.

'Careful with him now.'

The tinkling of those bells came again and he could see well enough their cause. Peri. A long line of the delicate creatures busied themselves over his leg, their silver hair shifting like worms, chiming as the strands met. They held fast to the fabric of his trousers. There were at least a dozen of the normally impossibly shy creatures, whose origins lay in a long-ago union of nymphs and woodland fae. The musical accompaniment was pleasant enough, until they set his heel to rest against the soil. They did so as delicately as they could, but his enraged muscles and bone flared like a bonfire. Pitch shouted his unhappiness to the woods.

'Put that away, this instant. They are trying to help you. Don't you dare burn anyone.'

Pitch blinked through his distress, wondering what the blazes the creature was on about.

It did not take long to realise. His hands were aglow with that miserable flame of his.

'That hurt,' he grumbled, but stifled the meagre show. 'And I'll burn you all if it turns out you are taking me from one trap to another.'

The stag shifted closer, lowering his head. Pitch leaned away from the pronged tips, and his back touched the trunk. The coarse hair at the stag's mane shifted.

'What we're trying to do is get you out of our woods. Strangers are not a good thing to have amongst our trees, not with the Hunt about.'

The speaker finally deigned to show themselves. A small pair of scaled green hands emerged from the thick ruff of fur beneath the stag's chin. A head came next, no bigger than the pad of Pitch's thumb, rounded and wrinkled like a walnut shell, the same hue as one too. Making for a stark contrast to the creature's forest-green body, which was smooth and scaled as a snake. Pitch had not seen a hobgoblin in a while, on account of the creatures normally preferring to hide away in the branches and toss pine cones, or indeed walnuts, at passersby. 'Come now, everyone, give our visitor some space. He seems a surly one.'

Pitch was grateful for his rescue, but cautious. The peri leapt off his leg, the tinkling of bells growing mad as they scattered, drops of quicksilver rushing off into the undergrowth. The brilliant light of the will-o'-the-wisps had shifted away, and for the first time, Pitch had a clear view of what had become of the hunter.

He was lying in a rather disconcerting heap a few feet away. The angle of his head was unpleasant. A narrow trickle of blood ran from his nostril, almost prettily, with all the colourful light playing against it.

'Is he dead?' Pitch knew which answer he'd prefer. If he could stand, he'd break the man's neck himself.

The hobgoblin clambered off the stag's shoulder and slid down the animal's foreleg, nimble as a spider down a web, coming to rest on the splay of a hoof.

'Either that or he will wake with a terribly stiff neck. Won't be many who'll miss him here. Been a thorn in our side awhile with his hunting...not that we begrudge him looking for a meal...' The stag shifted, huffing a breath through rounded nostrils. 'I know, Cornelius, I know. You begrudge it well enough, seeing as it's your kind he's trying to put in his pot, but it was his methods that were darkest of all. You know well enough how cruel his trap is, young man. And he checks them so rarely that any animal caught is likely to starve before he puts his knife to them.' The creature leapt from its place atop the stag's hoof to land next to Pitch's ruined ankle. There was something of the snake in the sinewy way the hobgoblin moved, a quiet elegance despite its less-than-elegant appearance. 'You did a fine thing, saving that doe. Cornelius is indebted to you.'

The stag dipped its wide head, and despite being intolerably uncomfortable, Pitch squirmed a little at the praise.

'Stop with all the bowing nonsense.' He reached a hand towards the animal. 'Bring yourself closer, help me to my feet. I need to get back to my companions.'

'Don't be ridiculous,' the hobgoblin admonished. 'You're not standing on that foot anytime soon. I'd be surprised if you've not broken some bone in there.'

So would Pitch. Just the merest flex of his toes made his eyes water.

There was no sign of his usual rapid rate of healing. His bones should be beginning to knit already, the torn flesh closing over, but he was in no state to trudge his way out of these bloody woodlands. Not even close.

He eyed the stag. The animal was broad and muscled. Getting onto his back was going to be torturous, but then so was having to listen to Silas's endless lecturing about getting oneself into stupid situations if he did not find his way back soon.

'Horns, over here, now.' He waved the stag closer. 'Help me to my feet.'

'Not horns, you tit. Antlers.' This was not the honey-voiced hobgoblin. This was harsh and deep as the distant thunder, which chose that moment to rumble, making the speaker sound ever more dramatic. The earth bulged, a small peak rising in the soil just beside the trap.

In reality they were half the creature their theatrical voice made them sound. A gnome poked it's head out of the dirt and decaying leaves. Their peaked head held a cap of damp soil, their long pointed nose dripping with brown fluid. 'I say we strike him over the head again, drag him out of the woods and dump him in a field where the Hunt can find him. Clementine? What say you?'

'I say, Tuppers, that's a tad extreme. And we are not abetting the Hunt in any shape or form. There's nothing to say that this is the creature the Herlequin is searching for anyways.'

Tuppers, pleasant chap he was, pulled himself fully from the soil. He was smaller even than Gilmore, which was to say his height barely lifted him to the stag's knee. He was far more rotund than the Holly Village earth elemental though. A belly that would make a fine pillow.

'What the fuck is a Herlequin?' The name was vaguely familiar, but a strike to one's head and a break to one's ankle tended to blur the mind.

'The one who leads the Wild Hunt.'

Now that was more familiar. Pitch closed his eyes. 'Do tell me that's not the Erlking's little band of merry men?'

'The very ones.' The gnome spat black dirt. 'Haven't been seen around in a very long time, and no one misses them. But here they are, storming about again. The Erlking declared it his royal right to hunt down the ones responsible for killing all those bluecaps in the Forest of Dean. Says everyone is to be on the watch for a pair of strangers. One big as an ox, the other pretty as a picture.'

'Oh for fuck's sake.' Pitch gave up trying to reach for the stag and slumped back against the trunk. 'I knew I should have burned down that whole fucking forest the moment I stepped foot in it.'

The will-o'-the-wisps flared their colours, frightened squeaks coming from them. The hobgoblin tsked again.

'No need for such talk.' Clementine's wrinkled face grew a few more wrinkles. 'And we don't want any part of that spat. Especially considering that same pair of strangers is said to have gone on to save the spirit of the forest. Heard they put an end to a witch-bottle maker's trade too, opened a lot of cages...set free enough birds to spread word a fire daemon had been the one to save them.'

Pitch stared down at the creature standing by his ankle. His wound ran crimson into the leaf litter. Clementine's scaled feet would be bloody before long if the hobgoblin did not move.

'Nice reward on offer though,' Tuppers said. 'A golden apple from the UnSeelie Court, grant you your heart's desire in a single wish.'

'Oh, and I'm sure there are no nefarious attachments to that prize.' Pitch tried to move his injured leg himself, a hand beneath his knee, trying to bend it. But he felt every shift of flesh around the wound, every twinge of split bone at his ankle. This was a fucking disaster. He was going to have to ask for their help. The knowledge was lemon juice on a cut. 'Are they nailing up wanted posters on noticeboards, then? How do I look in the drawings? Terrible I'm sure, for there is no artist alive who could capture this beauty.'

Pitch eyed the trunk, deciding that one of the jutting gnarls would work nicely as a lever. He reached for it.

'What do you think you're doing?'

He drew in a breath, ignoring Clementine. He tensed every muscle he knew how and leaned his weight into his arm. Right, a simple countdown would do. One, two...he pushed himself onto his knees.

What a fucking mistake that was.

The only fire that burned was made of injury and broken parts. He squeezed his eyes shut. He might have screamed; he certainly fell over flat on his back, panting through the throbbing pain. The will-o'-the-wisps were a storm of pretty colours around him. Laughing at him, he supposed, at his stupidity in imagining he was capable of anything productive. The stag nudged his shoulder, stamping a dark hoof.

'Yes, fine. I know,' Pitch said. 'Stupid idea.'

'What the bloody hell was that in aid of?' Clementine cried, scales clicking as they got themselves all ruffled with annoyance. 'Sit damned well still.'

'While you wait for the Hunt to arrive? I don't fucking think so.' Pitch swiped at the will-o'-the-wisps, which swarmed him.

'They aren't trying to hurt you. None of us are.' Clementine was exasperated. 'But if you go screaming and bringing attention to yourself like that, we can't vouch for who might hear you and think they'd like that golden apple. You can be sure there are some naturals out there who don't take kindly to someone killing bluecaps...or boggarts.'

'Boggarts?' Pitch rubbed at the tears that pain had forced free.

'One got murdered down Mordiford way. Word is it's the same killer.' Clementine eyed him meaningfully.

Pitch exhaled, the sigh taking a little more of his strength. 'That word would be very wrong. But if you truly don't wish to be part of all this bullshit, then let me get to my feet, will you?'

One of the will-o'-the-wisps darted to his side, the faint silhouette of their form visible in their glow—a miniaturised human for all intents and purposes. It was the unique one, with colours not set to one hue but rather all those of the rainbow. It held out a hand no bigger than a freckle on Charlie's face.

'Piss off.'

The wisp prattled at him in a squeaky, seesawing spewing of dialogue that Pitch could not understand a word of.

'Go away.'

The dejection that filled the minute face almost had him apologising. Almost.

'You're not much for taking help from others, are you?' Clementine said.

'I'm not one for having it offered.'

'Let the giant get him up.' Tuppers picked at his teeth with a dirt-packed nail. 'He'll be here momentarily.'

Pitch propped onto his elbows. 'Who will be here?' His pulse had already raced ahead. There were only so many giants he knew.

'The ox.' Tuppers scooped up a handful of earth, spat into it, and rolled it between his palms. 'Found him wandering about, calling for you, I assume. Stomping around like a one-man herd.'

'Silas?' Pitch was faintly aware it may be unwise to mention the ankou by name, fugitives as they were, but who would not know Silas Mercer on sight? He was unforgettable. 'Silas is coming?'

'Well, now that we aren't leading him astray, yes.'

'Why would you do that?' Pitch cried.

'Didn't you hear the hobgoblin?' The gnome's voice dipped lower still with frustration. 'But it's not only the Hunt. We're hearing tales that the kodami spread word through the trees black magick is about, too. We want strangers out of our woods. Now here, get this on your wound. Seems you are taking your time with healing.' The gnome stepped in, and with no warning at all, smacked the dollop of mud on torn flesh.

'Fucking, fuck...gods.' Pitch fouled the air with discontent, nearly blind as his vision wobbled and fizzled. He could just make out the hobgoblin dancing about in front of the gnome.

'He's supposed to stay quiet, Tuppers!'

The woods were a vague swirl of colours and shadows, Pitch's senses nudging at the very edge of consciousness. The brightest shades were the will-o'-the-wisps, swarming around an odd hulking shape.

The strange creature made no sense to Pitch's fading coherence. It seemed a chimera of man and beast, one side tall and broad and striding forward at a rush, the other shorter and angular and bobbing up and down elegantly.

'Pitch? Christ almighty.'

Not a chimera at all. Something altogether far more wonderful. The two pieces split, taking proper shape. Silas came at him at a run, roy-al-blue coat like summer sky around him. And at his side, the doe Pitch had freed.

'Sickle.'

Was all Pitch could manage to say before his elbows gave way beneath him and he slumped back against the damp earth.

CHAPTER 18

Silas gathered up the silent, bleeding prince as carefully as he could manage. But despite his care Pitch stifled a moan against the Inverness's black lapel.

'I'm sorry,' Silas whispered.

'Stop being sorry...I fucked things up nicely on my own. Please go.'

'Follow the stag.' The hobgoblin waved the animal forward. 'He'll lead you back the way you came.'

'Thank you.' Silas offered a nod, for it was all he had to give. He peered down at the gnome. 'And to you too.'

'For poisoning me with dirt?' Pitch muttered.

'For not throwing the dirt at you.' Silas hoped he might receive some note of amusement with that. And was mightily relieved when the daemon pinched him gently at the breast.

'Get on with it.'

Silas did as he'd been bidden, his head spinning with what the array of creatures had told him; the vile hunter who'd assaulted Pitch...and paid dearly for it, the Wild Hunt with their royal decree, the golden apple reward, the need for the ox and his pretty picture to leave this forest as fast as they could.

Silas followed along after the stag and the doe. With the stag's magnificent antlers and the wreath of will-o'-the-wisps about his neck, there was small chance of losing sight of them.

Silas sent a silent curse the way of every divot in the ground, every fallen tree he had to manoeuvre around or over, not for himself, though it was unpleasant enough, but for fear of bothering the man in his arms. Pitch, though, was quiet. Enough so to be worrisome.

'How are you doing?'

'It is I who should have voiced that question to you by now,' Pitch said. 'Are you...are you well, Silas?'

'Yes. Perfectly fine.' It was true. The bruised ribs would heal soon enough. 'I promise. It was a vision of sorts. We shall speak later of it.' When they were safe behind Sybilla's hexes, away from listening ears. Pitch nodded, his cheek grazing Silas's collar. 'It must have looked awful. But I think I shall recognise the signs if it were to happen again, and I shall try my utmost to give you warning before my theatrics next time.'

Another nod. A long silence.

'Perhaps, next time too,' Silas continued, though more tentatively, 'you will wait for me, so I might come with you when you run away?'

'I acted the fool...again. It was a stupid thing to do. Just say it.'

'You were frightened.'

There was heavy but empty air, just the crack of undergrowth from the deer and Silas himself as they moved steadily through the woods. As a roll of thunder plagued a distant sky, Pitch spoke.

'I am not healing quickly, Silas. And I'm not sure I could even fend off the damned fae in the Wild Hunt with the state I'm in.'

'You won't need to fend them off. I am here, and Sybilla and Matilda.' Silas glanced up but could see little of the sky. 'Hastings too. We shall be at the Sanctuary before this Herlequin chap even learns we were passing by.'

'Do you have any idea how irritating you are when you talk like that?'

'Yes, actually. You make it abundantly clear.' Silas buried a kiss in Pitch's putrid waves, hiding his consternation behind the gesture. The sooner they were on their way, the better. Silas was keen to put all aspects of this interlude behind them.

At their quickened pace, the journey was not long, and the deer held back as the trees thinned around the edges of the clearing. All but one of the will-o'-the-wisps kept their places around the stag's cage of antlers.

The delicate rainbow colourings marked out the single wisp that hovered in the space between the animals and Silas. Snippets of sound came from the tiny thing, like the twittering of a slightly demented bird.

'Thank you all, so much.' Silas leaned into a shallow bow as he bade the creatures farewell, ignoring the prince, who clucked his tongue. 'Go now, and keep yourselves safe.'

He stepped into the clearing, to find it devoid of life. The fire had been damped and the ashes kicked and scattered so they blended back into the ground. At a glance it would be hard to say if anyone had been there at all.

There were no voices evident, nothing of Sybilla and Charlie in conversation, nor the rattle of harnesses to announce the horses.

Pitch raised his head. 'Are we lost?'

Silas took a moment before he answered. He thought perhaps they were exactly that. Or worse...the deer had not been friends after all. Which made no sense. The creatures had clearly been caring for Pitch. The daemon was annoyed by the gnome but had hardly declared him an enemy. Was this the wrong clearing, then? Perhaps the deer were poor navigators?

'Silas? Where are they?'

He'd waited far too long to reply, and now the prince shifted about, trying to get out of Silas's hold. 'Pitch, wait.'

'They've left us?'

'No, of course not.' The daemon was so ready to be abandoned. It was infuriating. 'Sybilla would do no such thing.'

'The Valkyrie will do what she wants, or what she's told.'

'Why on Earth would she be told to leave us?'

'There's a mad Seraphim in her carriage. Who knows?'

'Has that hit to the head concussed you? She would not leave us–'

'Of course I wouldn't leave you here, but nor could I leave the others to search for you. You've taken your sweet bloody time.' Sybilla stepped out from the shadows on the far side of the clearing, and Silas only just caught himself from gasping with relief. 'Gods, I thought you might be fucking in the woods somewhere, but it looks as though you've had a boxing match instead.'

'Charlie and Edward?' Silas asked before Pitch could get out an angry word. 'Where are–'

'They are safe in the carriage.' She strode over, peering hard at Pitch's leg. 'What the blazes has he done to himself?' She touched at the tatters of his trouser leg.

'He stood on a hunter's trap, after freeing a doe.' Silas hesitated. 'The hunter wasn't much pleased.'

Sybilla's gaze darted to him. 'I thought I heard a shot beneath a crack of thunder but dismissed it.' She tried to lift Pitch's coat folds, which displeased him greatly.

'What the blazes are you doing?'

'Are you shot as well?'

'No. Stop touching me.'

'Why is the wound covered in dirt?'

'Because a fucking gnome decided rubbing dirt into an open wound was a wonderful idea.'

'A gnome tended you?' Sybilla frowned.

'A hobgoblin was there too,' Silas said. 'The creatures of the forest bade us leave quickly.'

While Pitch wriggled in his arms, demanding to be put down because he was not a fucking invalid, Silas quickly filled the Valkyrie in on what had been said about the Wild Hunt and its Herlequin.

'The Wild Hunt is far more than a diversion, then. What a fine mess.' Sybilla stepped back, leaving the way clear for Silas to move ahead. 'I suppose it is probably too much to hope that this Herlequin is as big an imbecile as the last. They were a veritable bull in the china shop, here for causing havoc, and so busy with it I hardly think they noticed when Mr Ahari dispatched them. Silas, get Tobias to the carriage, quickly. I'll tend him there, but we must move on. I should never have allowed him out of the shielding of the damned copse.'

'Why are you all talking about me like I'm not here?' Pitch demanded. 'I will not ride in that cabin, Valkyrie.'

'Tobias, you'll get in the fucking cabin. That's the end of it.'

The first pattering of rain played at the woodlands, glancing at Silas's face as he wrangled a daemon turned slippery as an eel. If not for the pain

Pitch's ankle caused him, he'd have been out of Silas's arms by now. As it was, Silas had to hold him far too tightly to ensure he didn't end up in a pile on the ground.

They paced across the clearing.

Sybilla peered up at the sky, visible in this open space. The clouds were thick and low and she did not seem pleased with what she saw. 'Matilda's not come back yet. And the storm is getting closer. Silas, you'll have us on our way as quickly as you can.'

She strode ahead to where hint of the carriage and Hastings's paler shape lay beyond the trees. Silas did not move quite so quickly, thinking of his injured passenger and how silent he had fallen. It was not Pitch's complaining, but another sound that interrupted the unsettled quiet.

The colourful will-o'-the-wisp had not left them. It bobbed about in the air, most enthusiastically telling Silas something or other.

'Go away,' Pitch muttered.

'Do you understand it?'

'I understand that its squawking is hurting my ears.' He covered the offended ear.

Silas glanced over his shoulder. The will-o'-the-wisp seemed to have heeded Pitch's command to leave. It zigzagged about, weaving up and down, moving so quickly that trace of its colours were left behind like true rainbows in the air. The critter dashed back into the woods, taking its soothing light with it.

CHAPTER 19

S ilas was certain now the horses were being influenced in their direction. They had been travelling for a decent couple of hours in increasingly miserable weather, and he'd barely had to pull on the reins. Well, that was to say he'd not needed to direct the bays, with the horses always choosing the northwest direction at any crossroad before he'd even lifted his frozen hands to guide them. But he certainly needed to keep them in check. His arms were beginning to ache from the number of times he'd reined them in, convinced they would have sought to gallop the entire way to their mysterious destination if allowed their heads.

At least the forced movement helped keep him warm. And the cold had numbed the lingering ache around his bruised chest. He was as good as healed now and fervently hoped the same could be said for Pitch.

Silas wiped his face. The rain was unrelenting and bitterly cold. The storm had grown noticeably louder, the flashes of lightning more brilliant.

There had been no sign of Matilda. If the elemental had managed to pass a message to Sybilla, he'd not been privy to that either. He'd been in the driver's seat alone for some time. And after Sybilla and Pitch had both suggested he worry less and drive more, and Charlie had declared Silas would make himself ill from fussing, he'd not called out again to enquire as to how everyone in the cabin was faring. He endured the empty space at his side unhappily but grateful the daemon was not subjected to the brunt of the icy conditions.

A dip in the road lay ahead, a place where a rivulet had swollen to a rather fast-moving stream across the path.

'Whoa, there.' Silas persuaded the horses to slow. There was no way to tell what state the roadway was in beneath the flow of murky brown water, so he erred on the side of caution. His muscles flexed as the bays showed their unhappiness with easing the pace. Silas was pleased with his decision when the carriage rocked back and forth pointedly, the wheels shifting through hidden depressions in the swirling water.

He waited for unhappy shouts to come from the cabin, and was not sure if he preferred their absence.

The carriage cleared the stream, and he let the horses have their heads, so as to negotiate the opposite incline. With all the groaning of wood and rattling of cinches and harnesses, Silas had no clue Sybilla was out of the cabin until she was hauling herself up beside him.

'Oh Christ. You caught me unawares. Why did you not ask me to stop?' But really the answer was evident. The Valkyrie moved like an aged seaman on her ship, settling on the seat beside him with practised ease. 'Is everything all right?'

'He is sneezing.'

'What? Who?'

'Tobias. I think he has a damned cold. He should barely have a sniffle, let alone a cold. Why did you not tell me the full extent of his woes?'

With both of them deeply hooded against the weather, Silas did not have to look her in the eye.

'I did try, at the stables as we readied the carriage. But it has been a tumultuous day.' Silas cleared his throat. 'There has scarcely been chance to speak of it again.' A woeful excuse, and he knew it.

'No chance to tell me the Berserker Prince is weak as a fucking lamb?'

Silas did glance her way, but he saw only the fabric of his own hood. He'd assumed Sybilla knew Pitch's full identity; she'd been the one to tie his tongue, after all. But her words reminded Silas this was not the only secret he'd been keeping.

'I told them,' he blurted, like a firework suddenly lit. 'In the Fulbourn, I let it slip that he is the prince.' Silas had not known the weight of his secret until it was being shed. 'They suspected already...after he survived the Gu and the...' He stopped there. He'd not breathe the Alp daemon's name. 'I made a terrible mistake, I didn't know I could be heard. Now they know for certain who he is.'

Sybilla sat beneath her hood awhile, the carriage rattling its way over a road that grew increasingly rutted by the heavy rain.

'I'm not sure it truly matters anymore, Silas. Regardless of his rank, the Morrigan know he is the one they want, and have likely known since Gidleigh Park.' Silas's grip on the reins tightened at mention of the place. 'And after the lengths you went to, to retrieve Edward, it is clear he is important too. There is nothing more vital now than getting the both of them safely to this blasted Sanctuary.'

'I'd feel a damned sight better about doing so if we had Lalassu and Sanu with us.'

Sybilla sighed. 'As would I, Silas. But do you not think they would be here if it were possible? Or was the right place to be in the circumstances?'

'Are you suggesting they have better things to do than protect the man who is being hunted the length and breadth of this country?'

Sybilla shifted beneath her folds, the rain loud against the stiffer leather of her coat. 'Sometimes the best protection is distance.'

'What a load of rot,' Silas fumed. 'He is vulnerable, Sybilla. You've seen it. This is far worse than how he was after Goodrich Castle. At least then he still had the flame, he could still defend himself. He is vulnerable now as he's not been before.'

'Which would have been very, very useful to know before we headed off on our little journey. I've given him a sleeping draught to settle him because he was driving me mad with wishing to be out of the cabin. I've never known him so...so fearful. And I see why. He's not healing as he should. I'm quite certain his bone is still fractured, and the skin has barely begun to knit. He is cut and bruised badly from a strike to the head that might have left barely a bump before. Even when he let himself get pummelled in the boxing ring, it took a decent few rounds to damage him. Damn it, Silas. What has happened? Was it the Fulbourn?'

'No. Well, that drained him, certainly. But it was made worse when he went to see Edward. The angel meddled with him again, Sybilla. He has placed a seal on his flame.'

'Why would he do that?'

A vicious snap of thunder stole Silas's answer. The horses shied, dragging the carriage far too close to the muddy gutters. 'That thunder seemed close.' Silas worked to bring them back on track. 'Still no word from Matilda?' He grunted as the bay on the left resisted him.

'Nothing.'

'Does that not worry you?'

'Very much so. But it is midway down on a long list.'

The world shone white and brilliant, and both Silas and Sybilla twisted in their seat, trying to catch glimpse of where the lightning originated. That particular strike was gone before they could turn, but only a few seconds later another took its place: a sear of white due south, piercing the ground with three prongs, a design not unlike Pitch's tattoo.

A great wind struck the carriage, bullying Silas's hood, trying to unbalance him from his seat with its fierce rush. The carriage was pushed forward, spooking the unsettled horses. Silas wrenched his attention back to keeping them on the road, but his mind raced.

'Has the storm not tended west until now?' He raised his voice against the strength of the wind. 'Or is that another front there to the south?' He tried to peer past his hood. West. Where only a faint haze of grey sat now. The ominous darkness of earlier gone.

'It is the same storm.' Sybilla stood and turned to rest one knee against the seat, holding fast to the metal rung that trimmed the carriage roof, her gaze on the land behind them. 'And from the suddenness of the shift I'd say its certain now there is nothing regular about the weather.'

'Matilda? Or the Hunt?' That last did not sit well to think on.

'The Hunts I've known did not include air or water elementals, but those were before the time of the Morrigan, nothing is as it bloody seems anymore.' She shouted to make herself heard over the beating of the rain upon the carriage roof and the wind hissing across the open landscape. There was no sign of a decent tract of forest to shelter in so far as Silas could see. The rain came down as though Enoch had decided to wipe out the world with another flood. 'And if it is Matilda then she is using all her might to vex something in her path. I don't like either of the possibilities. Nor do I like how it has shifted far closer than before.'

'But it's not following us, is it? The hexes you've placed on the carriage, they keep us hidden. That's what you said.' Silas's pulse pounded in time with the horses.

Sybilla cursed and dropped down heavily onto the seat. 'And that's what they do. I did not make the tale up.'

'I'm sorry, I'm just –'

'Concerned. I know. So am I, Silas.'

Silas shivered with a sudden thought. 'What if I've drawn them our way somehow...'

Sybilla held the edge of her hood back so she could look at him. 'Why would you think that?'

'Perhaps when I fell to the vision it betrayed us somehow. I could see that altar, those birds...what if somehow they saw me?'

'We can both sit here and drive ourselves mad with such thoughts.' She touched his shoulder. 'Keep your calm, best you can. The storm is well away yet, and we have no reason to believe it on our trail. But best you keep those horses at the fastest pace you dare. I shall check on the others and see if the angel will deign to tell me more of our destination, in particular, how much bloody further it might be.'

Silas's greatcoat was succumbing to the wildness of the wind, the rain finding a way in where it had not before. He was about to ask Sybilla if he should slow the horses just a tad so she might alight, when the Valkyrie stepped off the moving carriage in a whirl of darkness. She did not fall but drifted down, her coat lifting out behind her. Silas spied what he thought was a silver-threaded black shirt beneath, fluttering as though torn. Until he realised it was not fluttering at all, but making very distinct movements up and down. Silas wiped at his eyes, but by the time he focused again, Sybilla was pulling open the door of the carriage and he lost her from view.

Silas was quite sure he'd just seen his first glimpse of the angel's wings. In this lifetime at least.

The rain turned to sleet, making it difficult to keep eyes open as the tiny flecks bit at Silas's face. And the horses were lagging. This was a perilous path, with the road growing muddier every mile and a thin mist descending over the land around them. Silas could no longer feel his lips, and felt bottled in, with no clear sight of what lay ahead. If another carriage burst out of the haziness, it would be no surprise, for he'd not hear a thing with the rain and wind that buffeted them. But no other fool would be travelling as quickly as they did in this weather.

With each flick of the reins, he despised himself. Already the horses were driven by unseen forces; now he added his own hand to their urging. He must slow them. The plumes of white billowing from their nostrils and the heated steam rising from their lathered bodies left the two bays in a cloud of their own.

'Ease up now.' Silas could barely feel the leather between his fingers and worried it made him too harsh upon their bits. 'Whoa, now. Steady.'

They fell into a trot, a restless one that he was only barely in control of. Even his voice did not soothe them as it had before. The blasted wind making it difficult to be heard.

He opened his mouth to call out again when the road ahead dipped away. The muddy slope caught one of the bays unaware and the horse went down on its knees. The other screamed as it fought against the drag on the rigging. The downward angle encouraged the carriage's momentum, the tremendous weight giving the animals no opportunity to recover.

Silas leapt out of his seat, jumping over the footboard, throwing himself in front of the carriage shaft. The rod slammed against his back, and he grunted as the full weight of the laden carriage drove at him, the forward tilt of the footboard forcing him to bow his head. He ground his teeth, his arms straining against the weight pressing against him. His feet sank up to the ankles in mud, with no solid ground beneath to give him purchase. The downed bay fought to stand but seemed caught in its straps.

'Shit.' Silas hissed.

The carriage jerked unkindly against his shoulders as someone alighted.

'Silas, Jesus!'

He caught sight of a figure dashing past, rushing to the side of the horse tangled in its trappings. The flash of auburn gave them away.

'I've got him, I've got him,' Charlie cried.

Silas was too occupied with the tonnage bearing down on him to see exactly what the lad was doing until, suddenly, the terrible pressure upon his spine relented.

The downward slide of the carriage stopped.

He lifted his head. Silas could just make out the lad's legs, and his hands against the bay's belly as the horse found its feet. Christ almighty, had he just lifted the animal?

'Charlie? Charlie are you –'

'Fine. But Silas, my god, what were you thinking?' Charlie raced to where Silas was barricaded in like a third horse in the harnesses. 'You could have been crushed.' His eyes were wide with alarm. 'Are you all right?'

He was fine, perhaps he'd ache a little in his shoulders later but the carriage had been in more danger of breaking than he had.

'I'm fine. A crick in the neck perhaps, nothing more.' He ducked under the shaft and traces, removing himself from reach of two sets of hooves. But the horses were far too exhausted to consider giving him a kick. They nuzzled one another, heads sagging. 'As for you though, Charlie...'

'Don't you dare. I just found you practically under a carriage, trying to carry the whole bloody thing on your back. All I did was help a horse to its feet.'

'Helped, or lifted?'

'Both.'

The pin-prick sleet outnumbered the raindrops now. Charlie wore only his frock coat, a simple, far-too-thin affair of plain brown. This was not the place for such a discussion, but Silas glared at him.

'What if you had gotten tangled in the straps and the horse fell on you, or kicked you?'

'None of those things happened, Silas.' Charlie met his gaze, chin high so he could look Silas right in the eye. 'Will you not acknowledge that

I can fend for myself and others?' He raised his arm, brandishing the bracelet. 'This makes me helpful, and I intend to use it.'

'You have no idea how reliable that bracelet is.' Silas straightened, hoping to intimidate the lad into seeing sense, but the glint in Charlie's eye only brightened. 'What if it fails you when you need it most?'

'Then I die having done a few decent, worthwhile things. Starting now, repaying you for all the times you've saved me so far, by ensuring you weren't squashed flat by a coach.'

Silas nearly swore aloud. This ancient connection between them had gone quite far enough. He'd not allow its strange influence to push the lad into foolish things.

'You are not in my debt, Charlie.' Silas hoped whatever god or fate or fortune had unified them at the loch that day heard him now. 'And I wasn't about to *be* squashed. Do you know why?' His temper pushed him on before Charlie had a hope of answering. 'Because I am not bloody human, I'm not even truly alive. And I've died enough times to know I will keep you from that experience for as long as it's in my power to do so.' Oh, he was shouting now. Quite losing the plot. 'I have no idea how many people I have lost, but I know it's too great a number. And I am in no way ready to lose you, so stop doing stupid bloody things. Do you understand me?' He snapped his mouth closed, or at least assumed he did. There was not much feeling upon his face anymore.

Charlie stared at him. Blinked. And hurled himself headlong at Silas, who had no choice but to open his arms and accept the incoming cannonball. 'I didn't understand half of what you just said, but I love you too, Silas.'

'What? No, that's not...well...yes, I am very fond of you.' Silas sighed, enveloping the lad in his arms. Mostly to return the hug, partly to try and shield him from the terrible weather.

'Merciful gods, do you think when next you are trying to woo one another with your enormous talents, you don't almost break my neck in the process?' The daemon's words were as frigid as the air.

'Oh god, Tobias is awake, and I'm hugging you,' Charlie mumbled against Silas's coat. 'I'll never hear the end of this.'

Pitch was indeed awake. He'd opened the cabin door, scowling at the rain and Silas in turn.

'Leave them be, Tobias.' Sybilla was already outside, standing by Hastings whose mane was slipping from where it had been wrapped about the back wheel of the carriage. The dapple grey had played a part too, it seemed. Perhaps Silas had been a little hasty in deciding Charlie's act so foolhardy.

'The horses are spent,' Sybilla said. 'And it will take some doing to pull the carriage from this mud. Charlie, help me unhitch them from the harnesses. I'll have Hastings pull the carriage clear.'

'Right, then.' The lad pulled from their embrace and headed to the horses at once.

'Shall I help you?' Silas offered.

'No.' Sybilla shook her head. 'Give yourself a moment, Silas. Perhaps you can grab Charlie's greatcoat before he's soaked through?' She patted his shoulder. 'Probably best you're not there if he decides to carry one of the horses up the incline.'

With a wink at Silas's scowl Sybilla moved to join the lad in unharnessing the bays. Feeling a mite foolish, but unrepentant, he turned to Pitch who had closed the door and now leaned against the sill of the open window.

'Did you truly hurt your neck with that sudden stop?'

'No,' Pitch said. 'But that is not to say you have permission to go carrying carriages about on your back again.'

Silas smiled, taking in the sleep-rumpled vision who gazed back at him. 'How are you feeling? Your ankle?'

'Fine. Never better.' The bruise above Pitch's eye had turned the yellowish-grey shades of an older bruise, the cut was a thin line of black. 'So when might I expect my invitation to the wedding, Mr Mercer? Clearly that is the next step for the two of you.'

It was a ploy to distract him from more serious questions, but Silas would play along. Even though his teeth chattered and the wind sought to fill the hollow where the carriage had come to a halt.

'Oh, we intend to elope. A quick affair at Gretna Green, the Blight and Morrigan be damned. Would you pass me Charlie's greatcoat please?'

'Elope? How terribly romantic.' Pitch passed the coat through the open window, his face damp from the elements.

'A pity it's not in a church though. I dare say you'd have looked wonderful in a bridesmaid's gown.'

'You know I would have.' Pitch pulled back, sliding the window up slowly, an indecent smile on his face. If he was hiding any discomfort, he was doing it very well.

Silas bent against the sleet, and waited while Charlie and Sybilla walked the horses free of the rigging, hooves sucking at the wet mud, tired animals straining. As Silas held up the coat so Charlie could slip into it, the first snowflakes fell.

Delicate lace among the hard cut of the sleet, the flutters of soft white danced around them like dulled will-o'-the-wisps.

'What the –' Sybilla began.

Matilda came down with the bright white snow, her long black hair like vertical streams surrounding her thinly clad body. She landed right atop the carriage roof, causing Pitch to throw open the door with a shout, only to curse a moment later as water flowing from her gown poured over the edge of the roof, nearly drenching him. He slammed the door closed.

'Sybilla, I fear they know what direction you travel in now.' Matilda seemed starved for breath.

'The Wild Hunt? How can that be?' Sybilla handed the second bay to Charlie, and moved to peer up at the elemental who crouched on her haunches atop the carriage. There were thin trails of black coming with the water that flowed from Matilda, as though a dye in her hair ran free. 'What has happened?'

'You tell me. They had been holding to the west for a long while but suddenly diverted, intent on a woodland area to the south-east. I tried to get close enough to learn why only to discover they have their own elemental with them. An airy little cow who knows how to whip up a decent storm front.'

'A woodland?' Silas did not think he could grow any colder. His gaze shifted to the carriage. Pitch stared back at him from behind the glass, his expression grim.

'That's what I said.' Matilda watched him too. 'What went on there?'

'We had an incident...Pitch was hurt. A hunter's trap – '

'And he bled...no small amount either.' Sybilla balled her fists. 'Shit. Are they using blood magick to guide them?'

'Why are you asking me?' Matilda scowled. 'You're the magick angel.'

'And angels don't bleed, we burn,' Sybilla returned. 'I don't understand all the intricacies of blood magick, it's unique to maleficium. I haven't exactly had a band of sorcerers to study.'

'Well, there's no doubt they use it,' Silas said. 'Did you not say it was in the tarts?'

Pitch was slamming down the window before Sybilla could offer a reply.

'The tarts?' Snowflakes settled on his nose. 'Why the blazes did no one mention that to me?'

'There's been things to occupy us, in case you haven't noticed.' Sybilla frowned at the ground, scratching at her neck absently. 'Silas, you said they performed a blood ritual at the greensward too?'

He took a breath, forcing back the image of the young man having his throat slit. 'They did, yes. Though I'm not sure what purpose it served there.'

'Fortified the circle, fed the panlong...' Sybilla paced as she muttered.

'Whatever it was,' Silas nodded. 'The sorcerer Nemain has an appetite for bloody magick.'

'This reminiscence is wonderful, but utterly unhelpful.' Matilda declared bluntly. 'Suffice to say, that bunch of misfits have powerful sorcery at their disposal and you need to move along.' Silas found himself under her watery gaze. 'The Herlequin is a brute. He'd put you in his shadow, Mercer, and he pushes his riders hard.' Her gaze shifted to Sybilla. 'And you have a bleeding daemon in your carriage who may or may not be leading them straight to you.'

'I'm not bleeding anymore,' Pitch retorted. 'I likely have earthworms nesting in the wound from the damned soil, but no bleeding.'

'But it was.' Sybilla swore, rubbing at the back of her neck. 'And there are stains on the seat...the cloths I used...'

'Your hexes are doing something useful.' Matilda coughed and the snowflakes shuddered as they fell. 'Whatever trace of you they have, it's not strong enough to see them on top of us right now. But how long till that changes?'

'We need to abandon the carriage,' Sybilla declared.

'And then what?' Silas frowned, gesturing to the landscape that grew increasingly laden with snow. 'We go on foot?'

'You fly.' The elemental declared. 'The Valkyrie has wings, she needs to use them.'

'Oh, that is absolutely not happening,' Pitch declared from the relative comfort of the cabin. 'I'm not flying.'

But Sybilla was nodding, thoughtful. 'I can fly them, but not all at once.'

'Then take who you can, and I'll put some miserable weather between the hunt and those who stay behind.' Matilda braced against the rooftop, a weightlifter preparing to rise. 'Not making any guarantees about it though. Between me and that little bitch with the Hunt, we're stewing up the weather something awful. Not sure how much control of the elements I'll be able to keep.'

Pitch gripped the edge of the sill, his face far paler than it had been just a moment before. 'And where the blazes are you going to flap to, Sybilla? We don't know where the fuck we are going, and the angel didn't exactly draw us a map.'

'There are Order strongholds about, and places safer than this. They'll have to do for now. I'll come back for you as soon as I can.'

'Those bays look rested enough to me,' Pitch said. 'I'll ride.'

'My gods, this is the fool we are relying on?' Matilda touched a toe to the edge of the roof, sending a fresh torrent of water downward to where it forced the daemon back into the cabin with an unhappy shout.

'Can you take Charlie and Edward together?' Silas asked of Sybilla.

'Don't worry about me, Silas.' Charlie was handling the wild talk of flying far better than the prince. 'Please just get Edward to –'

'I can take them both.' The Valkyrie was decisive. 'They are lithe enough. But you, Silas, shall take some figuring out when I return.' She jerked her head towards the carriage. 'And he may require another knock to the head to put him out for the journey. I know his aversion to flying.'

'It is far more than an aversion,' Pitch called out from somewhere in the depths of the cabin. 'It is against my religion, or creed, or whatever it need be.'

They both ignored him. 'Silas, you'll take him on Hastings for now. She will be able to follow my lead.'

He nodded.

'Speaking of your horse,' Matilda still crouched in her rivulets of black-and-crystal-blue water. 'Best you put her back to rights. The White Horse and a snowfall will work together nicely. Time she shows her true colour.'

'Agreed.' Sybilla's gaze went to her mount. Hastings stood so still that she appeared as though a statue, the snow piling on her haunches, dulling the strong grey of her dapples. No. It wasn't the snow at all, Silas realised. The dapples were fading.

'Right, I'm about done with standing here now.' Matilda coughed again, and the sound that came was the rather unpleasant gurgle of a blocked pipe.

'Are you all right?' Silas blinked snowflakes.

'Be better if I'd never agreed to join the Order, but there we have it. Now get on with you, the lot of you. I'll do what I can but I'm about run dry. Get them where they need to be, Valkyrie.' Matilda stood up– and continued on up, rising as the snow fell. 'Good luck to you all. And prepare for some bad weather.'

Her form whittled away until there was nothing to see of her at all. From the south came the ominous roll of thunder.

'Bad weather?' Pitch said, incredulous. 'Does she think this a lovely fucking day?'

As though winter itself heard him the skies released. And what had been a fluttering of icy flakes became a downpour.

CHAPTER 20

Not just snow but a biting wind. One that pushed itself up Pitch's trouser legs and etched its freezing self into his skin.

'Shit.' He clung to the doorframe, not daring to test his ankle too much just yet. The pain was not quite so intense as before. That had to count for something, surely? And his headache had definitely improved. He sneezed, something he'd been doing too frequently for his liking, and discovered he was wrong about his headache.

'Charlie, make sure the bays are untacked. Let them go free,' Sybilla shouted from somewhere in the white blur of the outside world. 'Silas, remove Hastings's saddle. It will be easier for the two of you without it.'

The ankou called back, though his exact words were stolen by the wind and another of the ceaseless murmurs of thunder.

Pitch shrugged on his greatcoat with inelegant aplomb in the confined space, fighting down the ever-ready panic that choked him. If they forced him to fly, he wasn't sure he wouldn't just crumble altogether. He felt sewn together with weak threads.

'All is well, all is well,' he muttered like a loon while he dressed. 'Keep your wits, keep your wits.'

Edward was huddled in the corner of the seat, layered up with so many blankets that the poor sod looked as though he were part of some strange burial rite. As Pitch fumbled with his buttons, the lieutenant stirred. His eyes opened.

Pitch could not help shrinking away, pressing himself back where there was no room to do so.

'Tobias. It's me.' Grey eyes soft, Edward regarded him.

There was space to breathe again. 'Well, that's...how are you?'

'Not so terrible as I might appear.'

Was the fool man trying to smile? Amidst all this mayhem?

'Edward, we are to separate. Sybilla will take care of you and–'

'I know. I understand. Tobias, we are so close.'

'To the Sanctuary?'

'To everything.'

Pitch was in no mood for cryptic speech. 'Fine. Great, wonderful. I have to go.'

He braced his hands on either side of the doorway, steeling himself for the effort it would take to step down. Snow drifted in, settling on the seat he'd just vacated, and on the blankets covering Edward. Outside voices were muffled by the density of the fall.

'He's trying to protect you, you know.' Edward spoke quietly but managed to be heard above the weather. 'From the weight you carry. I know you feel made small, but he has done this for your own good –'

Pitch tensed, barely feeling the twinge at his ankle as he shifted his weight. 'Edward, you are a decent man who has been dealt a terrible hand.' He paused. 'I'll not forgive myself or the angel for that. I see now I was like you once...so enraptured, so desirous of his attention that we fail to realise that those soaring above us rarely look down. And when they do, it is not for our own good, or our protection, or anything of us at all. It is to serve their purpose. To meet *their* desires. To right their mistakes and create new ones.' Wind finally snuffed out the last stalwart candle still fluttering in the interior. Fixed above the vacated seat, its flame had lasted through impossible odds until then. 'Please tell your Holy One, if he's not already listening, that if it turns out I did not succeed in killing him that day upon the cliff, and should I survive what is demanded of me now, then it shall be *my* purpose to find him, the true monster, and seek vengeance for what he's stolen from us, you and I.'

The door on the far side of the carriage opened, Sybilla appearing through the flurry of snowfall.

'Silas has Hastings ready for you, Tobias. Go on quickly.' She clambered into the carriage, stripping the blankets from Edward, who had not yet let his eyes wander from Pitch. He nodded when Pitch met his gaze, mouthing something which looked an awful lot like *thank you*.

Pitch pulled up his hood and stepped from the carriage. He hoped to do so with dignity, with grace even, after such a dramatic speech, but his ruined ankle had another plan. The moment he had his foot on the carriage step, Pitch saw stars.

'Sweet fucking blazes,' he cried, and lurched forward to escape the pain.

'Steady.' The ankou loomed out of the white haze like one of the damned storm clouds that chased them. 'I have you.'

Which, of course, he did. With the snow pelting down, Silas grabbed him by the waist, holding him so only the tips of Pitch's booted toes could touch the whitened mud.

'I'm fine. I just lost my balance is all.'

The ankou grunted. 'Very well. Do you wish to ride behind me or in front?'

Because even though the world was caving in and their enemies were chasing them down, the ankou found time to offer Pitch what he so rarely had. A choice.

But there was no decision to be made, not really.

'In front.' With a great mass of ankou at his back.

'Right then,' the ankou said. 'I will do most of the work to get you up, but perhaps you can grab hold of Hastings's mane and pull yourself –'

'I know how to mount a horse, you dolt. Get on with it.' He gave Silas's arm a quick squeeze, to dull the sharpness of his words.

The mounting was not too unpleasant. Silas did indeed do most of the work, his height convenient alongside the tall mare, his strength hugely arousing, despite the fact that it was actually cold enough to freeze one's balls off. There were a few seconds of discomfort, Pitch would not deny, as he swung his injured leg over the horse's broad back, but he convinced himself he was not seeing stars this time, only snowflakes catching the light. Silas used the carriage wheel as a mounting block, making sure he did not lay his weight heavily when he brought himself down on Hastings's back.

He slipped his arms around Pitch and took up the reins. 'All right?'

'Fine, yes.'

The ankou served as a windbreak of sorts, but there was no avoiding the fine churn of the snow, which settled on Pitch's eyelashes and insisted on finding its way up his nostrils. It was as he lowered his head to shake tiny icicles clear that it struck him: Hastings could be a snowflake herself. She was entirely white, the grey dapples no more.

'Do you see that?' Or maybe Pitch had suffered a head injury after all.

'Her coat?' Silas returned. 'Yes, beautiful, isn't she?'

There was no denying it. The white was so pristine, almost glowing against the snowfall. There was a sense of utter purity about the animal. Of not a single dark stain of the world being able to cling to her.

Silas turned the mare about, or more likely the horse turned itself about. The snowfall was all-consuming; there was barely a speck of the landscape to be seen. If the ankou had a clue which direction to take, it would be a marvel.

'Try to stay alive until I can return for you, won't you, gentlemen?' Sybilla called.

Pitch peered into the alabastrine surrounds. There was a shadow of sorts some few feet away, which might have been the dark angel.

'Take care,' Silas called. 'Charlie, do not let go, do you hear me?'

'Yes, Father.' Pitch smiled at the lad's dry reply and Silas's irritated harrumph. 'The same to you. We shall all be perfectly...oh...oh my god...those are wings...you have wings...real ones...Silas, you should see this!'

But neither he nor Pitch could see much of anything at all.

Sybilla called on Charlie to focus...and hold tight. Through the haphazard to and fro of the snow came a strong, purposeful gust of air. Another swiftly followed. The snow blasted back at them, and Pitch closed his eyes, turning his head from the onslaught.

He'd stood near the launch space of enough angels to know when one was taking flight. He could just make out a smear of darkness twisting through the white, a column of centred movement as Sybilla bore her passengers aloft.

'I can't see a bloody thing, damn it.' Silas lifted a hand to shade his eyes, as though that would help him see through thick snowfall.

'I think that is entirely the point. Let's go, Silas.'

The ankou sighed, a despondent sound. 'Pitch...I don't think I could bear it if...'

'Nothing shall happen to the lad, Silas.' Pitch defied the gods to prove him wrong. He'd slay them on their pedestals should they do so. Silas's misery would be immeasurable. 'Now we should go too.'

It took the ankou a moment before he came back to himself. 'Yes, of course. Move on, Hastings. Fast as you like.'

The mare did move on, setting off in a direction Pitch suspected was her choice alone, following the invisible thread that existed between a Horseman and their mount. Sybilla was now their guiding star, in a sky they couldn't see.

'Oh blast.' Pitch winced as the horse's gait rocked him too far forward, finding bone in unwelcome places. 'Don't you dare trot, you silly nag.'

'Does your ankle still bother you?' The carriage and its abandoned rigging was swallowed by the storm and the growing sea of white upon the ground.

'It's my cock and balls that concern me. Do you have any idea what damage a wither can do?'

Silas's laughter was no more than the shift of his chest against Pitch's back. 'Trotting is definitely prohibited, then. I'll see no harm come to anything between your legs.'

'What use would you have for me otherwise?'

'Exactly, my dear. None whatsoever.' Silas's embrace tightened before slackening once more. 'This is not so easy as I imagined though. I fear I'm going to slide straight off her back once we have some speed.'

'True, but we can't have her walk all the way to the Sanctuary.' Their coats snapped in the wind, and Pitch spat out a length of hair the wind was determined to shove down his throat.

'No. We cannot.'

While he and Silas pondered the most pressing of issues, the well-being of their family jewels, Hastings took the matter in hand. The mare's mane defied the bothering of the wind to slither around Pitch's waist and down his legs, forming stirrups of a sort beneath his feet, putting an extra weave around his wounded ankle, bracing it. He was locked in place, his lap blanketed by hair whiter than the snow that fell.

'Well, this is...oh.' Silas shifted, edging back from where he'd been pressed up against Pitch. 'Oh my.'

Pitch glanced to one side, but with his hair whipping about it was hard to see much. He used his hand instead, reaching for Silas's thigh, finding him likewise woven into Hastings's mane. The horse whinnied, tossing her head as though ensuring the weaving tight enough. Her muscles tensed beneath Pitch's thighs.

'Silas, I think you should hold –'

Hastings burst into a gallop, a headlong charge into the white ether that would have sent both him and Silas tumbling off her back if not for the fact that they were so neatly strapped in. There was wriggle room enough to lean forward, press his good foot into the hair-sewn stirrup she'd made for him, and rock his hips in time with the motion of the horse with no fear of flattening his assets. But there was as much chance of falling off the mare's back as there was of saving his eyes, and nose, from watering with the mix of startling speed and chilled air.

Silas was a looming presence at his back, his arms brushing Pitch's own in time with the rhythm, his breath the one hint of warmth where it glanced against Pitch's ear.

How the mare could see a bloody thing, he could not imagine. But she could see well enough to plough her way through the land. And plough it was, for the snow was thick, her hooves kicking out sprays of white as she drove forward.

There was some sense of rise and fall in the ground beneath them, of travelling over uneven terrain. They passed through a thin woodland at one point, Silas pushing Pitch down without warning as a branch glanced over them, drawing a grunt of complaint from the ankou when its snow loosened upon him.

'I thought I might like snow. I've decided I do not.'

Pitch laughed, despite being cold and wet and sore. 'Much better to look at through a thick pane of glass with a glass of whisky in hand. Brandy for you, of course.'

'Christ, can you imagine how wonderful that would be right now?'

Even with Hastings's mane weaving between them, the motion of the gallop pushed Silas against Pitch's back in a way that made it very difficult to imagine much else at all.

The White Horse ran on. Her pace was blinding. *Actually* blinding. They could have reached Scotland – he wouldn't doubt it possible with the speed – and he'd be none the wiser. All the world was a blur.

His stomach was beginning to ache with the need to lean into the gallop. Not to mention the difficulties of resting more heavily upon one foot than the other. His hip thought very little of the pose, the muscles spasming enough to make him wince. He'd been fighting a sneeze for a while, but there was no stopping it now, the only redeeming factor being the startled sound from the ankou as Pitch's arse shoved against him.

This propensity for sneezing, the dripping nose and slightly blocked ears signified a cold, Sybilla had informed Pitch. As though he had not suffered indignity enough, now he had a pointless purebred ailment.

'Do you hear that, Pitch?'

'A sneeze, I'm told.'

'No, no, though the way you manage to sound both infuriated and immensely satisfied when you sneeze is endearing...but listen...in behind the storm. Something is there.'

'If this is your way of saying you'd like to stop for a moment, then just say it, man.' By the gods, please say it. Pitch took ahold of the reins, which Silas held loosely in his grasp. 'Come on then, stop, nag. Silas has had quite enough.'

The ankou did not protest when Pitch tugged against Hastings's mouth. The mare tossed her head, and did not seem keen at all to move from earth-shattering speediness to a more modest walk. He gave another tug, gentle enough but clear. The mare dropped into a trot for a few wince-worthy moments and then to a walk. The horse was not happy though, sidestepping and shaking her head.

'Settle down, you damned –'

'Hush, quiet a moment...' Silas cupped a hand to Pitch's shoulder. 'I hear something out there.'

There was wind, there was enough snowfall to be faintly heard, there was of course the ever-present thunder, but the ankou was right. Beneath that came a rumble, a drumming against the earth. Pitch's skin crawled.

'That sounds a lot like horses at a gallop,' he said. 'Too fucking many of them.'

Hastings snorted, turning about in a circle.

'How are they so close?' Silas leaned forward, his chest pressed at Pitch's shoulder. 'You're not bleeding are you?'

Pitch surveyed the offending foot, as best he could considering it was wrapped up in Hasting's mane. 'Not so far as I can tell, but I can't feel my toes let alone a bleed.'

Silas flapped the reins. 'Hastings, race on. Go.'

The mare's whinny was a blade upon the air. And her takeoff came from deep in her haunches. They were returned to their flat-out run in an instant.

If the rumbling behind them continued he could not hear it over the whip of the air against his ears. His head pounded, right beneath the hunter's cut. 'How long do you think she can keep up this pace?' he shouted.

'Long enough, I hope.' Came the very dissatisfying reply.

Pitch was readying to tell Silas so when he was halted by the unmistakable movement of something in his pocket. Not his greatcoat, but the lighter coat beneath. 'Shit...what the fucking...' He dug his hand down behind the blanketing of Hastings's mane.

'What's wrong?'

'There's something...my pocket...'

He left half the words behind, distracted by the squirrelling. His fingertips touched at something smooth and cold.

And that something tapped at his fingers like a frantic sailor sending an SOS.

A rainbow fled his pocket. A squeaking, maddened rainbow.

The will-o'-the-wisp hovered in front of him, so close he was liable to go cross-eyed with looking at it. The creature had taken a vaguely human shape, translucent, as though a delicate work of blown glass. It stabbed a pointed finger to the way ahead. Chittering like a creature possessed.

'It is trying to tell us something,' Silas declared.

Pitch elbowed the ankou. 'What a brilliant mind you have, fair ankou. Do you speak will-o'-the-wisp also by any chance?'

The snow glistened with all the hues of the creature, sunrise oranges, strawberry, lavender, and forest green, all of which glowed brighter as the will-o'-the-wisp grew more and more irritated with being unheard. Abandoning them, it dashed to Hastings's ear, hanging on like a sailor to a crow's nest. The squawking and pointing continued, but this time it had found a suitable audience. Hastings curved her neck, snorting hard, and found a new burst of speed, turning them sharply to the left. The few threads of her mane that were not holding Pitch and Silas in place, those at her ears where the will-o'-the-wisp stood, rose and twisted about one another. An intricate display that became all too evident, all too quickly.

'Is that...' Silas began.

'Please tell me that is not us being thrown from this horse.'

Beyond the woven diorama of what appeared to be Hastings herself, with her riders dangling at the ends of lengths of mane like downed, oversized kites, the hue of the real landscape remained an unappealing blur of white.

'It does seem to be the case.'

'Silas,' Pitch cried, his delicate threads of resolve straining. 'I don't wish to be flung.'

The beacon of light between Hastings's ears, the spectrum of colour that was the will-o'-the-wisp, turned to face them.

A sharp squeak, a jabbed finger to the left.

'I think that's a signal.'

'I will not be flung, damn it.' Pitch grabbed a handful of mane, but the mare was already slipping her hair away from his legs, unbinding him from the snug, secure, and warm position.

'I don't see we have much choice.' Silas wrapped his arms around Pitch's middle. 'I'll not let you go, don't worry.'

'This is ludicrous. Where is she sending us?' A length of Hastings's mane struck at the thin skin on the inside of his right wrist. A violence that saw crimson bloom. 'Fuck...she just cut me.'

A few strands of hair pressed against the wound, and his blood flowed along them as though Hastings had opened his vein.

Silas cursed right against his ear. 'What has she done?'

But there was no time to reply. Hastings released the bloodied strands from Pitch's wrist. They hung like a ghastly scarf of scarlet down her neck. But the rest, still pristine white, she used to swaddle them. The will-o'-the-wisp, damn it to any hell that might exist, gave them a salute.

And the gesture marked their launch.

The White Horse lifted them off her back and flung her riders, as though they were a stone from a slingshot, her mane peeling away as they flew through the air. Pitch crushed his curses behind his teeth, his body so tight against Silas's they were almost as one. The ankou held him. Wrapped about him as they shot over the ground, whipping over the snow with only a foot or two to spare.

The speed was as impressive as the mare's gallop, but where the blazes were they headed? Pitch squinted through watery eyes.

Out of the stark nature of the land, grey shadows loomed. A blink and he saw that it was not shadows at all. A forest.

'Shit, Silas!'

'I see it.' The ankou curved in over him in a more thorough way. Pitch ducked his head, refusing to see which tree trunk was going to break them in half. He was held in Silas's shadow, embraced in the armour that was the ankou. And never had Silas's presence seemed so...large.

He swore the ankou cast a shadow. An inflation of the man that was breathtaking. One capable of opening a hole in the forest.

'Brace.'

Silas shattered the illusion with his sharp warning. He jerked his shoulder, throwing himself around and taking the brunt of the hit that came. They drove through shrubbery that snatched at them like the hands of the starving. Silas grunted, his shoulder hitting something firmer, their trajectory shifting, their bodies flipping. Pitch peered up at the forest canopy.

A solid thump announced a landing and a startled gasp came from the ankou. Pitch was now a passenger on a living sled. They tore along a short distance before the sodden earth brought them to a standstill.

'Silas? Are you all right?' Pitch struggled to free himself from the ankou's still-tight grasp, catching sight of an odd speck of whiteness on his own wrist. Like a tiny patch of lichen right over the site of the cut Hastings had inflicted.

'I think so. Give me a moment.' Silas's grin was a little wobbly, and he definitely winced as he sat up. His hair was caked with mud and twigs, more dirt brown than black. 'You?'

Pitch held up his hand, gesturing at the blot on his wrist. 'Fine, fine, the nag saw fit to patch me up at least. Are you sure your bones are intact?'

'Quite sure. I didn't strike anything much, remarkably.' Silas's gaze shifted over Pitch's shoulder. 'We have company.'

The will-o'-the-wisp darted in through a widened path through the trees, barrelling through the gap, which narrowed even as Pitch stared. Two sturdy ash trees leaned back towards one another, blotting out the light their separation had allowed in. There was the reason Silas did not have any broken bones to contend with. The damned forest had bent to accommodate them.

'Do you think trees so dull now?' Silas shifted onto his knees, rubbing at his back and making a face as shreds of his greatcoat came away.

The rainbow creature made the first recognisable noise Pitch had heard. 'Shhhhh.' Turquoise hands bade them stay down. As though either of them was about to bolt off. The will-o'-the-wisp went back to jabbing fingers out beyond the ash trees.

The ground shook, actually vibrating beneath Pitch's knees. He looked to Silas, and they spoke without uttering a word, both rising to their feet. Silas embraced Pitch around the waist and lifted him so his feet barely touched at the ground. He moved them both back the way they had come. And Pitch was too distracted by what they sought to see to protest being carried about like a child's doll.

Silas settled them in behind one of the ash trees, where a parting in the shrubs allowed them to see some of the landscape beyond the forest. 'Keep down.' He took Pitch's hand, tugging him in closer.

The Wild Hunt was close. Pitch glanced at his injured foot, reassuring himself that he'd not reopened the wound. The bandaging Sybilla had fixed was in place, the remnants of the gnome's soil peppered his skin. But no blood.

He saw Hastings' plan now. The reason behind her seemingly appalling mistake in cutting him.

Not a mistake at all.

The will-o'-the-wisp dulled their glow and settled in front of them, hands splayed, bracing itself like a rugby player, as though daring the Hunt to try to get close.

A rough wind played at the edge of the forest, though it failed to reach them where they stood. With the surging of the air came a chance to view the Wild Hunt, the snow sweeping back like a curtain, revealing players on the stage.

The riders were half a mile away at least, despite the thunderous sound of hooves. Pitch tightened his fingers around Silas's hand.

The Hunt raced along, surrounded at their horses' feet by a blue-grey mist, a contrast against the endless white. Their number seemed considerable, with many riders of differing sizes, but the jumble of horsemen was chaotic and shifting, and the distance too great to be certain. What *was* certain, though, was that Matilda had understated their leader.

The Herlequin.

The elemental had called him a brute, but it was hardly enough to cover it.

Even from this distance, with their view obscured, the cloaked rider dominated the landscape. He was massive in comparison to those who rode behind, all their cloaks flying in a messy show of heraldry. The Herlequin's horse would likely stand a head taller than any of the Lady's mares, a necessity for the load it endured.

'Have you ever seen a fae like that, Pitch?'

'Never. I've not fought a bruiser in the ring like that either. He's at least two of you and a bit more added together.'

What the blazes were they feeding them in the UnSeelie Court?

Silas ran his thumb around the concealed wound on Pitch's wrist. The odd covering resembled a snowflake, melted in place against his skin. One shade whiter than his own hue. No hint of crimson. 'She wounded you intentionally,' he said softly. 'She has saved us.'

The Wild Hunt was racing in entirely the wrong direction, intent on the blood-stained horse.

'It would seem so.'

The cacophony lessened, the trembling dirt settling as Sybilla's steed drew the blue mist away, leading them northeast. The Herlequin could still be made out for quite some time, a hulking shape peaking above his hunters like some breathing mountain.

Finally though, they vanished. The squall of the snowstorm engulfing them. The roll of thunder travelled in their wake.

Pitch exhaled. But neither he nor Silas made to move. Silas lifted Pitch's hand to his chest, and they drank in the silence.

The will-o'-the-wisp settled itself on Pitch's shoulder, but he was too boneless with relief to shoo it away.

The relief was fragile though. His mind crowded with new and obvious concerns. First and foremost, what the blazes did they do now?

CHAPTER 21

Pitch was not the first to pull away. And Silas only did so in order to peer down at Pitch's ankle.

'How is it? Did it hurt you when we landed?'

'No. But look at the state of you.' Pitch tutted, lifting a scrap of Silas's greatcoat, which had been shredded to within an inch of its life, like curtains at his back. 'Your coat is ruined.'

'Oh shit, no.' But it was not the greatcoat he was bothered about. He shrugged that off with no regard and proceeded to spin about, trying to peer over his shoulder. 'Is the Inverness all right? Please tell me it's not torn, too.'

'Good gods, Mr Mercer, are you going to cry if I say it is?'

'Are you going to berate me if I say yes?' He scowled. 'Foolish question. You'd relish the opportunity to taunt me.'

Pitch blinked, surprisingly insulted. 'It is your lucky day. I think myself too tired to ridicule you. The coat is intact.' Astonishingly unscathed. Pitch watched while Silas checked each button. 'But it is just a coat, Silas. My concern lies with the body beneath it. That was quite the blow you took to land us.'

'I assure you, no harm done. And it is far from just a coat. It is a gift from you. One I do not think I have thanked you properly for.'

'No need to fuss. I hardly sewed the bloody thing.'

'But you had it sewn *for* me.'

Pitch took the ankou's proffered arm, grateful for the excuse to lean. The wildness was so much heavier since it had been made quiet. Silas's arm slipped around his corseted waist and held him close. So close their thighs and hips met. With the rush of their escape tingling beneath his skin, it was difficult not to let his mind drift and imagine how easy it would be to start something, here in the dirt, desirous of something other than fear to make his heart thump. Perhaps the ankou thought it too, for his eyes were heavy-lidded, and his lips parted as though he were considering a kiss.

But the will-o'-the-wisp put paid to any notion of an irrational rut. The creature darted at him and returned to where it had been buried before, in the deep folds of his coats.

'No.' Pitch pulled away from Silas and drew open his greatcoat, slapping at the pockets of the lighter one beneath. 'No, that is not your blasted nest. Get out, out.'

When the critter showed no sign of itself, he shrugged off the greatcoat entirely.

'Pitch, it is too cold for undressing.'

Silas received a light slap for his attempt to intervene. A momentary reprieve for the will-o'-the-wisp, who suddenly reappeared between them, nattering in that intolerable way of theirs.

They brandished a very familiar object, one almost as large as they were. The creature hugged the piece of amber as though it were a treasured heated water bottle.

'How the fuck did you get my earring?' He did not even recall retrieving it after the hunter had stolen it. 'Did you go back for it? It's not really that pretty.'

A snort and something much like a hiccough was his reply. The will-o'-the-wisp was either very excited or very annoyed, but something caused its colours to swirl over the surface of its curious blown-glass-like figure. The blasted thing had given itself eyes, two dots of white crystal, with tinier dots of black at the centre. No eyebrows, no lashes, just these unblinking orbs. It was horrendous, like one of the awful dolls children seemed to adore.

A jab-jab of moss-green fingers followed. More chittering. And darting.

Silas moved to speak, and Pitch held up his hand. 'If you say it wishes us to follow, I truly shall lose my temper. I can see it well enough.'

The ankou's lips twisted as he deadened his smile. 'Can you help us tend his injury?' He directed his question at the wisp.

There was no chance of interpreting the enthusiastic nodding and slapping of the earring like it were a drum as anything but a yes.

'Then, what do you say?' Silas asked of Pitch. 'Hastings was happy enough to follow the creature's directions, and I certainly hear nothing untoward here – the bandalore does not stir. Do we assume the White Horse has left us in good company?'

Silas's light-heartedness could not hide all his concerns. He was deeply worried – Pitch knew the lines upon his face well enough now – and working hard not to show it. The weight of their circumstance pressed upon Pitch's shoulders. Gods, he was tired.

'Silas...what do we do?' He rubbed at the bruised flesh on his forehead. It still pained him to do so. 'I mean truly, what do we do now? We have no horses...' He swept a hand down at his leg. 'I am walking wounded. We don't know where the fuck we are going. This is an utter disaster.' He could barely stand to hear himself, how pathetic he sounded.

But Silas's gaze softened. 'It is far from ideal, but hardly a disaster. Hastings knows where she left us, which means Sybilla does, and in turn the Lady and the Order. Plus, the Herlequin has been led astray. Let's get you somewhere you can rest, first and foremost.' He took a step forward, and Pitch took one back.

If the ankou touched him, he might do something reprehensible, like burst into tears. Pitch had made a fool of himself far too many times this day.

The will-o'-the-wisp came between them. Pitch accepted the interruption gladly. The shining creature fluttered up in front of him, forcing him to squint with its tiny brightness. The wisp cradled the earring in one purple arm and patted Pitch's cheek with the other. In a voice not so squeaky as it had been before, it told him a tale he couldn't understand a word of. He could read nothing in their disconcerting crystal eyes as the wisp touched at the earring, and then pointed into the forest, before returning to their unsettling fixation with caressing his cheek.

'Right, that's enough then.' Pitch blew a breath, rushing the creature away.

The will-o'-the-wisp retreated and made a short sound that might have been *Do you understand?*

'I don't understand a bloody word, but lead on. And let it be known, if it is a trap of any kind, I shall pluck you apart, piece by tiny piece, and those eyes shall be first.'

The creature very definitely scoffed, and if those eyes could have done so, he was sure they would have rolled.

When Silas moved to lift him, Pitch gritted his teeth and said not a word. Cradled in the ankou's arms once more, he scowled at the forest as they moved into its depths.

And deep it was. They walked on for a long while, near on half an hour Pitch would estimate, and not once did Silas's hold waver, nor did the ankou shift his shoulders in any discomfort. Pitch studied Silas through his lashes. Those shoulders were broad and magnificent, but the Herlequin's own would have put them to shame. The Erlking had a giant leading his Wild Hunt. And if his strength matched his size...and he were to find them...Pitch shivered, closing his eyes against the thought of Silas facing up to such a creature. For he would, certainly, if it came to it. The ankou would not hesitate, which frightened Pitch every bit as knowing he could do little to aid him in any fight.

The snowfall had hardly penetrated this deep in the forest, the heavy canopy stopping much of it. There was a surprising number of evergreens here. Very few of the trees were not brimming with foliage in hues of autumn and pale hints of summer. The forest was dense with growth, Silas having to pick his path carefully and turn side on at times to negotiate the way.

They were being watched. But not very stealthily, and the will-o'-the-wisp was clearly darting about in greeting of some members of the hidden audience. He heard the tinkling bell sounds of peri, caught the stirring of a kodami or two, the tree dwellers matching the texture of the bark nearly perfectly. He'd not have noticed them if they did not mind him doing so, but he couldn't help a niggle of unease. The gnome in the other forest had spoken of the kodami spreading word of black magick. The trees were like an enormous spiderweb across the country, all connected in the peculiar way nature allowed. He and Silas certainly had friends in the Forest of Dean, and the woodlands where he'd rescued the deer, but what if the lure of a golden apple from a fae court saw the loyalty waver? Fuck, they only needed to prick his finger with a pine needle and it may see the Hunt return.

A tawny owl made no attempt to hide itself, hooting at their passing and dragging him from his thoughts. They had little option but to be where they were, and hope it was the right place to be.

'Look, Pitch...how magnificent,' Silas whispered.

At first he thought the ankou referred to the will-o'-the-wisp's antics. The creature was whirling about in tight circles, doing so at a speed that marked its colours upon the air. It was pretty, but what lay beyond was far prettier.

The crowded nature of the forest peeled away, revealing the clearing at its heart, one dominated by a single great oak. It was the most aston-ishingly large tree Pitch had laid eyes on, and green as though it were the middle of spring, not dull December. The clearing was devoid of all other foliage save for a thick covering of moss, strewn with glowing toadstools that cast their glow up against the far-reaching branches of the oak, highlighting it like it were an actor upon the stage. He'd not begrudge Silas his reverence – the ankou was sighing with approval – for it truly was an awesome sight.

This tree was a beauty, dripping with age, as a lady at the ball dripped with jewels. A very rotund lady. Silas could have held hands with his twin, and the girth of the trunk would have hidden them both. The oak was gnarled and twisted in many of its limbs, with a rounded opening down low on the trunk, like a natural entranceway into the tree itself. Not unlike that upon the rowan tree Charlie's bracelet had enabled to grow in the Fulbourn.

Pitch's open-mouthed admiration was replaced by gnawing unhap-piness at the thought of the lad. Of what had become of Charlie...and Edward and Sybilla.

'The prodigal child returns at last.' The voice moved like groaning timbers on a ship.

Silas set Pitch down, gently as he could in a rush, and reached for the bandalore. 'Where is that coming from?'

Pitch eyed the bandalore with fresh dismay. 'Gods, tell me it is not a teratism.' He had assumed them all to screech and holler like Black Annis, but perhaps he'd jumped to conclusions.

'No. It's a leshy. But I don't know anything of them. The bandalore is a precaution.' Silas peered about. 'Do you see where they are? I hear the tune, but I can't fix on it.'

'A leshy?' Pitch said, rather dumbly. 'No, I can't see anyone.'

He knew what one was, of course: a spirit of the forest, of the same ilk as the stag in the Forest of Dean but more likely to be found on the continent in the easternmost forests of Europe. They could, like the stag, assume whatever form they wished so long as it was of the wilderness. From the direction of the voice, he suspected it lurked in the branches of the oak.

'Well, you're staring right at me, in an impolite way, can I add.' The joins in the voice creaked and groaned. 'Can't make myself much larger, though I'm hoping for another foot or two come the next century.'

The will-o'-the-wisp looped around one of the oak's lower branches, holding up Tilly's earring to the thickset limb. There was a substantial burr halfway down the branch, the bulging deformity of wood growth that tainted many a tree, squatting like a giant cowpat upon the bough.

'Yes, yes. I see, Will Scarlet. You're practically sticking it up what would likely be my nose if I bothered to grow such a thing. You've been gone a long while, young one. Now you bring us quite the prize.'

Silas stepped in front of Pitch, a frown knitting his brows. 'Who is there?' His deep timbre was much more pleasant than the leshy's, though Pitch was likely biased. 'Show yourself.'

'There, Silas.' Pitch pointed to the burr where the will-o'-the-wisp fussed. If he squinted just so, he could make out two slashed lines of black: what might pass for eyes in the folds of the burr, which itself was the colour of a mouldy, though ripened, pear. A hint of the leshy's aura surrounded the bulge, evident now that he peered so intently. So dull he'd nearly missed it. But not, Pitch realised with alarm, because of any sickness within the tree. It was *he* who was unwell.

'Well spotted, boy,' the leshy declared as the will-o'-the-wisp, Will Scarlet, took Tilly's earring and darted down to the opening in the trunk, disappearing inside.

'I'd like my earring back, if you don't mind. That does not belong to it.' Pitch took a hesitant step forward. It wouldn't do to cower behind Silas all day. But his show of stamina was ironically brief. One rock forward and he was cursing at his fractured bones, clutching at his knee and, damn it, in need of assistance once more. 'This is intolerable!' he shouted, loud enough he'd probably bring the Herlequin back to the forest on the strength of his voice alone.

'Careful.' Silas was alarmed, too much so to hide it. 'Don't start bleeding again, Pitch, for god's sake.'

'Which god would that be then?' He did not make it easy for Silas to steady him. 'Because I'd say most of them are getting a right fucking laugh out of all this.'

'Gracious heavens,' the leshy tutted. 'What a fuss. We've heard you were cantankerous, daemon, if that's what you are, but no need for the private show.'

Pitch glared up at the burr. 'What did you just say?'

'That you are a cantankerous, impolite specimen?'

Silas let out a low groan. 'Pitch, don't let him upset –'

'You said, "if that's what you are." Do I not seem daemonic to you?'

The oak's branches swayed, despite there being no hint of the blustering winds that had followed them on much of the journey.

'You are strangely hued. I'll not deny it. And far less brilliant than I imagined, for all the tales.'

'The tales?' Silas interrupted before Pitch could ask about his lack of brilliance. 'You know who we are?'

There was a pause. And when next there was a voice, it was certainly not the leshy's groaning tones.

'Saviours of the Forest of Dean.' The sound brought to mind summer days, warmth, and open skies. It bore a feminine lilt, though Pitch knew more than one man capable of such a lovely whisper. 'Deliverers of the Fulbourn.'

Pleasant or not, Silas swore and Pitch jumped, nerves on a knife edge.

'Damn it. Show yourself at once,' Silas demanded. 'I've had quite enough of being sprung upon.'

'Listen here, young chap.' The leshy huffed, its annoyance rustling leaves. 'You'll not speak to Robin that way.'

'It's all right, Major. I should have announced myself better.'

They, Robin presumably, stepped from the opening in the oak's broad trunk, long slender legs unfolding in a languid way. They appeared womanly, at least in the way a purebred may define such things, with most of the curves and bulges expected of such a creature. But, just as it was for Pitch himself, there was a blurring of the lines so many sought to draw between man and woman. Robin bowed their head and leaned forward to accommodate the narrow opening. Flaxen hair, long to their narrow waist, shifted around them like the reed the creature so resembled. They were thin to the point that it stole a little from their beauty. But there was so much beauty to be had that it was quickly overcome. Flower petals, barége sheer and a touch creamier than the white of snow, clung to their flat chest and around their jutting hips, caught in an endless cycle of fluttering away from their body and regenerating once more. Revealing, in rotation, the absence of breasts but so too the absence of a shaft.

At a guess Pitch would assume them fae, but he had to search hard for sign of the creature's aura with his weakened sight, and Silas was ahead of him by a heartbeat.

'A hamadryad...fae of the trees.' He sounded as awestruck as he'd been on seeing the oak. 'Pitch, it is one of Tilly's kind.'

Not exactly. Hamadryad were life-bound to one tree, the oak, Pitch would assume. Which accounted for its immense growth. Tilly, in contrast, was a freer spirit, able to align herself with any she chose.

Robin watched them through eyes not rounded but scalloped at their edges, with irises the yellow of a daisy's centre. The hamadryad was not much taller than the changeling, but by assumed appearance, Pitch decided they must be older.

'Tilly?' Their question lifted like birdsong. 'That is what they have called my kindred? How very beautiful.'

'Kindred?' Silas marvelled. 'You are related to the little changeling?'

'Your kind might call us sisters.' Robin inclined their head, and a cascade of tiny petals fell, mimicking the snow, of which there was no evidence here in the heart of the forest. 'You must be the one she names and loves as Sy. Welcome, Mr Mercer.'

Silas of course took the endearment with all his usual restraint in such matters, blushing and looking inordinately pleased.

Pitch found it his turn to be observed.

The dryad cocked their head. 'A creature of sad but incredible beauty. You can be no other than her fire man.'

Pitch let out a shuddered breath.

Robin's wheat-gold hair was lively, as though it carried its own breeze. A shift at their ear revealed Tilly's earring had found a new home.

Silas touched his shoulder, his face bright with what they both understood. They were among friends.

'Doesn't seem much of the fire about him. Strangest aura I've seen in a while.' The leshy shook a branch, the way an indignant lady might flick her fan.

'And that's just as well.' Robin's melodious voice helped the daemon forget how damned cold he was. 'You wouldn't like him burning down Sherwood now, would you, Major? Now come, gentlemen, come and rest yourselves. We'll see if we can't make you more comfortable on that foot, Mr Astaroth.'

'Pitch.'

'Pitch.' They smiled. Their teeth were nearly the same daisy yellow as their eyes, not altogether pleasant, but that glint, that vibrant hint of life...he knew it so well. He was taken aback by how much it pained him to be reminded of the changeling. 'You've had a trying time of it and both look as though the very weight of the British Isles is upon you.' Will Scarlet chittered in the fae's ear. They nodded. 'Wonderful idea, Scar. Would anyone like some dewberry mead?'

'Yes, please.' Silas, polite and suitably restrained.

Pitch had no time for such things. 'Oh fuck, yes.'

CHAPTER 22

Dewberry mead, as it turned out, was delicious. Silas drained his third cup of the sweet liquid, which was not so gluttonous as it seemed, for the cups themselves were hollowed-out acorns. Bigger acorns than he was familiar with, yes, but still not so large as a glass of brandy.

He sat with his back against the oak, a surprisingly comfortable position, considering the hardness of the wood. Perhaps that was more to do with the mead, and the prince who rested with him.

Pitch sat propped between his legs, using Silas's raised knees like the rests on an armchair. A trio of meliad nymphs strummed on tiny harps, woven from grass and strung with spiderweb. The toadstools pulsed their light slowly, in a pretty mimic of candlelight, while peri and brownies and a gnome or two danced on the thick moss of the clearing and enjoyed the mead with impressive vigour.

Silas ran his fingertips up and down the length of Pitch's arm. They had removed their coats, dressed now in only shirts and trousers, and the corset for the prince of course, but neither were the colder for undressing. Pitch's ankle had been packed in fresh soil and wrapped in layering that looked and glistened like morning dew. He'd not made a fuss. In fact his sigh at receiving the compress had been nearly sinful. Silas had been relieved to see that the gashes had all knit firmly, with no chance of a bleed from there. Now they just waited on the bones beneath to heal.

The oak was warm, as though it stood in the summer sun. The formidable branches fanned out and cascaded down to umbrella the entire clearing in their embrace.

'Have you ever seen such a sight?' Silas sighed.

'Hmm?'

Silas tilted his head as he brushed back Pitch's hair. 'Were you sleeping? I'm sorry to wake you.'

'I am exhausted, but I don't want to sleep, not yet.' He traced his finger down Silas's shin, laughing when it caused a shiver. 'Do you think anyone would notice if we never left this forest? Just stayed here, drunk on dewberry mead?'

Of course they both knew the answer, but Silas shook his head. 'Absolutely not. We'd need a cottage though, don't you think? Where should we build it?'

Pitch lifted a finger, pointing towards a place across the clearing where ferns grew in great numbers, fronds swaying with all the activity. Silas hadn't seen such a gathering of folk since the Marquess of Ailsa's fateful ball. He hurried his thoughts on, not wishing to be reminded of the tsukumogami who had watched there, nor Ronin with all his broken pieces.

'Just over there would be perfect, don't you think?' Pitch said, a tender slur to his words. 'But you shall need to do all the building. I'm far too delicate for such things now. I shall supervise.'

'I'm sure you shall, very thoroughly.'

'I warn you, I'll insist my carpenter be shirtless.'

'Is that right?'

'Perhaps entirely naked. So I can ensure you have not stolen any of my tools, and admire your arse when you bend.'

Silas took a moment to gather himself. 'A harsh taskmaster indeed.'

'Well, I'm not averse to being told what to do in return.' The daemon lifted his chin, drawing his head back to look up at Silas. 'I can be a very good boy, can I not?'

His lips glistened with the honey-rich mead, and the toadstools' light did wonders against verdant eyes. Silas was kissing him before the daemon could bat his lashes again. Slowly, as though they had all the time they could wish for. He ran his fingers over Pitch's belly, where the stiffness of the corset sat above a hardness of an entirely different kind. He traced a path all the way up to Pitch's throat, relishing the soft moan his touch drew.

'You can be...' Silas was hoarse with want. 'A very good boy indeed.'

They played a game of tag with their tongues, being foolish about it, laughing against each other's mouths when one managed to dig their teeth into the other's lip.

Oh, they were drunk. No doubt of it. And it was bloody fantastic.

'Decent mead, isn't it?'

Robin's question did not cause them to break apart in a hurry. Silas kept his lips pressed to Pitch's for another heartbeat before he looked up. The prince's sigh was indecent.

'Oh, it is truly divine.' Silas knew his smile all crooked, his eyes no doubt sparkling with the effects of the drink. He was painfully hard in his trousers. 'Sorry, I fear I am quite drunk.'

'Why do you fear it?'

He gathered up his flighty thoughts. 'You understand our circumstance. This is hardly the time for levity.'

'I think rather the opposite is true. You are much in need of rest and enjoyment.' Robin smiled their yellow smile. They certainly had the same childish happiness about them as Tilly did.

Silas sobered. 'You knew much about us...through the jewellery, I presume.' Fine strands of gold drifted as the dryad nodded, offering another glimpse of the earring, which adorned their left ear. 'Does it enable you to speak with Tilly directly? Do you know how she and her mothers fare?'

A waver moved through the happiness. 'No. I'm afraid not, on both counts. The earring is more like...' They searched for the word. 'A decree, her instruction. The flower embedded is her insignia.'

Pitch cupped his hand to the back of Silas's neck, playing with his hair. 'Decree?' His laughter was derisive. 'You make her sound like royalty.'

'Well, I suppose we are worth as much as a prince or princess, when it comes to our value in court play. The Erlking certainly prizes us.'

Pitch abandoned Silas's curls and braced himself against his knees so he could shift more upright. The movement was no help at all against Silas's groin.

'He prizes you? How so?'

'The Wild Hunt that searches for you?' Robin said. 'It last rode out to retrieve the likes of me, and my kindred. The UnSeelie Court does not grow as Lokke pleases. His riders were sent to retrieve the dryads, capture as many as they could steal and make slaves of them so he'd have gardens to boast over and his court could flourish. Their hunts were halted by the Order, but not before dozens of my kindred were taken. With the way Lokke works them, they do not last long.'

Silas winced. 'That is why Tilly was hidden with the purebreds?'

'When she was newborn.' Robin nodded, a tiny moth darting from their ear. 'The UnSeelie Court think your Tilly dead.'

'She very nearly was,' Pitch yawned. 'If she'd caused me to step on one more brooch, I'd have sent her to her maker.'

'Stop, that's an awful thing to say,' Silas chided gently, but his grin was wide.

'I can only be honest.' Pitch nestled more deeply against Silas, rubbing his finger over a mark on his trouser leg. 'So the Hunt has not bothered you for some time, it seems?'

A nod of Robin's head sent a fresh shower of petals falling. 'We are fortunate Lokke's interest in finding us waned, some time ago. Another plot must have occupied his interest.'

Pitch glanced up at Silas, and he was sure the daemon's thoughts followed his own: the Erlking was busy with sorcerers instead, and angels.

'Lokke is the Erlking's true name?' Silas asked.

'It is. He was no more than the court jester once upon a time, until his head filled with plans of grandeur.'

'And then he murdered and connived his way to the UnSeelie throne,' the Major grumbled, the burr now a bulge halfway down the trunk, nearer to them so he might be heard. 'Deception, conniving, and false promises are his forte, and they got him to where he is. His court is full of the same. The more trouble that elf can cause, the happier he is.'

The harps lifted with a more jovial tune, a hearty polka-inspired piece.

'What's he want with you two, then? What do they all want, for that matter?'

'Major.' Robin settled a fine-boned hand upon the trunk. 'There now. Even if they would tell us, they should not do so. Knowledge is a double-edged sword. We willingly play our part in sheltering these gentlemen, but we'll not deepen our inclusion in the troubles of the world any further. What we don't know is less likely to harm us.'

'If only that were true,' Pitch said, quietly, as though he did not intend to be heard at all.

The burr puffed up and deflated, moving like a puce-coloured chest. 'Then best they are retrieved soon. Lokke is no fool, nor are the fresh witches who run about, making a foul mess of the balance of things. That mare of yours had a fine plan, but it may not serve us long. I'll not see you end up in that putrid court, Robin. You know he still covets you.'

The dryad glanced at Silas and must have seen his consternation, for they clapped their hands and declared, 'More mead, and we have some honeysuckle bread almost done.'

Pitch went limp in his arms. 'Truly? I've not tasted that in ages.'

'You're hungry?' Silas asked, pleased.

'For honeysuckle bread, always.'

A gnome, a chap who could have been Gilmore's twin, poked his head through the soil right beside Silas's foot. 'The leg. Good?' He was prone to very brief sentences and had said barely more than three words as he coated Pitch's ankle in mud earlier.

'Yes, thank you.'

'Snot gone?'

'I'm not sneezing anymore, if that is what you are asking.'

'You do seem better,' Silas admitted.

'Far better than the Valkyrie managed.' Pitch held his acorn upside down, letting the last drop of mead fall to his tongue. 'I barely feel a thing, though that is perhaps the liquor.'

'Why is it that Sybilla could not help you?' Silas frowned at the lounging prince. His injured foot was bare, but on either side of the bandaging, his skin was its usual alabaster, pink beneath the nails, the warmth of the clearing keeping him comfortable.

'Because I would not let her, and threatened to hurl myself under the carriage if she told you.'

Silas frowned at the gold-strewn strands atop Pitch's head. 'Why would you not wish to be healed? You left yourself in pain?'

'We are hardly strange bedfellows, pain and I.' He ran his hands along the place on Silas's leg he knew to be ticklish. A distraction that would not work this time.

'Pitch, there was no need for you to –'

'There was. I needed very much to learn how disabled I am. How long it would take for such a wound to heal. I needed to know if I was capable of healing on my own. Perhaps if you'd all been more forthcoming about your blood theory, I'd have taken a few extra precautions.'

'Are you lying to me now when you say you are feeling better?' Silas demanded, some of his intoxicated good humour leaving him.

Pitch sat up, and turned whilst he shifted onto his knees, moving in so close that his thighs brushed at the hardness still raging between Silas's legs. 'Oh my.' He cupped Silas's cheeks with his hands. 'You sound as though you wish to slap me, yet you feel as though you have other things in mind. The two need not be distant cousins.'

Silas made a play at being stern, but truly who had a hope when faced with the likes of the daemon? 'Answer my question.'

'What shall I get as a reward if I do so?' Pitch kissed the tip of Silas's nose, his breath rich with the mead, his customary bittersweetness hinted at beneath.

'My thanks.' Silas swallowed, his mind a merry-go-round of other ideas.

'Lovely, but I think you have better prizes to offer.' Another kiss, this one to the top of Silas's cheeks, Pitch's face so close that their lashes grazed.

Silas's moan had a life of its own. 'Stop, we are not alone enough for this.'

'I'll darn well say.' The oak downed a few leaves over them in place of an icy-cold bucket of water. 'There are young-uns here too, you know. Bit too early for them to lay eyes on such things.'

Pitch scoffed. 'As though they have not seen the animals rutting in the woods. We would be far lovelier to watch.'

Silas was not so horrified by the idea as he would have been were he sober.

There was a chuckle from the burr. 'As all creatures who fornicate seem to think, but it's not pretty to see, no matter how lovely you are.'

And with his gentle insult delivered, the Major took himself away, the burr slinking along the trunk like an enormous squirrel beneath the bark, disappearing into the foliage higher up.

Pitch planted his hands on Silas's raised knees and used them to lever himself to his feet.

'Where are you going?'

The prince held out his hand. 'Showing you how much better I feel. Dance with me.'

Silas's mood lightened. He took Pitch's hand but mostly used the tree to pull himself to standing. 'You do recall how terrible I am?'

'My toes shall never forget.'

The brownies went a little mad with excitement at seeing them move into the centre of the clearing. The hairy folk were not much bigger than the peri they danced with, which meant most of the naturals on the makeshift dance floor barely came halfway up Silas's shin. The peri tinkled like silver bells as everyone shifted to accommodate the new arrivals. Robin stood off to one side, the dryad moving to a tune known only to them, slightly out of step with what was played. A contentment hung about the creature that was contagious.

'I hope I don't tread on someone.'

'I shall be able to help with that.' Pitch removed his remaining boot, the sock too, and promptly stepped one foot onto each of Silas's.

'What is this?'

'That gnome is glaring daggers at me. He thinks it too soon for my ankle, so this shall appease him. I will be a passenger only.'

The nymphs must have recognised Silas's hesitancy, for they adjusted their tune to a much slower waltz style. Silas settled one hand across Pitch's back, offered the other to the prince, who promptly took it, and they began to sway. He carried Pitch's weight, keeping watch for sign of any upset, but the daemon was, so far as he could be, at peace. The gentle to and fro continued, no fancy steps or twirls, a simplicity Silas thought would garner rebuke. Instead, Pitch rested his head against Silas's shoulder, humming along softly to the music. At times he raised his chin to seek out Silas's lips, and over the course of a dance or two, his hand found its way down to rest upon Silas's arse.

Later, much later, when the nymphs laid down their harps and the brownies and peri bade their adieus and tinkled off into the forest, Robin led them to the edge of the clearing where a patch of the dewberries grew. They touched their hand to the shrub, and the foliage parted low and wide, revealing a hidden alcove inside. Large enough for a daemon and ankou to lie.

They had to crawl on hands and knees through the parting, but not a single thorn scratched them nor prickle bothered as Pitch went ahead first to find his place. Silas soon settled beside him upon a layering of moss that would rival the most sublime mattress. The opening in the brambles closed over, giving them privacy.

There was not much space to be had, which was fine because they did not wish for distance. With the late hour, night now well and truly fallen, darkness should have been heavy in their cocoon, but the toadstools outside threw just enough light to bathe them in a grass-green haze. They grinned at each other, Pitch's knees against the ankou's thighs and his hands already beneath his shirt. Hidden and alone, their veins humming with mead, and their cocks twin swords of want, they sucked on stifled laughter and one another. Silas did not take Pitch fully, they were enjoying fumbling about with each other too much in the cramped space, and remained mostly clothed. Fingers tunnelling beneath trousers and drawers, flirting with the lace on Pitch's corset and teasing at the hooks, undoing just one at the bottom, searching for hidden delights.

To outsiders it must have appeared as if wild pheasants were caught in the shrub, with Silas too broad to be remotely clandestine in the space. His hair snagged in the spindly fingers of the brambles when he sat up to shift himself so he could sink between Pitch's legs and take the daemon in his mouth. His shoulder nudged at the shelter again when Pitch had Silas roll onto his back so he could return the favour. And what a return it was.

To watch the prince's lips stretch around his shaft, to feel its tip strike the back of Pitch's throat and hear his fervour as he sucked and teased, made a man's eyes roll and his breath stutter. Much to Silas's chagrin, he was powerless to hold out too long, and Pitch was soon raising his head, wiping at his lips.

They both needed time to catch their breath after that, but the daemon needed far less.

'Do the Crimson Bow, will you?' It was what Pitch had taken to calling it when Silas held them both in his grasp at once, his broad hand uniting their pricks as though they were one engorged member.

Silas still panted, and his skin was sensitive to the touch, but he did not wait too long to oblige the prince his fancy. He sat up, his head just shy of the overhead canopy. Pitch spread his legs, settling them either side of Silas's hips, shuffling in so he was close enough for Silas to hold their cocks together. There was a certain awkwardness to the position, but the moment Silas began to slip his fingers up and down their differing lengths, rubbing them in unison, neither of them cared a damn about much else at all.

Pitch dug his forehead into Silas's shoulder, moaning his pleasure there. The rhythm took up speed, and as their tips dampened, the prince sat up, spine stiffening as though the corset covered him from neck to arse.

'I'm close,' he gasped. He threw up his hand, grabbing at the tangle of branches overhead. Loosening a shower of dewberries, and laughing so hard Silas nearly lost his grip. 'Don't stop...don't stop.' The laughter morphed into a cry. 'Oh, fuck..gods. I'm coming. The moss...'

Silas grabbed for the pulled tufts they'd placed at the ready, and only just managed to cover their cock heads in time. Pitch grunted and arched and pulsed, and as much as Silas desired to wait and watch, see every grimace and hear every whimper, the daemon's release tipped him over his own burning edge.

He exhaled, a noise coming from him that lay between groan and shivered cry. Pitch's body still twitched from his own pleasure, but his gaze never left Silas as they rode out his climax together. Pitch covered his hand, murmuring filthy words of encouragement as Silas came, holding on as heat and seed shot forth, soaking the moss till it was saturated.

They returned to the world in slow, rocking measure. Pitch's smile could have swung the pope towards debauchery.

'Do you think the forest will mind what we did with her groundcover?'

Silas chuckled. 'I truly hope not. I'd hate to think how she might show her disapproval. But it worked, mostly.'

He tossed the punished moss away. His hands were only a little sticky, and their clothes were spared as they'd intended.

'I'll make it clear it was your idea if we are in any trouble.'

Pitch cleared away fallen dewberries before he flopped down onto his back, tucking himself away and undoing another clasp on the corset. He declared himself too tired to take it off entirely when Silas made the suggestion.

'It doesn't bother me.' Pitch yawned. 'And it's pretty. Those brownies are likely to steal it. Is it bothering you?'

'Not at all.' It was so very pretty indeed.

Lying down on his side, Silas waited while the prince nestled in and found where he was most comfortable: his back to Silas's belly, his arse just shy of where Silas's balls ached happily. Wrapping an arm around the daemon, he bade the prince a drowsy good night. Pitch slept before Silas, who stayed awake until he was sure his lover slept peacefully.

Silas had no idea what time it was when he woke with an urgent need to relieve himself. He'd been deeply asleep, no dreams to disturb him. He gingerly, and regretfully, disentangled himself from Pitch, who had turned around at some point and now had his face pressed up against Silas's chest.

'Where are you going?' he mumbled, rolling onto his back, eyes still closed.

'Nature calls.'

'What does it say?' Pitch muttered, screwing up his frankly adorable nose.

'That I must pee.' Silas leaned over, delivering a parting kiss. 'I'll be back in a moment.'

'I know you will.'

Silas paused, his chest tight. Finally, the prince realised; Silas was true to his word.

The daemon curled himself into a ball. Silas was on hands and knees readying to leave when Pitch spoke again.

'I fed from you...just a little...' He was mumbling, as though this were dream speech, but Silas heard every word crystalline clear. 'I didn't take much, Sickle. I hope you don't mind.'

Silas had to swallow hard before he could answer. 'I shall never mind. It is yours to take.'

He waved a trembling hand at the brambles, and they parted to allow him to crawl free. The sooner this was done, the sooner he could return. He got to his feet with a sigh and stretch. There were thin hints that morning was breaking. The air was tinged with a blue-grey light, the toadstools standing dull and snuffed of their glow.

He found his coat and Pitch's, neatly folded side by side at the entrance to the tiny alcove. They'd been discarded beneath the oak when Silas had last seen them. He hoped Robin had not heard anything too untoward when delivering them.

Pleasantly warm as he was, and not intending to be long, Silas left his coat where it was, with the bandalore tucked in its favoured pocket. Boots on, Silas moved across the clearing.

There was no sign of the dryad, but the burr was there, one black slit marginally wider than the other to watch him.

'Morning, Mr Mercer.' The Major had himself out on one of the lower branches whose length reached all the way to the perimeter of the clearing. 'I should have thought you'd need far more sleep after all your activity.'

Silas's face warmed. 'Morning, Major. I need to step out.' He gestured vaguely at his belly. 'Beyond the clearing I presume?'

'Certainly.' The tree sounded mildly affronted. 'But not too far, mind. Sherwood is a large forest and good at getting people lost in her, which suits us fine for the most part.'

'I understand. Thank you.'

'He knows you're gone? Won't wake up and try to burn us all down, will he?'

'No.' Silas wished he could have found more amusement in the assumption. 'He will not. I won't be long. Is Will Scarlet about? I don't recall seeing much of them last night, and I haven't thanked them properly.'

The burr made a movement that might have been a nod toward the oak's entranceway. 'Sleeping.'

Silas thanked him again and stepped beyond the clearing. He was not ready for the bracing chill that came. 'Christ almighty.' He considered retrieving his coat after all, but this was to be a short journey. He'd be done in the time it would take to go back for the coat.

Silas carried on.

CHAPTER 23

When Silas thought himself at a discreet-enough distance, he answered nature's call, sighing with the relief. Done, he stretched his arms overhead, trying to work out the kinks formed after a night spent without a pillow beneath his head. Several satisfying cracks later, he turned to head back to the clearing. A faint trickling of water caught his attention. A stream or brook not too far off. A place to splash his face and wash his hands of what the moss had failed to remove of last night's exertions.

That was memory enough to warm a man through to the core. With a covetous grin, Silas traipsed further out into the forest, where slivers of faint morning light were having much more luck with pushing through the canopy. It struck him, only then, that they'd not heard the grumble of a storm in quite some time. The Herlequin, it seemed, had taken his unsteady weather with him. Good riddance to both.

Snow lay in patches over the ground, thin layers nothing like the depths that Hastings had had to deal with when she carried them to safety. His uplifted mood wavered at the thought of Sybilla's horse. How long should they wait here for her return? Not that they had any other choice right now. He must speak with Robin about horses when the dryad woke. He'd feel a hell of a lot better knowing they could at least *try* to race off if an attack came.

It did not take him long to happen upon the water. A spring bubbled up through lichen-covered rocks and ran away in a narrow and very shallow brook that serpentined through clusters of dogwood, whose red new-growth shoots provided rare splashes of colour in the December landscape. The splay of several elder trees, which looked suspiciously purposely planted in a rough circle, grew amidst the dogwood. With superstition decreeing that elder kept the devil away, Silas could only guess what rituals may have gone on between the boughs.

He rested a knee upon one of the rocks and splashed the cold water against his face.

'Shit,' he hissed, a shiver running the length of his body with the slap of the icy liquid. But gracious, it was refreshing. The water was sparkling clean, unlike that of the pond he'd dunked himself into.

To think that time with the kappas was barely a day ago. It felt as though they'd all lived a dozen lifetimes since.

He shook off his hands and was playing with lewd thoughts of returning to the prince and making them dirty once more when several delightful little asrai made themselves known, leaping like translucent trout from the shallows of the brook to greet him. Young ones, whose giggles were like raindrops on a tin roof, trying to outdo one another with leaps and twirls and backflips. Their orbs of fluid swirled happily when he congratulated them on their acrobatics.

Was I the best, ankou? said one, who truly was not. Their twirls had showered Silas with a spray of unwelcome iciness. But he gave a non-committal nod and shake of his head.

'It is so hard to choose, really. You are all very impressive.'

The asrai insisted on him judging a race next, pleading with him in their watery tones. With a glance around at the lightening forest, Silas agreed. He'd not been gone long, and Pitch needed rest not arousal, so it was best Silas gave himself a moment to clear his head. Sherwood had proved herself a safe haven. So long as Silas kept near the clearing, a little spectator sport sounded very amusing. Besides, he knew it was asrai who had led Pitch to him at the greensward. He owed them this small consideration.

'Just quickly then, and not too far.'

The asrai splashed themselves up and down, over and over with such fervour that Silas had to take a step back to avoid getting any damper. Finally they settled and sat themselves atop the water, like large marbles of clear crystal. There was some semblance of a lineup, then the race was on.

Silas followed after the handful of asrai, who rolled themselves along the water's surface and down the brook where it meandered through the elders and out to where more dogwood and buckthorn stood sentinel along the waterway. He jogged to keep up and actually got quite absorbed in the competition. It was hard-fought between two particular asrai, the rest trailing out behind in varying degrees of distance, including the poor inept twirler, who was last of all.

'Come on then.' He slowed to give encouragement. 'You're not out of the race just yet.'

Which was a lie, for there was no way this poor thing was going to catch their faster brethren, who had now moved around a slight bend and out of sight. By the time Silas and the dejected asrai found them, they had moved on to another game, which involved diving for minnows.

Silas bade them farewell and turned about.

The very faint cry of a child reached him, barely caught over the boisterous splashing. He stepped away from the brook, straining to hear.

There. Again. A little one calling for their mother. At once Silas strode towards the sound, horrified at the thought of a youngster lost in these woods. What if their family had stopped to take shelter from the snowstorm? An unnatural storm created in part because of him. It was far too cold for a babe to be wandering about. The chill would claim them quickly. Silas broke into a run, homing in on the sound, which grew louder as he approached.

'Mumma? Where are you?' Their voice wobbled and hiccoughed with the strain of tears and distress.

Silas hurried, pushing his way through the undergrowth, which seemed determined to make the way a challenge. 'Hello?' he called. 'Hello there, it's all right. Just stay where you are. I'm coming.'

He was puffing by the time he dragged himself clear of a bramble that had lain in wait beneath a less thorny dogwood. His jerked his shirt arm free, scowling at the tiny tear left behind. A good thing he'd not worn his coat, then.

A wet and violent sniff announced the youngster. There was no telling if they were a boy or girl, for a bonnet covered their hair, and in the trend of the very young, the child wore a dress. This child was young indeed, more so than Tilly, he'd guess. They wore no coat, only a rather bedraggled pale yellow slip, and one of their slippers was missing, the other with notable holes near the little toe. Their tiny toes were a worrying shade of blue.

'Are you all right?' Silas asked.

They stared at him with bugged eyes, red with crying, their nose twin rivers of mucus, and took hurried steps away when he approached.

'It's all right, I won't hurt you.'

He didn't blame the little thing for disbelieving that. He dropped to his knees to make himself, if only mildly, less imposing.

The child dashed off, sobbing and calling once again for its mother.

'Shit.'

He followed suit, distantly aware he was fast losing track of his direction, but with flashes of the yellow slip not far ahead, he was certain he could catch the little runaway before long. He was almost proved terribly wrong a moment later, losing sight of the child when they darted around a big ash. By the time Silas reached it, crunching through a patch of snow, there was no sign of the lost one. But something had disturbed the first of the morning's twittering birds, for they fell abruptly silent.

Likely that something was him, crashing about in the forest as he was. 'Are you there? I truly mean no harm. Just let me catch you.' Christ, what a preposterous thing to say.

A shadow shifted in the treetops: the spread of wings as a bird alighted from a branch. He glanced up but caught only the darkness of a swift-moving shadow.

Silas bit at his lip as he surveyed his surrounds. He was in an endless tangle of trees and shrubs with narrow pathways between, trails best for deer and creatures far smaller than he. Whichever direction he turned, the snow-dusted ways each looked the same.

The Major had said it...Sherwood enjoyed getting people lost in her...and Silas had not minded the leshy well enough.

A quiet whimper brought him away from his thoughts.

There at the base of a dead birch, the child huddled with knees cradled to their chest, dirty cheeks marred with pale lines of tears.

'There, there.' Silas advanced slowly. 'Let's find your parents, shall we?'

The child lowered their head and pressed their forehead against their knees. There were twigs caught at the back of the bonnet, a white fabric once but dirt-stained now. Silas dropped into a crouch, keeping a cautious distance, not wishing another chase through the woods. It was very quiet where they were, and it bothered him. Almost as much as the bird he'd glimpsed. It'd been a decent size and very dark.

His throat worked as he tried to keep the fear down.

Not every single raven in the British Isles was the Morrigan's servant. If it truly was a raven he'd seen, though it could well have been his wild imagination taunting him. He touched at his pocket, looking for the reassuring bulk of the bandalore.

'Christ,' he said beneath his breath. So much for a quick jaunt into the woods. Would he never learn to carry the scythe at all bloody times? But he did not need it to hear the melodies, and there was no song of the naturals here. Not for the child, nor for the bird that had spied on him from the treetops. 'Come now. We really must go, little one.'

He'd have to take the child with him back to the clearing. Robin and the Major could decide what to do with them. Silas could barely stifle his impatience to return to Pitch. 'Give me your hand. You must come with me.'

The time for coaxing had passed. Silas leaned down, ready to pick them up whether they cared for it or not. He had one hand upon their slender shoulder when they looked up. They curled a lipless mouth into an ornery smile, revealing gums crowded with jagged teeth.

The low, dreadful caw of a raven came from the trees.

Silas froze.

And in that finite pause, the harpy's melody, loathsome and rough as it was, sang beneath whatever illusion fought to keep it hidden.

They lunged, teeth flashing, eyes sagging into that horrid melted appearance the unfortunate harpies were graced with. Silas threw himself backwards, narrowly managing to avoid the first attack.

There was another straight after, the harpy's speed catching him off guard. They drove at him, releasing their soot-black wings, shifting their feet from a child's to a monster's in a heartbeat. Now instead of a slippered foot, it was a scaled leg with dangerously pointed claws that aimed at him, searching for where to impale him. Silas dropped onto his side, executing a quick roll to move himself out of reach. He needed to get back on his feet, but the forest was not favouring him. Silas gasped as his panicked roll landed him up against the trunk of a tree, right against his ribs, winding him.

A claw raked his back. His shirt tore as easily as his skin, but the blow was not terribly deep. Not yet. Shallow luck came his way, for the harpy was too fevered, too eager to land blows, and their strike set them off-balance. Their wings caught at the shrubbery. Silas scrambled clear on hands and knees, seeking desperately the best way to go. But it was forest, forest, and more forest around him. His hesitation was costly.

The harpy landed on his back, flattening him to the ground. The creature bit down on his shoulder, driving its numerous pointed teeth through his skin.

Silas roared his hurt and fury to the trees, reaching back to try to catch ahold of the creature who gnawed on him. The wretch was slippery, their wing tips equally as sharp as their teeth, and Silas's arms were soon cut and bloodied with trying to dislodge his passenger.

He was so busy seeking not to be eaten by a foul-smelling child-monster that the rumble beneath him nearly slipped his notice.

The disordered drumbeat of many hooves causing the earth to shudder.

'Fuck...fuck.' Silas coughed, tasting warmth and copper.

He forced himself upright and at last snagged ahold of a coarse leg, the scales roughing his palms like gravel. Silas gritted his teeth and hauled against the struggling creature. The harpy was ripped from its perch upon his back. Silas got his other hand upon that same leg and twisted his shoulders, gathering momentum. The harpy screeched. Silas threw the creature against the birch, where it had huddled as a lost child to deceive him.

With the weight of Silas's rage behind it, the blow was tremendous. The harpy's cry broke along with its back. Silas heard the snap as body met dense wood. The creature gurgled where it lay, wings twitching, dark drooping eyes full of hatred.

Silas was on his feet just a moment when a fresh assault began. The raven he'd spied earlier returned, coming in like a furious shadow, flapping and scratching and darting too swiftly for him to catch. The bird was more annoying than dangerous. Silas winced at catches of claw against his cheek, cursing the creature for its bursts of speed that left him lunging at thin air. The trembling beneath his feet steadily intensified.

He should be running, not swatting at the bird like it were a giant wasp. But run where? He would not go back to the clearing. Not if there were any chance that place remained the haven it had seemed. It was he who had wandered too far.

He who had chased after a goddamned illusion.

Silas punched at the air, and his fist met a low-hanging branch, the sudden stop reverberating up his arm. 'Shit, idiot!' he shouted at himself.

The clatter of riders was unmistakable now and seemed to come from all directions at once. There was no one way he could be certain of to run. Even if the bloody raven had backed off long enough for him to see clearly. So Silas chose randomly and sent a hurried, brusque prayer to the goddess to help him choose wisely.

He covered his head and ran, past the dead birch, towards what he hoped was the furthest place from the clearing. He kept his eyes to the ground that shook beneath him, ignoring the swoops of the bird taunting him. He knew it a fruitless dash before it had begun. But he'd not stand there for the Wild Hunt to find him. Let them chase him down. He'd not go to his knees with a raven pecking at his scalp.

Silas ran, and Sherwood Forest shook herself apart.

Good god it sounded as though all the trees were toppling around him. And then it struck him. Not the raven. But the song of the Wild Hunt itself.

A shrill, discordant wreck of melodies, all clambering over the top of a central, sonorous, contralto note. One so deep it alone could be responsible for the rumble of the earth.

Silas threw his hands to his ears, seeking to halt the dreadful symphony. But the orchestra sat in his head; there was no escape. Silas ran on, lungs aching, ears bleeding, heart sinking. The few trees whose leaves still clung to them let them fall now, the chaos that closed in on Silas shaking them free.

He recognised one of the melodies at precisely the moment its owner found him.

The Dullahan's whip came from behind, blazing a white line at his side, reaching ahead before curling back to wrap bony joints around his arms and pin them to his sides. The vise-hold cut off his cry, and a hard jerk pulled him off his feet. Silas hit the ground, dirt filling his scream-widened mouth. The Dullahan wrenched on the whip, digging bone into soft flesh and flipping Silas onto his back. He'd not stay there. Bones be damned, he'd not lie there to be trampled.

Silas rolled onto his side, grunting as he managed to get onto his knees.

The Wild Hunt drew in from all directions, an abundance of cloaked riders. They were hidden in their folds but must have been slender of form, for even with the layering, they did not seem so substantial. Ravens flew among them, and several perched upon the haunches of the horses, the equines foaming at the mouth and squealing with displeasure when commanded to halt. The headless horseman was nearest to Silas, holding his whip lightly as though assuming him not foolish enough to attempt an escape.

Silas dragged in rough breaths, desperate to ease the pressure of the bones.

The Dullahan's shoulders shifted beneath his grey cloak in the manner of someone glancing in another direction. Silas caught a movement off to his right: the shuffle and rearrangement of the riders assembled there, reining their horses aside – stepping back, out of the way of the one who moved through their ranks.

At first he mistook the approaching rider for a shadow cast by one of the monolithic trees, an aged elm shifting in the breeze. But it was no tree, and there was no wind besides. The horse moved closer, a massive black shire with stark white hooves as large as Silas's head. This animal would have put Lalassu in its shadow, large as she was, but there could be no lesser mount for the brutish rider being carried.

The Herlequin's horse sank hooves deep into the undergrowth, drawing their master near. There was no naming melody to announce them.

There was something else.

Silas watched, pulse rabid, mouth so dry he could barely move his tongue. His blood was thick beneath his skin, burning as though his heart pumped fire.

A strange sound escaped him. Recognition a mighty blow.

The Wild Hunt's leader was Nephilim.

CHAPTER 24

Pitch awoke with a jolt. The rude awakening tore him from a rare, pleasant dream. He reached out, eyes still shut fast, and patted the ground, searching for the body that should be warming him. He found only moss, cool moss at that, instead of the brick wall of flesh and bone expected. He opened his eyes and sat up, head throbbing at the sudden movement. Will Scarlet dashed up into the air, brightening the confines of the shelter with its rainbow colours.

'Were you sleeping on me?' He brushed at his shoulder, where he was quite certain it had been perched. 'You damned well were, weren't you?'

The will-o'-the-wisp had the gall to smile at him, revealing tiny teeth the colour of plums. But it would certainly not receive a smile in return. Pitch's stomach was not settled, and he rubbed at it absently.

'Where is he?'

Will Scarlet shrugged, tittered. It tilted its head, hands in prayer and touching at its temple. The damn thing was telling him it had been asleep too.

How many blasted times this week had Pitch woken alone now? He'd never had so much issue with keeping a man in his bed; usually it was he who was kicking them out. Now the one man whose presence he craved with a fool's addiction seemed to have an aversion to sleeping late and preference for leaving Pitch to wake alone.

He sought to calm his disquiet. Last time he'd succumbed to such worries, the fool oaf had just been off having a godsforsaken swim.

Pitch had the vague sense of having woken earlier, of mumbling something to the ankou, who had been getting up...for what? To relieve himself. That was it. But he'd said he'd be back in a moment. How many moments was it now? Pitch could not decide if he'd been asleep a long while or just a minute, though he was groggy enough for the former. He rocked onto his knees, a wry grin forming at the loosened state of his trousers. What a pleasant evening. With all that mead and cock sucking, and daft talk of building a cottage in the woods, Silas speaking of a life lived as though they were joined in strange matrimony. Lucky the alcove in the dewberry bush was so compact, for at one point he thought Silas about to take the knee and propose. Daft bastard. But for a luxurious moment, Pitch had become a daft bastard too, imagining safe peace at the ankou's side.

Now though, the faint light of day arrived, bringing with it a slight headache and need for water. Pitch was almost done adjusting the corset, which had slipped on account of being half undone, smoothing his hand over the boning and trying to keep his thoughts away from the events that had transpired after he received it. He buttoned his shirt next, thinking how much warmer he'd be with a coat, when muted cries came from the clearing. Will Scarlet whipped its tiny glass-blown figure about, its squeaks taking on a note of alarm he did not like.

'What is it?'

The will-o'-the-wisp dashed through a thin space in the brambles, vanishing at once and leaving no reply.

'Damn it. I asked you a question.' Pitch waved his hands about, searching for the place where the brambles had opened to allow them entrance. 'Open up, you fucking...' He paused, took a breath. 'Please...allow me to leave.'

At once the branches shifted, snaking back. He crawled through the low archway that formed. 'Thank you.'

On his hands and knees as he was, he saw the coats before anything else. The sight of the royal-blue Inverness made his unsteady stomach clench.

'He went to take a piss, idiot,' he chastised himself. 'Didn't need to get dressed up for it.'

But still, it was Silas's coat he reached for and not his own herringbone as he got to his feet. Pitch tested his ankle carefully before deciding it could take his weight this morning. At long, fucking last. He cradled the Inverness and took in the sight that greeted him. Gathered in front of the Major Oak were gnomes, peri, and brownies, and upon the tree itself, peeking kodami. All faces he recognised from last night but their expressions far less jovial. The sombre air made the hairs stand on his arms.

Robin was on their knees, their back to Pitch, petals fluttering in a circular motion as though a mini whirlwind focused on the hamadryad alone. The attention of every living creature in the clearing was set upon something Robin held.

'What's going on?' Pitch demanded. 'What is this?'

The burr was low on his trunk, only a foot off the ground. 'The asrai bring grave news, I'm afraid. Now I'll ask that you keep your calm –'

'Where is Silas?' Pitch's bellow had all the forestkind jumping. Will Scarlet hid itself in Robin's hair. One of the younger brownies burst into tears. 'Tell me where he is, now, or I swear to the gods I shall tear this forest apart.'

Barefoot but with neither time nor patience to stop and put on his boots, he stormed towards the hamadryad – the only one not to startle at his bellow – ignoring the stiffness in his hip. Flecks of dried-out soil fell from the compress at his ankle, but he barely paid it any mind, too intent on what the dryad held. For a pulse-stopping moment, he thought it might be the bandalore. It was round certainly, but it quickly became clear it was not the ankou's scythe. It was an orb of water, not unlike the crystal balls the Order entertained the purebreds with at seances. Only this one was not solid and stationary but fluid and swirling with hints of a current. An asrai. And not a healthy one at that. Threads of brown marred the clarity of their water.

'This is what has you all looking as though the sky has caved in, then?' Pitch snapped, aware he was being less than charitable but caring little. 'A sick asrai? That's it?'

There was some muttering at his comment, which only infuriated him further. The tension stuck to him like prickles to a trouser leg. Far more was wrong than this simple creature being ill.

'The asrai brought us word, Pitch, a warning that has cost them dearly.' Robin looked up, and Pitch despised them for the mixture of pity and grave concern that carved their features. 'The Wild Hunt has entered the forest, and he is found.'

'Who is found?' It was the most foolish question he'd asked in four hundred years.

'Your ankou.'

The clearing rocked on its axis, and if not for the nudge at his shoulder by Will Scarlet, there was a chance Pitch might have tilted along with it.

'Silas?' The second most foolish question he'd asked. But he could not fathom this nightmarish exchange. For that was what it had to be – a nightmare.

'Yes. The Hunt closes in on him. He wandered too far out into the forest, beyond where it was safe. A harpy led him astray.'

'A harpy? A fucking harpy?' Pitch was squeezing the words out, a mix of rage and terror rendering him nearly speechless.

This wasn't happening.

This was *not* happening. He'd gone to sleep in Silas's arms not a few hours ago. Fuck, he could still taste the ankou.

'We must gird the heart of the forest. We will keep you safe here for as long as we can, as he wished.' Robin handed the asrai to a gnome with a beard like tufts of mushrooms. 'Do what you can, but we cannot return them to their source now. No one must leave the clearing. Keep them comfortable as you can.'

'As he wished?' Pitch stared down at the flower-petal-shedding fae, certain he must be in a dream state. An obscure laugh erupted from him. 'You are making it sound as though you work in his memory, that he is dead.' His voice rose so high that even Will Scarlet cringed.

Robin moved to his side. 'Please Pitch...' The hamadryad did not touch him; they were that smart at least. 'He placed vital importance on your safety. You must be guarded well, and the only place to do that is here, in the heart of the forest where the Major and I are strongest.'

'*My* safety?' Pitch blustered. 'I don't give a shit about –'

'We are Sherwood's heart, Robin and I.' The Major would have been puffing his chest if he had one. 'A safehold for the dryad and any other the Hunt has seen fit to pursue these past centuries.' Was it Pitch's strained mind, or were the Major Oak's branches lengthening, widening? 'They've not got what they've come for, not once. No reason that will change today, if we put our minds to it. That ankou will fight his fight out there, and we shall do so here.'

'*That* ankou,' Pitch hissed, 'has a name. He is Silas Mercer. And if you think for the remotest moment I shall just stay here hiding in the godsdamned brambles while he deals with the Hunt, you are a fucking moron.' Despite how fiercely he spoke, he moved numbly, his head aching, his chest impossibly tight, scanning the edges of the clearing as though Silas might have left giant footsteps to mark his path. The forest was vast. Run in the wrong direction and it would be too late. He cut off that train of thought and distracted himself by pulling on Silas's coat. It was laughably too large for his much slighter frame, and running out behind him like a ballgown's train with their difference in height, but wearing it went some way to loosening the knots in his chest. 'Tell me which bloody direction...point it out now. Tell me.'

'Pitch.' Robin tried to barricade him.

'Tell me!' He was shouting again, which was a miracle in itself, considering he could barely take a breath.

'I will not.' Robin was firm. 'He would never forgive me, to begin with, and you are in no state to take on the Wild Hunt, especially one who associates with sorcerers.'

Pitch touched at one of the coat pockets and his stomach roiled. The bandalore was there. Silas had not taken it with him.

Gods.

'My state is none of your business to decide,' he snarled, suddenly desperate. 'Tell me the direction, you vazey cretin, or I shall –'

'Do what?' Now it was the Major Oak's time to bellow, only his came with a showering of sudden autumnal leaves and a gasp from their natural audience. 'Set fire to a singular hair upon the Herlequin's head? If that colossus fellow has any to begin with... There was a bald chap once...thin as a rake, half the size of this one, with eyebrows white as the unnatural snow falling. About two hundred years past, would you say, Robin?'

'I'm not sure it's very important right now, Major.' Robin, ever the fucking diplomat.

'I am truly out of patience,' Pitch growled as well as any wolf.

The branches to his right rose and fell, in mimicry of a shrug. He had little doubt they had grown, for he could no longer see the brambles where he'd lain with Silas. The branches were favouring growth towards the ground, rather than up, as trees normally went. Their tips were only a balled fist away from the moss.

'Well best you find some,' the Major Oak said. 'That pissy excuse for fire won't scare them, any more than it scares us.'

Pitch hadn't even realised he'd brought the flame to hand until then. Gods, it truly was appalling, the lonely flicker upon one fingertip, the unimportant brightness beneath his skin. His ankle may be nearly healed, but the rest of him was quite broken. Will Scarlet hovered close, balling up a fist the colour of gilded gold and shaking it towards the Major, an odd little ally, apparently disliking the summary of Pitch's inadequacies just as much.

'I have no intention of scaring them,' Pitch said. 'I intend to beat the living daylights out of them.' He brushed the will-o'-the-wisp out of the way and strode towards the edge of the clearing. He did so with only the barest of limps, sending peri scattering out of his way, clipping a few of the toadstools with his bare feet as he made a determined path to where the leshy had not yet lowered his boughs. 'I will find him myself.'

'You cannot leave, fire man.' The Major spoke quietly in an even quieter clearing.

'It is precisely what I intend. And call me fire man again at your peril.' It was Tilly's own stupid name for him, for one. But he was neither man nor fire daemon, and if the leshy reminded him of it again, he'd pull off ancient branches one by one. After he'd found Silas, of course, and given him the talking to of his life. His many lives.

Led astray by a harpy? Had the ankou not learned a blasted lesson in Highgate Cemetery?

Pitch was so busy distracting himself with the ear-bashing he was going to give Silas that he was paying no mind to Will Scarlet's chirruping. Which was, as it turned out, a warning – to watch out for the girder of a tree branch standing in his way. Pitch collided with unyielding wood and sent a myriad of curses the tree's way.

'Get your fucking stick out of my way, leshy.'

'We cannot do that.' Robin stood surrounded by a circle of the toadstools, which were all now shining far brighter than his own flame. 'I'm so sorry, Pitch. He would not want it. I think you know it, too.'

Pitch did not know what he hated more, the Major's pugnacious prattle or Robin's soft empathy.

He definitely despised the dryad's awful, correct assumption. The very last thing Silas would want was for Pitch to come rushing headlong into the mess he'd made. But the ankou was also an idiotic oaf who would know full well there was no chance in all imagined hells Pitch would sit by when he was endangered.

He moved quickly, headed towards the rapidly shrinking gap he'd been aiming for. There was no edge of the clearing anymore. Rather a tangle of branches coming from overhead, and ivy pushing up from the ground, birthing from the soil like spring had suddenly struck.

'No.' He broke into a run. 'No, don't you dare. Let me go.'

A sturdy branch pointed its woody finger at him, pressing at the centre of his chest and holding him back. Another caught him from behind, wrapping about his waist and lifting him off his feet.

'Put me the fuck down, now, leshy.'

The Major drew him back across the short distance he'd made, moving him through the air over a frightened gathering of brownies and peri who huddled together near the hamadryad. Robin was speaking to them, but Pitch was making too much of a fuss to hear a word.

He shouted and protested and swore in every language he knew. Will Scarlet was with him, chittering no doubt about how he should calm the fuck down and listen to reason.

A part of him was doing just that. There was sense to be had in keeping himself safe here. Waiting it out. Letting the ankou deal with the Hunt. The oaf was far more formidable now than when they had first met. And surely the fucking Order or the Lady or Sybilla would decide it time to get off their arses and show themselves?

It was sensible to stay put.

But sensibility stood no chance against the overwhelming idea of losing the ankou.

Pitch pressed his smouldering hands against the wood, singeing the bark.

'That is unkind,' the Major grumbled. 'We seek to help you.'

Pitch didn't want blasted godsdamned fucking help, just as he didn't want a sleeping behemoth in his belly, nor an angel's scar upon his back, or to be hiding here with the brownies and gnomes while Silas was in harm's way.

The Major held him at a slight distance, and there came a splintering sound. A great split formed down the tree's middle, and two folds of wood opened like doors on a crudely carved wardrobe.

'Don't you dare.' Pitch struggled, but was ultimately pushed into the innards of the tree, a hollow of a size more than ample enough to hold a slender, panicking prince. He was to be sealed in.

His fear got away from him, slipped its collar and had his heart crashing against ribs. 'No, no don't do this.'

'It's all right, Pitch. You will be safest there,' Robin called from where she stood at the centre of the clearing with her gaggle of naturals. 'That is my home.'

'Your home is too fucking small.' The folds of the tree began to move back in place. Doors being closed. Locked in darkness. 'Not the dark.' He knew himself wild-eyed, practically spitting his plea, slapping his hands against the steady wood. 'Don't put me in the dark.'

'Robin, he's having a turn,' the Major declared as though Pitch were a child who'd just soiled their nappy. 'And he won't stop burning my skin.'

'He's frightened, Major. You can see that as well as I.'

'It's us who should be frightened, if he's the one they think will right all the wrongs.'

'That is truly not helping. He's not deaf.' The discussion played around him as he fought not to lose his mind entirely. 'Pitch, do try to take a decent breath. We seek only to protect you.'

Protecting him by confining him. This felt little different to being sealed away in the abaddon. A scream was building at the base of his throat. He was damned awful at holding his nerve, since Seraphiel had buried the behemoth. As though that beast had devoured his fears before, eating at them with teeth made of rage.

The sections of wood creaked, moving on invisible hinges to close.

'It will not be dark, I promise you, Pitch. Please trust me.' Robin blew at the palm of their hand and sent a swathe of petals floating his way. Each one glowed like the toadstools surrounding the hamadryad. The petals slipped in through the narrowing crack between the portions of wood, which drew slowly back as the oak reformed his trunk.

Will Scarlet dashed through the gap. The will-o'-the-wisp settled on his shoulder, tittering in hushed tones, sending its colours to every dark inch of the tree's innards.

With such a bathing of light the darkness was pushed away, too far away to plague him.

Will Scarlet made itself comfortable against the black collar of the Inverness coat, settling in and giving him a pat that might have gotten it slapped were Pitch not so desperate for reassurance.

The trunk closed over, the wood settling without a sound. And his view of the world narrowed to a small gnarled peephole in the ancient tree.

CHAPTER 25

The Nephilim halted his massive steed a mere step from where Silas knelt on the ground. The stallion's chest loomed over him, blocking his view of most of its rider, who in turn was so heavily clad in layers of dark fabric that even if Silas had dared try to move, he was unlikely to see much more than shadow.

The horse and rider's spectre engulfed him, stifling the emerging morning all but completely. Silas craned his neck, seeking out the rider that had his blood churning: akin to having his veins filled with boisterous, tiny gnats.

He yearned to see what he might find atop that horse, yet loathed the idea as well. What lay beneath those heavy layers of fabric? Silas knew not all those who had been born of angel and woman became fearsome goliaths. If he were to rip off that hood, would he see monster or man? Perhaps a bearded, frightened fool, hardly different to him?

'What do you want with me?' He already knew the ultimate answer, of course. They wished to finish him. But why was their rush now stalled? 'Answer me.'

Not a one of them did. The silence was cloying. The wait painful.

Silas was pinned by the Dullahan's whip, vulnerable as he'd ever been with the bandalore still in his coat pocket back in the clearing. Thought of the clearing left him reeling. Christ, surely the leshy and the dryad knew of the Wild Hunt's invasion of their forest?

They would have Pitch spirited away by now. They *must* have spirited him away by now. Silas would not call on the bandalore. Not least of all because he'd never risk betraying the daemon's location, but also because it felt inordinately right to have it remain where it was.

The other riders flanking the Herlequin were far less substantial than their leader, lithe beneath their cloaks, and not so numerous as the shaking of the ground had suggested. Three on each side, their horses unsettled and cracking their bits against their teeth.

Surely this number of riders was not responsible for the quaking of the forest floor? Or was this only a portion of the Hunt, the rest elsewhere?

The thought spilled ice into Silas's veins, cooling the heat there and allowing quiet terror to trickle in. He could try to break himself free of the whip, a move unlikely to succeed and more likely to see him trampled by the Herlequin's mount, but at the very least it would keep this party occupied. Distracted from the forest's heart, where he fervently hoped his precious daemon no longer waited.

'Well this is quite the vigorous conversation. Am I being accosted by mute fools? The silence is rather dull.' Such bravado, and not a whit of it real.

The stallion held perfectly still, only a faint huff of white coming from its nostrils as it breathed, with the Herlequin as statuesque as his horse, and his darkness a mere shade less than his mount's.

'You trespass in this forest, Herlequin.' Silas could barely stand the weight of the silence. 'The Wild Hunt is banished from this world.'

Did the Nephilim recognise one of his own? There'd been no sign of anything from the rider, not even that he was aware of the man kneeling in the dirt before him.

At last the creature spoke. And what a noise it was.

'The Wild Hunt has no boundaries.' The scratch of his voice was like wind-tossed branch tips across a windowpane. Silas winced, hunching his shoulders. Jesus, he'd have preferred the Nephilim stayed silent. 'The Erlking's riders cannot be banished, no matter how your masters wish it were so, ankou.'

Ankou...perhaps the Nephilim did not *see* Silas after all. Or perhaps, after so long, there was nothing left of his original life left to notice.

Oddly, that foolish notion pained him. Silas had no wish to be known for the perversity of his birth, but nor had he ever been so aware of the distance stretching between him and the living.

Silas fought off foolish, ill-placed melancholy. He stared at all he could see of the Herlequin: a gleaming silver stirrup on which rested a boot so large that he could have slid both his feet into it at a push. The leather was strange, a whirling pattern that suggested animal skin, though of what species he could not guess. One not of this world, he suspected.

'The Erlking has made a grave mistake in siding with sorcerers and errant angels.' Silas rose as high as the Dullahan's hold would allow, which was further than he'd thought possible. The headless horseman was being merciful with his whip, his cuts not deep nor too painful. 'It will cost the UnSeelie Court dearly.'

Branches and glass met again, this time in one calamitous sound that was very likely laughter. 'Grave mistake? Says the man of death on his knees in the dirt, his masters nowhere to be found.' The Nephilim's voice felt as though it was scraping the skin from the channels of Silas's ears. 'You have partnered with the daemon too long; his belligerence coats you.'

Silas's gut twisted with the desire to reach out and tear the rider from his horse for mentioning Pitch at all.

'I'd say far more than Tobias Astaroth's belligerence coats him.'

Silas's terror stretched and widened at the new voice. He turned his head, the only part of his body allowed such freedom, to search out the speaker. 'Crane.' The name escaped him as a dying whisper. Cool fear evaporated, replaced once again by heat. A heat borne of rage, not merely the closeness of another Nephilim.

Balthazar Crane edged back the fringe of his hood, settling it so Silas had a clear view of his aura-touched face, the familiar thin threads of silver snaking from him. The only aura Silas had yet been able to see.

And one he had come to detest.

No melody arrived with the other ankou, but Silas did not need it. Crane's appearance was imprinted upon his mind. A portrait that would stay with him forever. Crane's betrayal of Silas had been shocking, but nothing compared to the part he'd played in sending Pitch to that upstairs room at Gidleigh Park House. Delivering him to the Alp daemon while knowing what she intended.

Silas seethed, repulsed anew by the unforgivable abuse.

Crane touched at his spectacles, urging the dull silver frames up his nose. His ridiculous muttonchops were as flamboyant as Silas recalled, but the ankou's face was so utterly commonplace, so devoid of any hint he was such a treacherous bastard.

'Hello, Mr Mercer.' Balthazar Crane's air held more flint than when they'd last met. 'Lovely to see you again. How is your pretty daemon? No, wait.' He fluttered a gloved hand. 'Don't tell me. We'll learn soon enough.'

The ankou's smile was a match to Silas's kindling of tinder-dry fury. He abandoned his attempt to keep his wits, to hold his audience's attention from the forest's heart.

'You fucking bastard.' Unadulterated hatred poured from him, and its suddenness, its ferocity caught them all unawares. Silas drove himself to his feet, taking the weight of the bones with him. 'I will kill you for what was done to him.'

He threw himself at the stallion for balance, driving the barbs into the horse's soft chest. The Herlequin's horse screamed and drew back into a half rear, but Silas was already moving, turning, hauling the Dullahan and his binding with him. He lunged for the traitorous ankou as though there was not a mass of horseflesh and a weighty bone anchor seeking to hold him back.

Silas was vaguely aware of the fact that he'd made far more ground than seemed tenable and had not been impaled to his core by the whip's teeth. The Dullahan's blue roan danced about, its long mane fanning as the animal tossed its head. Silas sought to lift his arms from where the whip held them pressed against his sides and found slight movement possible.

It buoyed him. His anger fed on the possibility of freedom and pushed him another step closer to the Morrigan's ankou.

'Bring him down, you fools! Herlequin!' Crane shouted, pulling hard at his horse's mouth to turn the steed about. 'Get him down, now!'

Silas imagined his hands around the other ankou's neck, squeezing the goddess-granted life from him. Just as he'd done in the Fulbourn with the teratisms. Silas let sharp loathing consume him.

Too late he noticed the loom of the Herlequin.

The blow was staggering.

A punch to the back of the head laid Silas out, flat on his face, a mouthful of decaying leaf litter burying his tongue, and him unable to do anything about it with the whip in place. Before he could spit, he was grasped by the hair and dragged up and off his feet, lifted high before being driven back into the ground, slammed on his back. All the air was pushed from his lungs, the light wavering as the blow threw him to the edge of consciousness.

He blinked, odd sounds coming from him as he fought for breath. A heavy foot was planted on his chest. Boots of strange whorled leather crushed his hope of inhaling.

The Herlequin leered over him, his hood removed.

Through starlit vision, Silas took in the creature pinning him down and holding him more completely than the whip, still loose enough to allow a small freedom of movement that Silas had enough sagacity to keep hidden.

The Nephilim was only part monster, mostly human, with all the usual limbs.

The humanity of the creature's mother was evident, but what a terrible babe he would have made. His angelic and purebred blood had not mixed well.

A slashed mouth and blackened teeth lay beneath a solitary, bloodshot eye, which sat centred over the bridge of a nose broken terribly and healed in a grotesque and crooked way. One side of his face looked as though it were melted, hanging longer than the other at the jowls, while on his head, tufts of hair clung to a scalp badly scarred – burns which brought to mind the scarring he'd seen upon Pitch's back, when the amuletum failed at the greensward.

The comparison and the thought of his daemon brought on fresh resolve, and Silas tore his gaze from the silent Nephilim to seek out the ankou. 'Your false goddess has not made you' – Silas coughed, gasping – 'any less of a coward, Crane.'

'Look at you, all brazen and defiant.' Crane exaggerated a shiver. 'Little wonder you have a prince on his knees for you. You are quite the sight when riled.'

Silas bit the inside of his lip, determined not to rise to the bait on offer, sickened to recall it was he who had revealed Pitch's true identity to this fiend and his miscreants.

The Nephilim shifted, grinding his heel into the shallow valley between Silas's ribs. Crane removed his glasses and took a moment to polish the glass with a handkerchief he pulled from his pocket.

'I know it likely a waste of my breath.' He huffed at the glass, holding the spectacles aloft, squinting as he inspected them. 'Since I've been told you are incorruptible. But as my brother, I'd like to give you one last opportunity nonetheless, for we'd make a formidable team. Join me, Mr Mercer. Devote yourself to the goddess Morrigan, stand with us when the Watcher King rises, and you and I shall be his lords of the dead, together.'

Silas sought to laugh, but with all the pressures upon him, the Dullahan's viselike whip and the Herlequin's tonnage, the sound resembled a death rattle. 'Piss off,' he wheezed. 'Never.'

Crane shrugged. 'I didn't think so. You are far too settled in the daemon's bed. And who can blame you? He's a fine specimen to fuck, by all accounts. But you can't say I didn't give you the opportunity to avoid unpleasantness.' He lowered the hand raised to inspect his glasses. By the time it hung at his side, the spectacles had transformed.

Balthazar Crane flexed his fingers around the handle of his scythe. A dagger, its stiletto blade squared and tapered to a fine point, dull and mottled metal the shade of midnight shadows.

'You'll have to move, Herlequin. I must pierce his heart.' Crane jerked his head at the Nephilim, who'd not yet released any of the pressure he brought to bear upon Silas's chest. 'Keep a heel to his head and hold him steady. He's bound to flinch.'

A black-teeth-baring snarl crossed the Herlequin's lips as he raised his foot from Silas's chest. A ripple went through the surrounding riders of the Wild Hunt, who formed a near-perfect circle around them. The only stillness was where the Dullahan sat upon his roan, silent and watchful.

'Make haste here.' The Nephilim's hideous, grating voice forced a grimace from Silas. 'Iblis will be done with the daemon soon enough.'

'Harm him, and there will be no world safe for you. I swear.'

With a throaty sound that crudely mimicked laughter, the Herlequin pressed his boot down upon Silas's head.

'Your lover is not who should concern you now, Mr Mercer.' Crane knelt, straddling him at the hips. He held the hilt of his blade with both hands. 'This is a waste, I'll not deny it. A pity he has you so beguiled that you cannot see sense. I do hope he was worth it, for that daemon is costing you everything.'

Silas blinked, particles of dirt finding their way from the Herlequin's boot to his eyes. He was bound and threatened and helpless, but did not resent why. Or for whom. 'A price I pay gladly.'

The ankou sighed and raised his dagger overhead. Whispers from its blade caught at Silas's ear. The dark goddess. Her promises glinted like diamonds and were sweet as mead. Morrigan's lure was viciously strong. She desired what her sister possessed with a hunger that twisted every fibre of Silas's being. But the ankou was right in one thing. Silas was beguiled. And it would take far, far more than divine promises to sway him from the daemon's side. Or from Izanami, the goddess who'd put him there.

Crane plunged the dagger into Silas's chest, shoving it between ribs, sinking it deep to where an unnaturally beating heart lay.

Silas's cry tore at the air, a cacophony of sound not entirely his own. Izanami laid her echo upon his pain. The goddess thundered in to clash with her sister as the Morrigan's scythe searched for Silas's anchor point.

The tether that connected him to his goddess.

And to this wretched world.

CHAPTER 26

Pitch dug his dull, embered nails into the wood. So, he did not have a raging flame – each fingertip glowed with little more strength than that of a glowworm – but so damned what? He was strong, tenacious, and his reputation alone would give the Wild Hunt cause to falter, surely. He should not be here, kept away like a damned princess in her tower.

'I shall burn you down, you cockless, witless imbecile, if you do not release me.' He uttered the demand for the hundredth time, and was fairly certain Will Scarlet sighed.

'You shan't,' the Major barked back. 'Because you can't. We all know it. At best you've scorched me a little, which is terribly rude, considering. Do you mind?'

With a snarl Pitch lifted his glowing fingertips away but gave the inside of the trunk a decent kick for good measure. The will-o'-the-wisp tittered angrily and shook a bright fingertip his way.

The leshy grunted, the rustle of resettling branches easing the pressing silence.

'Will someone at least fucking tell me what is happening out there? In the woods...' He disliked the silence that followed far more than all the quiet that had come before. 'Robin?' he snapped. 'Major? I swear by all the Celestials' holy sphincters, if someone does not say a fucking word, I shall kick a hole in this oak.'

Will Scarlet placed itself at the peephole and delivered a small tirade of chirps to the outside world.

'Calm down, Scarlet.' Robin's voice came from close without. 'Fine, yes, you are right. Our silence is doing him no good.' Scarlet backed away from the hole, crossing its tiny translucent arms and nodding, setting off a prismatic show of colour as its inner light shifted.

'What do you know of Silas?' Pitch demanded. 'Is he harmed?'

'No. He holds his ground.' Robin spoke smoothly, with great calm. As though it might rub off on him.

'Does anyone come to his aid? The Order? His horse?'

'There is no sign of anyone,' Robin returned. 'Do they know where you are?'

They *should*. Sybilla should know exactly where they were, thanks to Hastings. But the White Horse's continued absence, despite the Wild Hunt's appearance, made him inordinately uneasy. 'Of course they do.' He would try to convince himself, if no one else.

'Then we just need time. That is all. I'm sure your ankou can handle himself until help arrives.' Robin's grim determination was pitiful.

Pitch wrapped Silas's coat tighter about him, gathering up its copious length like it was a blanket. His hand found the hardness of the bandalore, his ankou's scythe.

For a foolish moment Pitch thought perhaps if he took it from his pocket and held it upon his open palm, it might...what? Fly off to find Silas?

For fuck's sake, it was a weapon not a butterfly. The bandalore just sat there, the stained boxwood a pleasant warmth against his skin, its dirty string partly unwound. He traced the swirl in the centre of the rounded disc, moving his finger over wood that had come away from the encounter with Black Annis changed, the hue deepened to mahogany with the blood spilled that day. Blood spilled by the bandalore's master.

Pitch shoved the scythe deep into his pocket, a choking lump in his throat. He paced the three strides each way he could manage in his woody confines, the discomfort in his ankle all but a whisper. If the ankou left him...if he lost Silas here...

They were supposed to navigate this quest together. The ankou had *promised* him that was how it would be.

Pitch was light-headed, suffocated by his own thoughts. This reliance upon another living being was astounding and devastating, and the most confounding of things. Why the blazes did the purebreds seek out relationships with such passion? It was insanity. The sooner the quest was done with, he and the ankou could part ways, and sense would return.

He could be done with this weight, too. The silent wildness, that firebird at his core, was draining. Pitch sought to ignore it, but he was leaden, straining at the seams with an inferno suppressed.

He dug his nails into the fine flesh at his wrist, as though that could possibly relieve the pressure.

Scarlet came dashing at him, squeaking and squawking.

'What the blazes is wrong with you?'

The creature darted in and jabbed an angry sunflower-yellow finger at the red mark on his wrist.

'It's none of your fucking business what I do to myself.' Pitch brushed off the scowling creature. 'Go to Silas, if you wish to be helpful. I won't miss you.'

Scarlet folded its tiny arms and jabbered utter nonsense. He was about to tell it how unflattering its voice was, and what a waste of air it was for it to breathe, when the drag of the leshy's burr sounded through the wood.

'What is it?' he called.

'Quiet.' The Major's reply echoed in the hollow interior. 'Keep quiet. They are very close.'

Pitch considered ignoring the instructions in favour of demanding answers, but he held his tongue and pressed his eye to the peephole.

Robin knelt at the centre of the clearing, surrounded by gradually widening rings of toadstools, a circlet of petals rotating overhead. Their fingers were splayed, the tips pressed to the ground on either side of where they rocked back and forth, eyes tightly closed, flaxen hair shifting like wind-gentled wheat.

Pitch strained to listen for signs of what went on beyond the barrier, but he might as well be buried in a pine box beneath the earth. Robin's chin jerked up, as though they were held by a collar and the chain were wrenched.

'They see us.' They threw back their head, and the rotation of the petals quickened. 'Sweet mercy...they are strong.'

'Who?' Pitch demanded, forgoing the silence. 'Who is it? Is it the Herlequin?'

Robin shook their head in a slow back and forth. 'No.' They raised their arms, extending them to either side. Long, sinewy limbs lengthened further as Pitch watched. The dryad's fingertips touched at the foliage that grew at the boundaries of the clearing. New brambles and vines pushed from the soil, their leaves the brilliant green of new growth. Faint creaking came from the Major Oak, and the branches Pitch could see added themselves to the barrier, tangling in with the thorns and ivy.

The heart of Sherwood Forest was reinforcing itself.

'Tell me who sees us.' Pitch leaned his weight against the wood, pressing into it in the vain hope that perhaps, with the leshy's attention elsewhere, he might find an escape. 'What is going on? Fucking gods, tell me.'

'Angels.' Robin barely freed the single word.

'More than one?' Pitch pressed flattened palms against the wood.

'There is more than one.'

'More than one angel?' he repeated, incredulous.

'There are three.' Robin spoke as though the weight of the entire forest were upon them.

'Fuck...fuck...' Pitch renewed his escape attempt with fresh fever, putting his shoulder into the wood. 'Open up, you idiot.'

The oak shuddered with each of his blows, but he was no closer to getting out of the trunk than before, and now he had an ache along his collarbone and a bruise where his temple had smacked the wood in his panic. Pitch set his eye to the peephole once more.

Peri landed upon the dryad's extended arms, while will-o'-the-wisps gathered in their hair, entwining themselves into the strands. Brownies assembled close to the fae, inside the circle of toadstools, which were now glaringly bright.

'We shall not let them have you. Do not be afraid,' Robin said.

That was not what he was most afraid of. 'You need to let me out,' Pitch shouted while Scarlet buzzed and whimpered nearby. 'They will destroy this forest to get to me.'

Destroy every creature frantically throwing their meagre weight into fortifying the clearing. Gnomes were poking their conical heads through the earth at the perimeter, like stupidly inadequate traps ready for the footfall of any who should breach the thick walls of vine and wood. And kodami, normally happy to watch from behind the bark they so resembled, could be spotted moving about in the brambles, like clandestine snipers readying themselves.

It was insanity. Half these creatures could be picked off by a hungry falcon. They stood no chance against angels and sorcerers.

'Did you hear me, Robin? Major?' Pitch slammed a balled-up fist against the wood. 'Set me free. It is me they are after. This defence is useless. It could never hope to be enough.'

'Perhaps not.' The Major's voice moved through the timber. 'Perhaps all we can offer you is time, but we offer it willingly. You are a friend of the forest, fire daemon, for all else you may be. We do not forgo a friend in their need.'

They were kind words, he supposed, but very stupid. 'I am not the sort of creature you should befriend, you moron. Forgo me, and be fucking quick about it.'

A deep rumble menaced the clearing, the vibration coming up through the ground, tickling at Pitch's bare feet. Twin cries of terror rose from Scarlet and the creatures out in the clearing.

'Hold fast, hold fast now,' Robin called, a note of desperation clinging to their words.

'Shit.' Pitch grabbed at the will-o'-the-wisp, who was taking prime position at the hole in the oak. He held the delicate creature as gently as his haste would allow and shoved his eye to the opening.

Across the clearing, at Robin's back, a glow seeped through the foliage. Wide and round as a carriage wheel, brighter than a rising sun. Bone white at its heart with the tinges of a golden fire's glow at the edges.

A golden fire, like that which burned beneath Lord Enoch's Ophanim throne.

'The angels have a damned halo.' If Pitch had not leaned against the wood, he likely would have collapsed to his knees. Will Scarlet made a dolorous sound, and he glared at the tiny critter. 'Do you even have the faintest fucking idea what a halo is?'

Scarlet's widened, unblinking eyes managed to remain locked on Pitch, even as the creature shook its head.

He turned away, peering through his ridiculous view-finder. The answer was very simple. A halo was, for him, and for these creatures, the end.

'Robin, get them out of here. Run, you idiot.'

But the fae, may all the gods damn them, remained on their knees, or rather, their roots. In the brief span of time he'd looked away, the dryad's transformation was astonishing. Their lower body did not resemble anything human now. Instead, there was a network of roots stretching across the clearing, a woody spiderweb with the dryad a spider at its centre. Their arms were thick as jungle vines, their fingers tangling through the wall of forest, surrounding a space brightened not just by the halo's glow but by the myriad of creatures within it. The sight was really quite glorious, but all the work being done to stave off the angels amounted to little.

Robin raised their head, though their shoulders remained slumped with duress. 'They are so very strong, daemon.' Their voice was the hush of a pile of dry autumn leaves. 'I fear I cannot hold them back much longer.'

The pain filling their features made Pitch flinch. 'Then don't,' he said. 'Let go. Run. Find the ankou, help him instead.' Because it was *not* too late for such things. 'Take your protection to him.'

Behind the dryad, the halo's scar widened. Great hefts of foliage came away, the forest racing to replace the dead and dying limbs with new green shoots. A pointless struggle that was going to destroy this forest, and all who lived in her. Because these imbeciles called him friend.

The thought struck hard, left him breathless and filled with the strangest sorrow. Thank the gods he'd never felt like this leading his legion. If loss had so bothered him then, the Berserker Prince would have been done with centuries before now.

'Run, you fool!' he shouted. 'Damn you, go. Find the ankou, you cannot fight the angels.'

'Nor can you.' Robin was defiant, a glint in their daisy-yellow eyes, the beautiful scalloping at their edges seeming to sharpen.

The glare from the halo brightened, and the woven barrier shuddered. The splintering of wood was terrible, the crack and snap and anguish of bones breaking as the halo's power carved its path, umaking the fortress even as it sought to reassemble. A melodic hue and cry ran through the snarled limbs and rose up from the creatures who offered their strength to the dryad's trees.

Pitch fought to steer his mind clear of Silas, of his absence in this hour of great need. Of the few things that would keep the ankou from his side at such a time.

'Robin, we cannot hold them back,' the leshy cried, and the Major Oak trembled as though struck by the axe of a giant.

Pitch shifted about in his confines, a rat trapped. His pulse was so quickened that there was no beat, just a hum in his chest. Scarlet buzzed about him, tiny fists balled, mouthing off who-knew-what in its strange language towards the growing chaos outside.

'I am begging you, Major' – and Pitch loathed begging – 'release me.'

There was not enough air in the godsdamned trunk. Pitch opened up Silas's coat, desiring the coolness of the air, but not prepared to remove the Inverness entirely.

Scarlet squealed, stabbing a pointed violet finger towards the ground. The wisp dove downwards, letting its rainbow hues highlight what it was indicating.

Sections of the Major's oak had turned an insipid grey, the sickly shade of the unwell.

'What is that?' Pitch crouched down, Silas's coat spilling around him. He tugged at it so it would not touch where the oak was tainted and peered closer at the discolouring. This was the ghostly grey of a long-dead tree, one turned white with time and weather. Pitch touched a finger to the damage and recoiled at the tingling against his skin. 'Magick,' he whispered.

What fouled the Major Oak was not so pure a thing as death. This was the work of angels. Of divine magick.

'I'm not done for yet,' the Major declared, though he did not manage the lie very well.

'Bullshit. They are killing you.' Pitch shot to his feet, pressing up to the peephole. 'Robin, for the gods' sake, just go!'

The dryad lifted their head to find him. Pitch hissed through pressed teeth. One side of their face already suffered as the oak did, gone ghastly grey with petrification. Some of the brownies were already turned to stone, trapped at an active moment, one with an arm raised as though to ward off the evil encompassing them. Several of the gnomes' heads were turned to ashen peaks where they stood sentinel around the border of the clearing, and the toadstools had not escaped unscathed, most of the illumination now coming solely from the glare of the halo. The incoming assault had widened its girth. The circle of dead and dying foliage would be wide enough now to accommodate Lalassu and Sanu walking side by side. Thought of the horses only served to deepen Pitch's agitation. Where the bloody, blazing hell were those infernal animals?

'We can withstand this a while longer.' The dryad's efforts to speak were awful to witness, with one cheek jagged and hard as a cliff face.

'You are dying. Don't try to be a fucking hero, you fool.' But Robin lowered their head, sending more new growth to race towards the halo's mark. Pitch's ire rose. 'You're too pathetic for this, look at your tree.' He punched at the mix of stone and wood for good measure. What was a bruised knuckle amongst all else? 'Your oak is dying too, stupid, idiot fae. You are outmatched.' The dryad's gold-wheat hair hung limp, its vibrancy being stolen along with much else. Pitch swallowed. 'Do not sacrifice yourself for someone who does not wish to be saved.'

He sagged with the release of saying it aloud. Gods, he wished this over with. Let them come, let the angels destroy what Seraphiel had made of him. What did he fucking care if this world had Azazel for a master, if the Severance War finally took a turn one way or the other? What did he truly fucking care? He was no longer a part of any world, not this one, nor Arcadia. Pitch was...well, he had no idea what he fucking was, apart from the reason everyone who came near him was endangered.

The reason Silas was nowhere to be seen.

Pitch turned from the sight of Robin and their feeble mission to protect him. He shoved his fingers through his hair, pulling at the roots until it stung. 'I'd feel it...would I not? If he fell?'

Scarlet chirruped, dangling by one hand from his shirt button, patting at his breast with the other. Trying to soothe him.

Could all that mattered be lost so simply? Without a sound. Without so much as a whisper. Or a whistled note?

Of course it fucking could.

The stony creep of petrification rose higher up the inside of the Major's trunk. The oak could not suppress his groans. His timbers were splitting, light was seeping in through the hairline cracks in the wood.

A crack large enough for Scarlet to dart through. Pitch was barely quick enough to stop them.

'No, you idiot.' Pitch snatched the wisp from the air. 'Keep out of sight.' He held the squirming critter, too tight no doubt. 'And stop moving about or I shall burn you to a crisp. My flame is big enough for that at least.'

A snort of dismissal came from beneath his curled fingers.

'Do as I say.' Pitch let a hint of menace, an old friend of his, creep into his voice. 'Or you shall discover that rainbows can be melted.'

Satisfied with the sudden stillness in his hand, Pitch released Scarlet and turned his attention to the dying oak. 'Major, it is time to stop this thwarted attempt to protect me. You've done all you can...and I thank you for it, but you know as well as I it is not enough.'

'Can you save them?' The leshy's exhaustion drained Pitch just to hear.

'Maybe.' A lie most likely, but the halo was not making as terrible a mark as it could. If it were an Archangel or Seraphim seeking entry, they'd have done so ten times over by now. Perhaps Iblis had been trapped too long in this world, and his halo suffered for it. 'But not alone.' Pitch considered the options, his thoughts calamitous. 'The gnomes, they are tunnellers, and your roots reach far. Have the gnomes build a path for the forest folk to escape through, and you show the way. Get them out of this clearing or they will all die. Do you understand?'

'Yes.' A hiss of air and little more, but the earth around Pitch's feet began to stir, the niggling of roots beneath the surface.

'Let me out, now, sir.'

The tree exhaled, the wood settling like the timbers in an old house, the cracks widening with the expansion. But nowhere near great enough space for Pitch to step through.

'A little more, quickly.'

The wheeze of grinding wood was laboured, and the cracks widened by only the merest margin. An agonised moan drew from the timbers. Scarlet chittered and its colours trembled as it caressed the tired old oak where the stony grey had not yet trespassed.

'Break,' was all the Major managed, but Pitch took his meaning and ran with it. Quite literally.

He turned his shoulder, aiming for where he recalled the parts of wood meeting to close him in – a place where weakness could be exploited – and took as large a run up as possible in the confines.

Pitch hurtled forward...and through.

The wood shattered with the delicacy of fine glass. Far easier a break than he'd expected, and the sudden coming apart threw off his balance, which hardly needed any help with being off-kilter on the best of days. He was rescued by one of the gnomes, a rotund fellow of a height not common to the earth elementals, who ducked his head beneath Pitch's thrown-out hand, providing a prop that kept him on his feet. He gave the gnome a grateful nod, then dished out instructions.

'Gather everyone in the clearing, lead them into the oak.' Pitch tossed the command over his shoulder, already making his way to Robin's side, damp soil squeezing through his toes. 'Tunnel them out of here, do you understand? No one is to remain.'

'But Robin is here, we cannot leave them. They need us for –'

'Whatever succour you've given to the forest, it's done with now.' Why did gnomes never just do as they were told? 'Get the blazes out of here, damn you. Don't test me, for it won't end well for you.'

'Yes, sir. Going now, sir.'

The gnome's cries for assembly rang out. The brownies and will-o'-the-wisps gathering near Robin did not take much persuading to follow the call once Pitch levelled them with a glare. They scrambled over the spiderweb of roots that covered the ground, taking a wide berth around him, gathering the kodami as they went.

He reached Robin's side and found a narrow crouch space in the bulge of roots. The toadstools closest to the fae were still shining with weak light, but those further out were stubby rock markers. Pitch's eyes locked upon the huge crest-shaped hole where the halo sought to puncture the natural barricade. Robin's vines and brambles formed a thick frame around the edges as though the destruction were a horrid, massive painting.

'Robin, stop, let it go.' He laid a hand on their narrow shoulder. The dryad shook like the proverbial fucking leaf, despite much of their lower half holding the grey tinge of the magick. 'Enough. It is divine magick, you –'

'I know what it is, daemon.' They slipped the words through clenched teeth. 'And those angels have no right to bring their destruction to my forest.'

'They are not overly fond of the rights of others,' he said bitterly. 'They are going to destroy Sherwood, and you, if you continue to fight them. Stand down.'

'But what of you? The ankou told us we must...'

'Silas is not your master, and he is prone to absurd amounts of fussing.' *And if he does not return to fuss again, I shall fall to endless pieces,* Pitch thought. 'The ankou would never expect you to place yourselves in such a position. He would despise what is being done to you here. Go, Robin. Keep the forest alive.'

Robin glanced at him, eyes dull, the daisy yellow fading. 'But it is you who must live.'

Before he could dispute that, the dryad cried out, their gaze shifting to the left, to where the petrification crept along their vine-snaked arms, turning Robin's lengthened fingers to stone.

'Shit.' Pitch grabbed at their shoulders. 'Stop fighting. Let the fucking barrier down.'

A thin sliver of the halo's light pierced the barricade.

Horrified cries rang out from the fleeing forest folk. Run. They cried. Run.

Which is what Pitch *should* be doing.

Find Silas, and keep running. Escape in the chaos.

The clearing shone with the purity of the halo's white-and-gold-dashed glare. The forest's bulwark shattered. Pitch threw himself over the helpless dryad.

Placing himself right back where it had all begun.

In the path of a halo's strike.

CHAPTER 27

Pitch regretted his decision to play living target immediately. To know what it was to be struck by an angelic flame was to know that it should be avoided at all costs. Yet, here he was.

The pain of impact was astonishing. A strike at his shoulder, just above Seraphiel's mark. He may have screamed, rather uncouthly, as he tumbled through the air, flipped over and over by the power of the blast. There was no telling where up began and down ended, and his head filled with a strange hum. Not a melody or anything pretty, just a resonance that deadened everything else. Silas's coat tangled around him, wrapping him tight about the legs. Pitch's back was alight with inglorious flame, and yet he only found concern with how badly burned the Inverness would be if the fire was not put out at once. Silas would want his coat when he returned. And Pitch had bloody well ruined it.

While his thoughts jumbled, his flight came to a violent halt. Pitch was slammed against the Major Oak, where the leshy was all but entirely turned to stone. He bounced clear and thumped down on his belly, landing against hardened moss. Thin shapes skittered out of the way, kodami perhaps, slow to heed the evacuation order.

The sudden stop nearly knocked Pitch senseless, and certainly did knock the air from his lungs. His lip must be bleeding, for there was a tang against his tongue.

'Pitch. Pitch!'

He thought for half a heartbeat the ankou called him, but realised before he'd finished wondering, it was not. He knew every intonation of Silas's voice too well. Robin called for him, the fae's horror echoing faintly in his ringing ears. Pitch groaned, testing how well he could turn his head so he was not face-first against moss grown hard and rough as coral. He was fearful that some of his fingers were broken. He hoped for dislocation at best but the throb at his right thumb suggested that was too optimistic. The waft of his smouldering flesh was appalling, not least of all because of the memories it stirred. Twice now he'd received a direct blow from a halo; twice he'd survived. The scent of charcoaled skin had been different on the Hellfield, of course. Seraphiel had struck when Pitch was in his true Dominion form, but purebred or daemon, no one smelled pleasant when they burned.

Gods, he was hazy, floating somewhere between conscious and not. It took a moment to recognise the sound of footsteps approaching, feet crunching down on the solidified moss.

'Pitch, please...get up. You must –'

What Robin intended to insist was cut clean from the air, the dryad falling silent in a way that had Pitch fighting to lift his head.

'Robin?' He bubbled the name through blood-rich lips, the humming in his ears keeping it dull. Pitch frowned, at a loss as to which muscles must be used to move from prone to standing.

Hands grasped the back of his collar and dragged him roughly to his feet. The righting was nearly as violent as the crash-landing had been. He was shaken with a force that had his aching head snapping back and forth and tugging cruelly against the burn on his back. He wasn't even certain the flames were out.

'Your Highness.' The snarl licked at Pitch's deadened ear.

He fought to clear his vision, to make out the surrounding shapes in the blur. The air shifted with the unmistakable currents of an angel's aura. Not one, but two. The dryad had been right about there being more than one angel, but they'd spoken of three. Where was the last little bastard hiding? But seeing a foot ahead of him was hard enough, and looking around was out of the question with the way his vision rolled and tilted and his knees felt made of jelly. So Pitch studied what was right in front of him.

The angels, one to either side, held his arms as though they meant to crush his bones. They were indistinct silhouettes, but their auras were clear and notable for how they lacked the usual vibrancy of an angel's morphing colours. These lackadaisical spectrums seemed stuck on one shade only, a rather insulting mud brown that shifted to ditch water beige and back again. Angels, preening arseholes they were, usually pranced about like peacocks on display, showing off a collection of colours in their auras the way a colonel showed off his medals. Pitch could only hope it meant the cretins manhandling him were unwell. That would be lovely. And might account for why the blast had not done far more damage. Halos were a conduit for an angel's inner flame. An ailing angel was less likely to cause as much harm.

'Who the fuck are you?' Pitch could barely understand himself. His mouth was thick with blood.

'Ensure he is secured.'

The command came not from either of the two angels who were lifting Pitch off his feet but another who had yet to reveal themselves. Not that they really needed to step out of whatever dark corner they hid in, for Pitch knew Dr Severs's tone.

The human form of Iblis. The Watcher angel who had imprisoned them at the Fulbourn. One tended to remember a creature like that. Pitch squinted, trying to make out if any of the shapes around him were the good doctor. He looked away quickly when his gaze found the crouching greyness of the hamadryad. They'd been made statuesque where they knelt, every inch of them petrified by the cruelty of divine magick.

'A pity Silas did not tear you apart as he did those teratisms, dear doctor,' Pitch said. 'But plenty of time for that I suppose.'

He really was making an appalling mess of speaking. One of the angels near him actually turned their head to avoid the flying blood.

'A threat is more significant if it is real, Mr Astaroth.' Iblis had not yet shown himself, or if he had, Pitch had not yet gotten coordinated enough to notice him. 'The ankou would need to exist in order to tear anyone apart, but I regret to inform you that is no longer the case.'

Of course the comment was intended to inflame, and of course Pitch should have kept his calm, but he went quite mad regardless.

'Liar! Fucking liar.' Pitch lashed out, kicking out feet that had barely been touching the ground as it was. The jolts caused to his shoulder were more than a little eye-watering, but he persisted. He was aiming for angelic balls, but the angle was impossible, rage and trauma making him foolish. He ended up imitating a person seeking to skate the ice for the very first time, legs flailing. An appalling display of ineptitude which did nothing to strengthen the threats of extreme violence he was levelling at his captors. One of the bastards had the audacity to chuckle.

'This pissy Mary had them trembling on the Hellfield?'

'Less Berserker Prince, more fucking Imbecile Prince, I'd say,' said the other, so smug Pitch wanted to scratch his eyes out. 'You sure we've got the right daemon, Captain? This one doesn't seem much of anything to worry about. Crying over a fucking dead man.'

Not crying. Not dead. Not crying. Not dead. Pitch's addled brain worked the thoughts over and over.

'Secure him to the tree. Let's have this done with.' Dr Severs was direct, gruff, brooking no nonsense, and the angels in his service worked quickly to heed him.

Pitch was shoved against the broad stone girth of the oak, and they landed him so all his weight pressed upon the fresh wound. There was no holding back a scream. A horde of stars appeared before his eyes, and it took all his focus not to land himself in the darkness of unconsciousness. Good gods, he was pathetic.

It was through blinked tears that Pitch had his first glimpse of Iblis.

The angel was just as he recalled, wearing the unimpressive face of Dr Severs, a dull face with a square jaw and sagging jowls beneath, his eyes set slightly too close together to be pleasant. The only change of note was the absence of bristling muttonchops, the angel now clean-shaven. He was clad in those dreary black cloaks the Morrigan favoured, his bulky shape not flattered by the drape of material. All in all, Iblis was every bit as unimpressive as he'd been at the Fulbourn.

Odd he'd not used his halo at the asylum, but then, the Morrigan had been ill-prepared for the arrival of an idiot daemon and his ankou. And perhaps it would not have served a purpose against a daemon with all his faculties. Iblis had just been held off for a good long while by a haphazard cluster of forest dwellers. Embarrassing, really, considering what a decent halo was capable of.

The cold cinch of fear caught at him. Did Iblis's strength falter because he'd already been busy with dispatching an ankou in the woods?

Pitch forced a shallow breath between his teeth. There was no place for paralysing fear here. He could not imagine the ankou gone for a moment. He yearned to touch the bandalore, find some reassurance there, but he was not about to betray the scythe.

'Hold him steady, very steady.' Iblis raised his arm and pointed towards Pitch. He spoke in hushed tones, uttering the language of the angels.

A flash of heat seared Pitch's lips.

'Fu...' was all he managed before he could not utter another word. His lips refused to part, sealed with invisible thread he could feel pinning the swells of flesh together. Magick, of course. Divine. But of a level so low that it should have been easily repulsed, not nearly enough to silence him...were Pitch still the powerful Dominion he'd been created.

'It seems I owe an apology to the blood witch. The Berserker Prince truly did wound himself in a simple trap.' Iblis's gaze fell to Pitch's ankle. 'And is having trouble healing. I thought all that blood around the trap a ruse, that you had realised the use of blood magick and sought to divert us. But that was the plan of that stupid horse, seeking to lead us astray, forgetting the djinn are hardly the only masters of illusion. Macha has developed a useful aptitude for it, knows how to sniff it out when it's being used.' He reached beneath his cloak and withdrew a handful of pure white, or rather, mostly white, strands. Crimson stained the fine lengths he held.

Pitch spewed maddened curses against the backs of his lips, as powerless to stop his gagging as he was to prevent tight shackles being snapped over his wrists, a short thick length of metal between them forcing his hands almost palm to palm. His arms were lifted with brutish disregard, and his hands shoved against the tree. Every second of the rearrangement was a torment for his wound. His cries felt as though they might shatter his clenched teeth. But gods...Hastings...these cunts had killed Sybilla's mare. They had brought down one of the Lady's horses.

'Make sure he can't move about, Zaquiel.' Iblis tossed away the clump of Hastings's mane as though discarding rotten fruit. Pitch's hatred blazed hot and pure. 'I'd like a word with the prince before he is dealt with, and I want his full attention.'

'But, sir, should we not –'

'There is time. He is alone. Now do as you are told.'

Pitch stiffened. Not from pain now or fear and anger, but at mention of being alone. He struggled against the tide of possibilities that came at him. If they had dispatched Hastings...could they do worse? Pitch shook himself. Refusing to listen to his fears. He was *not* alone.

'Yes, Captain.'

Zaquiel, another impossible survivor of the Day of Ruination and the Flood, complied with a sharp half bow. How many of these pricks had survived along with their captain? This angel was nearly as dull as Iblis in appearance, with uninteresting brown hair cut suitably for a banking clerk, eyebrows too bushy by half, and a figure notable for neither litheness nor overindulgence, falling plainly in the realm of unremarkable. A purposeful disguise perhaps? They were all so very average that few would give them a second glance. Their humdrum brown auras were the most interesting thing about them.

Zaquiel stretched to tamper with the cuffs that bound Pitch. He leaned in so close that Pitch's nostrils filled with the ripe tang of sweat and leather. Next came a solid clunk, a click and clack, as though a lock were being assembled. The angel shoved at the metal that connected the cuffs, a violent jolt that knocked Pitch's head back against the tree. He struggled as best he could, but his best was far, far from good enough of late, and he could not risk fainting with the pain. Within moments he was locked fast to the remnants of the Major as though the ancient oak were a giant magnet and not wood-made-stone at all. Pitch groaned and dug his bare heels against the tree, trying to ease the pressure at his shoulders. With his toes barely able to touch the ground, he was like a sack of heavy grain, his wrists taking all the weight of his body.

'Stand back now.'

Zaquiel and the other angel, the only thing making him less dull than his fellow soldier the hint of auburn in his hair, did as they were told, and Iblis stepped forward. He drew the halo from beneath the folds of his cloak.

Well, the semblance of a halo. What a miserable piece of weaponry. A knife of sorts, though one created from an assembly of parts, the joins in the claret-red metal running like black horizontal veins along a blade that had a crooked left lean. Little wonder Iblis had not seen fit to flash it about before now.

The angel stuck its pointed tip against Pitch's belly, down low near where the corset flared a little over his hip bone. Measly in appearance as it was, the halo was bitingly sharp, cutting through the corset's boning, and into his flesh. The angel barely appeared to exert himself.

Pitch's anger burned. It was a damned fine corset, one that was holding him together, and the fucking angel dared put his blasted blade through it.

With the penetration of the blade into his body came a stirring. At long, long last, the faint restlessness of the wildness. The beast murmuring like a hibernating bear disturbed. Reaching out to where Pitch was impaled, circling the wound, as a predator around an injured beast. Pitch moaned against his gag, a sound the angels mistook for pain.

'We shall put you out of your misery soon enough,' Iblis said, though thankfully he did not punctuate the statement with any cringe-worthy villainous grin. He spoke as though stating a simple truth and dug the knife in an inch further. 'But my master would like to know your secrets, angel-slayer.'

Iblis turned the blade, and searing pain followed. The wildness slunk around the halo's invasion, but kept its distance, no bloody help at all. Pitch tried to pull his belly in, alleviate the burn, but the tree he was pinned against gave him nowhere to go.

'Where is it they are trying so desperately to take you? Do they truly believe because luck was with you once, when you destroyed one maddened Seraphim, that you can stop us heeding our master's call?' The smirk upon the angel's face said he gave that idea little value.

Pitch poured his hatred into his gaze, for his lips would not allow him to tell the angel what he thought of his questions.

The wildness slipped away, quickly as it had appeared. Falling back through whatever crack had formed in the seal to allow it forth. But its brief reappearance buoyed Pitch no end.

His eyes stung with the flame. A fire greatly reduced but more than enough, he knew, to ensure his verdant eyes now raged with tiny infernos.

Pitch knew it was so by the subtle flinch that came from the angel and the wildly unpleasant shift of his knife tip.

'Your theatrics do not impress me, daemon.' Iblis scowled, and lied. 'And you stretch the patience of those above me.' He raised his free hand, a conductor readying to start his orchestra. 'Let this be done with. Let him see you.'

CHAPTER 28

B althazar Crane's blade searched its way through Silas's innards. And sweet mercy, it was horrific in its relentlessness. Silas's cry slipped between lips bitten together, pushing through cracks formed when pain overwhelmed him. He'd tried so very hard not to indulge the ankou with a cry or even a whimper.

Silas's body convulsed, his knees lifting, back arching, shoulders digging into the soft ground as agony took hold. And he was so very close to calling on the bandalore, demanding the scythe heed him, return to him and help end this. But as soon as the thought crossed his agonised mind, it was banished by a strange certainty it should not be done. That he was the bandalore, and the bandalore was he. And he did not need that scythe to exact his will.

Just as his time in the Fulbourn had shown him.

All the while the Nephilim stood over him, boot pressed so hard against Silas's forehead that if the knife did not end him, the crack of his skull would.

Crane twisted the blade, searching for the heart of the goddess. Searching for Silas's unnatural beat. Morrigan's ankou, traitor he was, buried his goddess deep. The loosening inside Silas was a whitewash of devastation, clearing a tumultuous path to the place where the tie that bound him to Izanami lay raw and delicate and ripe for unravelling. The power of Crane's dark goddess was eye-watering. This was not the same ankou Silas had encountered on the road to Gidleigh Park House.

As Silas drew blood from his own lips, his pain-struck mind filled with memory of his vision: the horrendous spectacle of ravens devouring teratisms. What part did that play here? A certain one, for sure. A part that bestowed Crane's blade with a power Morrigan should not possess. The goddess was strengthening. Just as the sorcerers claimed the Watcher King to be.

Crane muttered beneath his breath and dragged his blade free. Silas gasped as the serrated edge carved a deeper cut into his ribs.

Silas panted into the relief of the knife's withdrawal, returning to testing the Dullahan's confining hold. There again was the slackness in the whip's embrace, one the headless horseman did not attempt to correct when Silas shifted his arms and squirmed as best he could against the coils of bone. He was barely impaled by the shards; only one or two had broken skin. The oversight seemed strange. Or perhaps the horseman was just so certain that Silas could not escape, he did not bother too greatly.

He could not move his head with the Herlequin's boot upon him, nor could he shift his eyes far enough to get a glimpse of the Dullahan. From where he lay, all he could see was the Nephilim's single eye, his dry and cracked lips pulled back to display blackened teeth, oversized and with jagged breaks giving them the appearance of stalactites hanging from grey gums. If it was a smile, it was a truly foul one.

Crane stepped closer, back into Silas's scope of vision. He held his blade over Silas's face, the metal coated and dripping with blood. The scythe transformed itself once more: twin blades off a singular hilt, more deft at probing all the space beneath Silas's ribs and reaching the heart that eluded the ankou so far.

Silas rolled his hips, digging his heels into the ground where he'd already dug a hole in his failed efforts to free himself. For all the carelessness of the Dullahan's hold, each attempt at freedom had been as futile as the last.

'You are found wanting, Crane.'

The ankou ignored his remark, looking to where Silas knew the Dullahan to be upon his mount. 'Take him to the brook. Over there.' He jerked his chin to a place beyond Silas's head.

Before Silas could truly fathom what Crane intended, the Herlequin withdrew the pressure of his boot, and the whip tightened around Silas's middle. He was dragged along the ground with no regard, sticks and stones catching at Silas's underside, shredding what remained of the back of his shirt and dragging his trousers low. He thought himself about to be made naked, adding insult to injury, when the faint bubbling of the brook met his ears. The narrow stream of icy water he'd foolishly chosen to go to, instead of returning at once to the clearing and his waiting prince. Christ, let Pitch have fled this madness.

Take what you want from me, just see him safe, Silas begged his goddess.

If Izanami gave any sign she'd heard, it was lost with his dunking in icy waters. The familiar surge of revulsion arrived, and thousands of years of habit had Silas crying out, pleading. 'No! No, wait!'

Silas barely had the words free and the Herlequin was there again, with a hand this time instead of a boot. He planted his enormous palm to Silas's face, squashing his protest, crushing his nose, and pushing him beneath the water. The brook was not deep. When Silas's head hit the rocky bed, his face was barely beneath the surface.

But his mind did not care. Under was under.

The familiar terror rushed through him, as much a part of him as his own skin, as attached as the lashes over his eyes. Despite his work at the pond with the kappa, the well-stained fear took its place, knowing it intimately. It shoved aside resistance as easily as a crumb swept from a tabletop, leaving him nearly mindless in his panic to lift his head above water. A creature of terror-borne habit, automated to flail and cry and lose his fucking mind at finding himself submerged.

Crane struck. Drove his blade down once more, his image flickering as Silas's cries bubbled the water.

The twin blades were buried higher up his chest, piercing through lungs emptied by Silas's screams.

The agony was a much-needed slap to the face, a punch in the guts that, quite unexpectedly, did the very opposite of what Crane must have intended. It did not paralyse Silas. Rather, it jolted him from his panic, knocking sense in as water endeavoured to wear it away.

Silas coughed against the press of the brook. There was no time for this. This ridiculous, pointless panic. And he *knew* he could overcome it. Bloody hell he'd sat at the bottom of that pond with weeds and kappa holding him down and survived it. He'd only reemerged because Pitch had disturbed the waters. The prince had searched for him. Traipsed out into the chill and drizzle and lost his wits when Silas could not be found.

He could not abide the idea of Pitch reliving that moment.

Silas's cry thrashed the water. Here he was, acting the godsdamned fool over an ancient fear. There was no changing what had happened that day in the loch, nor did he desire to. Charlie's family lived because of it. Silas's last moment, one of fear and sacrifice, had lasting consequences. All of them were astounding.

All of them had brought him here. To a place where he knew Balthazar Crane could search for an eternity with his sinister blades and find nothing.

Silas's heart wasn't here to be found.

He'd left it in a bower of brambles. In the hands of someone frustrating beyond endurance, and so full of beautiful cracks and wonderment that he was impossible to look away from.

To *be* away from.

A gentle prodding at his back sealed his resolve. The brush of the asrai as they gathered beneath him, reminding him of what old fear sought to erase. He was not alone. Not here in the water. Not anymore.

Silas's bellow churned the water. The asrai drove him upwards. And the sudden motion had his captors set on the back foot. Quite literally, for the Nephilim stumbled, taking his pressure away long enough for Silas to get his face above the surface. Crane's blades drove deeper, cutting off Silas's cry. He could not tell the asrai to stop their pushing, and so his impalement worsened. With breathless agony Silas endured the rending of the blades, which felt sure to pierce him straight through.

'Hold him! Hold him, you fool.' Crane was flustered, the dampness doing him no favours with keeping his grip.

If the Dullahan heeded him, there was no sign of it. The loops of the bones remained slack enough that Silas entertained hopes of freeing his right arm. But the goddess's blades pierced his lungs too deeply for sudden movement. The silhouette of the Herlequin swept over him, the massive creature resettling at Silas's head, reaching broad hands towards him.

The shriek that filled the air did not come from Silas. The monstrous sound, one that sought to tear free the few leaves remaining upon winter limbs, caused Crane to start, twisting his blades.

A choked laugh jumped from Silas.

'What is that?' The Herlequin's hiss was the blast of a steam engine.

'A skriker…a hound of death.' Crane eased the pressure on the scythe. 'Of small concern to us, but do not let your Hunt be distracted.'

The shriek came again. Much closer this time, even to Silas's water-filled ears. Christ almighty, had he ever heard such a beautiful sound? Forneus had found him.

'Surround us.' It was as though an entire ballroom had dropped all its chandeliers at once. The Herlequin's call superseded the ear-piercing sound of the skriker. The order was meant, Silas presumed, for the assembled fae of the Hunt, their exact location hidden from him where he lay. 'Find your places, be at the ready.'

Another cry rang out. Not a shriek this time but a hoarse and awful scream. The foolish grin upon Silas's face widened. Bloody hell, never would he have imagined the ugly sounds of a teratism could be so welcomed. *His* teratism. There was not a doubt in his mind.

The Herlequin glared down at him. 'What is that? What do you know?'

Oh, he knew many things. 'Know of what?' Silas found his own voice rough.

'Don't piss around, Mercer.' Crane's face was set in furious, hard lines. He pulled the scythe's blade free from Silas's chest. The sudden retreat had Silas wheezing, struggling to catch his breath. 'Get him up, get him up now.'

The Herlequin did so with a hand wrapped around Silas's neck, dragging him to his feet like he were a butchered duck. With the Nephilim's formidable height, he was able to dangle Silas so his feet were just neatly clear of the ground. With enough wriggling, Silas could touch his toes down, but it was hardly enough to reduce the intense pressure at his throat.

'Let me snap his neck now and be done with it.' Metal grated against wood, the Nephilim's words torture to listen to.

'He's no mortal man. You will finish nothing that way,' Crane snapped. 'Only a scythe can end an ankou.'

'Yet yours fails to do so.' The Herlequin's grasp tightened with his anger.

Cries rose from the assembly.

'Hold your ground.' But the Herlequin's order was buried beneath screams.

Chaos descended around them: flashes of movement, and a chorus of bestial snarls and growls that bounced between the trees, the heavy press of hooves upon the earth as horses shied and whinnied. The Dullahan's mount lunged backwards, going down low on its haunches as it backed away from the brook. With the Nephilim's hold on his airway taking its toll, Silas viewed it all through eyes watering and with mouth widened to suck at air that barely filtered to his lungs. Seeing the Dullahan's horse shift, he tensed, expecting to feel the bones tighten cruelly, but the horseman, intent on steadying his mount, let the coils slip too much. Silas pulled his right arm free, the bone tips scratching his skin, tearing his sleeve.

'What are you doing?' Balthazar Crane's fury lit his words. He jabbed the scythe towards the headless horseman. 'Hold him, Dullahan. I command you, *hold* him.'

But the headless horseman paid him no heed. As Silas's vision fluttered with black specks, the Herlequin's chokehold nearly too much, the Dullahan's bone whip slid away entirely. Its owner took it with him as he turned his roan and raced off towards the sounds of the fight raging deeper in the forest.

Take the blade.

The voice made Silas startle, its brush like a feather to the back of his neck. Izanami's presence spilled through him, a warmth that chased off the chill of the water and offered air to starving lungs.

Take the blade. He was my child once, and you are yet.

But dangling from the Herlequin's grasp, Silas was hardly within snatching distance. So he'd follow the goddess's command another way. Silas shoved one hand against the bulk of the Herlequin, using it to lever himself before he kicked out with all the strength he could muster. Luck was at last upon his side. His length played in his favour, and his swing saw him able to strike the toe of his boot against Balthazar Crane's wrist. The heavy impact drew a shocked, pained cry. With his vision more clouded than clear, Silas watched the scythe fly from the hands of its ankou. The blades glinted as they dropped into the brook, vanishing beneath the surface.

The Herlequin shook Silas, a violent thrust back and forth that would have broken his neck if he were not being braced by the Nephilim's hand. He put both hands into trying to loosen the grip about his neck and sent both his feet in an assault against the huge creature that held him. Silas kicked back blindly, relishing the blows that landed against a solidness the Major Oak would envy. But this was a long way from freedom and even further from where the scythe had landed. Crane cradled his hand against his belly as he waded back into the brook.

'Fuck, fuck...where is it?' He slashed at the water with his free hand, dropping to his knees, the brook's flow up to his waist.

Take the blade.

How Izanami expected Silas to do anything but fight to breathe, he could not say.

'Quickly, ankou.' The Herlequin's order sounded near as horrendous as the skriker's battle cry within the woods, a battle Silas hoped to all gods the hound was winning, because he himself was so very near to passing out.

'I need a moment.' Crane held his hand over the unsettled waters and closed his eyes, preparing to summon his blade just as Silas could have done the bandalore.

As he *should* have done the bandalore, god damn it. Silas blinked through tears forced by lack of air, but his head was suddenly, oddly clear.

Take the blade?

Christ almighty, he was such a slow bastard at times. He had another scythe at hand. Silas went slack in the Herlequin's hold, let go of all resistance, and opened his mind to intention. He slumped his head forward, closing his eyes, hoping fervently that the giant would fall for the ruse, and lessen his hold so Silas could breathe well enough to think straight. He turned his thoughts to the blades beneath the water, to calling on the scythe to heed him – to listen to its new master. For Silas was the firstborn among Izanami's children. Her Pale Horseman. And bloody hell, he *would* get his way.

His blood thundered in his ears, deadening the sounds of the teratism and the hound that fought for him. His veins sought to tear themselves from his skin as his call went out. The silent summons was delivered to a scythe being pulled at by two masters. Silas felt the trembling of Crane's hold upon his blades, tenuous and much disturbed by Silas's sudden arrival.

'Stop him.' Crane's protest was muffled, as though he was submerged in search of his scythe. 'He's trying to steal the blade.'

Any hope of a slackening in the Herlequin's grip vanished at that. The leader of the Wild Hunt scorched Silas's ear with his rasping voice. 'Whatever you intend here, Brother, it is all for a lost cause.' Brother. So this fiend did see Silas for what he was. For *part* of what he was, at least. It was an age since he'd been Nephilim. 'Give up. Let go. For your prince is long dead.'

Sick fear filled Silas. 'No.' Had he actually spoken? It was hard to hear anything over the roar of his own heartbeat.

'It is certain. And you can be sure the angels did not give him an easy death.'

Silas had the vague sense he should be enraged, or at the very least furiously indignant. Instead, there arrived a despondency, an utter, desolate surety that the Herlequin spoke the truth. The certainty hung from him, his bones turned to lead beneath his tattered clothes and bruised skin.

'He's dead...' Silas echoed the words as the hold around his throat finally eased. He took in a breath, but the air barely made it down to his lungs before a sob expelled it.

Pitch was dead. And had died alone.

Why was the Herlequin smiling? There was no darker day than this. The birds should fall from the sky, the trees bend in sorrow. That fucking brook had no right to bubble so merrily.

Silas's feet touched the ground, but his legs had no strength to hold him, and when the Nephilim released him, he collapsed to his knees, hands landing in the dirt, his desolation a shroud he'd never be fit to carry.

He'd failed. And lost so profoundly it paralysed him.

The distant sound of splashing reminded him of the other ankou's presence. Of the blade he'd sought to own. But what did any of that matter now?

'Keep him down awhile longer, Herlequin.'

Balthazar Crane needed not to have given any such command, for Silas couldn't recall how to get off his knees. Nor did he *want* to. He wished to sink into the ground, be buried as he'd been a thousand times before. Hide from this appalling misery. Was this why he was spared remembering each lifetime? No creature could survive a grief such as this, no matter the god that pulled their strings.

What an awful thing it was to feel love. It left a man ripe for tearing apart.

He pressed his forehead to the ground, the bruises made by the Nephilim aching. He could not bear this.

The skriker's cry rent a hole in the air. The hound was close. So close that Silas was certain he'd see him if he could only find the impetus to raise his head. But what was the point? He had nothing to fight for now. Despair crushed him down, heavier even than what he'd felt when the teratism shared his vision.

He did not move when a black shape passed by, sending up flares of mud in its haste. Nor did Silas move when the Herlequin released a horrendous scream that made his bones quiver.

His grief was a quagmire, and he'd not fight its pull. Perhaps, if he was lucky, it would drown him. Finally. Once and for all.

Thick fangs drove into his arse cheek, a crushing bite that even misery could not deny.

Silas bellowed his unhappiness, jolting upright. Clarity rushed in like a dam bursting. Pitch was not dead. The certainty that had consumed Silas was a goddamned lie. Pitch had not been stolen from him. For Christ's sake, Silas was death's messenger. A loss of such magnitude would never escape him.

He was utterly, immovably certain.

'Shit, you are a foolish man,' Silas cursed himself for falling prey to the Herlequin's mindplay. 'Get off your damned knees.'

The hound had already moved on. Forneus was set to the task at hand, as Silas should bloody well be. He pressed to his feet with a cantankerous hiss, his butt cheek throbbing where the hound had made his mark.

A collision of two great bodies shook the ground.

The skriker clung to the Herlequin's broad back, his jaws locked on the creature's shoulder, both of them releasing sounds that would sit well in hell, but the sight nearly comical for all the Nephilim's failed efforts to dislodge his passenger. He stumbled about, huge feet slippery upon the leaf litter which seemed to have turned itself to ice beneath him. The bulk of his massive arms prevented him from reaching easily for the biting, tearing hound upon his back, and the Herlequin became an absurd, maddened ballerina, seeking to dislodge the creature who ate into him.

Silas turned his attentions back to the ankou.

To where Balthazar Crane stepped from the brook. His scythe was in hand, water gleaming on his ridiculous muttonchops, his eyes glinting with a fever not borne entirely of grim purpose. There was fear there too.

Silas drew on all his ample height, looking down on the turncoat. He barely recognised his own voice when he spoke. 'Your time is done with, Mr Crane.' Venom impaled every word. 'You will relinquish that blade to me. Now.'

CHAPTER 29

The whites of Iblis's eyes seeped into the dull brown of his irises, tangling there as the brambles had done so valiantly around the clearing. The angel's body stiffened in the way of one expecting a blow. He was muttering, so low and soft Pitch could not make out the words over his own grunts of discomfort.

A subtle shudder ran through Iblis, before his body relaxed.

'There you are, little prince.' The voice that emerged from between the angel's lips was not his own. 'Give your secrets to me.'

A ludicrous request. And if Pitch could have moved his lips, he would have sneered. As it was, the best he could manage was a sniff and a roll of his eyes.

Iblis's smile was wooden, his eyes a horrid blend of his own and...another's. Pitch's blood ran cold. Understanding what he was seeing. Scrying. Of an order few could manage. This was intensely powerful divine magick, to scry through another living being, rather then through an innate piece of onyx.

Pitch was not certain who stared out at him – and was not sure he wished to know. If it was one of the sorcerers, their mastery of divine magick was deeply concerning; and if it was not, then it was an angel of the highest ranks, a Cultivator he had not the slightest inclination to meet.

Iblis began to chant. His flat tones could be mistaken for droll mutterings wafting in from a monastery, so close to a hum that it was difficult to discern if words were being spoken at all.

Pitch's body hummed too, but with instinctual alarm. A dire predicament had become infinitely more so with the hidden observer, and yet he was still abandoned by the blasted wildness. A power that had been nearly uncontrollable only a week ago was now a loafing, lazy passenger. Pitch shifted, working his wrists against the stone-lodged cuffs while trying very hard not to disturb Iblis's blade. As it was, he was bleeding. The heat spilled beneath the corset, running along the slanted muscle at the inside of his hip and being channelled towards his very unhappy cock. For the first time, he regretted a lack of drawers, which was truly the most farcical thought to have while hanging at the mercy of avenging angels, but at least it was some distraction from the dreary singalong. It pained Pitch's ears to listen, even though there was a noticeable rhythm now to the odious tones, and a quickening of the pace. One that pulsed in time with his own heart, which in turned raced harder and faster with each word the angel uttered.

Pitch grunted against his gag – feeling altogether very odd.

Which was saying something, considering the wrecked state he was in. Iblis sidled in closer, bringing his mouth level with Pitch's ear. Gods, he hoped his underarms reeked. It was the very least the Watcher angel deserved. Iblis's breath stirred the hair hanging around Pitch's ear, and his monotone uttering sent a thrill of shivers scrambling along Pitch's spine.

Was that worrisome? Was he afraid? Why could he not decide?

This was the type of moment where a daemon's foul mouth usually served him well. A vulgar suggestion of what the angel could do with his tongue would normally be flung out to unsettle the occasion. Instead, Pitch was muted, and rather...well, he was feeling peculiar. That hum of alarm beneath his skin, the panic that had plagued him of late, wasn't gathering strength. It was...lackadaisical. What a fantastical word. He truly must use it more often. He grinned behind lips that could not shape a smile.

Lackadaisical. Lacka...daisi...cal. Imagine trying to teach that word to the ankou? Pitch breathed through his nostrils, exhaling the last shreds of jittery alarm. He wished he could speak. He wanted to ask them when Silas was arriving at the little party. He wanted to tell him about lackadaisical.

'Be honest with me.' Iblis's words, or rather whoever sat at the back of his eyes, found their shape. 'Be honest with me.'

The words touched at Pitch's mouth like the tips of a feather. He rolled his head back and forth but wasn't sure he wanted to avoid them. Something was definitely off-kilter, and yet, at the same time, he could not recall feeling so relaxed in a long while. The angel traced his finger along Pitch's lips and took up his humming once more. The black of his pupils blew wide, obliterating the brown that was already being strangled by the whites. In the onyx depths, another eye opened.

Pitch flinched, only to find his skull thumping against stone. Where had that wall come from?

'He played with you, didn't he?' That voice. It was familiar. That godsdamned voice. 'Seraphiel had a purpose for his little mindless prince. Show me what it is. Be honest with me.'

Pitch coughed against the fastening upon his mouth, vaguely aware that he needed to swallow desperately, but it was as though his mind and body could take on only one thought at a time. And all he could think, all he could hear in his head...was Azazel.

Pitch was eye to eye with the Exarch of Elyssiam.

'Be honest with me.' Iblis's mouth moved with his master's words, his tongue shaping the words Azazel wished delivered, words spoken in the fiercely guarded secret language of the higher angels: the Cultivators. How could he have forgotten the lilt? Seraphiel had carried on with it more times than Pitch could remember.

He slipped his heels from where they pressed against the stone to try to ease the weight on his wrists.

His tongue itched. Itched to speak of what had been done to him. Itched to reveal the secrets of Blood Lake. To be honest with the Exarch.

With each of Iblis's resonating hums, Pitch's mind softened. Became less his own. And though he thought he knew why – magick and all that nonsense – he cared too little to protest.

What harm in telling the Exarch of Seraphiel's meddling? Pitch need not be loyal to a bastard who had imprisoned him, who had twisted him up inside so badly that he did not recognise himself.

He stared at Iblis, who was but a few inches away. Stared into the eyes within the eyes. Should he speak up?

He blinked, startled by a sudden image of the ankou, of Silas scowling, shaking his head. Warning Pitch to say nothing?

Why did everyone always wish to keep him silent? He wanted to talk. To be heard. He'd never had a voice.

He was property. The property of the Lord of Arcadia, of the King of Daemonkind, of the Seraphim. And none of them wished to hear their chattel speak. They preferred their servants silent. Submissive.

And besides, Silas wasn't here. He'd lied. He'd said he would be here. Promised he would not leave the mad prince alone. That he'd protect Pitch.

That he loved him.

Pitch's body jerked with a fit of bitter laughter. Wetness dribbled from his nose as he snorted his disdain. Had he actually believed the ankou could ignore all his foulness and find a creature beneath to *love*? Whatever the fuck that meant.

'Be honest with me.' Azazel's voice caressed him, filtered through into painful, raw places. 'Tell me your secrets.'

Did the angel truly wish to listen?

That would be a first. Having an audience who listened to him. Who heard when Pitch said he asked for none of this and he resented, to his very core, being made a vessel for Seraphiel. He didn't want to go to Blood Lake, gods damn it, and fix someone else's mistakes. He wished he'd never stepped foot in this fucking world. For then he'd never have met the ankou. Silas made Pitch's mind hurt, knotting it into unrecognisable shapes, deluding it into imagining there was a place for him at his lover's side.

The ankou was not here. He'd not kept his promise.

But the Exarch would. And they promised to listen.

So tell him.

The idea perched in Pitch's mind, a canary in its gilded cage, beautiful and delicate and begging to be regarded. He *wanted* to speak. The Lady had trapped his tongue. His silence had been forced on him with yet more of the violence to which he was accustomed. But here...here Azazel just asked him to speak.

Iblis ran his thumb across Pitch's lip once more. He stared into the eyes of his enemy and was nearly...nearly what? Overwhelmed. Overwhelmed by the desire to speak up.

Pitch shook his head, trying to break away from Iblis's touch. Overwhelmed...strange thought, was it not? But he truly wished to speak...and Azazel wished to listen.

Pitch shrugged his shoulders, barely bothered by the painful tug at his hands. His moment of pause rushed away in an instant. He jutted his chin, mumbling against the sewn barrier of his own lips.

He wished to speak.

To tell them everything he knew.

Iblis caught on quickly and touched the tips of his fingers to Pitch's mouth. Freedom was instant, rushing in with the air Pitch dragged through his widened mouth. The iciness of it prickled the back of his throat.

Breathe. Breathe.

Familiar words. Who'd said them to him?

'Be honest with me.' Azazel's honeyed voice drew him back. 'But hurry now. We don't want to be interrupted, do we?'

Pitch was the centre of the Exarch's world. Not at its periphery, or hidden in a Sanctuary like a dreadful secret. 'No, I don't want to be interrupted,' Pitch whispered.

'Then take a breath, and speak.'

He drew in a deep lungful, as directed, and the words spilled from him in a rush. 'Truly, if the man weren't such an oaf, I wouldn't need to bloody breathe so much. For I'd not be so worried all the damned time that he'd be hurt.'

Iblis blinked, and the angel sharing his eyes blinked a second later. The strange echoed imaged was mildly disconcerting to see and stirred a sense of unease that Pitch promptly ignored.

He had an audience who wished to listen. That was all that mattered.

'Who?' Iblis brought Azazel's voice very close. Far too close really, but Pitch's desire to speak was too assuaged to mind. He spewed his thoughts.

'Silas Mercer,' he replied. 'Who else? That very tall, very broad man who is out there in the forest somewhere when he said he'd be here, with me. He lied, didn't he? He's run off the moment he could, hasn't he? You can tell me.' But even if Iblis looked as though he intended to reply, which his befuddled expression made difficult to determine, Pitch gave him no chance. Unsealing his lips had been akin to opening a floodgate. Pitch could barely keep the words from tripping over one another and was irritated by the need to take a breath. 'I mean I shouldn't be surprised. I'm not so likeable really. I know it. That's why I made myself so beautiful, so utterly divine to look at, because it distracts from the putrid mess that lies beneath. But he must be more the fool than I thought, for he seems to think he likes the contents of this pretty package. Can you imagine, the man claims he loves me.' Pitch laughed and he was bright and airy, and not even sure where he was anymore, only that all this needed to be said. 'But I'm rather new to all this, so I'm not entirely certain if I feel the same way. What do you think? I have him in my thoughts for more minutes than there are in a day. I want him to touch me, even when we are not fucking. And the fucking is superb, did I tell you?' For that also had to be said.

'You did not, and I did not ask,' someone replied, though who, Pitch wasn't sure and did not care. He was a pot boiling over.

'I'm not sure why it's so wonderful. My dear Sickle is well-endowed but hardly the largest cock I've had, and I tend to come far too quickly where he is involved. It must be all the hugging. He's prone to far too much hugging. I abhor hugging, hand-holding makes my toes curl, but I find myself wondering when he is next going to drag me into one of his ceaseless embraces. He kisses me, a lot. Far too much but I only complain half the time I should. Is any of that love, do you suppose?'

'By Dagan's light, what's wrong with him? He's prattling like a lunatic,' said Zaquiel.

It was the first reminder in a very long while that two other angels completed Iblis's party. Pitch didn't even know the other chap's name, the one who'd been especially rough in his handling, but that was hardly of importance. There were urgent words to be spoken.

'Oh, you have no idea how much is wrong with me, dear fellow.' Pitch grinned, knowing how crooked it was upon his lips. But that was what happened when he thought about Silas. The world went topsy-turvy, entirely the wrong way about. 'But that's the thing, you see. He doesn't seem to care about the monster I am. Even though he knows Seraphiel has made me one.' He faltered, his thoughts slippery for a moment, the tickling in his throat finding a sharper edge.

Iblis blinked again, his master doing the same only fractionally later. 'A monster? And what sort might that be?'

Pitch shrugged. The halo cut at him and the cuffs reminded him he was going nowhere at all. 'I don't know, and that is the honest truth.' He did not feel so well. There was a heaviness upon his tongue he did not like. 'The Seraphim has placed something inside me...I think...or added something...I don't know. Until very recently I thought it was going to spill over, and I'd lose myself entirely. The wildness is a power far beyond my own, I think. Or perhaps a magnification of it? I'm not sure. Do you know?' Iblis watched, waited. As though he knew perfectly well Pitch would not pause long enough for any decent chance to answer. 'I wish I knew, because it terrifies me, more than ever now, because I have him. I don't want to hurt him. I am so frightened, all the time, that I'll do damage I cannot repair. If I hurt Silas, I could not bear it.'

The prickling at his throat spread, reaching to the back of his mouth. He was suddenly conscious of how hard and cold the stone was at his back, of how the burn he'd suffered throbbed so punishingly, like a clock marking time.

Time.

How long had he been hanging here? He looked away from Iblis and the Exarch to where the dryad was entombed in horror.

'He doesn't need to worry about being the one to damage the ankou.'

Pitch jerked his head towards the chuckled muttering that came from the angel at his right, the fellow with harsh hands and an auburn tinge to his hair.

'What did you say?'

'Now, Mr Astaroth, never mind Harut. Return to our conversation.' Iblis, or rather Azazel's, pleasant manner was a drenching that washed away consternation. 'You say the Seraphim you destroyed gave you this power?'

Pitch replied without hesitation. 'Yes. I didn't want to kill him, you know. I deeply regret it. It tears me up inside to think on. And I still don't understand how it could happen. I mean, he was killed by his own ministrations really. Because at times I utterly lose control, and I know that is not a new thing for me...I'm the Berserker Prince after all...but it's been far worse since he brought me here...and...made me a bigger monster than perhaps even he intended. Seeing as I managed to kill him and all.'

Pitch didn't realise he'd been staring down and telling all this to the lengths of his coat, rather Silas's coat, until Iblis gripped his hair, an unkind tug forcing his head up.

'And why would Seraphiel need a monster? What was the purpose of all this? Did he seek to create greater warriors for Enoch?'

'Well, that's the story they both told, I believe. But it wasn't the truth.' He spoke quickly, fearing he'd lost favour here somehow, with how tightly the angel held his hair. It wouldn't be right to upset those who wished him to be honest with them. 'I wasn't defending Arcadia or helping to make the Dominion greater warriors of the Hellfield at all. I was made for this world.'

'This world?'

Be honest with me. Azazel had truly pleading eyes. Even if they were a bit horrendous, nestled within Iblis's own. *Be honest with me.*

The urge to do as the Exarch bade was titanic.

'Yes, this world. And what it holds.' Titanic, and yet...Pitch couldn't help but think it would be nice not to have such an odd sensation in his throat, and something more pleasant at his back. He was hurting. Quite a lot. But he'd agreed to dangle here...had he not?

'What did Seraphiel seek to protect here, then?'

Pitch sought to smile but hesitated, unsure of what he found amusing. 'Oh he's not protecting anything. He wishes to destroy it.'

Iblis shifted on his feet, running his tongue over his lips before Azazel's voice came from him once more. 'Destroy what, little prince?'

Pitch flinched, and that tickling in his throat forced him to clear it before he could speak. 'Destroy the...' His gaze shifted to Robin once more, lifting to follow the lines of their petrified vines to where a gaping hole punctured the brambles. Gods, he felt odd. 'I want to see Silas now.'

'That can be arranged, as soon as you answer the question.' The Exarch's words dripped with syrup. Pitch could barely drag another of those precious breaths into his lungs. 'Tell me what your angel seeks to destroy, sweet one.'

A ripple of something terribly unpleasant caught at Pitch's gut. 'I don't like that name.' Onoskolis had called him that as she violated him. The ripple strengthened, bitter and coarse and indigestible. 'I want to see Silas now.'

'Forget the ankou.' Brusque talk, the harshest from Azazel thus far. Iblis blinked. He may have gritted his teeth. 'My apologies, Your Highness. Tell me, which name do you prefer?'

'I prefer...' He closed his mouth on the astonishing, mortifying truth. Pitch would not be that honest, not even as the saccharine words Silas bestowed on him pressed at the back of his teeth, brushed at his tongue, yearned to pull free. This truth was Pitch's. Not even the angel who listened could take it from him. He squeezed his eyes shut, searching for illumination in the darkness, inordinately afraid that if he told Azazel he liked it best when Silas named him "darling," the Exarch would destroy all hope of ever hearing it said again. 'I prefer Pitch. Please let me see Silas now.'

'Very soon. I promise you.' The angel was so fixated on honesty, why would he lie himself? 'Pitch, be honest with me, what did Seraphiel seek to destroy?' Azazel's voice was full of comforts, warm furs in winter, a hot bath after a long day's ride, while Pitch was sore and aching and so very tired.

'He intends me for Blood Lake –'

Scarlet burst from a crack in the tree like a deranged fledgling leaving the nest too soon. Waving rainbow-hued arms about, chittering madly in its indecipherable tongue, its immovable eyes giving it a crazed look.

'Get rid of that bloody thing,' Iblis, and not the Exarch, shouted. So damned close his breath made Pitch's eyelids flutter.

'I don't want you to hurt that creature,' Pitch said. 'They are not too awful to have around.'

Will Scarlet flew like a bee drunk on honey, avoiding three frustrated angels, who were in danger of hitting one another rather than the tiny will-o'-the-wisp. Scarlet darted straight at Pitch and slapped his cheek. The most ineffectual, insipid slap he'd received in a long history of such things, but by the Archangels' taints, it bothered him. He'd just declared the bright flittering critter moderately bearable, and this was his reward?

'That did not hurt at all.' Pitch's tongue continued to heed the Exarch's demand for honesty. 'But I am greatly offended that you think so little of me.'

Harut brought an end to the miniature assault by backhanding the will-o'-the-wisp against the fortified tree. Scarlet's startled cry was short-lived. It dropped to the churned soil at the angel's feet, and Harut kicked its tiny body, barely larger than a plum, sending mud and leaf litter flying.

Pitch turned his head, peering around his own arm to try to catch sight of the rainbow, distantly aware that it hurt his shoulder terribly to do so. 'That happens so often to those around me,' he whispered. 'I wish it were not so.'

'Focus, daemon.' Iblis and his master returned with hard fingers on soft skin, squeezing Pitch's jaw, forcing his head about. 'Forget the unimportant things and return to what you were telling me.' Iblis's voice was not his own once more. His grip was tremendous, giving Pitch no recourse but to stare into those eyes within eyes, into the fastening hold of the Exarch who pinned him despite what must be an enormous distance between them. Azazel was on his throne in Elyssiam. The world of the purebreds had long ago been made unreachable for him. 'Tell me what Seraphiel seeks to destroy in Blood Lake?'

Pitch stared at Iblis. Blood. There was blood upon the angel. A tiny trickle oozing from one nostril. There in the whites of his eyes too. Splatters like ugly snowflakes around the abyss where Azazel waited impatiently.

'You're bleeding.' Pitch stated the very obvious and irrelevant truth. 'Answer me.'

Of course he would. Pitch wanted nothing more than to speak the truth. 'The halo. Samyaza's halo remains in Blood Lake.'

There was utter stillness around him and within the angel who listened. Iblis's pupils flared wider, the black submerging all the angel's own colour, the Exarch taking over completely. 'The halo survives?'

'In Blood Lake, yes. That's what I said.' Pitch bit down hard on his lip, skin splitting with the pressure. His eyelids fluttered, confusion gripping him. 'Didn't you know?'

Shouldn't Iblis know? Should Azazel? Fuck, why was it so hard to keep his thoughts in a row? He glanced down, seeing royal blue, and the dugout in the earth where Harut's boot had dispatched Scarlet.

The will-o'-the-wisp had slapped him. Shaken its head. Tried to stop him?

'And you are the vessel that would destroy the halo?' Where had the angel's comforting timbre gone? Azazel sounded...well, there was venom where there'd been sugar coating before. Pitch sucked at his bleeding lip. Should he answer that? He was not so certain as before.

Be honest with me.

Iblis stroked his chin and touched at the corners of his lips, and Pitch replied, 'I am the vessel.'

The angels who flanked him were restless, impatient. Why was everyone so impatient all of a sudden?

'You, who are at our mercy?' Iblis's laughter joined with that of the angel's he carried, and neither was pleasant.

Pitch frowned into the odd phrasing. 'At your mercy? I thought you just wished to listen to me?'

One of the angels snickered. Iblis did not smile.

'We've heard enough. Hold his legs.'

Barely had the other angels done so, their hands on Pitch's knees, their feet stomping his own hard against the tree, and the halo pierced deep, sliding through flesh and sinew and other places he could not name. Pitch released a strangled cry, bucking against his restraints, tearing fresh pain from his burn.

'You fucking cunts,' Pitch spat. 'Don't touch me.'

But Iblis was done with listening. He sank the blade deeper still, reaching into the abyss where the wildness usually lurked. He placed one hand above where the halo impaled Pitch's belly, scowling as he worked the weapon like a thief with a lockpick.

'Why is he still moving?' Zaquiel nearly deafened Pitch on top of all else. 'What are you waiting for?' He kneed Pitch's thigh, ensuring he could barely shift his hips against the penetration of the halo.

'Shut your mouth,' Iblis hissed, all semblance of pleasantness gone, working his wrist as he adjusted the angle.

'Oh fuck.' Pitch's own curse slipped through bloodied lips but was not born of pain. The halo's prodding was all levels of unpleasant. Godsdamned awful, as though his belly were filled to the brim with serpents all moving at once. But unpleasant was very different to painful.

Iblis made a strange sound, something between a snarl and a growl, and he dragged the halo free, taking a step back, wiping Pitch's blood absently against his cloak. The angel's own nose bled profusely, his eyes a map of crimson ruin as his Exarch ruled them.

'The Seraphim has a seal set upon his monster.' The words bore the weight of Azazel's voice upon them. 'A sleeping beauty who I would very much like to wake on my own terms.' Iblis peeled his gaze from Pitch, taking Azazel with him, and fixed on Harut. The angel's composure slipped, his startle obvious, before he gathered himself and bowed his head.

'Your Majesty.'

'That halo is no use here. You will need more to destroy this vessel, but there is still more to learn of where this rat and his ankou are bound for. Deliver him to the Morrigan with all haste.' Iblis turned back to Pitch. His lips shifted at the corners, jerking up as though someone's fingertips dragged at the skin. 'Now I understand why my lord calls to my maleficent children. Thank you, little daemon, for being so delightfully honest with me.'

Iblis's eyes closed in a slow blink, and when the lids were raised again, there was only the drab hue of Dr Severs's eyes to see. Pitch's blood thinned.

'Where has he gone?' Desperation sank into him. 'He promised...he...the Exarch said I could see...Silas.' The word was less than a whisper, more a breath of pained air, but it was the only sound that made any sense at all.

The magick slipped away, mist at sunrise retreating, leaving his mind naked, flayed bare and raw.

Oh gods, what had he done? What had he just been *made* to do?

'You heard His Majesty.' The voice of Dr Severs returned, unremarkable and plain. Not girded by his master. His shoulders hunched, the curve in his spine evident as the weight of Azazel left him bent. Good. Let him suffer. 'Harut, we must summon the Hunt. They will be done with the ankou by now. Ready him.'

Zaquiel reached for whatever mechanism had Pitch pinned so solidly to the tree, and Harut stepped away, withdrawing something from beneath his cloak, but Pitch barely noticed the movements. Barely registered all the damage he'd just done. How he'd blathered to the ruler of Elyssiam, the very creature the halo was intended for, of the weapon's existence.

Done with the ankou.

While Pitch was here spilling his fucking guts, had the Herlequin managed the unthinkable? Bile seared up his throat, parching the lingering prickle there. He was dizzy with horror, with pain, with the magnitude of what had been done, and what *might* have been.

Hold it together, you imbecile.

He'd lost his marbles once too often, fearing the ankou gone. And each time he'd been wrong.

Silas survived.

Surely Pitch would feel the Earth tilt, see some of the stars slip from the sky, if that were not so. He would fucking *know* if that stupid oaf was gone for good.

Pitch dug a heel into the neck of his panic, stomping it down. The bandalore was right here, in the pocket of Silas's coat. Its master did not need it.

Silas survived. And so Pitch must too.

He took a breath. Sucked it up his nostrils like it were sugar and cocaine and all the white fluffy things he adored. *Breathe.*

A long mournful note rang out as Zaquiel released Pitch from where he hung. The angel did not try to halt his fall, and Pitch's legs were unable to support the rest of him, bringing him to his knees. Harut held a curled white horn to his mouth, the pearlescent surface twisting the paltry light, as he blew a summons for the Wild Hunt. The echo of the singular note resonated deeply through the clearing. Pieces of Robin's hair chipped away, falling in macabre imitation of their petals.

Pitch put up little struggle as Iblis resealed his lips, silencing him anew. He wished to be gone from this place. Taken far from where he could cause more harm.

He had tried to run, he had sought to hide, and here was the result. A debt he could never repay to a forest that had given him its all.

Iblis's instructions were absently given. The angel was distracted, his gaze shifting between Harut with his horn and the opening burned through the brambles.

Pitch's fragile instincts locked in on the glances, even as Zaquiel behaved like an utter prick, grabbing his coat near enough to the halo burn to agonise. But Pitch barely whimpered.

The Watcher angel was unhappy.

Pitch's mind raced, finding its way, throwing off all that lingered of Azazel's hex. Did the Wild Hunt not heed the angel's summons?

Hope dared bloom, a mangled, ugly little flower, but one that pressed through the cracks regardless.

'Again,' Iblis snapped.

Harut obeyed. And the solemn note from the horn hung cold and lonely in the air. The forest held its breath, defying the angels and holding silence like a shroud around its boughs. Pitch swore the grimace upon Robin's petrified face was not so terror-stricken as when he'd last cast it a reticent glance. Was it possible the hamadryad was not so easily felled?

Did they see what Pitch saw? A trio of angels too disturbed to bother concealing their unease. Pitch smiled like a madman behind unmoving lips .

Oh the Hunt was not done with Silas at all. For the ankou was not done with the Wild Hunt.

And the truth of it was written all over Iblis's mediocre face. The angel was fucking furious.

A sob of relief entwined with laughter behind Pitch's sealed lips, and he loosened a positively marvellous string of vulgar taunts at all the angels. Wonderful vitriol that was wasted upon this party, who paid him as much attention as a mannequin standing in a dress shop.

Pitch's delightful, momentary smugness vanished with the next few simple words from Iblis.

'We shall take to the sky. Wings, gentlemen.'

CHAPTER 30

S ilas pursed his lips, his eyes locked on the scythe in Balthazar Crane's beefy hand. He was not a small man, the other ankou, but to Silas's eye he certainly seemed so in that moment. The ankou's aura coiled in tight against his body, tentacles retracting, seeking shelter.

'Oh, Mr Mercer, you shall have to do far more than ask for my scythe.'

Glaring, Crane wielded his scythe one-handed, as though readying for attack, but he was afraid. It was written all over him. And well it should be. He suffered a noticeably broken wrist, and the fight between skriker and Nephilim was ripping holes in the air, with both creatures making sounds not fit for ears to hear. More distantly the teratism made its mark upon the forest with equally unsettling noise, fighting off an enemy Silas had yet to lay eyes upon.

How had he ever imagined himself alone here?

His lips shifted into the briefest of smirks before Silas reshaped them, letting his tongue curl, ready for the note he would need. And in one long exhale, he called on Izanami's lost scythe.

The whistled note cut at the air as well as any sword might. The finality of death was always sharp.

'Dullahan!' the ankou cried, for Crane heard all that Silas's note contained and the seething unhappiness of the goddess he'd betrayed. 'I command you –'

Whatever he thought to demand from the absent headless horseman, Silas did not learn, for Crane's cry was consumed by his efforts to keep hold on the scythe. He lurched bodily forward, and it was miraculous the ankou kept his footing. His fingers curled about the hilt. He slapped both hands to it, a choked cry escaping him as his broken wrist was forced to action. The ankou's feet braced, body tilted back, as though he were wielding a kite so huge that it threatened to lift him from his feet.

But the scythe did not seek to rise to the sky. It sought to heed the note Silas whistled to it, to return to the true messenger of death.

'Fuck...' Crane spat, veins bulging in his neck with the strain upon him. To his credit, or rather that of the goddess Morrigan he bowed to, the ankou put up a considerable fight, proving himself no walkover. Crane held a depth to his strength that had not been evident on their first encounter. At Gidleigh Park House the traitor seemed more sycophant than challenger.

Not so now.

But good luck to goddess and turncoat, both. Silas had no time for either. This was not where he needed to be.

With Forneus's screech and the Herlequin's jarring cries chaotic in the background, Silas drew on deeper reserves, his own note strengthening. His call was greater than that of a hundred sirens unified as one. His lungs sent forth more air easily, as though he'd inhaled all there was available in the world and it was at his disposal now. The note would not end until his cause was met.

And that end was so exquisitely, tantalisingly close.

Crane's heel slipped in the mud, a damp and unexpected ally in this forest of friend and foe. The ankou's precarious balance shifted irreparably. The twin blades ripped from his grasp and arrowed straight at Silas.

He met them halfway, snatching the weapon from the air, settling it in his grasp as he ran on.

Crane had no time to get his wits about him before Silas was on him, landing his full considerable weight upon the slighter ankou. He heard joints pop beneath him, heard the ankou's curse fly free with a gasp.

Silas's skin tingled, the goddess feeding on his fervour. 'Traitor.' He ground out the word. 'Your goddess's end will come as surely as yours.'

Balthazar Crane's eyes widened, and he tried to speak, to utter his last words. Silas slipped his hand around the ankou's neck and held him in readiness for the blow they both knew was coming. The blade shivered at his touch, the metal warping like tin in the midday sun. The twin blades merged, and confusion emanated from the scythe like a fine sea spray as it threw off what remained of the goddess who had stolen it.

Crane stared up at him, revealing in the depths of his eyes the shadows of divine sisters at war. The ankou was still defiant, still raging, but through his eyes alone. He did not seek to shake off Silas's hold nor slither from beneath his weight.

'I wanted more time.' His eyes bulged with speaking through a choked throat. 'I just wanted more time...a year...it is not enough.' The ankou's last moments were pitiful. 'I don't want to die.'

'You have no say in the matter.' Silas leaned close, made sure his words could be heard over that of the warring skriker and Nephilim. 'None of us do. And if your betrayal has harmed Pitch again, I'll hunt you down in the life that comes after this one, and you'll know no peace there either. You deserve none.'

'Silas, please –'

Death came as quickly for Balthazar Crane as it did a beggar on the street or a king upon his throne. Without apology or recourse. Swift and final.

The only difference here, the ankou saw it coming, arriving in all its macabre beauty.

The scythe he had wielded just a few moments before now drove itself deep into his heart, searching for, and finding, what had alluded him when he did the same to Silas.

Izanami reclaimed her blade and cut away the foetid tether that had granted Balthazar Crane a power he'd chosen to abuse. Silas twisted the blade, as She swept the ankou from Her service. The force of the disconnect was bone-jarring. Silas grimaced, weathering the unpleasant discord that ran through the blade: a very human stew of regret and angst, desire, delusion, and, at the very last, desperation.

Silas shuddered, and pulled the blade free.

His blade.

The metal hummed, the vibration tickling at his hand. Silas felt Izana-mi's pleasure as surely as he felt his own deep sense of relief. Her blade returned to its original form, a pair of silver spectacles, no more impres-sive than the bandalore. On meeting the ankou the first time, Silas had wondered why on Earth he would need glasses. Of course Crane hadn't, they were costume, a convenient disguise for his scythe. But he *had* been blind. Those glasses had granted Balthazar the extra time he'd been so desperate for. Greed had killed the ankou as surely as the blade just now.

A high-pitched, frantic yelp had Silas rising to his feet and turning about in time to see the Herlequin raising the struggling skriker above his head, his wide hands set at the hound's haunches and neck, his knee raised so his thigh was laid flat. Forneus's black fur was made darker in glistening patches, wounds bleeding, his enormous black tongue lolling as he fought to free himself.

'No!' Silas screamed and lunged.

The Nephilim fixed his central eye on Silas as he brought Forneus's body down. The hound's shriek was tainted with anguish and cut off cruelly as the Herlequin broke the skriker's back against his thigh. The terrible crack of the hound's spine was all Silas could hear as he dove at the Herlequin, incandescent with rage.

It was like diving against a wall of solid stone, and for a moment Silas feared for his own neck with the sudden stop. But though the Herlequin was a massive beast, Silas was not insubstantial. The Nephilim staggered back, and Silas threw his weight behind the glance of his blade.

'You fucking bastard.' He stabbed wildly into the endless pleats and folds of the Herlequin's cloak and clothes beneath as the Nephilim tried to peel him off. Thoughts of a wall of stone returned when the blade seemed to find impenetrable layers. Firm resistance threatened to dislodge the scythe from Silas's grasp as his fury, his grief, made his blows too frenzied to be precise.

The Nephilim snarled and delivered a mighty punch beneath Silas's chin. The strike threw him away and brought on stars and mottled vision. Silas landed hard against what he thought was a true stone wall but was likely one of the many wide-girthed trees surrounding them. A punishing blow that snapped the scythe from his hold but achieved little else. Forneus lay unmoving, no hint of his crimson glare. Silas's chest was hollow with the skriker's loss, a loss he knew resonated through countless unremembered years. His heart ached as he searched about, near blind, patting at the ground in the hopes of finding the lost scythe, the tug of anguish threatening to overwhelm him if he stilled for a moment. But barely was he grounded and Silas was being gathered up again. Fingers bit at his thigh as another hand clasped at his neck, hard upon his windpipe. The Herlequin raised him, just as he'd done the skriker, hoisting Silas overhead with barely a grunt, as though he were a belt won in the ring and no heavier.

Head pounding, some teeth likely shattered, Silas fought the appalling hold, wriggling his hips, kicking about with his leg that was not pinched into submission by the numbing grip of the Nephilim. It must have been like trying to keep hold of an oiled serpent, but the bastard managed it. Christ almighty, the strength of the creature was truly monstrous. Or Silas was too weakened to prove a foil. His kicking and shifting about only earned him a more brutal hold upon the neck, joints wrenching as body and head moved in differing directions.

'You are worse than your dog, Brother.' Glass slid and made fine cuts against Silas's ears as the Herlequin spoke. 'For you at least should put up a fight worthy of your lineage. But you have never been a fighter, have you, ankou? For here you are, a pathetic servant of death, when you could have lived in glory for our lord and father, who shall return.'

Live for Samyaza? Silas would sink to the bottom of that loch a hundred times over to elude such a fate. But there was no chance Silas could reply; he could barely draw enough air as it was. All efforts with his free arm and leg, trying to land a blow somewhere, anywhere that might be useful, were as effective as a wind-whipped flag. Silas coughed against the chokehold. The contorted ruin of Forneus's body was all he could see.

The Nephilim was right, was he not? Silas was pathetic.

The skriker had given himself up for a master unworthy of the sacrifice.

Silas's fevered attempts to free himself shuddered and fell apart. He hung like a true corpse above the Herlequin, ceasing the futile game of hide and seek he played with anguish. Why not let it win now? It would always find him. Find any living thing. There was no escaping loss...death...sorrow. He was going to lose Pitch...of course he was. Silas had spent thousands of years losing all he knew and loved.

A dreadful sound came from the Herlequin, another which sounded too much like corrupted laughter. The creature braced, grip tightening, and he tossed Silas away. Not downward, as he'd done with the skriker, but out towards the trees again.

Silas could not find the impetus to do anything but let the momentum take him. Let the hulk of an oak or elm or birch bring him to a violent, gut-tangling halt. Why had he ever cared which tree was which? Pitch was right. It was pointless, uninteresting. And all trees would die. Silas would lose every single one of them, too.

He struck the nameless timber, and thumped to the forest floor, his cheek upon the damp soil, his mood so wretched that repair seemed impossible. Which was not the least he deserved, considering all those he had failed this day.

'I'm sorry,' he whispered, sending tiny fragments of decay floating about as he sank deep into the sands of melancholy. 'You deserved better than I.'

A silver glint drew his eye. The spectacles lay not an arm's reach away from where he wallowed, bruised to his very core. They shone again, as though there was something to brighten for in these bleak woods.

'Take the scythe, Brother.' The Herlequin's breadth stole the light. The scythe dulled. 'You suffer. Deliver yourself from your own misery. Redemption lies in that blade, ankou.' The Nephilim had seemed large before. Now he was a mountain looming over Silas as he lay. 'Take up the blade, Silas Mercer, before you do more harm. Give yourself the end no one else cares enough to give.'

Silas blinked, the sting of tears blurring the Nephilim's horrid features, the hang of skin and rot of teeth, the crooked path of his nose. The creature was right. One simple strike and this would all be over. He would do no more harm. Pitch would truly be safe if there were not a fool stuck to his side. Silas felt himself sinking into the soil, the weight of his failures heavy upon him.

There was a momentary flicker, a sudden thought, delicate as the drop of an eyelash. What failures? What harm? He'd fought hard, he loved harder...his prince needed his oaf. And Silas needed to be at Pitch's side like he needed...air to breathe.

Awareness set off bells that peeled alarm. This was all too familiar, this tug-of-war in his head. Silas shrugged his shoulders, tried to raise his cheek from the ground, lift his head despite the heaviness of tightly weaved despair. 'Stop this. I need...'

Another wave struck, a tsunami too monumental to withstand. Silas dropped his head, tears burning as they fell. A new, fresh, bullying certainty took hold. The goddess had wasted her time dragging him from the depths that day in the loch.

'The blade, ankou. Take it to your throat. End your misery.'

With a groan Silas reached and found the glasses at his fingertips, as though they yearned for his touch as much as he for theirs.

'Bring forth your scythe. The power to end this lies with you alone. Bring on your demise, bring on peace.' The Herlequin's words ran like warm honey against Silas's senses, no longer pernicious to hear. The seduction was undeniable, nimble and arousing as a lover's touch.

Silas curled his fingers around the rim of one of the lenses, a soft moan escaping.

'Quickly now, Silas Mercer.' Sweeter than honey this time, so rich Silas thought he could taste the Herlequin's words melting upon his own tongue. 'Before those arrive who would steal your right to reprieve and your chance is lost.'

The scythe, new and pliant and willing, rearranged itself. It brought forth the compact, sharp, little blade he required, a simple wooden handle squat and perfectly snug in Silas's palm.

He exhaled. Christ, what a relief awaited him, a final rest from so much endurance. He was exhausted...he was... Silas touched the edge of the blade to his throat, the metal icy, his blood warm where it spilled at once.

He was...

'Now, deeper. Let your blood run, Silas Mercer.'

He was Silas Mercer. He was ankou. He was a hundred other curiosities.

But he was not ready to leave.

A brittle protest sought to rise to his lips.

'Cut your throat, ankou.' The Herlequin's voice returned to its foul origins, cuspate as the blade Silas held.

The Nephilim pushed him, brutal now, impatient. And shockingly powerful. The creature's physical strength paled alongside this...this murderous mindplay. Even as the clouds parted in Silas's head, even as he realised this was the same game played earlier, when he'd thought for certain Pitch was dead, shaking off the Nephilim was like trying to crawl up from the deepest, darkest pit by his fingernails.

The weight of escape lay ten times heavier than the despair that had trapped Silas to begin with. He could not stop the press of his hand, the slow driving of the blade harder against his flesh.

He could not help *feeling* as though this was what he longed for. Even as his reasonable mind screamed for him to cease. The Herlequin had his claws deep.

Silas choked out a sound, gurgled his refusal, and all the while his blood ran faster. The cut widened.

Herein lay his true end, by the one instrument guaranteed to bring it about. And the Nephilim knew it. He could not kill Silas, just as Crane had said. But he could guide the ankou's hand to kill himself.

A resolute and mournful note rang out. Nothing of death's note or naming melody, but the deep thrum of a horn's blow.

The burden upon Silas's mind lessened by the tiniest degree, but it was more than enough. With a gasp he let his hand fall from his throat. The blade was rimmed with his blood, his hand shaking at the release, his arm barely able to hold him as he propped himself up.

The Herlequin shifted, his cloak swaying over the rot and dampness of the forest floor as he turned to peer towards the sound. The echo of the lone note clung to the treetops and soaked into the bark that peeled from the trunks.

The Nephilim turned back to Silas, his grievous face contorted with what might be fury, or concern, or exhaustion. A level of all three, Silas suspected. It was only now he could see the toll it had taken on the creature to bend Silas's will. The tufts of hair upon his rondure head were damp with sweat, and he dragged in his breath through the narrow slit of his mouth. The Herlequin's bloodshot eye sat amid a wreckage of barely human skin. He fixed it now upon Silas, like the blaze of a lighthouse beam.

They stared at one another, stuck in a stillness disturbed only by each of their laboured breaths. In that silence stretched endless questions, suppositions, and imaginings. What did this creature see when it peered at Silas? How much difference stood between them? And was there enough?

He couldn't bear the roar of quiet considerations. Couldn't chance the Nephilim finding a new way to poke at his fortitude again. That moment with the blade had been far too close for any comfort.

'Do you need to run to your masters, Herlequin?'

The taunt was foolhardy, no doubt. Silas was still on the ground, the Nephilim a living mountainside above him, but a kick or another blow he could endure; another twist of his mind, he was not so sure. He clenched the scythe, relishing his clarity. And before the Herlequin saw his intent, Silas lunged, driving the knife into whatever body part he could reach. It was a shin, he thought, or maybe just the leather of a high boot. Whichever it was, it made little mark upon the Nephilim and gained Silas a kick to the guts that crushed his stomach flat. He doubled over, coughing and retching, eyes streaming once more.

As he fought for a breath, he glimpsed the unmistakable shape of the Herlequin's black shire, the great horse moving to his rider's side.

Silas allowed himself a modicum of hope. Was the Wild Hunt truly at a retreat? Had the Order found them at last? Or better yet, had Pitch's strength returned, his flame sending his persecutors running?

The thoughts put a rod in Silas's back and eased the ache in his belly, and he pushed himself to sitting, leaning hard against the graceful, stalwart oak behind him.

'Dullahan!' the Nephilim roared. It was the second time the headless horseman had been called. And the second time there had been no response from the cursed rider. 'Hunters, heed me.'

The Herlequin's irritation was a brilliant concerto to Silas's ear. He barely noticed how the harsh words scraped at the inside of his skull.

The horn bellowed again, a baritone of a depth that plagued Silas's skin with gooseflesh. He braced, fearing he'd read things wrong. That this was not a call to retreat but rather a new ploy to entangle his mind. A lure that would drag him into the Wild Hunt, or have him try to harm himself once more.

But no such manipulations came.

Nor answer from the Dullahan, or any other of the Wild Hunt so far as he could hear. Silas let his hopes lift him.

'Perhaps your Hunt and the headless horseman have a sense you lack,' he said. 'They've seen fit to run when they know they are bested.'

Talking accentuated the ache of all the bruises Silas had gathered since this encounter began, but it buoyed him to taunt the creature.

The Herlequin mounted his stallion, somehow shifting his enormous bulk with finesse, and lowered himself onto a saddle whose thick leather was carved with intricate etchings. His horse sidestepped, plate-sized hooves barely missing the prone body of Balthazar Crane where it lay upon its back, the ankou's eyes wide and unseeing.

'There is no need for the Wild Hunt now, foolish brother.' The Nephilim turned his horse about, hard upon the reins. 'We have what we came for.'

With another yank at the leather, the shire turned full circle, broad hindquarters now faced towards Silas, a flick of the animal's tail close to his face. The hiss of it like a serpent.

But Silas was distracted, taking in the Herlequin's words and unpicking their meaning.

Silas saw the signs too late. The horse's rump muscles tightened, haunches dropping as it gathered to strike. The stallion kicked out. A blow aimed precisely for Silas's head.

Something jerked hard at his wrist, tugging him sideways. He had a moment, less than the blink of an eye, to glimpse the bones wrapped around his wrist, before the horse's hooves struck. And sent him into darkness.

CHAPTER 31

Z aquiel and Harut discarded their cloaks, revealing uninteresting
costumes of more black beneath, before they set to manhandling
Pitch away from the tree. To thwart them he did the worthiest im-
pression of a snake his beleaguered body could manage and was greatly
satisfied when Zaquiel cursed and slapped at the back of his head.

'Stand still, you imbecile.'

Pitch would do no such thing. He drew on the flame, paltry as it was,
making sure that at the very least he singed the angels as they unfastened
the cuffs briefly to wrench his hands behind his back and refasten them.
The nekhri contrasted the heat at Pitch's fingers, a heat that served only
to warm his own arse. The vainly-hoped-for reemergence of the wildness
failed to arrive. Harut released a nasty chuckle at the same time a kick at
the back of Pitch's knees forced him down.

'Why does the Hunt not answer?' Zaquiel hissed to his cohort, apparently unwilling to ask the question of Iblis.

Because Silas has cut them all to tiny pieces and used them as fertiliser
for his precious trees, Pitch muttered away behind his invisible gag, as
much to distract himself from Iblis's order to fly as to enjoy imagining
the ankou doing just such a thing.

'Hurry up,' the Watcher angel snapped, and Pitch's daydream was
rudely interrupted by a violent shove that cast him onto his belly, nostrils
filling with grit with the faceplant.

'Bastards,' he mumbled against his plastered mouth.

But it was far from over. His legs were wrenched back, and as though his day were not terrible enough so far, he was hogtied. His feet were brought back to touch his hands, where more metal fastened around his ankles and the snap of a lock joined one set of cuffs to the other.

You are fucking kidding me. Pitch pumped his hips in a far-from-sufficient attempt to get free. His nose streamed with all the pent-up efforts to scream his annoyance.

'Where is the ankou, the Herlequin?' Harut asked. The angel had an odd accent upon his words, a mingling of Arcadian with something else. Too long in the UnSeelie Court perhaps.

'Do not concern yourself with their fate,' Iblis growled, and it was truly a feral sound. 'Move the prince at once.'

'Iblis,' Harut protested. 'You've ordered us to the wing, in broad daylight. We should know if there is something –'

'Wrong?' Iblis bellowed. 'All that is wrong here is your failure to heed my order. Now move. Zaquiel, you shall carry him. Harut and I shall flank you.'

The Watcher angel was definitely rattled, his orders spitfire and terse. Dare Pitch imagine him frightened? His own fears and trepidation morphed into a wild giggle, one that had painful pieces of dirt whipping up his nose as he inhaled. His amusement earned him a kick in the side.

There was a surge of movement, through which he did his level best to be a giant pain in the arse for the angels who sought to grab his wrists and lift him like he were a fucking picnic basket. He rolled back and forth in the useless protest, jerking his bound limbs, delaying the inevitable.

He was caught off guard by the pinch of something against his belly, down beneath his shirt where a sliver of skin lay exposed between the bottom of the corset and the top of his trousers. If it were a stone he rolled upon, then it had developed a remarkable ability to move of its own accord, making a very deliberate trek up from his belly and around his hip to find his back. He let loose with a startled cry behind clenched lips as something crawled just beneath his trouser waist, following the line of material to nestle, of all places, in the dip of his arse cheek. He had a stowaway. And when tiny hands patted at his skin, in a deliberate gesture unlikely to be a trapped bug, Pitch suspected he knew its ilk.

He renewed his attempts to shake off the angels with extra vigour, and his passenger dug infinitesimal fingertips into the meat of his butt cheek, holding on for dear life when it should have allowed itself shaken loose.

'Idiot.' Pitch would wager all the whisky in London that Will Scarlet had just come aboard his sinking ship, and the stupidity staggered him.

A boon for Zaquiel though, as it quietened Pitch's protest enough for the angel to grasp the stubby length of metal connecting the cuffs and lift him.

A punishing gust of wind swept through the ruined clearing, bringing with it a sudden gloom, shadows he knew well.

Pitch moaned into his gag as the angels brought forth their wings. Sweet merciful gods. Flying. He could already feel his stomach dropping, his propensity to hurl when soaring through the air arriving.

The wind gathered strength, and the tips of Iblis's wings appeared in glimpses in Pitch's peripheral vision as the angel swept them back and forth. They resembled the wings of a dragonfly, very nearly translucent with a veining that glittered throughout as though diamonds were scattered. Angelic wings were nothing like the feathered atrocities purebreds imagined in their legends and myth. They were fine sheaths, tough as iron. Zaquiel lifted him clear of the ground. Pitch's shoulders screamed protest, the skin at the halo's fresh burn crinkling with cruel ferocity.

He almost longed for passing out, and the pain made it seem possible, but fate was having a wonderful day with him today, and he remained conscious.

They lifted off, wings scattering all that was still movable in the clearing: the lace-like leaves eaten away by the winter; the finer twigs; and even a toadstool or two, those that had been broken as the angels stomped across the way, their stone shapes not heavy enough to resist the powerful down-draughts. Robin remained ever still, ever statuesque, their webwork of petrified vines and roots spread around them.

Pitch hung his head, watching the hamadryad and their Major Oak become less and less. The wind whipped up, circling around them, raising the angels higher and higher.

Will Scarlet shuffled beneath his trousers, moving out from the crease of his arse, for which he was thankful, and travelling a little higher to pat at the bare skin beneath the boned hem of the corset, for which he was not. Pitch tilted his hips, a tight jerk that made muscles grumble, but it stopped the will-o'-the-wisp at least, Scarlet now too busy with holding on to bestow wasted comfort.

With the wound burning as though it had caught fire anew, Pitch hung beneath his captors and closed his eyes. All the better to pretend he was not lifting skywards towards a place where he could not keep his panic in check, and there was no ankou to do so for him.

Fuck, he was a calamity. Everywhere he went he left ruin behind. Sherwood, Goodrich Castle, the Fulbourn...gods, even Gidleigh Park House and the greensward. And in all those places, every time, there had been those creatures foolish enough to try to protect him.

No, that was not right. They sought to protect what lay *inside* him. He was a tool they all wished to utilise, whether it be for power or freedom or a taste of both. Even the folk of Sherwood Forest, kind as they were, did not care for a vile, cantankerous daemon. They cared about the secret he carried, what harm it could bring them. Just as those in Arcadia had minded him for his power, for the advantage he could deliver. It was the way of things. And Pitch had been unmoved by his isolation from true affection. He'd not been birthed to desire it and, hence, had never given a fuck that no living soul liked or even knew him.

Until the oaf, a man neither living nor dead, had messed up a perfectly adequate existence.

Something very nearly a sob tried to force itself against Pitch's pressed lips. His stomach lurched in time with each pulse of wings around him. And he tried to convince himself it was his hatred of flying that was knotting him up. He certainly despised it enough.

Fuck, fuck, he hated flying. Focus on that.

Not on the man he was leaving behind.

Pitch peered through eyelids parted just a crack. A dense fog surrounded them, no hint of the forest visible below. It was a mild relief not to be able to see how high he'd been flown.

The strain was enormous upon his arms and legs, tormented by their contorted shape, his spine curved in a most unpleasant way. Silas's coat bunched in the crease of his v-shaped body. Thoughts of the bandalore pulled Pitch from less pleasant considerations of a fall from this height. He wasn't sure if he hoped the bandalore was still with him or if it had tumbled out and would find its way to its master. Silas would be all the safer if it were the latter, but Pitch was a selfish prick. He did not wish it gone, to be so alone.

The angels flew in heavy silence, Iblis only visible every now and then as the fog thickened. An air or water elemental in the Watcher's service likely, though if it were the same one responsible for all the snowfall, they were more subdued now.

Even just thinking the word 'fall' had Pitch's stomach twisting, his nerves fraying ever-more.

Scarlet, thankfully, chose that time to move. Beneath all the layers, scrambling over the corset, finding its way up his back and using the firm ridge and lacework of the top of the corset to work its way around to Pitch's chest. There was an off-putting moment where the will-o'-the-wisp used his nipple as a stepping stone, and then he felt the brush of the tiny creature against his throat as it poked its head from his collar. He lifted his chin, wary of crushing his stowaway. It touched a tiny hand, a warm hand, to the lump at his throat, patting him again. Like he were some giant fucking flying pony.

It was sweet, sickening. Pitch reconsidered his efforts not to squash the wisp. Ridding himself of the careful, gentle gesture might be useful, as it was likely to see him come undone if it did not cease. He'd definitely shrug the wisp off soon. Very soon. Just, not yet. The will-o'-the-wisp's touch was also helping in the fight to contain his mania, his struggle not to think on what lay ahead...and down...if the angels decided to be done with him and let go.

Pitch and his passenger were flown through a world of stark white, pushed on by a strong wind that managed not to shift the fog but to glide the angels ever faster along. With the world a whitewash, Pitch could gather no sense of direction, and all talk among the angels had ceased. The wind hushed against Pitch's ears as he was moved further from forest and friend. There was a storm about, somewhere distant. He heard the faint murmur of thunder in the distance, as though a great bear slunk along in the clouds with them. The Wild Hunt riding beneath the angels? Or perhaps a diverting storm, one that would lure Silas in the very opposite direction. For the ankou was alive, Pitch would not believe otherwise. And if he drew breath, there was a chance he'd try to follow his idiot companion who'd made himself a prisoner. In Arcadia such a rescue attempt would have been laughable. Both White Mountain and Elyssiam had enough languishing prisoners of war to prove it.

Pitch bit the inside of his cheek. There was no *chance* Silas would follow, there was only utter certainty. He'd never been so sure of anything in his life. And by the Archangels' taints, it was a foreign, curious thing to have such faith. But equally terrifying.

He had no idea where the angels were taking him, but he knew what awaited would be far from pleasant. And with Seraphiel leaving him no better than a lamb to the slaughter, he had little to offer Silas by way of protection.

Scarlet nestled into him, bringing Pitch back to his senses.

The will-o'-the-wisp couldn't seem to get close enough. Was the blasted thing trying to burrow under his skin? At least Scarlet had sense to subdue its colours. Pitch caught no hint of a glow from where it bothered about at his collar, no rainbow hues reflected off the starkness of the swirling fog to draw attention.

The angels flew. And flew. Undiscovered. Uncommunicative. The storm mumbled away in the background, and it all became rather monotonous and strangely hypnotic. After all the violence and turmoil, this was a queer calm. Well, as calm as one could be when being whisked away by one's enemies, with arms and legs turning numb from being held in such a distorted way. In the lull Pitch could almost...almost...imagine himself still at the country house, wrapped in sheets and an ankou, his biggest decision how best to avoid Tilly and her games that day.

When one of the angels spoke, Pitch was startled out of an odd, and very unrestful, doze.

'Iblis.' Zaquiel was sharp. 'There is –'

'I'm aware. Keep your calm, damn you.'

The first words anyone had spoken in a decent while, and the conversation was stunted with concern.

'What do you propose, Captain?' Harut kept his voice low, the fog deadening it further.

'That we hold our course,' Iblis returned. 'She is not the threat she imagines. Hold your tongues.'

But Pitch had heard enough to encourage him to raise his head, even as his neck muscles cursed him for doing so. *She.* The tension surrounding the angels was palpable. Whoever she was, she was making a mockery of Iblis's assertion that she was no threat. The Lady? Showing her face at long fucking last? His breath caught, his throat strangled by fledgling hope.

The fog hemmed them in, giving the sweep of the angels' wings a deadened air. There was barely a sense of being airborne at all, which suited Pitch just fine, keeping his head clear enough of panic. He paid close attention to the group and was there to notice it when their flight path took a subtle shift, a veering to the left.

Pitch could not *hear* Zaquiel's displeasure so much as feel it in the hunching of his shoulders that saw Pitch shifted up and down, the quick mumble beneath his breath as he banked. But the change of direction did not bring the angels the change of fortune they must have sought. They'd not flown the new course more than a few minutes when Iblis erupted.

'Fuck, that whore persists.'

'Iblis, what would you have us do?' Harut cried.

'Send the daemon to Harut, Zaquiel,' Iblis barked. 'You have faced the Valkyrie in battle, have you not?'

It was not the Lady lurking in the fog; it was her angel. Her warrior. Rider of the White Horse. His fledgling joy faltered to think on Hastings, of what had become of the mare.

'It has been thousands of –'

'Do it!'

Zaquiel jerked at the unequivocal command. 'Captain.'

With no warning, not the slightest, Pitch was swung and then released. He sailed through the air, thrown like a newspaper towards the doorstep.

Scarlet was as unprepared as he and was whipped from his neck, managing to snag itself in his hair, dangling there like a heavy earring caught in the strands.

Pitch was hurled away from the meagre safety of the angel's hold. He cried out. He bloody well screamed. Harut swooped in, shifting his body so his feet jutted ahead of him, working his great shimmering wings with all the dexterity the angels were renowned for. As he moved, readying for the catch, he pressed his legs together, reshaping toes and heels to form a single great talon, though more hooked than any bird could manage, and thick and large enough to lift netted cargo with ease.

Pitch despised himself for being utterly relieved to see the angel manoeuvre himself in close, clearly readying to catch a falling daemon. The halt was problematic though, for Harut did not snatch him at the wrists but slid the great hook his feet had become around the backs of Pitch's bent knees. He found himself dangling upside down, swinging wildly back and forth, blinking through threatening blackness as the sudden stop nearly dislocated his hips. His bothersome side blasted him with pain, the old wound vastly unhappy. As was he.

Scarlet screeched its tiny lungs out, managing to drag itself to his ear, where it clung to the ear's curve as though it were the only solid ground left on Earth.

You can fly, you stupid cretin, he wanted to shout. *Save yourself and get the blazes away from here.*

Pitch shook his head, trying to loosen the wisp. Whatever comfort he might find in its presence hardly mattered now.

Will Scarlet would not be moved and nattered away in his ear. Encouraging him to what? Not be smashed to a pulp when landing upon the ground?

Harut swept right, doubling back on their direction, flanked at a cautious distance by Zaquiel still, but Iblis was nowhere to be seen.

Pitch hung like a pendulum, sweeping through the fog, which parted only momentarily before it rushed back in to cover the path of moving bodies. The wind strengthened, a headwind that whipped up the length of Silas's coat and flared it out on either side of Pitch's folded legs. Despite the strength of the breeze against them, Harut was unhindered, his wings barely visible as they drove up and down, the occasional glance of light against the whisper-thin skin all that betrayed their existence.

Pitch's eyes streamed with the touch of the air. Night air? Morning air? He had no fucking idea what time of day it was, nor what day in particular. Only that the pit of his stomach sought to find the back of his throat, and he was so very fucking tired of playing punching bag.

He blinked in crazed flutters as he sought desperately to clear his vision. His world was actually upside down, but it all looked the bloody same as it had done when he was horizontal. White.

A curse was flung from the fog.

'From the east she comes,' Iblis roared. 'Zaquiel, turn about.'

Pitch saw them then. A squall of company arriving. Not just *she* but *they*.

Sirin. At least a half dozen of the creatures, with their almost-human female heads, save for the hawkish noses and wide-set eyes, their bodies bedecked in colourful feathers.

The sirin battled against the wind that worked hard to drive them back, while a huge shape loomed at the back of their ranks like a great menacing storm cloud. A winged glory that Pitch watched from his upside-down perch, the blood roaring in his ears, his heart in all manner of disarray. Scarlet perched on his earlobe like a miniature jockey, squealing with unmistakable excitement.

As well it should. A Valkyrie in flight made for a formidable view. Sybilla swept towards them like a piece of night had grown wings. Pitch's pulse hammered. By the gods, she was magnificent. Even upside down.

A cawing cacophony soured Pitch's elation.

The whiteness of the fog took on a green tinge as he struggled to find the source of the noise. There was no easy way to move about where he hung, no pleasant twist of his neck to find. Scarlet went mad with chattering and poked at his jawbone, urging his head a certain way.

The way opposite to Sybilla's grand approach.

A huge unkindness of ravens bore down on them. Their clustered formation was like the warped fin of an ocean predator, slicing through the fog.

The Valkyrie would need all the sirin she had.

CHAPTER 32

S ilas came around, nursing a headache that far exceeded any he'd yet endured in this lifetime. Brandy could not hope to accomplish what a horse's hoof managed. His eyes were tightly closed, and for now he chose to leave them that way.

'Oh fuck.' He touched the side of his head where the throb was fiercest. His fingers came away sticky with cooled blood.

What the hell had happened? His thoughts were haphazard, clambering over one another in their haste to be seen. But the loudest of them was simple. A horse's rump, a flash of silver upon a broad hoof.

His stomach roiled, and he was faintly aware that his arse was damp.

Whispering came from his surrounds, hushed sounds Silas thought at first were only inside his pounding head.

Wake, ankou. You are needed.

He knew without any searching that it was a teratism who spoke to him. Needed?

'Shit.' Silas's eyes flew open, and he whimpered at the brightness that stung him. 'Where is he?' The world beyond his lids was blurred with light, his sight taking its sweet time to adjust. Silas needed to *see*, damn it. 'Pitch? Are you there?'

But he knew the answer already. There was an emptiness here that sat heavy as nightfall.

He is taken.

Silas staggered to his feet, trying to focus on the shapes gathered around him. 'Where, where have they taken him?'

The skies.

A scowl was a terrible idea, almost as bad as trying to stand so quickly after being knocked out cold. Everything tilted, including Silas himself. He threw out his hands, trying to find an anchor, and found a moving roughness he clung to. The teratism had survived. He had one ally here at least.

'Speak clearly,' he demanded. 'He is gone?'

The angels are on the wing –

'Angels? More than one?'

Three. The daemon with them. Alive.

Silas's vision cleared enough to reveal he was braced against the hunchbacked creature who had followed him from the Fulbourn.

'Why did you not protect him?' Silas knew himself unreasonable, terror making him careless. 'Why did you not stop them?'

Not only was Pitch taken, he was in the blasted air. Flying. His own daemonic version of hell. Silas shoved the teratism away, hard enough that the creature struggled to keep upright upon its bowed legs. Silas was being ruthlessly unkind, he knew it, but Christ almighty, what a nightmare. The angels had Pitch.

It was not just Silas's head fit to tear apart now. He left the teratism, reaching for the next solid thing, on his way to god-knew-where. His hand brushed at a column of stone, one he was faintly aware was out of place but was too anguished to consider.

'Enough of that, now,' a curt voice remonstrated. 'No need to be a bastard, after all they've done. They, along with the rest of us, were dealing with the Hunt when the angels took your boy. Can't be everywhere at once.'

Silas blinked, staring down at the gnome who stood before him, plump hands on hips. Silas recognised the portly fellow as the one who'd been especially attentive to Pitch's cup of mead the night before, even daring to ask for a dance, which the prince declined, preferring to stand on Silas's feet for the evening.

Oh god, how could it be that precious time was only just last night? Silas fought to steady himself, nearly overwhelmed by the crush of panic that came.

'How long ago was this?' *Stay steady, man. Keep your wits.* 'How long have I been out?'

Not long. Barely a half hour.

'Half an hour or so.' The gnome and the teratism spoke in near unison, the forest dweller's ears not open to the voice of the dead.

Silas knew nothing of an angel's speed on the wing, but he imagined that such an amount of time, assuming no interruption came, had put an intolerable distance between them.

And here Silas was, without even a damned horse. The enormity of the situation had him shaking, fatigue, grief and helplessness making him weak.

'Best come and deal with him,' the gnome continued. 'Don't think he can hold out for much longer.'

Silas frowned. 'Deal with who?'

'The fellow who stopped you from having your head caved in by that stallion.'

For the first time, Silas studied his surrounds. He had been returned to the clearing, but how different it was now to when he'd stepped from it just a short time ago.

'Oh sweet mercy,' he whispered. 'Robin.'

Silas tried to make his way to where the hamadryad knelt at the centre of the clearing, their hair mimicking Medusa's snakes, reaching out and down towards the ground to join the roots which spread in a myriad fashion over the ground. He was not so right upon his feet as he'd have liked, and one or two of the finer roots were crushed beneath his boot. They cracked and crumbled like a log weakened by fire, turning to dust beneath his weight.

Except it was not ash. This was stone. *All* was stone. The hamadryad had been made a horrific sculpture by the angels' invasion.

'They did this?' Silas shook with disgust and rage, struggling to find a path that would not see him ruin more of what had, just last night, been exquisite.

'Come away from there, you giant fellow,' the gnome cried. 'Let the forest find its way, don't break something that can't be fixed.'

Silas halted at once, balancing on one foot while trying to decide where to place the other. 'Robin is alive?'

'Barely a pulse to be had, but the leshy gave of themselves so it could be so. Sherwood Forest's heart still beats. It knows drought and flood and all manner of things sent to cut it down. The woods will find a way through this black magick, be sure of it.'

Silas glanced over at the stone pillar he'd been leaning against. Not a pillar at all. The Major Oak stood tall and proud, a magnificent if not damaged statue, standing sentinel over the insistent, defiant heart of the forest. There was a huge rent in the trunk now, not there when he'd left, with the splintering splayed outwards as though something had burst forth, tearing out.

'Tried to keep him in, but he's a stubborn daemon that one. He helped keep that heart beating, you know, ankou.' Silas turned at the gnome's words. 'Wouldn't let Robin and the Major give it all away for his sake. Saved a good many of the forest folk before those angel bastards got to him. And we're sorry, awful sorry, we couldn't do more to stop them from taking him.'

Silas found his way out of the embroidered rootwork, stepping carefully, being sure not to cause any more damage. 'I'm sure you did your utmost,' he said, his throat thick. 'And I thank you sincerely for it. Do you have any idea what direction they took?'

His thoughts tore him apart. Pitch was alive. The angels had not killed him, but why? Of course Silas was grateful; he was drinking in the knowledge that the daemon lived like it was the finest brandy, but sickened to imagine what could be done to a captive, weakened prince.

The Dullahan will tell us.

He spun to find the teratism. 'The Dullahan is still here?'

The creature's severe hunch made it so he could barely raise yellowed eyes high enough to look at him.

He waits for you. I will take you to him.

'Waits for me?'

The teratism did not linger to answer. The Blight's monster lumbered out of the clearing, dragging a rough-skinned foot through the leaf litter, the ankle's vile angle suggesting a break.

Silas was struck by a vision of Forneus, the skriker's back being broken by the Herlequin. Fists clenched and heart heavy, he followed after the teratism, fighting off thoughts of the hound, for he was barely keeping himself in check as it was. Another sorrow to think on and he might curl up next to Robin and never move again. He pinched the bridge of his nose, giving himself a moment, his gaze shifting to the ground where the soil was churned with mismatched footprints. One of them was notably bare. Goosebumps rose along Silas's arms, certain it was Pitch's.

A speckle of white against the dark soil caught his eye, and he latched onto the distraction: strands of stark white hair, peeking out from between the bulge of one of the leshy's frozen roots. Kodami scampered out from their various hiding holes, emerging from the petrified bark like pieces of it come to life. They watched as he crouched down, peering at the new discovery.

Horsehair. A bundle of it, tied with a simple piece of dark leather. He reached and pulled it from where it had fallen into a crevice of stone and soil. The kodami whispered, their voices like gentle sighs. A tingling ran through his fingers. His pulse quickened as he turned the bundle over in his hand. Bloodstains decorated the strands where the mud had not soaked.

Silas pushed to his feet so fast his head spun.

Hastings's mane lay in his hands.

Here was how he and Pitch had been found. At the White Horse's dire expense.

The Hunt must have known the ruse, somehow. Retraced their steps. Perhaps to where Hastings had taken a sudden, erratic turn to fling them into the forest.

And Silas had sealed their fate with his idiotic saunter through the woods. His good intent had led them all firmly into a hellscape.

He stumbled after the teratism, carrying another terrible loss with him. The Herlequin and his Wild Hunt had dealt two catastrophic blows so far: Forneus and now Hastings. *Dear God, do not let the angels deal a third.* He shoved the horsehair into his pocket. This may be all that remained of the mare; he'd not leave her there in the decay and sod. Sybilla must...oh Christ, Silas could not think on how Sybilla would feel with this news. Did she already know of the loss? Would it guide her here, or send her further away, to where Hastings had been brought down?

The teratism was well ahead of him but had paused, waiting until they were certain Silas saw before moving on again. The trees immediately around the clearing were dry and brown, not a single leaf upon a limb, drained of life. That changed as they moved out further. There was not much greenery of course, winter's embrace omnipresent, but the deadly taint of the angels' attack had left no stony touch here.

Silas almost stepped upon the first body, he was so absorbed in his worries. 'Bloody hell.' He jumped back, removing his boot from the slender hand that lay with fingers splayed as though reaching for him.

This creature was well past reaching for anything, their head sliced clean off, the wound cauterised into a rounded plate of crisp skin. Their cloak lay spread around them, Silas mistaking it at a glance for a huge pool of blackened blood.

'What has happened here?' He took in the rest of the scene. More bodies lay scattered about, all in the same state of decapitation. Some were curled upon their sides as though they had tried to ball themselves into unnoticeable lumps to escape their attacker. All were the same slender build, fine limbs and fingers too elongated to be human.

The Wild Hunt has fallen.

Christ, it had not just fallen; it had been decimated. Silas was so intent on the massacre that it took a moment to realise it was not the teratism's voice in his head. But another, far-less-familiar tone. One that barely rose above a languid sigh. 'Who is there?' He eyed his surrounds, glancing quickly over the wreckage of bodies.

Hurry, ankou. I have waited too long as it is.

But when a voice was in the head, rather than on the tongue, it was nearly impossible to discern where it came from. 'I don't know who you are.' Silas scowled, too tired for such things. 'Or where. Show yourself at once and stop this foolery.'

The teratism was at his elbow, touching his arm, before Silas finished speaking. *He is there. Waiting.*

They pointed, and the crookedness of their finger might have made it difficult to figure out where he was to look if the dancing of several peri along a huge fallen elm did not make it obvious. The slight creatures, floating strands of hair like gleaming silver thread, were clearly directing him, chittering as madly as Will Scarlet had ever done.

The last time Silas had seen that will-o'-the-wisp, it had been nestled outside the bramble alcove he'd shared with Pitch, far too close for its own good. A sudden yearning for a return to last evening nearly staggered him.

He made his way quickly to the fallen tree. The downed growth had apparently not long been horizontal, for there was no sign of moss or decay upon it and the breaks were fresh on young branches. The peri gathered in a tight bunch and danced over the trunk, drawing his attention to the far side, their motion joined by the tinkle of bells. Rather than navigate his way around the length of the old tree, and considering its bulk only went as high as his belly, Silas clambered over, pulling himself up to kneel on the wood.

His eyes widened.

The Dullahan lay next to the tree, his arm extended towards it, his hand lost beneath the wood.

The hand that bore his bone whip.

Silas's own hand went to his trouser pocket, searching for the bandalore, recalling at once it was not with him. Dear god, let it still be with Pitch. Let it be with him, giving him hope, if nothing else.

But Silas's thoughts were overtaken by a sudden, dire realisation. He had neither the bandalore nor Crane's spectacles, the blade he'd fought hard for and won.

Your scythe is with me. The headless horseman's whisper was a pine forest swayed by a breeze. *But I'll not return it unless you promise me you shall use it to break this curse, and not to destroy me.*

'You are blackmailing me?' Silas dropped to the ground, keeping a cautious distance. He searched for sign of the Dullahan's horse, of which there was none.

I am offering a deal. Sever the whip, ankou. I know you have that power. The ethereal whisper sent a chill over Silas's skin. *Hurry. I cannot withstand it much longer.*

'Do you think me foolish enough to go anywhere near you?'

Do you wish to save your daemon or not?

'Of course I bloody do.' Silas riled, struggling to fathom what was happening. The teratism had beseeched him to come here. The gnome said the headless horseman waited for him. None seemed afraid. 'But you are the Morrigan's servant –'

I saved you from the true aim of the Nephilim's horse. And I will be no servant to those maleficent fools. The hiss was caustic, enough to make Silas grimace. *Sever the whip. It is what binds me. Break the curse and you have me at your side.*

Truly, did this creature think him moronic? Besides the fact his attempt at blackmail was worthless–Silas could summon the scythe, and did not need this creature to simply hand it over–the Dullahan had cut him until his bones were on show, and hunted them down in the Fulbourn like a mongrel chasing rats. He'd eaten a piece of Pitch's flesh at Macha's command.

But, Silas had seen the bones about his wrist before the horse struck. And the gnome had said it too. The headless horseman had kept him clear of a catastrophic blow.

'Why do you seek my favour now? After all you've done?'

I don't seek favour, I seek release.

The peri went into a fluster, tinkling like miniature church bells in the grip of a fit, jabbing teeny-tiny fingers at one of the bodies lying nearby.

He yearns for freedom. The same as which you gave us.

This from the teratism, standing nearby, watching Silas, as all the gathered peri were.

'Freedom?'

'What's this then?' The gnome emerged from the soil, a few paces from where Silas stood in a quandary. 'Why's he still having to pin himself beneath that tree? Thought you'd be done and on your way by now.'

'Pin himself?' Silas shook his head, truly lost. 'Did the forest not trap him?'

'Only because he asked us to. So we obliged. We owed him, after he'd done all this.' The gnome gestured at one of the corpses. 'What? Did you think we forest folk went about cutting off all these heads? Best I saw was a couple of brownies tripping up one of the fae. It is the headless rider who is to credit for destroying the Wild Hunt.'

A grunt came from nearby. *The massacre has my hand upon it too.* The teratism was unimpressed with being overlooked.

Silas glanced between him, the Dullahan, the decapitated body, the gnome, and the jingling peri.

'The Dullahan truly did this?' He wasn't sure whom he was asking, but it was the teratism who answered first.

He truly did. The hunchback could not nod, seeing as their chin was already upon their chest, so they made a stunted bow instead.

My king has lost his way. The Dullahan's night-breeze whisper filled Silas's head. *He lusts after the Morrigan's promises and deludes himself that the Watcher King will grant him power in this world if he sides with the sorcerers. But the UnSeelie Court will fall under Lokke. If you want your blade returned, you will unbind me from the curse.*

Silas paced out his confusion. Delay was costly, a mistake here could see him pay a dear price, but the right choice could see him with an unexpected ally. 'What on Earth makes you imagine I can release you at all?'

I know what you did at the Fulbourn. Bent the Blight to your will. You are the messenger of death, and my curse is built from the dead.

'But that was human dead at the asylum, and an entirely different curse.' Silas ran an irritated hand through his still-damp hair. 'The whip is what binds you?'

Bones of fae dead. Those who fell at my hand, when the Seelie and UnSeelie Courts divided. I am punished rightly, but I serve the UnSeelie court, not the Morrigan.

Silas had no time for a fae history lesson. 'But your head...the Morrigan have it, do they not? Can they not control –'

They showed you nothing of mine in that asylum. Six hundred years I've been cursed. My head has long since crumbled to dust. They used some other to frighten you, whilst they stole a piece of your prince for their own magick. The sorcerer relishes dramatics. Words flowed like the wind upon a beach, the sand humming as it was swept through the air. *The daemon's debt to the UnSeelie Court is real, but was not sealed by pushing his flesh between the lips of a corpse. Hurry, ankou. Make your choice. Shall you use your blade? Free me as you did your dead?*

He may doubt the horseman's trustworthiness, but he did not doubt that of the forest folk, nor the teratism. And they had seen the Dullahan turn on his own kind.

'Do you know where they have taken him?'

Yes. And I am the only one with a horse to carry you there.

'Tell me where.'

It might have been laughter that pushed through the air like a shot arrow.

So you might kill me the moment I hand you back your scythe? No.

'Not unreasonable to be worried about that, if you ask me.'

Silas glared at the gnome who perched on the tree like a chap watching the races.

'I did not ask you.'

Set me free and I will take you to your prince.

Every creature watching seemed to hold their breath, waiting on Silas's reply. A breeze brushed at his face, where the blood was now stiff against his skin – a wound that would have been far worse had the Dullahan not intervened.

'Bloody hell,' he muttered beneath his breath. 'Fine.'

Our deal is struck? Your scythe for my freedom?

'My scythe for your freedom.' Lopsided deal that it was.

'You're going to trust the ankou, horseman? Just like that? How wonderfully dramatic this all is.' The unhelpful gnome now held a handful of wriggling worms, nibbling on them as he spoke. He was enjoying this far too much.

Silas Mercer is a man of his word. The teratism's voice brushed his mind.

There are few things more certain in all our worlds. The Dullahan raised his free hand and snapped his fingers.

A soft nicker had Silas turning. The Dullahan's blue roan picked its way through shrubbery and death towards him, ghostly quiet as it moved. The horse stopped a short distance away. And tossed its head. The spectacles flew from the roan's mouth. Silas reached for them. Clasping them tight, the metal uncomfortably warm and damp.

Now. Quickly. Take my hand off at the wrist. Be swift. Be sure.

The scythe hummed in Silas's grasp, eager for his hold, welcoming its new master without hesitation. He imagined the blade he'd need and set about reshaping the spectacles into a sickle, a hard blade he hoped decent enough for the task at hand.

As death's instrument found its form, the whispers began. The Dullahan's whip, the echoes of the remnants of the souls it held. Pieces only, an assembly of fragments of the fae that had once been. He sensed them now as he'd not done in the Fulbourn. But then, he was not the same creature as the asylum had known. Maybe the Dullahan was right in having such faith in him.

The peri scampered away, bells ringing, hiding themselves from what was to come.

'Are you ready?' The whispers intensified, but Silas heard little protest. Only expectation. The souls were eager for his blade too.

Are you? The voice of autumn leaves stirring.

'Yes.'

The Dullahan wriggled away from the log, until his arm was stretched straight. The horseman's wrist was visible, while the rest of his hand remained trapped beneath the log along with the whip. Silas would have to be precise or risk taking far more of the limb than necessary. But he was calm, certain the blade would know best where to strike.

Silas went to one knee and raised the sickle. A swell of strange hunger took him. The whispers rose, a cry of those who saw an end in sight. The magick of the fae came for him. Pinpricks of discomfort darted like wasps, the curse seeking to stay his hand. He did not even bother to brush them aside.

Silas struck down with the scythe, sending the sickle where wrist met the heel of the palm. Severing hand from limb.

The Dullahan's cry was raucous, a medley of voices.

The bones cracked beneath the log, causing it to rock where it lay. And those last tiny fragments of life fled, escaping the curse that had imprisoned them as much as it had done the headless horseman. The Dullahan's moan could have shaken the moss off stone. He rolled away from the log, free, clutching his handless limb to his chest. The roan worked around him, nuzzling its rider as he lay with his face turned towards the dirt and dealt with whatever pain the end of an enduring curse wrought.

Silas had no time to nurse him through a recovery. He got to his feet, the scythe already shifting, but he did not allow it to take the form of spectacles this time. That was Balthazar Crane's signature. And that ankou deserved no legacy here. Silas bent his will to reshaping the blade, imagining a much more worthy design.

The scythe took its new form; a ring of smoothed, gleaming silver, with a design etched in tiny pieces of emerald upon its surface.

Silas tilted his hand, letting what light there was catch at the verdant and silver, a lump in his throat. He slid the ring onto the middle finger of his left hand, where the fit was superlative. He rubbed his thumb over the etching: a pitchfork. A replica of the tattoo upon Pitch's back.

'Is it done, Dullahan?' Silas nudged his boot against the horseman's leg, where the fallen rider was worryingly still.

A faint hitch of the shoulders and an airy reply came. *I am Byleist, my lord Death. And it is done.*

Silas cared not for the title bestowed on him, nor for the horseman's true name. So long as this was not a terrible mistake, it did not matter. 'Then if you do not wish to lose another limb, Byleist, get on your feet and ready your horse. Take me to the prince.'

CHAPTER 33

The ravens swept in, stealing his view of the Valkyrie. Pitch lowered his head. The pressure at the back of his eyes was considerable, and his skull felt fit to burst with all the blood in his body forced there by his hanging and swinging about. Iblis shifted behind the other angels, spreading his wings wide, the thin translucent membrane like the skin of a drum, appearing far too delicate to endure even the slightest touch. But Pitch knew better. Angel wings were tougher than basilisk hide and capable of withstanding many a strike from a vestige before that daemonic weaponry could cause any ruin. Pitch closed his aching eyes. What he would not give to have his vestige to hand. At least then he would be remotely capable of defending himself, instead of dangling like a carcass.

His eyes flew open, escaping that unfortunate image. It was far too close to the truth.

Iblis's wings flashed subtle gold and braced at the air, sending him further behind Zaquiel and Harut. Pitch scanned his upside-down world, hoping for another glimpse of Sybilla and the sirin through the moving curtain of black created by the ravens. Was he delusional with all the blood in his head? Had he truly seen the Valkyrie at all, or was he so desperate for rescue that he was seeing things?

Pitch made the mistake of looking down, precisely when a thinning of the fog allowed a glimpse of their height. 'Fuck...fuck...don't do that,' he mumbled against his gag, eyes lifting and fixing on anything but the ground below.

They were so high that the landscape looked to be in miniature. Wonderful, now he was very likely going to be sick inside his own mouth. He wriggled against the churning of his belly, and Harut, irritated, glanced a wing against Pitch's face. The desperately thin edge sliced his skin this time, cutting off a decent lock of hair. At least the attack occurred opposite to where the will-o'-the-wisp still played at being Pitch's personal cheer squad. Scarlet patted him madly as Harut returned to steady flying.

'Iblis!' Sybilla's roar pushed through the feathered barrier of the ravens, who were less like individual birds and more a thick, clogging smoke that had a life of its own. 'You traitorous bastard. Do you think you can outrun me?'

Pitch's laughter hiccoughed behind his imprisoned lips. He could not see her, but by the gods the Valkyrie was here. And mightily pissed off by the sounds of it.

'I do not need to outrun you when I have what you covet at my mercy. Shall we see what happens when a sickly Dominion prince falls from such a height? You and I both know he is not at his best. I dare say it won't be pleasant.'

Iblis spoke with decent enough conviction, but Pitch had a vantage point Sybilla did not. The Watcher angel flew close to the barrier of ravens, looking this way and that. Searching. He didn't know where Sybilla was or where her attack may birth from. And Pitch had a front-row, upside-down seat to witness how nervous that made him.

Iblis banked and swept in towards the others, flying over the top of Harut and Zaquiel, making it impossible for Pitch to glimpse him no matter how much he twisted.

'Fly on,' Iblis shouted. 'Stop for nothing, get the prince to the Morrigan. If you are there before me, tell Nemain what has been said. Our lord must learn if what lies inside him can be vanquished or must be destroyed.'

Pitch's paltry flame stuttered. Vanquished? Now there was a thought he'd never considered: taming the wildness and making him Azazel's servant...instead of Seraphiel's. What a perfectly horrendous notion.

'You'll face Sybilla alone?' Zaquiel did not sound happy with it.

'Do you doubt my strength?' Iblis sniped.

'She is Valkyrie, here by decree of White Mountain, and with a halo not worn hollow by time,' Zaquiel returned. 'We are just –'

'We are Watchers. Azazel's most loyal. Did you not hear the words of the daemon? Samyaza's halo awaits, and with it a power undeniable. The Severance War shall finally be at an end, and we the victors. An army of Valkyrie could not subdue me now.'

Pitch listened, and the heat from his flame barely warmed a fingertip. Power undeniable. Azazel would subjugate this world.

Silas's world.

And Charlie and Edward's.

Tilly's.

Pitch winced to imagine the insufferable child fighting to grow in a world where Azazel ruled with the might of the Watcher King at his disposal. A world where Nephilim would roam. Where more monsters, created by angels, would plague her every waking hour.

And unlike Pitch, who was such a creature, those made by the Exarch could do far worse than push her off a window seat when she bothered them. The skriker could not protect her from those creatures, though the slobbering ball of mange would try.

All of it bothered Pitch. So very fucking much. And he had never been one for bothering. There was a reason his legion was known for its deserters. Prince Vassago had not been made for selflessness.

Pitch sagged. He was truly broken if he imagined himself fond of this vapid world, with its sweet shops and senseless parties...and handsome, bearded man who insisted on declaring affection.

Scarlet scampered down his neck, burrowing under his shirt, which must have been quite the feat considering the sweat and blood that soaked him. The will-o'-the-wisp had finally gone mad with fear, its tiny hands and feet tickling at his underarms.

'Get out of there.' Good gods, the idiotic creature would drown in his sweat if it did not asphyxiate on the fumes.

Where the blazes did it think it was going?

Harut quickened the stroke of his wings, rising higher again as Iblis fell back towards the tail end of this strange carriage of raven cloud. Sybilla, if she were still there, did not make herself known again.

A violent cry came from the birds, a unison that only vaguely hinted at their number, being more like the roar of one enraged beast. Harut jumped, the yank on Pitch's limbs nearly intolerable, and Iblis suddenly plummeted. The wall of ravens parted. The Watcher angel pressed his wings in tight against his body, sliding through the narrow space created by the birds and shooting downwards headfirst. The part in the feathered curtain showed only more thickness of the fog beneath, no hint of the ground now, for which Pitch was foolishly thankful.

Iblis's translucent wings spread wide, glistening and unsettlingly beautiful. When upon the Hellfield, Pitch had had little interest in angelic flight, commonplace as it was. But here...here it sickened him.

The ravens reorganized, closing in to form a prison once more. Pitch exhaled. It was the strangest sensation to hang there in silence while all around the world erupted, and a will-o'-the-wisp sought to find a hiding place between his shoulder blades. But he could not blame Scarlet for choosing to conceal itself, especially beneath the bunched drape of Silas's coat. Pitch would have done the same if he could so much as move a finger with ease.

Another raucous cry came from the black-winged mass surrounding him. And there too, faintly visible through the minute gaps, a flicker of yellow light. Zaquiel yelled something Pitch did not catch, something that may have been from one of the wads of languages spoken by the fae, but he was admittedly distracted by Scarlet's reemergence along his arm. The wisp was somewhere in between shirt and coat, and he could feel its struggle not to pull the sleeve down as it used it as a crude ladder to climb up. It was only the sweat on Pitch's body holding the material in place at all. Too hard a tug and the wisp would end up back near his armpit.

Pitch craned his unhappy neck and glimpsed a bulge beneath the coat arm. A strangely large bulge, considering how small the wisp was. A sudden blast of wind gave Harut a jolt that Pitch feared would shake him loose. A cry smacked against his gag, and he let his head drop, fingers clenching at air as instinct had him lunging for something to hold on to.

The wind surged, hurtling Harut forward, pushing the angel to breath-taking speed. Either they had just flown into a tailwind of astonishing magnitude, or an air elemental was lending their hand to Pitch's stolen journey.

The ravens moved in a dark whirlwind, a rotation that tightened with each sweep of Harut's wings. Pitch was lifted by the speed, dragged out behind the angel as Harut leaned forward to level himself with the sky before banking hard right, a violent move that swung Pitch out nearly horizontal for a heart-stopping moment. He whimpered against his gag, the sudden shift cruel against all the injured parts of him.

This helplessness was infuriating. The alone time in his own head repulsive.

Perhaps heart-stopping was exactly what he should aim for. He sniffed, the sound horridly moist.

Iblis had threatened Sybilla with dropping his prisoner, had laughed at the mess it would make of an imperfect Dominion prince. But what if that threat was the solution?

If Prince Vassago were completely broken, then he was no use to Seraphiel *or* Azazel. He may survive his injuries, he may not. Either way he'd be no use to anyone for a long, decent while as his bones knitted themselves back from fragments and his mind was remoulded from mush.

Perhaps it was the chill of wind-sped air freezing his sensibilities, but the idea seemed perfectly logical, so long as he ignored how furious Silas would be. But the ankou would see, in time, that it was for the best. That Pitch had given everyone who fought for him the only thing he could.

Nothing to fight for. A way out of this chaos. They'd all be free.

Silas would be free.

And hurting. He will mourn. Pitch shook off the thought. Better a few tears now than greater horrors later.

His mind set, his purpose fixed, Pitch bucked his hips.

His first attempt to shake off the angel had him nearly screaming his gag off, as pain wracked his entire body. But the angel lurched violently, spitting out an equally violent reprimand.

'You stupid prick,' Harut shouted. 'Stay fucking still.'

This hare-brained idea might just work, if Pitch didn't black out in the process. He readied for another wild thrash.

And flinched at a sharp pain at his wrist. He tried to lift his head to see what new affliction ailed him. A flash of yellow lit up the air.

The entire flock tilted, as though the sky had suddenly vanished from beneath their wings.

'Faster, damn you!' Harut shouted. No, he screamed it.

Another sharp tap came at Pitch's wrist, as though from beneath the nekhri cuff itself. For fuck's sake, he was so tired of hurting.

Pitch shouted his discontent into the bind – right as another blast of light, and severe tilt of the shrouding mass, had Harut hollering obscenities at his air elemental and ordering their wind ever faster. Pitch's neck cricked as Harut too was thrown off kilter by whatever it was rocking his raven-made boat.

A Valkyrie, most likely. Dark and mad and coming for Pitch. Gods, she was insufferable, ruining his plans to extricate them all from this freak show. If he hurled himself clear of Harut now, the Valkyrie would no doubt make some noble plunge to save him. Likely get herself killed in the process.

'We should kill this bastard and be done with it.' Zaquiel's voice, though Pitch could not see him from where he hung.

He'd not been called a bastard in at least a day. He'd rather missed it. Especially when it made the speaker as furious as it did here.

'You heard Iblis,' Harut returned.

A nasty burning sensation riddled Pitch's right wrist. And for a horrifying moment, he thought Zaquiel had decided to cut off his hand, seeing as he could not kill him entirely. A pat at his knuckles let him know Scarlet was there, up at the summit where he was bound.

But doing what? Was the wisp carrying a box of matches? Because it sure as blazes felt as though he was being stabbed with a head of smouldering sulphur. Barely had he begun to lift his head and his wrist was freed from its restraint.

His arm dropped, his hand, almost entirely numb after so long in that position, smacked at his hip, dragging a fold of Silas's coat with it, his arm dangling like an anchor below him. The pain at his shoulder joint was exquisitely intense, but that hardly mattered.

A will-o'-the-wisp was somehow, impossibly, granting his daemonic wish to plummet to his ultimate demise. Either the creature despised him far more than he'd imagined, or there were greater things at play here. Pitch dug his teeth into his lip as the blood returned to his limb. The dangling royal-blue coat covered his partial escape well enough for now, but it surely wouldn't be long before one of the dunderheads flying with him noticed.

How had Scarlet defied the nekhri? In Arcadia the metal could hold Nephilim bound in the bowels of White Mountain. What Iblis used here must be weakened somehow. With time, maybe? The weary state of the halo might account for that.

The pinch of discomfort moved to Pitch's left wrist, but desperate as he was to see what was being done, the muscles in his neck defied him. A spasm jerked his head back down.

Zaquiel cried out, and Pitch feared his release discovered. The ravens' cawing magnified, and a crack opened in the densely packed flock. Light, bright as the midday sun, poured in, highlighting the battle beyond the shroud. Pitch blinked madly, fighting to keep his eyes open in the glare.

There raged a storm beyond his prison. A blinding, flashing, maniacal storm that brewed between two angels.

CHAPTER 34

Iblis and Sybilla tore the sky apart with their angelfire. Or certainly the Valkyrie did. It was evident when Iblis's more paltry halo took its shots, for Pitch had no need to grimace at the brightness.

Both angels were silhouettes in the light show, but he could have picked Sybilla from any lineup, with the smooth roundness of her head and a particular heft to her shoulders giving her away. She flew slightly above Iblis, lunging down at the angel, her halo, her rapier pointed ahead of her like the prow of a ship breaking the ice. The sirin, the few Pitch glimpsed, focused their efforts on the barricade of ravens.

Brilliant white light pulsed from the rapier, swift as a piece of lightning moving at Sybilla's behest. But Iblis was quick where he was not powerful, and twisted out of strike range with irritating aptitude, wings cocooned against his body.

That was Pitch's last view of the confrontation, with the parting of the raven curtain closing over, the birds reassembling themselves despite the fierceness of the fight at their edge.

Pitch had no time to be frustrated by his obscured view. The burning at his left wrist grew intense, almost too much to bear. The tight clench of the metal released, and Pitch's arm was free.

The relief was utter painful bliss, and mildly terrifying. Pitch dropped, eyes flaring wide with the horror of the short fall. He hung like a trapeze artist beneath Harut, Silas's coat a draping curtain of blue at the back of his head. Most of his fingertips were numb and all his joints throbbed. Especially where Scarlet clung to his thumb, heavier than he'd known the wisp to be. The wisp pressed something into his deadened hand. A knife, compact, the hilt bigger than the blade. A whittling knife? Small as it was, it was double the size of the wisp, and yet somehow the creature had handled it to hack through his cuffs.

'The daemon is free!' Harut shouted, sounding only half as surprised as Pitch was.

The angel shifted his trajectory, body tilting upright, wings pounding the air to bring him to an abrupt halt. The stop swung Pitch forward, and he grasped at the opportunity the momentum gave him.

Pitch threw his body into the reverse swing, curling in on himself like the trapeze artist he wished he truly was. All he knew of the act had been glimpsed through whisky and boredom at a circus he'd only attended so he could bed the ringmaster when it was finally over.

The fellow had been a dreary fuck. Pitch should have watched the damned show.

Muscles he did not know he possessed, and overburdened ones he did, clenched and twinged like they'd suffered an electric shock, but the path of the swing was true. Silas's coat flared out behind him like a singular blue wing, and Scarlet screeched a battle-cry worthy of the Berserker Prince himself. Pitch's momentum took him just high enough that he could reach and plunge the knife into the swell of Harut's curious unified calves.

The angel let loose a gratifying bellow, slashing at Pitch with his wing and making blood run at his neck. But worse, far worse, the brutality of Pitch's blow brought on unwelcome transformation. Harut swore, appearing to lose control of his own abilities to morph his figure as he pleased.

'He has a weapon!' Harut screamed, while his legs took on bizarre shapes, none fixing long. All of them were precarious in their hold on the dangling daemon. That perfect idea of allowing himself to fall to his doom was abhorrently stupid in this stark new light.

'Steady, you fool! Do not lose him.' Zaquiel was somewhere nearby, shouting instructions Pitch thought fairly fucking obvious.

Scarlet squealed, its meagre weight painful when it was dragging at a fine strand of his hair.

'Fuck, fuck.' His vocabulary was reduced to that solitary word, his hand so tight around the whittling knife that he was likely to crush the hilt.

Harut was not steady. He let his passenger go. Or could not hold him. It hardly mattered which. Either way, Pitch fell.

From a staggering height.

His scream was trapped, a violent expulsion of sound against the back of his throat that burned.

And gods what he wouldn't give to *truly* burn now. Even if it were that winged inferno he'd seen in the vision with Edward. Anything to stop this fall.

But Pitch was a stone. And the wildness was trapped beneath its weight, unmoving. He flailed his arms, clawing at the air as though somewhere in the nothingness there would be a handhold. But even the ravens had abandoned him. Their cawing was still evident, but he plummeted through the fog unaccompanied by their black shadows. His stomach felt as though it was lodged in his throat. And his heart?... Well, that had stopped beating altogether. Will Scarlet, confound the blasted thing, fell with him, still tangled somewhere in his hair.

Pitch's descent reached a breathtaking speed. He was fairly certain he'd wet his trousers, absolutely certain all the screaming would ruin chance of ever speaking again. He would die with his lips knit together and his final cry embedded in the backs of his teeth.

He was so busy losing his mind that Pitch hardly registered that the knife he waved about like a mad conductor's baton was no longer a knife at all. Or remotely a baton.

What he clutched so grimly, as though it might spring feathers and fly him out of this nightmare, was rounded, smooth, with an embedded warmth that distinguished wood from stone, nestled in the curve of his palm like it ought to be there. Pitch snatched his hand to his chest. Heat seared his eyes.

Silas's bandalore.

Pitch's entire world narrowed down to those two circular discs, with their bloodstained string.

He fell, but despised it all the more now.

The air was a roar against his ears, the snap of the coat wild around him, and he wished he could imprint a message on this blasted thing so when he was a sack of broken bones with nothing to say, Silas would hear him. He'd know how sorry Pitch was for saying too little, and being far too much.

Too much even for death's blade to rescue. Far too much to deserve handling with any affection. Pitch closed his eyes. Fuck, he hated falling. And being silenced, when he had so much to say.

Scarlet punched him, right in the earhole. A fucking jolt to the senses if there ever was one. His eyes flew open, and he spewed a curse against his bind. The wisp dove under his chin, punching there too, forcing his head up.

Zaquiel. The angel was coming for him, one arm already reaching out, seeking to claim the falling daemon again. Pitch took up his clawing of the air once more, trying, albeit vainly, to make it more difficult to get ahold of him. All he managed to do was get himself tangled in Silas's coat, a slap of material over his mouth, a whip of it against his arse.

Zaquiel was a mere foot away. He was so close to grabbing ahold that if Pitch could coordinate himself, he might manage to kick the bastard's fingertips.

The sky lit up. Silver light streaked with yellow hues.

Zaquiel made a horrendous gurgling sound and grabbed at his own neck before he dropped from the sky. A bleak shadow stretched over Pitch, a darkness he feared was the ravens returned.

He was grabbed, a firm arm around his chest, his downward trajectory banished so suddenly that his chin nearly broke his collarbone. Pitch struggled, certain Harut held him, his world blurring through tears pricked free by the icy air.

'Hold still, or would you like to keep falling?'

He heard his rescuer's voice at the same time he saw the deep ebony of their hand at his chest. Pitch was struck through with bone-numbing relief.

The Valkyrie had him.

Sybilla wrapped about him, the astonishing shimmering plume of her night-struck wings distorting the air. 'Can you turn around? Hold on to me so I can free my hands?'

He would do anything the Valkyrie wished, kiss her feet and nibble at the crud beneath her nails, so long as she did not let him fall anymore. The turnabout was far from elegant, and Pitch hoped to the gods she could feel nothing of his damp trousers. But with Sybilla's assistance, the angel's translucent wings, brushed with midnight hues and catching the light as though it were from the moon and not a sickly winter sun, swept them both upright. Pitch wrapped his legs about her middle and his arms about her neck, keeping the bandalore held tight.

'There is a will-o'-the-wisp in your hair.' Sybilla eased into forward flight. 'With quite a lot to say.'

Pitch grunted.

'Dear gods, tell me they have not cut out your tongue, because nothing else would keep you this quiet.'

Pitch lifted his head from her shoulder, where he'd been resting like an exhausted infant, and gave her an indignant glare. He mumbled against his bind, shaking his head and tilting his chin, a weird performance he hoped might give her the necessary clues. The angel though, was distracted, her eyes set on the clearing sky ahead, and above, and below. Skies that had become settled, no longer wind struck, the fog peeling away to allow hints of pale blue winter to push through. Skies unsettlingly devoid of other angels and raven hordes.

'What are they playing at?' she muttered.

Pitch dared loosen one hand long enough to touch her chin and gain her attention. When Sybilla scowled at him, he jabbed his fingers frantically at his lips, only for a few seconds. That was all he could stand before he needed to cling to her again.

But Sybilla was no stupid creature. 'You can't speak?' The angel swore, and she shifted one hand from where it had pressed lightly around the small of his back. 'Don't let go.' He huffed and rolled his eyes. Did she think him a lunatic as well as useless? They were still ridiculously high in the sky. 'Tilt your head back. I need to see your mouth.'

On any other occasion, his reply would have been suitably crude, but Pitch was obedient. The Valkyrie brushed her fingers across the stone wall that kept him silent. The language of the angels whispered from her. How pompous that language usually sounded to him, revelling in its own vain exclusivity, but what utter music to his ears here.

The pressure at his mouth gave way, and his breath gasped free. And though his tongue was thick and the backs of his lips raw from the scraping of his teeth, Pitch's words burst from him. 'Silas...is he safe?' He rasped like he'd smoked all the cigars in Mayfair. 'The forest...Sherwood...did you see him?'

'No, I haven't seen him.' Sybilla flew them about in a wayward pattern, never keeping to the same height for too long as the fog faded around them. 'I'm sorry.'

Don't be sorry! Pitch wanted to scream. *Go and bloody find him!*

'Where the fuck has everyone been? Lalassu...she'll find him, won't she?' He was a flying bundle of knots, but none greater than the twist at the centre of his chest. 'Sybilla, you must take us to Sherwood.'

'We cannot go back. I'm sorry so much has occurred in my absence, but I couldn't return for you until I had Edward and Charlie somewhere safe. And I had no say over how far away that would take me.' Without asking the question, Pitch knew who it was who *did* have that say. 'But you had Hastings with you...so I thought...' The angel's fierceness wavered. 'Tobias...their illusion magick is so strong...they deceived us. The Order has been chasing ghosts. And Hastings...' It was the closest he'd ever known her to come to overwhelmed. 'Those cursed fiends of the Morrigan have killed –'

'I know. And I'm sorry.' That word was so puny, little wonder he used it, and meant it, so rarely. 'But you found your way through the deception. What of the others? Surely Lalassu sees her way clear as well? Does she go to Silas? He needs aid, the forest too.' It hurt his throat to speak so forcefully, as though the soft skin had forgotten already what it was to be vocal. 'If harm has come to the ankou –'

'Then you shall honour him by setting yourself to the task at hand.' Sybilla knew a thing or two about speaking forcefully, her mouth close to his ear, her words growing tendrils of ice in his heart. 'Because you know as well as I, he will give his all to protect you. To protect what needs to be done. I know you are hurting, Tobias, in all ways, but your belligerence is not what I need, your focus is. I have us shielded, we should be hidden enough that they cannot follow. But I shall not make the mistake of assumption again. Iblis and his flock appear to have retreated, but I do not trust it in the slightest. We must make quick passage north. I'll deliver you to where Edward waits –'

'Which is fucking where? How far away from Silas are you taking us?' It was already too far. The ankou might have kept the Wild Hunt from heeding Iblis's summons, but who was to say the tables had not turned? Damn it, Pitch was at much at the mercy of this angel as he had been the others.

'Edward is at the –'

'No, stop,' Pitch snapped. 'Don't tell me anything.' He gripped the bandalore tighter before admitting a more painful truth. 'Azazel watches through Iblis. I saw the Exarch in him myself.' Sybilla let slip a suitably vulgar curse. 'And...he forced from me the details...of what Blood Lake holds.' Gods, how many times would his will be overridden and disregarded? 'I was compelled with magick, and I could not hold my tongue.'

The Valkyrie's silence was far worse than any of her words could hope to be.

'For fuck's sake, Sybilla, it's not like they can waltz in and take the halo, is it? The lake is sealed three times over.' One for each of the Seraphim who had imprisoned the Watcher King. Their whereabouts were known to none but those who had created them. He tried not to imagine how the death of one of those angels might tilt the house of cards. 'And it's not as though the Morrigan don't suspect something of worth is there already. They are being called by the halo. And I did not put that fucking thing in the lake to begin with. It was not my mistake that gave it life, damn it.' He shouldered enough of Seraphiel's blame already. He'd not apologise for being so beaten down he had no fight left.

Scarlet tittered, its bantam voice raised. Sybilla nodded.

'I know he is very brave, Will Scarlet. And yes, those angels were very bad, very unkind.'

Pitch replaced one irritation for another. 'You understand the language of the wisp?'

'It is simple enough. Scarlet is quite enamoured with you, Tobias.' Sybilla resettled her arm around the small of his back. 'That wound at your shoulder needs tending. Does it pain you if I hold you like –'

'I'm not made of fucking glass.'

'But nor are you made of iron. Not today.'

True enough. Fatigue dragged at him. The cut in his belly was not altogether happy with being pressed against the angel. 'Mollycoddle me at your peril, Valkyrie. I am no weakling.'

Sybilla's wings beat with the sound of grass moving in a breeze. 'I could call you many, many things, but weak would never figure among them. The Seraphim was no fool. He saw what I and so many others fail to see at first. Your strength is astonishing. With all you have endured, all that has been taken from you, you persist. You defy. You survive.'

Normally, Pitch relished being fawned over and showered with flattery, the more sycophantic the better. But here, Sybilla's words needled him with odd melancholy, and he sought escape.

'Well, you can't be blamed for finding me intensely attractive. I know you've wished to bed me from the moment we met.'

The corners of her lips definitely twitched. 'I've no taste for pillars, most especially not yours.'

'No accounting for taste.'

'Just as well, for I dare say I'd be in a competition I could not win, were it otherwise.' Her chuckle was faint, her words said lightly, no doubt intended to further lift the morose mood. But talk of Silas, even if his name was not mentioned outright, dropped Pitch straight back into darkness. Sybilla must have felt him tense, for she spoke quickly. 'Tobias, he is a survivor like yourself. I'm sure we will all soon be back at the hall with Old Bess, rowdy with the drink and you and the ankou making us ill with your lingering looks and simpering smiles.'

His heart actually ached at that. Not just at the notion of being with Silas but of this being over. Of some semblance of a rowdy drunken party being possible. Of sharing company with those he might dare consider friends.

'I could have him bend me over the billiards table instead, if you prefer a show?' Pitch rubbed his fingers against the smooth steadiness of the bandalore, enjoying the Valkyrie's clucked tongue of disgust.

'And there you are, back upon my list of most repulsive, irritating people I know.' Sybilla's laughter bubbled, but the lightness was short-lived. Her body stiffened against him. 'Oh gods, I knew this was too good to be true –'

Ahead, the entire sky was illuminated, a stage lit by a spotlight that pointed straight at them. Pitch had no chance to turn his head before Sybilla moved them upright and swept her wings before her, like a villain in a pantomime twirling their cape in a dramatic flourish to cover their escape.

But this was no act of drama, rather a move of sheer desperation. With her wings shielding him, Sybilla turned about, embracing him so tightly he couldn't breathe. 'Hold on, Tobias.'

The Valkyrie was struck, and the blow reverberated through his own body. A brutal hit that forced a scream from Sybilla's widened mouth. The angel's wings burst into flame, a silent white blaze that ate into the onyx as she swept them wide again to drag them clear of the daemon she carried.

'Sybilla!'

The angel fell.

'Sybilla!' Pitch screamed again, trying to wriggle out of her hold, which was still inordinately tight despite the fact that the angel herself was being eaten alive by the halo's strike.

A strike of horrendous power. Pitch's confusion mingled with terror. If Iblis had nursed such strength all this time, why show it only now?

The Valkyrie's hold slackened, her wings afire but still beating, seeking to slow their maniacal descent. A brave though fruitless endeavour, considering she fought to carry his weight while massively injured. If she let him go, perhaps she could find a speed with which to dive and douse the angelfire. He knew it a tactic of the angels; he'd seen it done above the Hellfield.

A horde of pained sounds came from the Valkyrie.

'Release me!' he shouted. 'Syb, you'll not survive another blow, but they want me. They'll come for me...and you might escape.' It was a fraught and foolish idea, but with nothing else to offer, he'd glue himself to it. 'I'm begging you...let me go.'

Sybilla grabbed his chin, tilting his head with no gentleness, drawing them eye to eye. 'What is left of my magick goes to you, Tobias.' The words were harsh, forced through gritted teeth.

Pitch recoiled. Or at least, he would have if the Valkyrie was not pressing him so tightly. 'I don't want your fucking death wish, Syb. I want you to live.'

'But I have.' She burned, her wings consumed by an angelic inferno. 'And now it is what I want for you. To truly live.' She hovered in the enlightened space between life and death. The very same space that had given Samyaza the power to wreak his havoc, the power to imbue his halo with his divine magick. 'May the last of my divinity protect you, Tobias. You. Not what you carry, not the burden that is yours, but *you*. The daemon who has suffered enough.'

Sybilla brushed back a lock of his hair and breathed a word against his ear. A word of singular beauty, holding all the nuances of the angel, the fine threads that wove her together. Her true name. The one written by the creation fire on her soul when she was birthed from beneath the Ophanim Throne. A name known and understood by none but the angel who bore it.

Sybilla pulled away and smiled at him in that grim but determined way of those who knew that fate did not favour them. The flames licking at her wings shuddered, flickered...and snuffed out. 'Be strong. You know you are not alone. Do not despair.'

They touched down upon the ground. Pitch's bare feet met a coolness of soil that pulled him from the reverie of Sybilla's gift. He did not recall letting his legs fall from her hips, did not recall her gaining control of their descent. It must have been agonising for the angel.

But he was falling no longer.

The Valkyrie's eyes closed, her knees buckled. And he was not quick enough to stop her collapse. Pitch heard himself cry out, as though from a great distance.

'Sybilla, no.' He dropped to his knees beside her, shoving the bandalore into a pocket, while Scarlet keened softly at his ear and a tidal wave of anguish swept in with the sound. 'Open your eyes, Syb. I'll not have this. Take it back. I don't want your stupid wish. I want you to open your fucking eyes, damn you.'

A shadow stole the light, creeping over the Valkyrie lying so still on the ground, her once lustrous wings, made brittle by the heat, were now crystalline shards beneath her. As though she had landed upon a huge mirror.

'Sybilla,' he whispered. 'Please, come back.'

The faint whinny of a horse reached him. He knew he was being watched. Knew that something...someone nefarious observed his grief. And it enraged Pitch in a way he could not name. He was done with being stolen from.

He rushed to his feet, swinging about. 'Fuck off!' he roared.

A figure stood not two feet away from him. Cloaked, masked in those absurd feathers the Morrigan preferred. At their back, ravens drifted on the wing, arranged in two tiers, the birds mimicking bleak angel wings.

Pitch ran at them all, never more the Berserker Prince than he was now. Though it was not the wildness consuming him but the twin furies of loss and denial.

The figure regarded him in stillness, a glow at their left hand, a flare of light, blue as a glacier's depths around their gloved fingers. And again, the sound of a distant horse. This time the animal screamed. Defiant, threatening.

No ordinary creature.

And Pitch knew. He *knew*, and his heart swelled in his chest until there was no room for anything but certainty.

The Pale Horse.

Silas was here.

Pitch turned a vicious grin toward his watcher. They raised a gloved hand, the gleam of ancient ice flaring, and he was struck.

Right in the chest where his heart pounded, strong and sure. He knew a moment of insufferable pain before deep, drowning darkness arrived. Stealing him away.

CHAPTER 35

The Dullahan had his blue roan at a formidable gallop. The headless horseman rode one-handed, his handless limb tucked beneath his coat, and Silas's arm around his waist. The rhythm was almost soothing, the predictable, reliable pound of hooves near hypnotic, the pair of them moving as one. Silas was in no fear of slipping from the horse's back. Seated surely, as though he were in the saddle, his feet in the safety of stirrups. There was no sign of either though, just an extraordinarily beautiful rose-hued saddle rug beneath them, its intricate gold embroidery speaking of weeks of careful needlework. Or perhaps none at all.

Perhaps such beauty was easy to come by in the UnSeelie Court.

The Dullahan had discarded the uniform cloak of the Morrigan, and his celadon-hued coat beneath was extraordinary, high-collared, embellished with roped trim and more sophisticated embroidery. But beautiful as it was, the denseness of the fabric did not hide the startlingly svelte figure beneath. Hips sharps, waist terribly narrow, as though all the years of servitude had whittled the Dullahan to nothing.

What a strange turnabout this was. Silas's enemy now his hope. A dangerous agreement existed between them, but if there was chance of the unsettling union leading him to Pitch, Silas would not shy from risk.

The scythe hummed gently against his finger.

Sybilla's chorus reached him. Filling his head with a suddenness that had him inhaling sharply.

The angel's notes were ones of sheer and unadulterated beauty. Soaring high.

Are you unwell? The Dullahan's words were soft beneath the melody.

But Silas did not answer. He listened. Felt the long weight of the Valkyrie's years pushing her notes aloft. Notes that strove for freedom. That sought to disentangle from her near-immortal coil.

'She is dying,' Silas breathed. 'No, no. It cannot be.' He denied what he knew was certain. Sybilla's quietus reached across the miles, finding him, calling to him. Silas ran his thumb over the ring, the hum of the scythe making him shiver. He shook his head, rage bleeding into grief.

'Ride on, now. Fast as you can.' He pointed, and the ring flashed as he directed the Dullahan. 'There. We must go that way.'

Who is dying?

'My friend,' Silas snapped. 'Take us that way, at once.'

It may not be the way to the prince. The Dullahan's voice was the hush of sand through an hourglass. *Do you not wish to reach him now?*

'Of course I do.' Silas's fury grew as the notes elevated. Slipped higher from his reach. 'If you will not do it...'

He moved as though to dismount, his fright and panic making him insensible, for there was great distance yet to reach the angel.

The infernal headless creature sighed and threw back their arm, wrapping it about Silas to stop his angry departure. A strong grip, despite the lack of a hand.

You are as impetuous as he. Keep your seat, Lord Death.

Silas was far too distracted to reprimand the ridiculous title.

The gallop was flat out and stopped for no obstacle. Low hedges were cleared without adjustment of the horse's stride, as was the width of a shallow stream and the remains of a broken wagon which blocked a suitable thoroughfare. Silas moved into the motion of the jump as though he were an extension of the horse itself, leaning into the Dullahan, using his body to ease himself clear of the horse's rump as the roan soared. They rode in unison, a pair of dancers in a well-practised routine.

Horsemasters both. Silas had simply forgotten how masterful he was. And it had been Sybilla who was first tasked with reminding him.

She'd been patient with his vacant self. The Valkyrie had guided him while Pitch mocked him from the sidelines, laughing as Silas was unseated by the lowest of jumps or the suddenness of a trot. Sybilla was the one who had helped Silas remember his place upon Lalassu's back.

He winced, the air harsh, his eyes stinging.

How he needed those wondrous creatures now. Both the angel and his Pale Horse. But only one of them was within reach, and he could not let her slip away. The loss of the skriker had chipped a part of Silas away, and discovering Hastings's mane had scoured wounded parts rough. To lose the angel...he could not think it. Could not allow it. For if Sybilla could be overcome, what hope a tender prince?

Silas continued to guide Byleist, following the angel's song. 'Faster.'

Does my Lord Death wish to kill my horse too? Chollima has nothing left to give.

Silas's insides crawled, his skin too tight, his pulse frantic. He felt as though he might fly off the Earth at any given moment, made hollow by all his fears.

He rubbed again at the circle of silver and emerald around his finger. The etching would be rubbed smooth before long. In his mind, whilst Sybilla's notes played, he sent up a small prayer to the goddess, begging her to allow the bandalore to protect Pitch until he could reach him. Goosebumps pricked at the back of his hand, the scythe stirring. A wild notion found its way into his thoughts. He was master of two scythe now, and they were as much a part of him as his limbs, his tongue. Perhaps...perhaps...he could be heard, by a prince who needed to know he was not alone. Silas brought the ring to his lips. 'I am coming for you. Stay strong, my love. They will not keep me from you.'

He bit his lip, stifling the sentimentality that threatened to bring him undone. The gooseflesh settled.

No answer came.

Of course no bloody answer came. He was muttering to a piece of metal. No ordinary piece, granted, but he was treating the scythe like one of those blasted carrier pigeons that had failed to return Charlie's message in London.

Does your love reply, Lord Death? The Dullahan's voice drifted like the hush of satin on a dance floor.

Silas blushed. 'That is not your business. Do not intrude so.'

You are right behind me, speaking into my ear, Lord Death.

'Well, you need not listen.' Silas's frustrations had to go somewhere, so they landed upon Byleist. 'And don't bloody call me that. My name is Silas Mercer.'

That is not your true name.

They negotiated the crumbling hulk of a fallen birch, Chollima grunting as they landed before breaking once again into a headlong gallop.

'It is the only one that matters now.' Which was a lie. There was another that mattered far more.

Sickle.

The name had infuriated him in the beginning, for Pitch had meant it as a mockery. But at some point, when Silas was too busy adoring him to notice, the daemon stopped casting the name like an arrow and reserved it for moments when he was most at ease. When he could run his tongue over it and cause it to heat Silas's cheeks.

Silas bowed his head beneath Sybilla's dying. He clung to gentler things.

To a clarity that emerged from the desperate thump of hooves, the terror of the moment. That name was everything the prince could give. Pitch would never spout pretty, foolish words of adoration, as Silas did. But that look upon his face when he called his ankou Sickle...*there* was Pitch's declaration.

He swallowed, a catch at the back of his throat.

Lord Death...there is a horse.

Silas raised a weary head. 'What?'

There.

They had cantered up a rise, a hill like many others dotted around the countryside, and the onward view spread out before them. The sky was darkened to the west, a deeper bruise than the thin white above them here. Byleist drew in his horse. The stallion pranced restlessly. At the bottom of the gentle slope there was a small cottage, very much abandoned, judging by the wind-funnelling gaps in the simple array of wood panels. But it was what stood beyond that ramshackle building that had Silas sitting bolt upright, his fingers digging into the sharp bones at Byleist's hips.

'Lalassu,' he breathed, all the muscles in his body taut. 'Go, go, what are you waiting for?'

The Dullahan set his horse into a gallop and began racing down the slope with neither care nor concern for the pace on the uneven ground. They headed to where Lalassu reared in a stony act of defiance, hooves caught in a petrified reach for the sky.

The Pale Horse was turned to stone. Just as Robin and the Major Oak had been.

Her marvellous mane reached skyward. Long tendrils of hair were caught in their last movement, reaching at least three times her height above her. There was not a doubt in Silas's mind what she had been reaching for. Lalassu sought to steal a daemon from the angels.

Her tail splayed over the ground behind her and formed a brace to hold her as she strained upwards, lips peeled back to expose most of her large teeth. Her fury was evident in the wideness of her eyes and the severe flare of her nostrils. How sickening it was to see the mare so still. Her pale coat looked nothing like it should. Gone was the mysterious shift of hues, the moss and lichen shades that swirled like oil on water, and instead there was only a dull grey. Unremarkable. Utterly unsuited for her.

Sybilla's wavering song was so dominant in his mind that it took a few heartbeats before Silas noticed the solid, resonating tones of the Pale Horse's naming tune.

Djinn. Servant of lord and leviathan.

Leviathan he knew, for it was what the melody had named Lady Satine, but of lord he could only fathom a guess. The Lord of Arcadia?

But all that mattered very little.

'She's alive,' Silas cried. 'Under the stone, she's alive.'

Are you certain?

'You are the one who insists on calling me Lord Death. Do you not think I know it when life is gone?' As it would soon be with Sybilla, the angel's notes gravely weak. He needed to keep moving, the Valkyrie was not far, but bloody hell how could he leave Lalassu buried in stone? 'She's alive. How do we free her?' He could use the scythe perhaps? Or would he just end up shattering the Pale Horse into irreparable pieces?

I do not know. Nor, to Silas's irritation, did Byleist sound keen to learn.

Silas slid from Chollima's back and ran towards the mare, but no sooner had he begun when his breathless race to Lalassu came to a violent, gut-wrenching stop.

He saw what lay beyond the rearing horse.

'Oh shit...Sybilla.'

The angel lay far out in a neglected field that stretched like a bland canvas around her.

Silas broke into a run.

He ran past where Lalassu was frozen in her last desperate act, brushing his hand against her raised hoof, whispering a soft promise he would return.

The churned earth had him stumbling but not slowing. The angel's whispering notes dragged him on.

He dropped to his knees, his momentum sliding him the last foot to Sybilla's side. There was warmth here, and the strange waft of sweet ashes found him. A smell reminiscent of an extinguished hearth, and yet tinged with foreignness at the same time. He shifted through dirt...and glass? It was as though a great chandelier had shattered beneath the Valkyrie, who lay with eyes closed, lips parted to show a hint of white teeth. Her chest did not move with rise and fall of breath. Her normally bone-white curls were turned jet black, her eyebrows singed away.

Now the drift of smoke and tang of ash made terrible sense.

'Sybilla? Can you hear me?' He dared not touch her. He feared she may crumble to the ash she reeked of, and he had no wish to learn what damage had been done to parts of her he could not see. It was grave. He knew that much.

He *heard* it. Her song was more echo that real tune, a whisper of its regal self. Death was eating away at her melody, carving it into a shape Silas could barely recognise.

'Not yet. I beseech you, not yet. For there is great need of her here. Leave her to me, awhile longer.' He spoke with passion.

But there was no reply. Death had nothing to say, even to him, its servant. It left him to listen as it lured Sybilla, taking her where the simplest sparrow and mightiest angel all found themselves eventually.

Eventually. But not damned well now.

A fierce squall of defiance rose up within Silas. 'Not yet, I say. I am the Lord of Death, and I say not yet.'

He snatched the ring from his finger, held the scythe tight between thumb and forefinger. He was not sure of what he was doing, only that he wanted it done.

He uttered his command. *Keep her.*

Another test of the new blade. Had he truly vanquished this scythe?

The answer came swiftly. The ring softened between his fingers, and the metamorphosis was done in the wink of an eye. From simple circle to perilous hook, the type that might dangle from the rafters in an abattoir. The pitchfork etching graced the curve, reminding Silas of why he defied the gods.

He clenched his fingers around the short shaft and raised the hook above Sybilla's chest.

'Forgive me, my friend.' For Silas rebelled willingly, but he stole the Valkyrie's choice. And had no idea what that might mean for them both.

Before he could falter, Silas plunged the tip of the hook into Sybilla's chest.

CHAPTER 36

Sybilla's melody scattered, reminding Silas of the Morrigan's ravens, all shooting upwards in a startled crescendo.

He sank the scythe deep, crushing it through bone and heated flesh. And held on for dear life.

There was chaos in the melody now, as though the notes split in two, scrambling to play over the top of one another.

Confusion radiated from the scythe itself.

For Silas sought to defy their goddess.

Izanami, the deity who took those purebreds who had died on a new year's midnight toll and bound them in servitude for a desperately short year. Dangling life before her ankou like an unreachable treasure.

Though Silas despised Balthazar Crane, he understood the man's desperation to survive. To die and then be forced to work within reach of the living was tantamount to torture.

But the gods had no thoughts for such small things.

Just as Seraphim had no regard for daemon princes, and rebellious angels no care for the monsters they conceived. And fucking hell, Silas was tired of it all.

'Izanami,' he shouted. 'There is still time for her.'

His words came in jerky bursts as death fought the snag of his hook and tried to rattle its way free of his impediment. Silas wrapped both hands around the metal that shaped itself perfectly to his grasp, feeling every writhe of the fragment of life he pinned down. Sorrow, grief, hollow emptiness, all the marks of death sought to bite at him. Sharp lashings aimed to loosen his grip. 'Not this day,' he hissed. 'She is not yours yet.'

Good god, death was a monster. And an unhappy one at that.

'Fuck.' He spat the word, sinking the hook deeper. 'Not yet...' Silas strained against the mammoth, unstoppable tug of life's end. 'Izanami...damn it...grant me this so I might do your will. I need...I want the angel returned.'

The heat of the Valkyrie spread through the scythe, scorching his hands, causing him to feel as though his skin was melting into the metal. But he was not about to let go.

Death should serve him.

He had reclaimed Izanami's scythe, slain an ankou, and freed teratisms from the Morrigan's bastardised Blight. His ultimate aim was to help Pitch rid the world of the Blight entirely and extinguish the curse that twisted Izanami's own children, her lost souls, into monsters.

Death should side with him. Give him everything in his power to claim back the prince.

But instead it corralled Sybilla on, pushing her melody towards a horizon from whence it could not return. For all his rebellion, she was slipping from his grasp.

'Izanami! Do you hear me?'

Fool.

The goddess's voice, or rather his own, was a hot brand to the inside of his skull. Silas cried out, almost losing the tenuous hold he had upon the scythe, yet at the same time exultant.

He had drawn the goddess out.

Release her.

Izanami hitchhiked upon his own internal voice, which would have been far more unpleasant were he not distracted by something wonderful.

A strengthening of the angel's melody.

The notes finding some form.

The angel was joining the fight with him. The fight to hold on to some semblance of life.

'Sybilla...I have you,' Silas grunted. 'Stand your ground.'

Horseman, do you think yourself above death?

'I am no fool. You know that better than most.' Silas's arms were burning, the muscles screaming for an end to the terrible hold. He struggled to keep his thoughts in order, to find something that might tip the balance here. 'But your sister stole Crane from you. He was not hers to take, and yet she did so. Do you not want vengeance?' A shudder ran through him, a shift of his bones beneath his skin. There was not a deity in existence that did not crave retribution. But Silas could not hold on much longer. He needed more than Izanami's requital, he needed her approval. 'I wish to punish her in your name, and to right, once and for all, the ancient wrong done to this world. The Blight must be stopped. That is what all the Horsemen seek, do they not? Give me back the rider of the White Horse, and we shall bring you great honour.'

There was laughter.

Laughter, of all things...here at the brink of existence, upon the precipice where there was only one true master. Death was tearing Sybilla away, and its goddess laughed.

The sound was a steel brush moving beneath his skin, but Silas detected some real mirth with it. A gentler feel than the scorching heat at his hands.

How Samyaza would have loathed losing you if he knew what you were capable of, Nephilim. But do not deceive me, do not deliver false declarations. For I have raised you, child of the divine, and know you well. And never have I seen you more human in your desires. You fight not for me, nor for this world, or even this angel, but for him.

She did not name Pitch, for there was no need. Silas would not insult the goddess by denying it. 'So what if it is so? Is not a fervent purpose better than forced servitude?' His hands ached, his shoulders punished by the stranglehold he managed upon the greatest power the worlds knew. 'I seek what all do, for this to be over.' Sweat ran from him like the tears of a widower. 'I know the prince cannot escape his fate any more than I. We are both pawns, however powerful we may be, and I do not fight that. But can I not seek any reward for services rendered?'

With his strength faltering, his doubts crowded him. Who was he to seek to raise an angel from the dead? Who was he to covet one other above all else?

Silas cursed the gods, and banished his misgivings.

The Valkyrie would not be here if it were not for the games the divine played. Sybilla had served for time immemorial, loyal and steadfast and staining her own conscience to do what was demanded of her, and this was her deliverance?

To die in a field surrounded by fucking cowpats and emptiness? Fuck them all. This angel did not deserve this death, so Silas was removing her from it.

And as for the one he coveted...the prince had been created to fight an endless war. And was treated as nothing more than a bloody pack horse when it suited the higher powers. Never gently, of course. No, no. Only harshness for him. A soul given so little care that Pitch did not recognise what it was to be cared for at all.

'Fuck you all,' he spat between clenched teeth. He would be pushed about no longer. He would spit in the eye of fate and those she favoured.

His anger bubbled with the heat, and something rumbled in the pit of his gut like a bad stew not sitting well.

Silas's skin was taut. His muscles sought to bulge their way from beneath. He may be occupied with defying death, but it seemed to him that his shadow had grown, covering the Valkyrie who lay beneath him and stretching out into the field. A shadow. Had he always had one? He looked down on her, and the angel seemed further away, Silas higher above.

He felt greater, the world lesser.

Silas hauled on the hook, throwing back his head and catching his groan behind his teeth. Christ, he felt as though he were splitting open, and dared not glance at himself for fear he'd find it true.

But there...there...oh sweet mercy...was the Valkyrie's song. How beautiful it was, piece by piece rebuilding its splendour. Silas listened, enraptured, though he could not shake the sense of doing so from afar, as though he sat upon the moody clouds, not at Sybilla's side.

Horseman. Izanami's cry held surprise. Did her ankou's rebellion truly startle her? *Enough. Let go. Let go before you tip yourself over an edge I cannot keep you from.*

'Then you shall lose us both. I will not let go.' And how he meant it. Silas had never felt so enormous, so significant as he did then.

You are being a fool.

'Well, so be it.' The belligerence came easily, rolling off his tongue as though it had worn grooves there with frequent use. 'Perhaps a fool is more likely to get what he wants than a loyal servant. I have asked nothing of you, and you have demanded everything of me.'

His shadow grew, reached further and further beyond where Sybilla lay, her song delicate and wounded but trying desperately to remain. The shadow was his, certainly, but huge in comparison to the man it reflected.

Giant.

Silas's arms shook with wherewithal, his lips damp with strain.

He had been repulsed by his Nephilim blood since learning of it at the greensward. And his encounter with the Herlequin proved his repulsion well founded. But what if that blood made the difference here? What if this was what had astonished Izanami. That Silas was capable of holding Sybilla from death at all.

Careful what you reach for, Horseman. You are not as you once were.

'But I have always been more than an ankou.' The bumbling, cowardly man Mr Ahari had pulled from the grave had vanished between Holly Village and here. And Silas knew precisely why. It was far easier to be brave and stubborn and fierce when you loved bravely, stubbornly, and fiercely. 'I was Nephilim. That is why you made me the first of my kind. That is why the prince was entrusted to me to protect. And I will not fail him. I will do whatever it takes, do you hear me? *Whatever* it takes to be reunited with the daemon they have stolen from me.'

There was a sigh. One from the heavens, and another from far below on the field. He could feel them both from where he loomed large over the land. If he had lived, that day on the loch, if his brother had not drowned him, would Silas have been any different from the Herlequin? Would he have been greater? Or just a bigger monster?

A reprieve, that is all. No more is mine to give. The Valkyrie's end has come. Your intervention merely forestalls what will be.

'Just as your intervention does with me.'

Something wry brushed against his mind.

Do you think yourself a god?

He could imagine nothing worse. 'I think myself too short of time to be anything but immovable.'

Silas might have heard a goddess laugh.

Have your angel. Have your time. Neither shall exist for long.

The drag against the hook vanished. Silas was thrown forward. He didn't realise he'd closed his eyes until they flew open and he was wincing against a glare. Confusion reigned, and for one curious moment, he thought he must be on his feet, for the ground was too far away for him to be on his knees. But whichever it was, he was unsteady.

Silas threw out his hands. There was a longer moment than he expected before his palms found dirt. Dirt that cracked and crunched, those shards he'd noted earlier trying to pierce his skin.

Silas was on hands and knees alongside the angel. His enormous shadow was gone, as was the hook. His sense of impossible vastness had all but vanished. The glare was only the parting of the clouds above, enough to allow weak beams of late sunshine to grace the countryside and catch at Sybilla's eyes.

Her lids were barely parted. 'Silas.' The angel coughed, a hack like a farrier's rasp against a hoof. 'You brought me back.'

'I did. I hope you can forgive me.'

'It is you who must forgive me. They have him. I couldn't stop it...' The coughing seized her again, a dry, harsh sound that made Silas's own chest ache to hear. His hands hovered over her, unsure where to touch her, or if he should even try to move her from where she lay. He feared the way her clothing clung to her, as though sinking into her flesh. And at her neck, he saw it now as she shifted, the skin held folds it should not. The creep of burns slunk around from behind, where the damage must be terrible. He glanced at the broken shards around her. Truly they were like pieces of a once-grand chandelier, now smashed to pieces and jutting like broken stalks from a harvested field.

'Sybilla, please, stay still.' Though it was the very last thing Silas himself wished to be. Still. He felt the press of each moment, the drag of time as it widened the distance between him and Pitch.

The angel groaned, an awful grimace on her face. 'They have him, Silas. I could not stop it.'

'Hush, please, Sybilla.'

To watch her try to stir, when the pain of it was so evident, made Silas's stomach clench. There was a soft sound, like damp paper being torn, as the Valkyrie fought to sit up. Both he and the angel cried out. Sybilla's hand went to her back, while pieces of her front crumbled away. For a horrific moment Silas feared it was her skin, her roasted flesh that was flaking away in dark pieces.

'Oh Christ, stop, I beg you.' Silas touched his hands to her shoulder, and more of the stiff ash fell.

Her clothing, scorched through but intact while she had lain still. With the angel's movement, the illusion of solidity fell away, turning to dust and leaving her bare, naked, save for the cruel rippling of burns all over her breasts and chest. Whatever...whoever, had done this had left no inch of the Valkyrie unscathed.

And Silas had returned Sybilla into misery. Retrieving her from death, but not saving her from injury.

'I'm sorry...god, I'm so sorry.' He hovered, useless, abhorred by the part he played in this. She would heal, would she not? He almost retched at a sudden thought. What if he'd cursed her to live like this?

The Valkyrie rolled onto her side, breaking apart the ashen remnants of her trousers. Thick leather, her favoured costume, but no adversary to the heat that had consumed her. Silas's hands flew to his shirt. Tattered as it was, and likely not to offer much in the way of cover, it was all he could think of to cover the angel, who was now entirely naked before him.

She whimpered into the soil, one hand clasping at a piece of the broken crystal, her skin stretched nauseatingly tight over her fingers, shrunken by a fire that had killed her.

'I just need time...don't leave without me.' Her rasp was all the more disturbing now, for it spoke of a throat that had not escaped the flames.

'I won't. I won't leave you. I promise.'

He had promised the very same thing to Pitch.

Silas's hand shook. He could not make his fingers work well enough to slide his buttons free. He felt too large again, but not in a useful, astonishing way. Now he was the oaf once more. Clumsy, lost. The strange calm that had clung to him was sliding away, much like the clouds above. More and more sunshine was fighting its way through. As though there was reason to be bright and shiny.

The ring at Silas's finger hugged his skin, tighter than he recalled. Fuck, he wanted to kill Crane all over again for the distraction he'd caused. Never mind what Silas wished to do to the Herlequin.

Keeping him from Pitch.

Sybilla had not failed the prince. She'd died for him.

It was Silas who had fallen short.

'Bloody hell.' He gave up with the buttons, and ripped at his shirt, popping the top one free.

Keep your clothes on, my lord. Use this, but give me a moment to numb her pain before you place it on her.

The Dullahan stood at his side. He'd removed his elaborate coat and did not wait when Silas hesitated to accept it. He dropped it between them, sending whorls of bleak ash lifting. Byleist knelt near Sybilla's head. When the Valkyrie spied him, she jerked away.

'Don't touch me,' she wheezed.

Byleist's shoulders turned as he looked with unseen eyes to Silas. *She hears me. Few do.*

'Get away from me.' Sybilla was a cornered cat, hissing and spitting because it could do nothing else.

'Sybilla, it's all right,' Silas said quickly. 'He is with us.'

Dear god, let that be the truth it seemed.

The angel's narrowed eyes squeezed shut, her moan laboured and deep.

Byleist moved quickly, placing his remaining hand upon the Valkyrie's head, the other, the stump hidden in a draping cuff, rested on her shoulder. Sybilla wailed, a weary bellow of protest, and Silas was one heartbeat from punching the Dullahan away when the angel's cry evaporated.

She sighed, a long exhale that must have expelled every hint of air from her lungs. Her eyelids danced, fighting against closing entirely.

'What have you done?' Silas demanded. But not half as vehemently as he would have had he not noticed how the tension drained from the angel and her lips tilted. Of all things, she was smiling.

Numbing her pain. I told you. I am good for more than hitting you with a whip, Lord Death.

'You are a healer?'

I am many things. As it is with fae of my ilk. But I've not healed her, the angel must do that herself. I've simply enabled a way through the pain. Now, cover her over. We will move her beneath shelter. He pointed over Silas's shoulder, beyond where Lalassu still reared at the sky, towards the ramshackle cottage that barely held upright. *I can do something towards concealing us, but I think it unnecessary.*

'Unnecessary?'

Iblis and the Morrigan have what they want. There is no reason to return.

Silas faltered, the breath knocked from him. Not least of all because it was true. As Silas reeled, Sybilla touched his cheek.

'They want him alive, ankou.' She slurred a little. 'I saw him, I spoke to him. He is defiant, and brave, and knows he is not alone.' She pouted, a look that did not suit her. 'He had a will-o'-the-wisp in his hair.'

Surprise overcame fear for a moment. 'He had what?'

'Tiny thing.' Sybilla showed the measurement with thumb and forefinger an inch apart, a smear of blood at the base of her nail where taut skin had ripped. She seemed intoxicated. 'Like a little rainbow.'

Will Scarlet was with him? Silas could barely imagine it was true, but the notion lifted him no end. Why, he could not say, for the creature could not protect the prince any better than a gnome could jump a cloud. But Pitch was truly not alone.

Silas wrapped Sybilla, gently as he could, in the Dullahan's coat. More of the ashen remains of her clothing spilled away, and she was trembling when he lifted her, but she sighed anew as he settled her in his arms.

Byleist led the way back towards the cottage. His shirt was every bit as flashy as the coat, a rich gold, satin, billowing at the arms but fitted around the creature's all-too slender torso. Byleist moved with a grace Silas had not noticed before, a defined set to his shoulders.

Perhaps he'd bother to learn more of this strange creature someday, but for now all that concerned him was that the headless horseman's fealty continued. And was true.

The Dullahan stopped outside the cottage, taking up position to the side like a guard at the door of their master. Silas continued inside, negotiating the bowed doorway with an awkward stoop, frightened of hurting the Valkyrie any more.

Luck was with them, in some tiny measure, for the interior was not so tired as the exterior. There was a bed with a mattress of stuffed hay and a blanket the colour of gingerbread folded neatly at its end. The floor was swept, which seemed futile considering the gaps in the timbers that must let in every breeze that stirred. There was no such breeze about today. In fact, the stillness was unsettling, as though the world held its breath along with Silas.

He laid Sybilla down, gently as he could. The angel did her best to hide it, but the settling into the mattress brought on an agony the Dullahan's medicinal magick failed to overcome.

'I'll have him tend to you again.' Silas rose and moved to step away.

Sybilla grabbed his sleeve, forcing him to kneel back beside the bed again. 'He knows we will not abandon him, Silas. And I will be at your side when we ride to find the prince, but I beg you, do not be foolish and leave before it is time.'

'Before it is time? Sybilla, I am already long past overdue. I cannot promise that –'

A familiar steeliness forged its way into Sybilla's wounded gaze. 'That you won't rush in and do something utterly foolish? Keep your head, Silas. Steady your heart, or it will see you ended here.' Her surge of energy faded as quickly as it had arrived. The angel winced her way through a yawn. 'Gods, I must sleep, but you need to know this, Silas. The halo that struck me did not belong to Iblis. I saw his at work, and it was not enough, not nearly enough, to bring me down.'

Silas stared at her, his restlessness dimming. His focus narrowing. 'Then whose?'

'Tobias spoke of Azazel –'

Silas swore.

'No, no,' she said. 'It is not him. He would have to infiltrate White Mountain to gain entry to this world himself. He is scrying through Iblis.' Sybilla gave up trying to lift her head and lay flat against the mattress, her gaze never leaving his face. 'If the Exarch had struck me, not even you could have brought me back, my friend. But whoever Azazel has at his behest is immensely powerful.' She wrinkled her nose as though tasting a mouthful of cloves. 'I fear Arcadia has another traitor in the ranks, Silas.'

Sybilla's eyes fluttered closed, her breath coming in rapid gasps, the effort of the short conversation had left her drained. But damn it, she could not just finish there.

'Sybilla...what else can you tell –'

'There is much to tell.' Her eyes stayed closed, the bones seeming to leave her body as she slumped into the mattress. 'But I cannot manage it now...let me rest. Then we shall speak.' Another yawn split her mouth wide. The angel shifted herself beneath the Dullahan's coat, nestling in deeper. 'You have much to share too, I'm sure. But you promised me...you won't leave yet...'

'A promise I shall keep.' Even though it was like a nail through his heart to say it, to keep away from where he longed to be. Silas rose to his feet, and was halfway to the door when the angel spoke again, mumbling on the precipice of sleep.

'He'll have nothing to fight for if you are gone, Silas Mercer. Save yourself if you wish to save him.'

Silas leaned against the doorway, neither here nor there. All at once he was so utterly exhausted he could barely see straight. He pressed his fingers to the corners of his eyes. And when he opened them again, the Dullahan was there.

You should know that I lied to you.

'What?' Silas frowned.

I do not know the darker secrets of the Morrigan. I was a servant, as you are. The Fulbourn was the only stronghold I knew of. And you destroyed it. There was a pause in the delivery. *I do not know where they have taken your daemon.*

Silas stared at the headless rider, to where the creature's eyes might be. A strangled, disbelieving and wholly inappropriate laugh came from him. 'You lied?' Why the bloody hell had he ever imagined there would be truth? But confusion snatched at the frayed edges of Silas's mind. 'Then where the hell were we riding to?'

Was the fae biding time until the Morrigan found them? Or did he intend to deliver an ankou to the Erlking? Was the Herlequin lying in wait somewhere? Silas's addled thoughts tried to arrange things sensibly. But none of it made sense. If the headless horseman sought to bring him harm, he'd had ample time.

But Silas remained in one piece. Exhausted, still breathing, and now united with the Valkyrie.

The Dullahan shrugged. *I had not really decided. I was simply enjoying being free.*

Silas's mouth hung open. He was caught in a strange place, one between utter fury and insensible mirth.

The countryside was so still, barely the squawk of a bird to be heard, as he found his words.

'Do you know anything of value at all?'

That would depend on whether we consider the same things valuable. Every infuriating word said with the airiness of spring's morning breeze.

Silas's incredulity shifted back to annoyance. 'The angel the Valkyrie spoke of, then? Who are they?'

I do not know that creature. Only those who rode with the Hunt, and I do not rank them highly. They act with such blind devotion to their masters, a snivelling subservience that is not even forced upon them by a whip, as mine was. They are toady. I have never liked toads.

Byleist's disdain rattled his voice, the harsh scrape of a field of dead cornstalks. Silas found himself thinking, foolishly so, that Pitch would enjoy the challenge of this headless fae's company. The bluntness, the air of indifference would amuse the daemon, who enjoyed pushing at the bounds of a person until they found themselves acting in ways they were unaccustomed to.

Like thieving from death, and defying gods. And fearing nothing but losing what they treasured most.

Silas ran his finger over the ring. He barely recognised himself anymore, and that was not so terrible a thing as it could have been.

The hoot of an owl drew their attention. Silas raised weary eyes skyward. Byleist did the same in his way.

There flew not one but two owls, low and fast towards them, rushing in over the undulating landscape.

One tawny, one white as snow.

My lord? The Dullahan spoke flatly but Silas had no doubt of the concern being voiced.

He shook his head. 'It is all right.' It wasn't, but that was no fault of the owls. At least their arrival peeled away one thin layer of Silas's fear. Whatever had kept the Lady and the Order away before now, was done with. 'They are with me.'

Marcus the djinn flew at them, followed by the father of the tawny owl Silas and Pitch had rescued from the witch-bottle house. Or perhaps it was the poor sod they'd freed from the cage himself.

Either way, the presence of that bird was a consequence of a good deed, done by a daemon who didn't believe himself capable of such things.

The Dullahan shifted, drawing Silas back from bitterly sweet thoughts.

I do know something you may consider of value. That you shall need far more than a burned angel, a stoned horse and two birds, if you hope to reach your prince.

Silas shook his head. He stepped from the doorway and made his way to where Lalassu waited, her mighty elegance frozen in stone. Her sturdy melody had not faltered once since he arrived. A subtle reassurance that he'd nearly missed in his panic.

He set his hand against the mare's broad chest. Her heart thumped beneath his palm. A beat as sure and steady as Silas's own.

'You fail to tell me anything of worth, Byleist. In Sherwood, you said there was nothing more certain than my word, and you were right.'

Silas closed his eyes, Lalassu's heartbeat grounding him. 'I have promised Pitch I will never abandon him. So I shall find him, whether the entire Order is at my back or I am utterly alone. I don't need hope, to reach him. He has my word...he has far more. And no angel, god, man, or monster shall keep this distance between us.'

'The author truly created a world that is unpredictable,
intense and hauntingly human. It is an action packed
short story that fosters a lot of curious thoughts of a
futuristic and desperate society.'
Goodreds Review, 2021

D K GIRL

Danielle K Girl is an Aussie who lives in stunning Tasmania with her three furkids, cats Luffy, Sweetie and Ren.

Her idea of heaven is a farm full of rescued animals, with a vegie garden that sprouts peanut M&M's and chocolate wheaten biscuits.

Join the newsletter - Get a FREE D K Girl novella!

If you'd like to receive DK's monthly newsletter, and be first to know when a new book is ready, then you are in the right place.

PLUS, you will receive a FREE MM Dystopian novella for joining up.

https://daniellekgirl.com/subscribe/

Find D K Girl online:

https://daniellekgirl.com/

https://www.instagram.com/daniellekgirl/

www.ingramcontent.com/pod-product-compliance
Lightning Source LLC
Chambersburg PA
CBHW030513120726
47904CB00005B/1447